The Heist of the Hidden Heart

A Cozy Mystery

L.L. Gray

Heroic Rose Publishing

This one's for the brave hearts,
the book lovers,
and those who know the best treasures are rarely gold.

Contents

Your FREE novella is waiting

Want a free book?

Of course you do, what madness could possess someone to **<u>not</u>** want free books?
There's no catch - you do sign-up for my mailing list but you can unsubscribe at any time.
There's also no spam.
Ever.
Sign up here to get your free book!
https://www.subscribepage.io/havenwood

The Doldrums Are Not Romantic

THE WIND GUSTED DOWN Arcadia Avenue, blowing up loose snow and rattling the windows. Inside my cozy, if mostly empty, bookshop, I stayed snug and warm against the February chill, idly flipping through the pages of a graphic novel. The art was exquisite, and the plot would've typically captivated me, but I couldn't force myself to focus on the story. Every little noise had my eyes flicking towards the door in hopes a customer would walk in.

"If you want my advice, you should give it up," a grumpy voice said from near the floor. I glanced down to see Luna, the white rabbit who called Sullivan's Spellbooks her home, hop over. Her ears twitched as she jumped up onto a small step stool before landing on the counter right in front of me. Unconsciously, I moved my graphic novel out of the way to make space for her.

"Give what up?" I asked. A year ago, asking my great-grandmother's familiar for advice might've seemed like an absurd notion, but if the last six months had taught me anything, it was that Luna had a wise mind and a surprisingly good heart hidden behind her sharp tongue.

"The idea that someone is going to walk through the door. Even for Saturday, it's too cold out for foot traffic," Luna said primly, running a paw across her whiskers.

I sighed and let my head drop into my hands. "But I'm *so* bored. We haven't had a customer in hours."

"Well, why don't you straighten the shelves? Or finish your business course? Don't you have a paper due or something?"

"It was my final, and that was last week," I said, quickly reviewing my course schedule mentally. I'd taken some online classes so I could be a better small business owner. "I have another week before the next class starts, and I've already straightened, vacuumed, and dusted the entire shop. Twice."

"Why don't you read a book? You might have one or two lying around," Luna suggested dryly, twitching an ear towards the full shelves of the shop.

I held up the book I'd been attempting to read. "I was trying, but I'm finding it hard to concentrate."

"Perhaps try another book?" Luna offered. She thumped her foot on the counter. "Spellbooks? A little assistance, please?"

The floorboards under my feet rumbled, and a book fell off a nearby shelf with a thump, shuffling across the shining floorboards to bump against my boot. Now, most people would've been surprised by a talking rabbit, but they would've been absolutely stunned to learn that my bookshop was not only cozy but also sentient. Through what was an entirely unique ritual, my great-grandmother and her friend had somehow brought the shop to life. I was still hazy on the exact details, but Spellbooks and I had developed a partnership over the past few months that suited us both. I acted as Spellbooks' mouthpiece, just as my great-granny had, recommending the perfect book for my customers. Much like Spellbooks was doing for me now. I kept the building safe and the business running while Spellbooks gave me a place to call home. It was a more than satisfactory relationship for both of us.

I stooped to pick up the book, adding it to the growing pile of recommendations from Spellbooks with a murmured thanks. "Much appreciated."

Luna tipped her head to the side, eyes studying me. "You don't look as excited as normal for a good book. What's going on?"

I sighed. "Don't get me wrong, I love to read, but I need a change of pace. Things have really slowed down around here since Christmas."

Luna bobbed her head. "Yes, that happens after the holidays."

I glanced over at the rabbit. "Are there any town events coming up? You know, a big Havenwood, touristy shindig that I could volunteer for?" I asked hopefully.

"Shindig? Really?" Luna twitched her nose. "Ah, I see what this is."

"What are you talking about?" I asked.

"You're in the doldrums," Luna said knowingly.

I wracked my memory for something in Havenwood with that name, but nothing sprang to mind. "Like in the Dr. Seuss book?" I finally asked. "The place of waiting?"

"Yes. Boredom, lack of progress, stuck in a rut, all of it," Luna said as she cleaned her whiskers with her paws even though they were already pristine. "I find people get stuck in the doldrums after the holiday season, especially here in Havenwood."

"Why here especially?" I asked curiously.

"Well, we've just survived four months of back-to-back town events—kicking off with the Renaissance Faire all the way through to New Year's. Then what? Crickets."

"Well, what about Valentine's Day? That's coming up soon."

"I mean, sure, Havenwood typically throws together some kitschy stuff. Card making at library or how to make gourmet chocolate dipped strawberries at the Candy Cauldron but let's be real—how much enthusiasm can you muster for a holiday concocted by the candy and greeting card mafia?"

"Mafia? Really?"

"Why? What would you call them? And don't get me started on the weather. Snow is cute for about five minutes, but by February it's either turned into that gross gray slush or everyone's just over it. Cue the doldrums."

"When you put it like that..." I trailed off, losing my enthusiasm to even complete the sentence.

The bell above the door jangled, announcing the arrival of a visitor. I looked up excitedly to see Bella, my best friend, stomping snow from her boots.

"Hey Harper. Hi Luna," she called as she carefully slid a white pastry box labeled with her family's B&B logo onto the counter before unwrapping herself from the cocoon of winter gear, each layer falling away until she was just a regular human again instead of a walking pile of wool and down.

"Hey Bella," I said, already feeling my spirits rising. Mr. Wigglesworth, the shop cat, deigned to move from his fifth nap of the day to wind his bulk around Bella's legs, demanding scratches behind his ears. She gladly obliged before heading over to me.

"I need your help," she said, carefully opening the box.

"Anything." The reply came out a little more earnestly than I'd intended. Wow, Luna was right. I really *was* stuck in the doldrums.

Bella grinned and nudged the box closer. "Mama has been baking up a storm for Valentine's Day next week and needs some taste-testers. I offered your services. Hope that's okay."

Instantly, I grabbed some plates and forks from behind the counter, setting them out for her. "More than okay. You know I'm always up for tasting whatever your mom bakes." Bella's mom, Honey, was a brownie, yes one of the fairy creatures, although you wouldn't know it to look at her. Other than being on the shorter side, she easily passed for human, as did most of the magical residents in Havenwood. She was also insanely talented with baking. Maybe my day was looking up after all.

"I don't suppose you brought enough for me, did you?" Luna asked hopefully.

"Of course I did. I'd never forget the most important member of the team," Bella said, shooting a surreptitious wink at me.

"I knew you were one of the good ones. Well, what have we got then?" Luna said, her nose twitching.

"My mom's been baking all morning, trying out some new recipes: Love Spell Sticky Buns, Rose-Scented Love Knots, and Heartfire Molten Cakes."

I reached for one of the treats Bella was holding out but froze mid-grab, my fingers hovering over the plate like a reluctant claw machine. "Love Spell Sticky Buns? *Heartfire* Molten Cakes?" I raised an eyebrow and shot Bella a look. "You *do* remember the candy shop incident at Halloween, right? Imps? Pranks? Ringing any bells?"

Bella rolled her eyes and pushed the plate toward me. "Relax, Harper. There's no magic in these. Mom's just...really committed to the theme."

I narrowed my eyes, still unconvinced. "Are you sure? Because I'm not ready for another confection-based catastrophe."

Luna snorted and shoved her paws toward the plate like a tiny white diva. "Radish ruckus! Give me the molten cake already. I'll test it for curses."

Bella grinned as she passed out the treats. "Not a single spell, I promise. Mom just said she was aiming for life-changing deliciousness."

"Life-changing, huh?" I muttered, pretending to still be suspicious. With exaggerated caution, I grabbed a sticky bun and held it aloft like it might explode. "If I start reciting poetry or proposing to random passersby, you're both to blame."

Luna snickered around a mouthful of cake, and Bella just shook her head, muttering something about "a drama queen." I assumed she meant Luna.

I glanced at the rabbit who was waving a paw in the air as if overwhelmed by the sheer culinary experience of the molten cake.

"Parsley perfection!" Luna gasped, eyes rolling back in theatrical bliss. "Even if this cake was magically cursed, it's completely worth it."

"Don't worry," Bella cut in, clearly used to both of us. "I promise, there's no magic in any of these."

"Well, they sound amazing!" I sniffed the air appreciatively. "And smell even better."

"Yeah, well, I think Mama's bored. I had to escape before she stuffed me so full of treats that I started oozing frosting like an overfilled cannoli," Bella said.

"I can empathize. Not with the overstuffed cannoli, but with the boredom," I sighed looking around the empty shop.

Bella nodded sympathetically. "Yeah, that's February in Havenwood for you."

"The doldrums," Luna said knowingly as she delicately nibbled at the sticky bun.

"Exactly," Bella said, pointing her fork at the familiar.

I popped a bit of the delicately braided pastry love knot into my mouth. Rosewater and a hint of cinnamon combined in an unexpected but delightfully balanced flavor profile. "Is this a thing that everyone knows about? The doldrums, I mean," I managed around my bite.

Bella shrugged, trying to pull apart the sticky bun neatly. "Pretty much. But don't worry. Things typically pick up again in March. By the time the winter weather breaks, it'll be so busy that you'll wish for this time again, just so you can catch your breath."

"I'll take your word for it," I said. Bella had lived in Havenwood almost her entire life.

"Enjoy the quiet while it lasts," Bella said with a wink.

"If you say so," I said, unconvinced. Seeing an opportunity to beat my boredom, I couldn't resist nudging her a bit. "Any updates on reopening the Hideaway? You know I'd be happy to help you anyway I can." We'd discovered an old speakeasy under Bella's family's B&B at the end of December and there'd been talk about restoring and reopening it to the public. I'd be happy to pitch in if it meant I didn't have to sit around in my empty shop all day.

Bella sighed and shot me a look somewhere between appreciation and mild exasperation. "It's in the works...but there are a couple of things slowing it down."

"What things?" I pressed, tearing off a piece of the sticky bun.

"Mama and Papa," she said with another sigh, as if that explained everything.

I frowned. "Why? I thought they were all for it—a way to bring more people into the Oasis by broadening the business."

"Exactly! They love the *idea* of it. Mama just isn't keen on people traipsing through the basement. Even though it's a hidden speakeasy, she doesn't like the thought of guests wandering past the extra linens and shelves of jam to get there. She's insisting on a separate entrance," Bella explained.

"Might not be a bad idea," I mused. "Especially if there's drinking involved. You wouldn't want a late-night party disturbing anyone sleeping upstairs even if you do have those noise-dampening spells."

"That's what I said!" Bella threw her hands up. "But then Papa took that suggestion and turned it into a *whole* project. Capital P. Now he wants to build a new tunnel, complete with runes reinforcing the construction."

"Oh?" I asked, raising an eyebrow.

"Yeah, he's got this grand vision to keep the essence of the Hideaway intact while honoring Mama's wishes to not have anyone wandering around the basement."

"How does he plan to do that?" I asked.

Bella tucked a strand of hair behind her ear. "He wants this tunnel to come up outside of the house so there's completely independent access to the speakeasy. Then, he wants to top it off with a shed that has some super-spy, gimmicky entrance. A fake wall, a password-protected telephone, something like that."

I couldn't help grinning. "Okay, that actually sounds kind of cool."

"It *does*," Bella admitted begrudgingly, "but it also sounds like it's going to take forever. And I was really looking forward to the Hideaway's reopening to distract me."

"Distract you from what?" I asked, frowning slightly.

Bella waved a hand, brushing the question away. "Oh, I don't know. Everything, I guess. Maybe the doldrums are getting to me, too."

I watched her for a moment, the sticky bun forgotten in my hand. "Well," I said lightly, "if you need another distraction in the meantime, Luna was saying there might be some Valentine's Day events around town. Maybe we could pitch in?" I suggested, wondering at the look in Bella's eyes. Something was off, and I couldn't place my finger on what was going on with my best friend except that she didn't want to talk about it. Absentmindedly, I tore at the bun, popping a section in my mouth. It was still warm and gooey, swirled with cardamom, cinnamon, and a hint of nutmeg. The scent of the delicious buns filled the entire shop.

Bella licked the sweet, sticky deliciousness from her own fingers before answering. "Yeah, but the Valentine's Day activities are usually pretty low-key. Heart cookie baking at Pixie Pastries, 'love potion' making down at the perfume shop, writing love letters at the library, that type of thing."

"Oh, well, those sound...interesting," I said, munching on my sticky bun.

Bella laughed. "Trust me, those are more for the overnight tourists. You really must be bored if you're looking at any of those for excitement."

Luna gave me a look from her spot on the counter. "She is if she's contemplating embracing that nonsense. Don't tell me. Next, you'll be decorating Spellbooks in heart-shaped everything to beat back the boredom. I'm warning you, if I wake up to hearts all over my hutch, I'm getting my headband. The snow is great camouflage for a ninja rabbit. You'll never see my retribution coming." She struck a pose, holding my eyes unblinkingly.

I couldn't help but laugh. "Come on, Luna. Love isn't so bad. It's nice seeing people all happy and connected."

"Radish ruckus, that's what it is," Luna said. "First, it's paper hearts, then they're walking around like lovesick puppies. I've seen it before, you know. People get all starry-eyed, and, before you know it, they're writing poetry and gazing at sunsets."

I rolled my eyes but was still smiling. "That doesn't sound all that bad."

"That's because love might be blind, but it's also inspiring. Especially the aftermath. Why, all the great artists love to use their heartbreaks as a muse for their art," Luna said, her nose twitching.

"Wow, that took a turn," Bella murmured.

"You can't have love without heartbreak. It's how you learn to appreciate real love when it comes your way. Whether its romantic or friendship," Luna said with a sniff.

"Well, I appreciate this friendship, that's for sure," I said, raising my fork to Bella.

"Seconded," she said, tapping her fork against mine.

"And it's not just for the cake," I teased. "I swear."

Bella waggled a finger at me. "Hey now. Be nice, or I'll take that cake back."

I slid a protective arm around my plate. "Not the cake! I don't think I could bear that level of heartbreak."

Luna didn't miss a beat. "That's not heartbreak. I'll give you heartbreak. One minute, you and Finn are having fun, maybe even something more. Then his ex rolls back into town, drops the L-word like it's some kind of magic charm, and suddenly the timing's all wrong. Everything gets complicated, and you're left stepping aside while old flames reignite."

"It's not like that," I protested, dropping the banter from the moment before. "Seraphina still loves him. I couldn't stand in the way of that." Even I could hear the uncertainty in my voice.

"And now," Luna continued with a dramatic flourish, "you're swept up in the Silverthorne saga. Enter Gabriel, stage left. Tall, dark, and handsome with a side of magical prowess. But don't forget the real kicker: his mother. The Ice Queen herself."

"She doesn't have ice powers.," I protested, but even as I spoke, I could picture Vivienne's stern gaze, the way she seemed to see through everyone with those piercing eyes. I shivered. She might not have ice powers, at least, not that I knew of, but she certainly could freeze me to the spot. "And Gabriel's...different. He's amazing, actually."

Bella smirked. "'Different', 'amazing'—aren't those just fancy words for 'I'm falling for him but terrified of what comes next?'"

I felt a blush creeping up my neck and quickly tried to redirect. "Okay, fine. But let's not forget that someone else here knows a thing or two about rekindling love. How's Alex, by the way?"

Bella chuckled, catching the not-so-subtle deflection. "Nice try, Harper. But we're not talking about me and Alex. We're here to figure out why you're hesitating with Gabriel, especially since you're the one who shut the door on Finn."

I sighed, looking down at my half-eaten sticky bun. "I don't know. It's just...I'm not sure I'm ready to deal with everything that comes with it. Gabriel's wonderful, and Isadora's a ton of fun when she's back from her magic academy, but the whole most-powerful-family-in-town dynamic? Especially Vivienne? It's a *lot*."

Bella nudged me gently. "So, what are you going to do? Gabriel clearly makes you happy. Are you going to keep waiting for the perfect moment or just let yourself enjoy what's right in front of you?"

"That's the problem. I haven't seen what's right in front of me." I frowned, picking at the corner of the bun.

"What does *that* mean?" Bella asked, shooting me a pointed look.

"Just that I haven't seen Gabriel—or Isadora, for that matter—since the murder mystery dinner party I threw last month. Isadora left for school a couple of weeks ago and is buried under finals at the moment. I haven't even had a text from her in a week. And Gabriel..." I trailed off with a shrug. "He's been busy with family stuff. Or avoiding me. Who knows?"

Luna sniffed, clearly unimpressed. "You know what I think. If you have to ask yourself if it's the right time, maybe you already know the answer."

I smiled softly, appreciating the honesty, even if it wasn't what I wanted to hear right at this moment. "Yeah, maybe you're right. But don't let it go to your head, Luna."

"Too late. I know my value," Luna said, hopping down from the counter with a determined thump. "Just remember, Harper, love isn't something you tiptoe around. If you're going to jump in, make it a cannonball."

I stared after her, letting the words settle. A cannonball, huh? For a rabbit, she really had a way of making things sound deceptively simple. Bella laughed, and I couldn't help but join in. Maybe they had a point. Maybe it was time to stop worrying so much and let myself feel...whatever this was with Gabriel. It was almost Valentine's Day, after all.

I cut into the molten cake with the side of my fork, and, to my surprise, a gooey flow of raspberry spilled out onto the plate, mimicking real lava. "Wow! This is incredible!" I said, scooping up a bite of the rich chocolate and raspberry on my fork.

"Just watch out for the kick. Mama takes her creations seriously," Bella warned.

"What kick?" I asked, popping the bite into my mouth. It warmed almost instantly as an unexpected heat from...was that chili?...mixed with the sweet dessert. I clapped a hand over my mouth in surprise, searching for a glass of water.

Bella laughed. "I tried to warn you. Mama really embraced the whole theme."

I wiped at my eyes as my taste buds finally calmed down. "Yeah," I coughed, giving my chest a light thump for good measure. "Heartfire Molten Cake is *on point.*" I took another small, careful bite and shook my head in disbelief. "It's rich, it's bold, and it's hands-down the standout."

Bella grinned, clearly pleased. "Mama will love to hear that."

"Honestly," I added, holding up a hand like I was delivering a royal decree, "everything's incredible. The Love Spell Sticky Buns? A solid contender. The Rose-Scented Love Knots? A delicate, fragrant surprise. But the Heartfire Molten Cake? That one takes the crown. It's got the most punch—and I mean that in the best possible way."

"Clearly, you've been struck," Luna quipped, perched smugly nearby. "By flavor or by fate, who's to say?"

"Definitely flavor," I shot back, pointing my fork at her. "And let's not start waxing poetic about cake."

"Too late. I'm inspired." Luna sniffed dramatically and hopped toward the rows of shelves. "Love is like a molten cake—sweet, fiery, and occasionally leaves you gasping for breath."

"Speaking of love," Bella cut in, using her fork like a wand to point at me. "If you're so bored, why don't you throw some kind of Valentine's Day event here at Spellbooks? Mama could bring over treats, and you could host a poetry reading or something."

A spark of interest ignited inside me. "That's actually a great idea, and I really could use the distraction, but would poetry be the best way to draw in a sizeable crowd?"

"It would draw in Grimgor. He's pretty big," Bella teased.

I rolled my eyes. "Not what I meant. I was talking quantity. Not a single half-giant. Although he'd probably love a poetry event. The question is, would anyone else? I mean, don't get me wrong. I love poetry, but it just doesn't have a wide appeal, you know?" We paused, each lost in thought for a moment.

"Well, why don't we start with a theme?" Bella suggested.

"I suppose love is the obvious one. But what about love?" I mused. "New love, old love, unrequited love...the list goes on."

"Dating?" Bella suggested.

Luna's voice drifted out of the stacks. "Or whatever you call what you're doing with that Silverthorne boy!"

"Hey!" I protested and then drew up short. "Dating. That's...actually not a bad idea."

Bella threw up her hands. "That's what we've been telling you. Just admit you're into Gabriel and go out with him."

"No. Not that. I mean, yes that, but...wait. Focus on the shop."

"Not as interesting as your love life," Luna called.

I ignored her. "I meant with the dating idea. What about a blind date with a book?"

"What do you mean?" Bella asked.

"Think about it. We could wrap up books in paper and give them a couple of key words like 'mystery' or 'globetrotting' or 'spicy'. Maybe we could even pair some books with your mom's treats," I suggested.

"That's an idea with potential. Really lean into the sentiment of the holiday without the hearts Luna is so terrified of," Bella said.

"I'm terrified of nothing!" Luna shouted from somewhere in the labyrinth of bookshelves. "*Terrifying* is another thing entirely."

"We could do even more," I said, my mind already racing with possibilities. "What if we set up a 'blind date with a book' table? People could choose a wrapped book based on a blurb or quote, and—" I gasped, pointing at Bella like I'd just discovered fire. "What if two people pick the same book? We could match them up for a special Spellbooks date. Like, with a whole date kit! Drinks, a book, maybe even a cozy little corner for them to sit and chat."

Bella raised an eyebrow, clearly trying to keep up. "A date kit?"

"Yeah! A cute little package—some love-themed drinks, like hot chocolate labeled 'Cupid's Cocoa', or teas we could call 'Love Potions'. And some themed snacks from your mom. It could be the perfect setup for book lovers to meet. Spellbooks could totally be part of someone's love story!"

Bella held up her hands. "Whoa, Harper. Maybe you should slow d—"

I cut her off, my eyes widening as another idea hit me like a lightning bolt. "Wait! What if we sent them somewhere *really* romantic? Like...the heartwood tree!"

Bella blinked. "The *what* now?"

"You know, the one Benny and Clara told us about?" I said, practically vibrating with excitement. "That old legend about the heartwood tree? Where couples used to sneak off to get a blessing for their love? It's perfect!"

Bella stared at me. "You want to host an event, in February, in Connecticut, outside, in the middle of the forest?" she asked skeptically.

I hesitated for a split second, then nodded with absolute conviction. "Yes. Yes, I do."

"Girl, what was in that cake?" Bella demanded, examining my plate.

I walked back my previous statement slightly. "Well, maybe not the entire event, but a part of it, yeah. I think it would make it memorable. Unique. Maybe we could even share Benny and Clara's story."

Bella tipped her head to the side. "I don't think bringing up a double murder would be great for this type of event. It might *kill* the vibe you're going for."

I chuckled and shook my head. "I see what you did there. Yes, their story might've taken an unexpected twist, but they're together now. What better ending is there?"

"One that you'd have to explain without the ghosts and the murder," Bella said dryly.

"Fine, we won't mention them. But the heartwood tree is a good idea. It has a rich history here in Havenwood, doesn't it?"

Bella shrugged. "Maybe at one time, but I couldn't even tell you where it is. To be honest, it's been mostly forgotten."

"Well, it's time we refresh everyone's memories, don't you think?" I said as I pulled out my phone, tapping away, hoping to find a walking map to lead me straight to the heartwood tree. To my disappointment, my Google search turned up absolutely nothing.

Bella gently pushed the phone down. "Did you really think that a supposedly magical tree would be listed like a franchise restaurant on the internet?"

"No...I suppose not," I said, already feeling the doldrums creeping back in. However, I wasn't about to be deterred. I shoved the feeling aside. "But there must be a way we can find out where it is."

"Well, if you're set on this, I would recommend starting at the restricted magical section of the library," Bella suggested.

"The library has a magical section?" I asked in amazement.

Bella shrugged like it was common knowledge. "Of course. In a town full of magical beings, there has to be a place to safely store and share all their books. What better place than a library?"

"Why haven't you told me this before?" I asked, hurrying around the counter and grabbing my coat.

"It never came up," Bella said, staring after me. "What are you doing?"

"Going to the library of course. The heartwood tree won't find itself," I said, wrapping my scarf around my throat.

"And nothing I say is going to keep you here, planning a lovely, warm, bookish event in your nice cozy—and did I mention warm?—shop, is there?"

I shook my head. "Now that I know there's a magical section in the library and the chance of making my 'lovely bookish event' even more appealing by finding the most romantic place in all of Havenwood?"

Luna's voice floated out from the bookshelves. "Fluff and furballs, who in their right mind thinks the cold, dark forest is romantic?" The floorboards beneath my feet gave a faint shudder—Spellbooks, clearly siding with Luna on this one.

I ignored them both. "C'mon, Bella. You've got to admit, this is the most excitement we've had in weeks. Besides, what if we rediscover the location of the heartwood tree after all this time? Maybe they could make a whole town event next year, and we would've started it all."

"I'm still not sold on holding any sort of outside event in February, but planning something might be just what we need to shake off the winter blues," Bella mused.

"That's the spirit!" I said, holding out her coat, like a prize.

Bella rolled her eyes but couldn't suppress a smile. "Alright, you win. But I'm not trudging through all that snow to get to the library. We're taking my car."

"Deal," I said, shaking her coat a little. I think I would've agreed to almost anything that got me out of the boredom of the empty shop. I flipped the sign to "closed" as Bella bundled up in her winter gear.

As we stepped outside, the February wind barreled down the street like it had a personal grudge against us, its icy fingers clawing at our faces and stealing the warmth from our breath. But there was something else in the air—something that felt like the first hint of an adventure, a spark of excitement. I pulled my coat tighter around me, but it wasn't just the cold that made me shiver; it was the thrill of the unknown, of doing something different, something that might lead us somewhere unexpected.

As the car's engine rumbled to life, I imagined we were leaving behind the doldrums themselves, shaking off the weight of the past few weeks. Whatever lay ahead, it promised to be anything but ordinary, and I was more than ready to dive in headfirst.

Restricted Access

THE SCENT OF WELL-LOVED books and ink greeted us like a warm embrace as we hurried out of the cold and into the library. Through the door, I could see that the children's section was buzzing as kids played with the toys set up in the corner or ducked behind shelves in a game of hide-and-seek. The adults hurried around, setting up tables with pink and red arts and crafts, calling to the more rambunctious children to quiet down. I hadn't realized the library was such a popular spot on the weekend, but upon reflection, it made sense. It was a warm, free place to bring the kids, and, from the look on some of the parents' faces, it was a welcome reprieve from the norm.

By contrast, the foyer was calmer with only one person at the desk talking to Martha Morningstar, one of the librarians. Because the library hosted my book club, I saw Martha weekly, if not more often. She always had an air of grace about her and seemed completely unflappable.

That is, until this morning.

We quietly lined up behind the woman at the desk talking to Martha. Although you wouldn't know it unless you knew her, Martha positively radiated tension from the rigid line of her perfectly straight spine to the tightness around her mouth.

"I'm sorry, but as I said before that's not possible," Martha said. Her voice was low, but in the tiled foyer area, I could hear her easily. I shot Bella a look, but she shrugged in bewilderment.

There was no confusion in the tone of the woman facing Martha. She had striking red hair and, apparently, a temper to match. "I know there is a magically restricted section in this library. Look, like I told you, I'm a mage in training. Cassandra Bellamy. My tutor is *incredibly* well-regarded with an impeccable reputation. She's the one who told me to come," the newcomer, Cassandra, insisted, sliding what looked like a business card across the desk.

Curious, I craned my neck to get a look at the black card. On it was a stark white symbol, but I couldn't see well enough from this angle to figure out what it was.

Martha slid the card back towards Cassandra without picking it up. "And, like I told you, a business card of a woman I don't know will not work in this instance. To confirm your claims, I suggest securing a meeting with Vivienne Silverthorne. If she will vouch for your identity, then I can let you in. Until then, I'm afraid my hands are tied."

"I've tried to arrange a meeting all week, but she is apparently always 'indisposed.'" Cassandra added air quotes, a snide undertone to her voice.

"Well, it seems we are at an impasse," Martha said steadily.

"What if I show you what I am?" Cassandra offered, bringing a hand in front of her body.

Martha reacted with a speed that surprised me, clapping both of her palms over Cassandra's. "For your own sake, I suggest you do not. We take our secrecy seriously here in Havenwood," she said firmly.

Cassandra struggled for just a moment, but something in Martha's steady blue gaze seemed to wear her down. "Fine," she huffed, grabbing the card from the desk and spinning on a heel. She must not have known we were standing behind her because she crashed right into me, dropping her purse and scattering its contents across the gray tiles.

"I'm sorry," I murmured, crouching to scoop up a tube of lip gloss and some hand lotion.

"Let us help you," Bella said, dropping to her knees and sweeping up the loose change scattered across the floor.

"Thanks," Cassandra muttered. "Today is *so* not my day." She slung her hastily repacked purse over a shoulder and stormed out.

"May you find what you seek," Martha called out after her.

A rectangular black card on the tile floor off to the right caught my eye. "Wait! You forgot your..." the door shut behind her. "...card." I said, trailing off. It was the business card she'd tried to slip to Martha. The symbol emblazoned on the front of the matte black rectangle was simple yet arresting. A single lightning bolt surrounded by a laurel wreath. It looked vaguely Greek to me, like someone had a thing for Zeus. I sighed and stuffed it in my back pocket, refusing to leave litter in the library even if it wasn't mine.

Martha smoothed back her perfectly coiffed blonde hair as she stared after the young woman. "Well then. And I thought the most excitement I'd have today would come from the playdough and glitter," she murmured.

"She was a tad forceful, wasn't she," Bella said, glancing after the newcomer.

Martha shook her head, briskly returning her attention to her computer screen and scanning in another book. "You can say that again. Oh my. I may need a cup of tea before I can face all those children, especially since two of our volunteers called in sick today," she said.

"Well, I think you have the patience of an angel, dealing so gracefully with people like her on top of whatever event you're hosting," I said.

"Not *like* an angel, dear," Martha said with a wink.

My jaw dropped open but before I could utter or even formulate a follow up question, Martha continued. "Now, how can I help you ladies?"

Bella glanced over her shoulder to ensure we were alone and then dropped her voice to a whisper. "We'd like to access the magically restricted wing for research purposes."

To my surprise, Martha immediately stood from her desk and grabbed a set of keys as she smiled benevolently at us. "Of course, right this way." She pulled open the half-door blocking access to the area behind her desk and waved us through, latching the door once more behind us. After flipping over a sign that read "Taking a Chapter Break, Be Back in 5 Minutes," she led us through a door marked "Employees Only."

We followed her, but I couldn't restrain my curiosity. "Hey Martha? Why are you letting us in and not her? The other woman, I mean. Not that I want you to throw us out," I added hurriedly as we followed her into a tiny break room with a small table, three mismatched chairs, a refrigerator, and a microwave.

Martha chuckled. "Everyone who enters must either be known to me as a member of the magical community or have a pass vouching for their identity. Something from one of the governing bodies of supernatural creatures would do. Or from Vivienne Silverthorne herself. That type of thing." Martha lifted a shoulder. "She had nothing I could credibly believe, so I couldn't allow her entry. The same doesn't apply to the two of you."

A faint crash sounded from the main library, making me jump, but Martha just sighed and shook her head. "That's what I get for running a children's event when I'm short-staffed."

She opened a door, revealing a small broom closet, and looked around. Other than some neatly stacked cleaning supplies, it was cramped, but empty. To my surprise, she inspected the closet closely before turning to me. "Look, I'm sorry I won't be able to do the full tour for you, Harper. It is your first time, right?"

I nodded, but Bella jumped in. "Don't worry. I'll show her the ropes. No food, no fire, no talking too loudly."

"You've got it," Martha said with a relieved sigh, shutting the closet door. She selected an ornate key and pushed it towards the smooth middle of the door. She turned it dramatically.

I glanced at Bella, worried that Martha may've taken up miming and was practicing her new skills on us. Bella just held up a finger, silently telling me to wait. As Martha gave the key one more full twist, the closet door shimmered. I sucked in a surprised breath as the wood rippled like it was alive. The barrier between the mundane and the magical world wavered, revealing an entrance that seemed to glow with a soft, ethereal light where only a broom closet had stood a moment before.

Martha pushed the door open, and a faint breeze carrying the scent of aged parchment and ancient secrets swept past me. "This is a research-only facility," she said, her tone gentle but firm. "You won't be able to check anything out, I'm afraid. But I do hope you find what you're looking for. The card catalogue is at the back of the room and is quite useful."

"I remember," Bella reassured her.

"Please put any books you use back on the cart," Martha instructed. Another clatter rang out, this time louder and more urgent. The librarian sighed, glancing towards the door leading to the main library. "I suppose that cup of tea will have to wait." She glanced back at us. "To exit, just push the door—no need for the key on your way out."

She hurried off with a quick, "May peace be with you," her footsteps fading rapidly as she disappeared around the corner.

I pointed, dumbfounded. "Wait. Is there a—"

"Library in the broom closet? Yes. Keep up," Bella said, grabbing my hand and tugging me through the door.

I twisted, looking at where Martha disappeared in the direction of the library. "And is she—"

"Part angel? Of course. She's a *librarian*," Bella said as if that should explain everything.

It didn't, but what I saw next took my breath away and pushed any further questions out of my mind.

A Book Lover's Dream

As BELLA USHERED ME inside and quickly closed the broom closet door behind us, she muttered something about preserving secrecy. I, on the other hand, was frozen in place, completely struck by the sheer magnitude of the room we had just entered. It felt like I was living every book lover's dream. The air was cool and still, carrying the faint scent of aged paper and polished wood. The ceiling seemed to stretch up forever, while towering shelves lined the walls, filled to the brim with books of every size and color. Intricately carved shelves with delicate inlays caught the soft glow of the brass lamps hanging overhead. Rolling ladders attached to the shelves made me want to climb them and go for a ride while singing about books. I could almost hear the whisper of the wheels gliding as I imagined sliding one of them across the rows of tomes, exploring until I found my next great read.

In the center of the room, a single large oak table, scarred with the marks of countless years of study, stood solid and welcoming. The dark wood floor beneath my feet creaked gently, its rich grain catching the light in places where countless feet had worn it smooth. Leather armchairs, well-worn and inviting, were scattered throughout, positioned just right for settling in with a good book. Everything about the room spoke of history and knowledge, a sanctuary where time seemed to slow, allowing the luxury of getting lost in a book. As I looked around, I felt a deep sense of reverence, knowing this place was a haven for those who cherished the written word.

"Uh oh," Bella murmured, nudging me with an elbow and jerking her chin at the large table in the middle of the room. I forced myself to look away from the rows of books and focus on the only two other people in the room.

The two figures stood close, their heads almost touching as they exchanged heated whispers near the large table. The taller of the two, a slender woman with long silvery blonde hair clutched a stack of books to her chest and shook her head emphatically. Her companion, a disheveled older man wearing a tweed blazer and thick glasses that magnified his weary, bloodshot eyes, seemed flustered, his voice a low, urgent murmur. Though their conversation was too quiet to be fully understood, the tension between them was unmistakable. Finally, the woman tossed her long blonde hair back with a huff as the man stormed off in the opposite direction, muttering under his breath.

It was obvious we'd been caught staring, and I felt heat flood my cheeks, but the woman surprised me by smiling radiantly at us. "Ah, hello. How nice to see some young people using a library rather than the internet these days," she said, her voice warm, even though she shot a dirty look at where the man had vanished into the shelves. She snatched a leather-bound book from the table, adding it to the stack as she hurried towards us.

When she drew closer, I could see the wrinkles forming on her otherwise pristine, alabaster skin. Not that wrinkles meant much in the magical world. She could be anything from fifty to five hundred. It was hard to tell with some species.

"Yes, well, erm..." I trailed off, not sure what was appropriate to ask or to reveal. Inquiring into someone's magical background wasn't exactly taboo, but it was frowned upon in polite society.

Bella, having had more practice than I, was more adept in these types of situations. "Oh, we love the library," she gushed, nudging me. "In fact, I can't keep this one's nose out of a book. Although that could be the fact that she owns Sullivan's Spellbooks, Havenwood's preeminent bookshop. Have you been there yet?"

The woman raised a perfectly plucked eyebrow and shook her head. "No, I'm afraid I haven't visited Havenwood in a long time. It's nice to be back, though. I have an old acquaintance that I've been dying to see. It really has been too long. But you know how things are at my age. The days slip into weeks then months and years. Suddenly, you haven't seen each other in decades. But I'll have to check out this shop of yours. Sullivan's Spellbooks, was it?"

Leave it to Bella to work in a plug for my shop while making polite small talk. I smiled and nodded, feeling like a bobblehead doll. "That's right. I love all things bookish, but it looks like you do too," I said, waving at the stack of books in the woman's arms. The leather-bound one on top was emblazoned with the title *The Tempest Codex: Secrets of Elemental Skies.* "Are you interested in the weather?" I asked, thinking that was a safe topic.

She glanced at the book and shook her head as if surprised. "Oh. No, not really. I suppose it just caught my eye," she said, her grip tightening slightly on the stack. "I guess it's always handy to know if it's going to rain."

Bella shot me a quick look, and I could tell she noticed the tension in the other woman's response too. "Sorry. Were you re-shelving these? Are you one of the library volunteers? It's nice of you to help out during your visit," Bella said, grabbing a nearby library cart. "Martha mentioned being short-staffed today."

The woman smiled, her shoulders relaxing. "Yes, well, you know how it is. You volunteer at a library thinking you'll give back and get a little peace and quiet in return." The woman set the books down with a relieved sigh and smiled ruefully. "Honestly, I just needed ten minutes. I'm Sandy, by the way."

"Harper Sullivan. And this is Bella," I said.

"Hi," Bella waved.

"It's nice to meet you both," Sandy said

"And you. Is there anything we can do to help?" I asked.

"Only if you can take care of that old coot, Professor Hawke, for me," Sandy said, tipping her head in irritation at the scholarly, if somewhat rumpled, gentleman poring over a pile of books at the reading table.

"Oh?" Bella asked. "Was he the one who borrowed all these books? It seems like a lot for one person."

"Annoying, isn't it?" Sandy closed her eyes and shook her head. "Sorry, that was uncharitable of me, wasn't it? It's just that, he pulled all these books off the shelves and didn't even have the courtesy to put them on the cart before pulling out everything this part of the library has on local plants. You think one element of study would be enough for him," Sandy said, shooting the oblivious scholar a disapproving look.

"Well, let us help you," Bella said, grabbing onto the handle of the cart.

"No, I couldn't possibly ask you girls to give up your time to—"

"We insist. It's what we do here in Havenwood, isn't it? Help our neighbors out." I said firmly.

Sandy relented. "Well, when you put it like that, how can I say no?"

We made quick work of the re-shelving. Sandy seemed grateful for the help, though her gaze kept flicking toward the table where Professor Hawke was hunched over his stack of books. Just as we finished and wheeled the last cart back into place, Sandy shot him yet another sharp, almost disdainful look, her lips pressing into a thin line. I frowned slightly at the tension radiating from her, but before I could make sense of it, she turned back to us with a tight smile.

"Thanks for the help," she said, her tone light but a little clipped. "I'd better go see if the other volunteers need anything."

She grabbed a large purse and a stylish jacket from the back of a chair and headed toward the magical door, her steps brisk and deliberate.

Bella tugged me towards the back of the room with an eager glint in her eyes. "Come on," she whispered, "you're going to love this."

Bella stopped in front of an ornate cabinet set into the wall, its surface etched with glowing runes. She reached out and pressed her hand against a small, shimmering sigil on the side. "We'd like information about the location of the heartwood tree in Havenwood, please," she said, her confident request breaking the surrounding silence.

The cabinet responded with a soft hum, and suddenly, the entire wall of shelves next to us began to move. Books slid seamlessly along the shelves and through the cabinet as if they were on a magical travelator. Surprised, I looked at the side of the cabinet, but there was no hole. Yet the books kept appearing, rearranging themselves as though guided by an invisible hand. The titles glowed briefly as they passed by, making it easier to read. I watched in awe as the books danced around us, organizing themselves in a way that felt almost alive.

Finally, the motion in the cabinet slowed and then stopped, leaving three books standing on the completely mundane looking shelf in front of us. Bella grinned, reaching out to take them. "Looks like we've got what we need."

"How did...what...just..." I couldn't formulate a sentence.

Bella smiled at me in understanding. "I had the same reaction the first time I used the card catalogue."

"But there were no cards!" I protested.

"Well, we can't very well go around saying we talked to a magical cabinet to find the books we needed, can we? What if someone overheard us?" Bella asked, leading the way to the large reading table.

"I suppose so. But why do they need volunteers to re-shelve then?" I asked.

Bella shrugged. "Maybe the magic only works one way. I don't know. I never really thought about it before. Anyway, we got what we need. Divide and conquer?" she suggested, spreading out the books on the oak table in front of us.

Professor Hawke blinked owlishly through his thick glasses in surprise as we shrugged out of our coats and sat down. He gave us a once over and then returned to his mountain of books without a word. I glanced at Bella and shrugged, selecting the thick book bound in green leather and settling in to read.

I opened the beautiful book, *Roots of Power*, and quickly flipped to the chapter on the heartwood tree, immediately becoming engrossed in the detailed history. The author, one Lucian Holloway, spoke of the heartwood tree as a living nexus of magic, its roots deeply entwined with the essence of Havenwood itself. He recounted rumors that the tree was planted by an ancient druid or a powerful mage, but he stated the true origins of the tree remained a mystery, obscured by the passage of time and the deliberate secrecy of its creators.

"Anything?" Bella asked, leaning over my shoulder.

"It's not much, but it's interesting," I said, passing her the book. "What about you?"

"Same, but I think you'll want to read it yourself. The chapter on the heartwood isn't too long," she whispered.

The disheveled scholar across the table looked up and glared at us. I sheepishly fell silent and flipped through the much smaller *Lifeblood of Havenwood*. This author, Orin Fallowfield, seemed to explore different aspects of the magic and spells protecting Havenwood. I wasn't that surprised when the name Silverthorne popped up several times. Gabriel's family had helped found Havenwood and had used their magic to protect the paranormal beings here from the outside world for generations. I'll admit, thoughts of the handsome Gabriel distracted me for a minute or three before I shook myself and refocused on the task at hand.

According to Orin Fallowfield, there were many myths and misconceptions that had grown, no pun intended, around the heartwood tree. The tree's protective magic had been misunderstood over the centuries; its true purpose obscured by romanticized stories. Many believed that the heartwood blessed young lovers, extending its protective magic over them—a tale that had become so widespread it was accepted as truth. But the author suggested these stories were merely the result of rumors that had transformed into legends over time. The real magic of the heartwood ran much deeper and was older than these fanciful tales. It wasn't about protecting hearts or lovers but the protection of the town itself, its very existence bound to the ancient, unfathomable power residing within the tree.

Bella hadn't finished the much denser history by Holloway, and I was a quick reader. Instead of interrupting her, I turned my attention to the final book entitled *The Forgotten Leaves* by Isolde Greenbough. This book was solely about the heartwood tree. I scanned it, searching for any reference to a map or location. Ms. Greenbough covered much of the same information the other authors had, but I found myself drawn into her creative use of the written word. Apparently, the heartwood was so unique that there was a guardian appointed to watch over it and keep it safe. According to the text, no one truly knew who the guardians were or how they were chosen. It was rumored that they shared a bond with the tree, a unique connection to the tree itself. Ms. Greenbough wrote that some believed this bond was akin to the relationship a park ranger might have with nature, protecting the area from trespassers and poachers. However, the author seemed convinced that the connection must be more magical in nature—though there was no definitive proof to support this claim. The guardians' methods and identities remained shrouded in secrecy, with only vague references to their existence scattered throughout history.

"Find anything interesting?" Bella asked.

"Not really, but—"

"Shh!" the man across from us hissed.

I shot him a sheepish look and dropped my voice. "No maps or anything thus far," I said, flicking through the book and glancing at the pages just in case the author had included one later in the book.

"Wait, what's that?" Bella said, leaning forward.

"What?" I asked, turning back a few pages.

In the middle of the page was a small, italicized piece of text, offset from the rest.

"On the edge of Havenwood's embrace,
Where the boundary whispers in the wind,
Seek the heart deep within the forest,
Where the ancient roots begin."

I whispered the passage aloud, tracing the lines with my fingers as if touching the page would give me a clearer insight into the author's meaning.

Bella furrowed her brow in concentration. "Do you think it's pointing us to the edge of town?" she murmured, "Somewhere near the boundary?"

"And in the heart of the forest." I added.

"SHHHH!"

This time, a dramatic slam of the cover of a book accompanied the shushing as the professor across from us stood suddenly. A flurry of papers flew off the table from his explosive gesture, and he shot us a look that clearly said he blamed us for the repercussions of his passive-aggressive outburst. With a low, irritated mutter, he scooped up the papers and slammed them down on the table. Well, as forcefully as you can slam unbound papers. Then he stormed off toward the card catalogue.

Bella and I looked after him in surprise. People in Havenwood were usually much nicer than that. I could see how he'd gotten under Sandy's skin.

"Ignore him; what did you find?" Bella asked, waving dismissively in the direction he'd disappeared.

I quickly recounted the main points from the last book as I pulled out my phone and snapped a picture of the italicized verse before Bella scooped up the books and carried them over to the empty library cart, depositing them for later re-shelving. Bella came back, grabbing her coat off the back of her chair. "Hey, do you really think the heartwood blesses couples in love? You know, like that Fallowfellow guy said?" she asked.

"Fallowfield," I corrected. "And Clara and Benny seemed to think so." Suddenly, I slammed the heel of my hand against my forehead. "Clara! Why didn't we think of this sooner? She had a map to the heartwood, didn't she?"

Bella's eyes lit up. "She did! I think I know just where I put it after the New Year's Eve party. It's with the rest of the things we discovered in the Hideaway."

"So we might have a map after all!" I said, excitedly.

"SHHHH!" This time, Professor Hawke stuck his head out from behind a corner of shelves and actually waved angrily at us to be quiet.

"Is he for real?" Bella asked under her breath.

"Maybe we should head outside to talk," I murmured.

"Yeah. No kidding," she whispered back, wrapping her scarf around her throat.

A thought occurred to me as I shrugged into my jacket. "Why are you asking about the heartwood and couples?"

"Oh, you know. Valentine's Day. It must be getting me thinking about happy couples. You know, the ones who make it past dating." Bella's tone was light, but I could sense an undercurrent to her words.

Thinking back on her strange behavior in Spellbooks, I decided to press and asked gently, "Is everything okay with you and Alex?"

Bella hesitated, her fingers nervously twisting the tassels of her scarf. That hesitation was all I needed to know I'd hit the nail on the head.

"He's going to Vegas," she finally said, her voice barely audible.

I froze mid-motion. "Vegas? What do you mean, Vegas? Like *Vegas* Vegas? As in the other side of the country?"

"Yeah. He got a call yesterday. He's been short-listed for an extended residency, and they need an answer within the next few days. It's short notice, I know, but this is kind of a big deal. It's the type of job that could really launch his career and set him up for enormous success."

"And you didn't say anything to me earlier?" My voice came out sharper than I intended. I tried to modulate it down before the professor came back to give us another scolding. "Why'd you let me talk about blind dates with books? This is huge!"

She gave a small shrug, her eyes dropping to the floor. "I've been...processing."

My heart sank. Processing was Bella-speak for *I'm freaking out, but I don't know how to say it.*

I leaned against the chair, trying to wrap my head around the news. "So, what does this mean? Are you two going to try the long-distance thing again?" I paused. They'd dated before and only broken up because neither wanted to do an extended long-distance relationship.

She sighed, running a hand through her hair, the motion betraying her nerves. "Maybe? It's only for a couple of months, and it's a fantastic opportunity for him. But..." She paused, biting her lip.

"But what?" I asked, unable to stand the tension.

"They hire the top trainees out of the program to work there permanently. It's a great opportunity, Harper. I don't want to hold him back, but...it's all so complicated! I don't know what to feel. On one hand, I'm thrilled for him, but on the other I don't want him to go." She looked up at me, tears welling in her eyes. "Does that make me a bad person?" she asked softly.

I shook my head firmly. "Absolutely not. You're a complex person who can hold two emotions at the same time. Of course, you'd be happy for him. It sounds like a great opportunity. But I get your worries about the distance too. It's..." I trailed off, unsure of how to finish without making her feel worse.

"Complicated," Bella finished for me. She met my gaze, her eyes filled with uncertainty. "When he asked me what I thought, I froze. And then, when I tried to formulate the words, they sounded so wrong in my head. I think I might have wrecked the moment if I said anything, so I didn't. But now I'm worried that was worse. I was thinking of writing him a letter. Something heartfelt, you know? To let him know I want to try? That the distance doesn't matter. But..." She hugged her purse closer, her fingers twisting around the strap. "I'm scared. What if he doesn't feel the same way?"

My chest tightened at the sight of her so vulnerable. I reached out and squeezed her hand. "Bella, you won't know until you try. Besides, Alex loves you. That much is clear to everyone except, apparently, you." I tried to smile, hoping to lighten the mood, but the worry in her eyes remained.

"It's just...I don't want history to repeat itself," she murmured, her gaze fixed on the floor. "But I don't know how to communicate that to him. What if I say the wrong thing, and he stays, but then he grows to resent me?"

I reached over, giving her hand a gentle squeeze. "Neither of you know what the future holds. Just be honest—with yourself and with him. Whatever happens, you'll figure it out together, okay?"

She nodded, but I could tell there was still doubt lingering in her mind. I didn't blame her. After everything they'd been through, the thought of going through it all over again must have been terrifying. But if there was one thing I knew about Bella and Alex, it was that their bond ran deep—deeper than either of them possibly realized.

"I just don't want to lose him," she whispered.

I pulled her into a hug, holding her tight. "You won't. You're stronger together than apart. Don't let fear get in the way of that."

As I held Bella, whispering words of reassurance, a sudden gust of wind blew through the library, causing us both to pull back. Wind? In a *library*? The books rattled ominously. Then one by one, they flew off the shelves, pages fluttering like frantic birds. The overhead lights flickered, casting eerie shadows that danced along the walls. A chill filled the room, raising the hair on the back of my neck.

Bella's eyes widened in alarm. "What the—?"

"I don't know," I said, looking around frantically. "But I don't think it's a good sign. This can't be normal, right?"

The air crackled with an energy that was anything but welcoming. I smelled the scent of burned ozone as something snapped and popped behind us. I instinctively reached for Bella's hand, trying to keep us both calm as the chaotic scene unfolded. Just as suddenly as it started, the books ceased their flight, crashing to the ground in a disorganized heap. The lights steadied, the flickering ceased, but the chill lingered.

"What just happened?" I whispered, bracing in case the books started flying again. "Is there an angry ghost?" I glanced around, not wanting to relive the events of New Year's Eve where we'd helped an unsettled ghost find his eternal peace after he nearly caused a disastrous end to Bella's party.

Before Bella could respond, a familiar figure appeared at the far end of the room. Edmund Hawke, his face twisted in an irritated scowl, huffed at us. "Honestly, can't a man have some peace around here?"

Bella and I exchanged an astonished look at the unfounded accusation. How could Hawke think we were responsible when it seemed as if he'd caused this ruckus? Before I could formulate a response, Edmund stormed through the chaos, his frustration clear in every movement. He swept the books that hadn't fallen off the table into his arms, dumping them unceremoniously onto a library cart. He muttered under his breath the entire time, sending pointed glares in our direction before marching toward the exit in a huff.

I turned toward Bella, shaking my head. "That was... strange," I murmured. As I glanced around the mess, something caught my eye—a faint set of boot prints on the floor, almost obscured by the debris. They hadn't been there earlier. I frowned. Didn't Hawke know to wipe his feet before entering a library?

I glanced at the table and noticed a small leather-bound notebook he'd left behind. Curious, I picked it up. Bold, black letters on the cover read: "The Property of Professor Edmund Hawke." Flipping it open, I quickly scanned the pages. On the last page, the words "roots = magic" were hastily scrawled and circled, surrounded by messy, frantic notes. My brow furrowed as I wondered what he was trying to piece together.

"Hey! You forgot—" I called after him, but the slamming door cut me off.

I turned the leather-bound book over in my hands, then looked at Bella. "What should we do with this? I don't think we should chase after him. Especially after he was the one who caused all this mess," I said.

Bella looked around and nodded. "I don't want to annoy someone who can do this either. Besides, he already seemed upset enough that we were talking. Maybe we should just report him to Martha."

I nodded, my mind racing. "I'd much rather do that, to be honest," I admitted. "But how are we going to clean all this up?"

Bella looked around at the mess and sighed. "I think we should go tell Martha. She'd want to know what that guy just did. Then offer to help."

"You're right. Especially since she's so short on volunteers," I said, even though cleaning up after someone who was old enough to know better than to throw a hissy fit wasn't exactly how I'd expected to spend my Saturday. Still, I supposed it beat being bored in my shop. Barely.

We headed out of the restricted area and paused when we heard raised voices coming from the corner of the break room. Bella nudged me, and we peeked through the door to see Sandy and Professor Hawke near the entrance, locked in a tense exchange. "I told you, it's none of your concern," Hawke snapped. His wiry frame seemed to bristle as he glared at Sandy.

"And I told *you*," Sandy retorted, her voice icy but carefully measured, "that I've seen your type before. Always digging where you shouldn't be. Havenwood doesn't take kindly to troublemakers."

Hawke huffed, his glasses slipping down his nose as he adjusted his grip on the books. "Troublemaker? That's rich coming from someone who—" He cut himself off, noticing Bella and me watching the heated exchange. His scowl deepened. "Never mind. I don't have time for this nonsense."

With that, he spun on his heel and stormed out, muttering under his breath. The glass door swung shut behind him with a sharp thud.

Sandy smoothed her jacket and turned to us, her expression brightening in a way that felt a little too rehearsed. "Oh, hello again! Just trying to make sure our patrons respect the library rules," she said, her tone dripping with faux sweetness. "You know how it is—some people think they're above the guidelines."

Bella and I exchanged a glance. "Speaking of that," Bella said. "That Professor Hawke guy had some kind of magical outburst in the restricted section."

"Yeah," I chimed in. "But it ended with books all over the floor. He didn't even bother to attempt to clean up his mess."

Sandy's brows furrowed. "He can be difficult, can't he?" She sighed, then gestured toward the notebook in my hands. "Is that his? I can take it to the lost and found for you if you like. The kids' event is keeping everyone busy."

I hesitated for a moment, then handed it over. "Thanks. I think he forgot it in his rush."

"Not a problem," Sandy said, slipping the notebook into the crook of her arm. Her boots clicked on the polished floor as she led the way out of the break room.

Bella and I exchanged a glance before bundling up. I looped my scarf around my neck as Bella tugged on her gloves. "Well," she said, "we should probably let Martha know what we saw. She'll want to keep an eye on him."

We followed the sound of Sandy's retreating footsteps, but when we reached the front desk, Martha was alone, her attention focused on sorting a pile of books while a group of children bustled excitedly near the craft table. "Ladies!" Martha said, her voice bright despite the chaos. "Did you find everything okay?"

"There was a bit of an incident," I said hesitantly. "In the restricted section. Professor Hawke seemed agitated. We think he lashed out with his magic and caused a big mess."

Martha let out a sigh, shaking her head as she glanced at the group of kids across the room. "That Professor Hawke. I swear, he's as temperamental as some of these children. Though at least the kids clean up after themselves better." She gave a wry smile before turning back to her work. "I'll deal with him later. Right now, I've got my hands full. Reliable volunteers are hard to find these days."

Bella and I exchanged a glance. "Do you want us to stay?" I offered.

Bella nodded. "Yeah, we could lend a hand if you're so short staffed. Help you tidy up?"

Martha shook her head, making a good natured little shooing gesture towards the door. "Oh, I couldn't ask that of you. I'm sure you have much better things to do than get pink glitter in your hair and bits of red paper stuck to your hands with crafting glue or pick up a mess in the restricted section. Besides, we have spells for that." A crash sounded from the children's section and all our heads whipped around in that direction.

"Are you sure?" I asked.

Martha sighed and pushed to her feet. "Absolutely. I'll handle this. You two have a good day now, and don't you worry about a thing." Martha gave us a little wave before hurrying off.

"Well, good luck," I called after her. I leaned over to Bella and whispered, "Do you think we should lend a hand anyway?"

Bella looked at me and shrugged. "If Martha says not to worry, I believe her. She's got more patience than a saint on double duty. That woman could probably balance glitter, chaos, and a coffee cup without spilling a drop."

"If you're sure," I said, looking after the librarian uncertainly.

"I am." Bella linked her arm through mine. "Don't worry. If she needed help, she'd ask."

"Okay," I finally acquiesced, following Bella towards the door.

Bella nodded, her expression brightening as she adjusted her gloves. "For now, let's focus on finding the heartwood."

The thought of diving into something intriguing lifted my spirits too. I couldn't help but feel like the day's puzzles were just beginning.

Love and Linzer Cookies

As we stepped outside into the crisp February air, I glanced at Bella, hoping to broach the subject of Alex again. "So, where's your head at? With the whole Vegas thing, I mean," I asked, tucking my hands into my pockets to shield them from the cold.

Bella sighed, her breath visible in the chilly air. "I don't know. It's just...I don't want to hold him back, you know? I don't know how many opportunities like this he'll find in Havenwood, but the Oasis is here as is my family. I've always had dreams of running the B&B, just like Mama and Papa."

Nodding, I wrapped an arm around her shoulders. I understood her hesitation, but didn't want to push too hard. "Would you like to talk about it more or have a distraction?" I asked.

"Oh, a distraction, please," Bella said instantly. "I've already gone around this situation so many times in my head that I'm dizzy."

"Okay, how about we focus on something else? We still have the location of the heartwood to figure out."

"Of course we can hunt for the tree, but I still think it's not a great place to host a literary event at this time of year," Bella said.

A gust of wind blew down the street, making me huddle deeper into my coat. Bella might have a point about the timing, but right now, what mattered most was keeping her mind off the stress with Alex and finding the heartwood could be the perfect distraction. "You're probably right," I admitted with a small smile. "But finding the heartwood could be a good adventure—something to keep our minds busy. And hey, maybe it'll surprise us and turn out to be the perfect spot."

Bella glanced at me, her expression softening. "You're always good at finding the silver lining, Harper."

I shrugged, trying to keep the mood light. "It's what friends are for, right? We'll figure it out together."

Bella and I made our way through the parking lot, the stiff wind gusting at our backs as we hurried toward the car. Just as she was about to unlock the door, a familiar figure emerged from between two parked cars, making my heart skip a beat.

Gabriel.

"Hey," he said, his smile warm and genuine, sending a pleasant flutter through my chest. "What brings you two here?"

I could feel my cheeks flush slightly, and it wasn't from the cold. "Just doing some research," I replied, trying to keep my tone light and casual, though I was acutely aware of every detail about him—the way his curly dark hair fell slightly over his forehead, the way his eyes seemed to catch the light just right.

Bella jumped in, "How about you, Gabriel? What brings you to the library?"

He glanced toward the building, his smile softening into something almost reflective. "I'm here to help with the cleanup of the children's event. I like to volunteer when I can. It brings back a lot of memories."

My heart warmed at that. Of course, he would volunteer at a children's event—he was always so thoughtful. It was one of the many things I liked about him.

"Wonderful memories, I hope," Bella said.

Gabriel nodded. "My mom used to bring me here when I was a kid. She'd read to me when I was younger. I loved it so much that it became our thing. What we'd do together even when I got older. Sit in the same room and get lost in our own stories, I mean. I loved reading on my own while she was doing magic research."

The mention of Vivienne brought a mix of emotions—admiration for her power and influence, and a bit of intimidation as well. But the way Gabriel spoke about her, I saw another side of her through his eyes.

"Really?" I asked, trying to sound casual. "So, coming to the library is kind of a family tradition?"

He nodded, his eyes softening with the memory. "Yeah, you could say that. Almost as much as Sunday night dinners. This place has always meant a lot to her and to me, too, in a way."

I smiled, feeling a little closer to him with this small glimpse into his world. It was comforting to know that the library wasn't just a place of study for him—it was a place of memories, of family. But with that comfort came a twist of unease. Vivienne's presence was always in the background, and the more I learned about Gabriel, the more I realized that getting closer to him meant getting closer to her.

Since New Year's, Gabriel and I had been keeping things casual by unspoken agreement. He'd been traveling a lot on family business, though I wasn't exactly clear about what that entailed and assumed it was probably magical in nature. Besides, I'd been sorting out my own feelings. Before Gabriel, I'd been in a friendly situationship with my next-door neighbor, Finn. That is, until his ex-girlfriend, Seraphina, turned up out of the blue and declared she still loved him.

The kicker? Seraphina was one of the nicest people I'd ever met, and I really didn't want to get caught in the middle of any drama between the two of them—especially since she was moving back to Havenwood, and Finn was still my next-door neighbor. So, I ended things with Finn.

And then there was Gabriel...

The man I'd spent a magical and altogether thrilling Christmas Eve with. The man I was pretty sure I was falling more for every day, even if I wasn't ready to admit that out loud. Did I want to keep things casual? Easy breezy? I could do easy breezy. Right?

Not a chance, my subconscious whispered.

Gabriel's eyes flicked briefly to Bella, then back to me, and for a split second, I thought he was going to say something more. But then Bella, ever perceptive, cut in.

"Well, Martha's pretty swamped today," Bella said, her tone polite but pointed, clearly sensing the moment. "She'll probably be glad to have your help."

Gabriel straightened, the warmth in his smile returning full force, though I couldn't shake the feeling that something had been left unsaid. "I'd better get in there, then. Don't want to keep the kids waiting."

He gave us a quick wave before heading toward the entrance. I watched him go, my heart lingering on every step he took. The moment of hesitation on his part stayed with me, making me wonder what he had wanted to say.

Once we were in the car with the heater running full blast, Bella turned to me with a knowing look. "You really like him, don't you?"

I felt my face heat up even more and it wasn't from the fan blowing full force. "What? No...I mean, yes...I mean, maybe?"

Bella chuckled softly. "You might want to work on your delivery. Or you could be like me and write a letter."

I swallowed hard, wondering what I would say. I really wanted to get to know Gabriel better, but, if I was being honest, the person getting in my way wasn't me or him. It was Vivienne Silverthorne. She wasn't just *any* mother—she was a force of nature in Havenwood. Getting closer to Gabriel meant stepping into a world where she had eyes everywhere, where nothing went unnoticed, and she had incredible influence in town. What would happen if we tried a relationship, and it didn't work out? Would she take it out on me? What would that mean for my future here in Havenwood, where I felt like I was putting down roots for the first time?

Bella and I drove in silence, both lost in our thoughts and half listening to the cheesy love songs pouring out of the radio as she navigated the snowy streets. When we finally pulled into the driveway of the Enchanted Oasis, Bella's family's bed-and-breakfast, the warmth of the place seemed to reach out and wrap around us like a cozy blanket.

As soon as we stepped inside, the familiar scent of something sweet and decadent greeted us. From the kitchen, Honey's voice rang out. "Bella? Is that you?"

"Yes, Mama. And Harper," Bella called back, shedding her coat.

"Oh, good! I could use a second and third opinion. Your papa is being utterly useless," Honey called, her voice carrying a note of exasperation.

I raised an eyebrow at Bella and whispered, "Is everything okay? Your parents aren't fighting, are they?"

Bella rolled her eyes with a fond smile. "No. They're so in love it blows my mind, even after all these years. What she means is he's tasted whatever it is she's baked recently and told her he loved it."

"Oh. And that's useless?" I said with a soft chuckle.

"Yes. Adorable, lovely, but useless to her in her current baking frenzy." Bella nodded emphatically as I followed her into the DeLucas' large, warm kitchen.

Inside, Honey was bustling around, her cheeks flushed from the heat of the oven, while Antonio leaned casually against the counter, a satisfied grin on his face. The kitchen was filled with the sweet scent of freshly baked treats, and I noticed a tray of perfect heart-shaped raspberry Linzer cookies dusted with powdered sugar sitting on the counter next to an elegant dark chocolate and strawberry mille-feuille.

"There you two are!" Honey beamed, motioning us over. "I've been trying to select the perfect treat to set out for guests on Valentine's Day, but your papa here won't pick one. He says they're both already perfect. I need another opinion."

Antonio grinned, his eyes never leaving Honey. "They are perfect, *amore*. Just like everything you make. Just like you." He caught her up in his arms, spinning her around and giving her a quick kiss on the cheek before setting her back on her feet.

Honey blushed, smoothing her hair into place and waving him off with a laugh. "You're biased. Harper, Bella, please, try them both and let me know which one you like better."

Bella and I exchanged amused glances as we each took a cookie. The delicate shortbread melted in my mouth, the tangy sweetness of the raspberry filling balanced perfectly by the light dusting of sugar. It was, indeed, perfect.

We each took a slice of the dark chocolate and strawberry mille-feuille. The layers of crisp pastry, rich chocolate ganache, and smooth strawberry cream combined into a luxurious bite, the flavors melding together beautifully.

"Wow," I said, savoring the complex flavors. "This is incredible." I couldn't resist taking a second forkful. And then a third.

Bella nodded in agreement, her eyes widening as she took another small bite. "I don't know how you expect us to choose Mama. They're both amazing."

Antonio gestured at us emphatically. "See? That's what I've been telling you for the last ten minutes."

"Oh. Well. It doesn't hurt to have a second opinion. Or a third. But if you had to pick, which was your favorite?" Honey asked.

"Everything was delicious," I said earnestly. "But if I had to choose, the spicy lava cakes were the most exciting—such a fun surprise. Although maybe you could have something milder too for folks who don't like spicy?"

Honey tapped her chin thoughtfully, her eyes sparkling with inspiration. "That's a good point. How about a strawberry shortcake with layers of delicate sponge, macerated strawberries in a hint of rosewater, and topped with a mascarpone Chantilly cream? Garnished with chocolate-dipped strawberries and a dusting of edible gold flakes to make it extra special."

Bella, Antonio, and I spoke all at once.

"Yes. Yes, please," Bella said.

I raised my hand. "I volunteer as tasting tribute."

"That is a superb idea, *amore*!" Antonio chimed in.

Honey looked at each of us, a pleased smile blooming on her face. "I suppose that means I have some more baking to do." She paused, her lips curving into a grin as another idea struck. "Oh! And maybe I'll make a batch of red velvet truffles filled with cream cheese frosting. Bite-sized and decadent—they'd be perfect for Valentine's Day."

Antonio caught Honey's hand and kissed it, his gaze steady and full of warmth. "That sounds wonderful, but it also seems like a lot of extra work for you. How can I help? I'm at your service!"

Honey blushed, but her expression turned thoughtful. "If I'm going to get to work on these desserts, I'm going to need some sustenance."

Antonio straightened, his brow lifting in question. "What would you like, *amore*?"

Honey's grin widened as she considered. "How about steaks with your secret sauce and those crispy roast potatoes? Maybe some broccoli on the side to keep it balanced?"

Antonio chuckled, leaning in to kiss her hand again. "Now *that's* the best idea you've had all day. You take care of the desserts, and I'll take care of dinner."

Bella and I exchanged amused glances as Honey and Antonio shared a warm, lingering look. Watching the two of them work together like this made me hope I'd find that kind of partnership someday—though I wouldn't say no to being a taste tester in the meantime.

The way they looked at each other, like there was no one else in the room, spoke volumes. This wasn't just surface love—it was a deep, unwavering connection that had been built over years of shared experiences, joys, and challenges. It was the kind of love that felt like home, solid and comforting.

Bella nudged me, a small smile playing on her lips. "See what I mean?"

I nodded, feeling a sense of warmth that had nothing to do with the desserts or the cozy kitchen. Honey and Antonio's love was the kind that everyone hoped for, the kind that didn't fade but only grew stronger with time. It was the kind of love I wanted one day.

Watching Honey and Antonio interact made everything seem easy. They were the epitome of relationship goals. I nibbled on my mille-feuille as I watched them tease each other gently and Antonio snatch another cookie when Honey wasn't looking. Maybe love wasn't so complicated after all. Maybe it was just about finding the right person and holding on tight, through thick and thin, just like Honey and Antonio had done.

In that moment, surrounded by warmth and sweetness, I realized that love—like Honey's perfect desserts—was something to savor with all its complex flavors.

The Disappearing Woman

BELLA HELD UP A scrap of paper triumphantly. "Here it is!" she called.

I hurried over, recognizing the paper immediately as the map Clara Silverthorne had drawn over a hundred years ago. She'd wanted to escape her father's oppressive, rigid adherence to tradition and run away with her boyfriend and business partner, Benny O'Rourke. Together they'd run the Hideaway, a hidden speakeasy we'd found under the Oasis. We only discovered it because Benny had been murdered and his ghost was lingering in Spellbooks' attic. Now, Benny and Clara were together again, enjoying whatever the afterlife held.

I flipped the map over, just in case there was anything I'd missed. It had been a while since I'd last looked at it. After we uncovered it during the whole ordeal with the speakeasy, I'd pored over every detail of Benny's and Clara's belongings from Spellbooks' attic. But once the mystery was solved, my memory of the map had faded into the background, overshadowed by everything else. Now, as I examined it with fresh eyes, something new caught my attention. I sucked in a sharp breath. There, faint but legible, was a neatly written rhyme.

"Hey, Bella, look at this," I said, my finger tracing the faded ink.

Bella leaned in, reading aloud with a slight frown:

> *"Where lovers dream and legends sleep,*
> *Beneath the shade where roots run deep*
> *A secret kept through time's embrace,*
> *A hidden heart, a guarded place.*
> *At the edge where light turns dim,*
> *Speak the word to pass within,*
> *Whisper soft, a promise true,*
> *And ancient boughs will welcome you."*

Bella's eyes widened, and she looked up at me in surprise. "Harper, this wasn't here before, right?"

I shook my head, my thoughts racing. "No, it definitely wasn't. It's like...it just appeared." A thought struck me, and I couldn't help but smile, going a little misty-eyed. "Maybe this was Clara's way of helping. She did tell Benny to remind me I was 'holding the pen to my own story.' Maybe this is her giving me a nudge."

Bella smiled softly, looking down at the map again. "She must have wanted you to find this. Maybe she wanted you to find your happy ending too."

"What do you think?" I asked, looking at the map. "Do you think we can use this to find the heartwood?"

Bella shrugged. "If this is accurate, and that's a big 'if', I'd guess that the heartwood is relatively close to the Oasis. I wonder what that rhyme means though?"

"Not a clue. Perhaps people from a hundred years ago were more well-spoken?" I suggested.

"Is that even a question?" Bella snorted. "Have you seen what texting has done to the English language?"

"But it's so much more convenient!" I tapped on the map. "What do you think? Is it walkable?"

"Maybe. I suppose we could give it a try," Bella said.

"I'm up for an adventure if you are. Besides, even if we don't find it, I could use the exercise. Too many desserts recently," I said, patting my stomach.

"Yeah, it sneaks up on you if you're not careful. Especially with Mama in a baking mood."

"Isn't she always in a baking mood?" I teased.

"I suppose so," Bella allowed with a grin. "But I'm not in the mood to freeze on our walk, so let's grab some of the gear we keep around for guests in case they don't realize how cold winters get up here."

About ten minutes into our walk, I was glad Bella had suggested an upgrade to my normal winter clothing. Between the waterproof pants I now wore over my jeans and tucked into my borrowed heavy boots and the hand and foot warmers, I was positively toasty. If it hadn't been for the biting wind turning the tip of my nose into an icicle, I could've walked all day.

As soon as we entered the thickly wooded forest, the wind dropped away as if by magic. There was something peaceful about the crunching sound of our footsteps in the snow being the only thing to break the pristine silence of the forest. There was a clean crispness to the air as we tramped past stoic evergreens keeping sentinel in the otherwise leafless forest. Animal prints pressed into the light dusting of snow on top of a thin crust of ice that we broke through with our much larger feet. It felt as though we'd slipped through the wardrobe into Narnia, where winter whispered secrets, and magic lingered in every shadow.

Bella kept up a rambling monologue, pointing out good places for berry hunting in the summer or childhood play spots. I nodded and made all the appropriate sounds of encouragement to keep her talking. I was glad she'd perked up a little. The walk really seemed to distract her from her worries about Alex. Even though I'd realized within about two minutes that having an event at the heartwood in this season really wasn't feasible, I didn't want to interrupt her to ask to turn back. Instead, I tried to keep my nose warm and ignore the aching in my quads when it was my turn to break a trail through the snow.

"Look over there," Bella said, stopping suddenly.

I shook myself out of a cozy daydream of hot chocolate and another Linzer cookie in Honey's kitchen and followed her pointing finger, hoping that we'd already stumbled upon the heartwood. Instead, I saw a chain-link fence painted a dark green.

"I had no idea this was here," I said, my voice tinged with disbelief.

Bella nodded, her brow furrowed. "Rumor has it, it was put up decades ago, back when they tried to survey the area. No one's ever explained why they stopped—or who's maintained it since."

I raised an eyebrow. "But why put it up in the first place?"

Bella sighed, her breath visible in the cold air. "Probably some misguided attempt at controlling nature. You know, because that always works."

I smirked. "Ah, yes, the classic 'humans versus nature' trope. Spoiler alert: nature always wins."

Bella laughed, her steps crunching through the snow. "Let's just hope it doesn't win today. I'm not in the mood to lose to a forest or a fence." She gave a shiver and rubbed at her arms. "Whoever suggested that hiking in winter is a fun bonding activity definitely needs their head examined."

I smirked. "You're saying this isn't fun?"

"Let's just say, if we don't find the heartwood soon, I'm filing a formal complaint with the magical tree department."

Her sarcasm made me chuckle, but I followed her gaze back to the fence. As we crunched closer, the details became clearer—the paint was chipped and peeling, and parts of the metal were bent, as if someone had tried to climb it or crashed into it. "Didn't the passage in Greenbough's book mention something about a boundary?" she asked.

"Yeah, it did," I said, debating whether I should dig my phone out to double-check. But the idea of swiping the screen without gloves held about as much appeal as spending an afternoon with the odious Puddletons, who ran the other bookshop on Arcadia Avenue. Not my idea of fun.

Bella pointed ahead, her eyes gleaming with excitement. "I think we should follow it. If the heartwood was behind us, I would've found it when I was a kid. Let's see where this takes us. This way, we'll be able to follow the fence back in case we get turned around."

"Good idea," I said, but before the words were out of my mouth, Bella had already started tromping off toward the fence.

I trailed behind her, glad *Operation: Distract Bella from Alex Leaving* was a success, although I needed a catchier name. Given the cold and the slog through the snow, I'd already given up on *Operation: February Event Under the Heartwood Tree*, not that I was willing to admit that to her. I also wasn't about to voice my growing doubts that we could even find the tree, especially with just a snippet of text from a book, a riddle, and an old, hand-drawn map to guide us. Instead, I tried to entertain myself by coming up with better operation names as we walked.

A movement out of the corner of my eye caught my attention. I half turned, expecting to see some little forest creature sneaking out of its cozy home for a winter snack, although probably not as delicious as Honey's mille-feuille. Instead, what I saw stopped me in my tracks.

An old woman, dressed in a long dark dress hobbled from tree to tree, scraping at the bark and adding it to a basket slung casually over one arm. She had a gray shawl wrapped around her shoulders and a matching piece of cloth keeping her wild silver hair out of her eyes. It looked like she'd never heard of the wonders of Gore-Tex, polyester, or even fleece. How was she gallivanting through the woods like that without turning into a human icicle?

As if she heard my mental question, the old woman's head snapped up, her eyes meeting mine and holding my gaze. I froze, unsure of what to do. How did one greet a woman wandering around the woods in the middle of winter with nothing to protect her from the elements but a shawl? A wave was somewhat underwhelming, but running away screaming was probably considered rude. I stood there, staring at her, and suddenly empathized with a deer frozen in headlights. As soon as that thought popped into my head, I couldn't shake the feeling that I was prey. Which made her—

"Harper? Are you coming?" Bella asked.

"What?" I blinked and turned to see my best friend waving me onwards. I raised a hand in return. "Oh. Yeah. I just saw..." I turned back to point at the old woman, but she was gone.

Wingding in the Woods

"A WOMAN IN THE woods?" Bella asked incredulously as we trudged along the boundary fence, her boots crunching in the snow.

"Yeah, wearing a long dress and a shawl. To be honest, she kind of looked like the quintessential witch. You know, from fairy tales. Not the ones living in town," I clarified.

Bella smirked. "All the witches I know are sensible enough to dress for the weather if they decide to go on a hike in the winter. Although, I'm not sure of the new girl who runs the local bookshop. She has an idea in her head that people will want to read books outside under a tree in the middle of February," Bella teased.

"Ha ha," I said sarcastically. "But, I know I saw someone. Maybe I'll ask Aunty Agatha to see if she knows the woman I saw."

"What? You think they all hang out at a woodsy witch's wingding?"

I quirked an eyebrow. "Wingding? Really?"

"It's a good word and has the alliteration thing going for it. I'm sticking by it," Bella said with a smirk.

"Well, in that case, I suggest you—wait! What's that?" I asked, pointing.

The boundary fence sagged and, up ahead, I saw a section of it was broken and lay half buried in the snow. As we approached, I could see the twisted metal links, worn with age as if Mother Nature herself had slowly reclaimed it.

"What happened here?" I wondered aloud.

Bella frowned. "I don't know, but it could be a problem."

"What sort of problem? A big one? You don't think anyone broke it on purpose, do you?" I asked, a shiver crawling up my spine at the thought. Why did this boundary fence even exist? And if it was breached, did that mean Havenwood's protective spells were compromised? What could be getting in—or worse, getting out?

"I don't know," Bella said, her voice tight with concern. Then she pointed behind me, her eyes widening. "But I think this is it."

"Are you sure?" I turned to look, frowning at the empty glade. "This doesn't seem right. Shouldn't a heartwood tree be, well, a tree? That's just a clearing full of snow."

Bella unfolded the map again, smoothing out the creases on her knee as she compared the landscape with the faded ink drawing.

I peered over her shoulder, squinting at the familiar curves and landmarks. "The boundary is just to our left, and that enormous boulder matches this mark here," I pointed at the symbol Clara had drawn, shaped like a crooked house. "It has to be here. But...where's the heartwood?"

Bella chewed her lip, her brow furrowed. "Maybe we missed something?"

"What about the rhyme?" I suggested.

Bella turned the paper over, revealing the verse that had appeared on the back of the map. She read through it, her eyes narrowing as she thought it over. "A hidden heart...and lovers...it's gotta be something to do with love, right? Maybe the answer is love?"

I considered her words, feeling a flicker of something in my chest. "Yeah, but the rhyme says to 'whisper soft.' Maybe it's not enough to just know the answer..."

Bella raised an eyebrow, a smile tugging at her lips. "You think you have to literally whisper it?"

I shrugged, my heart thumping with the possibility. "Only one way to find out." I turned to face the clearing, taking a deep breath as I focused on the space between the ancient trees. Leaning closer to where the shadows thickened, I whispered, "Love."

The surrounding air seemed to shift, a soft breeze stirring the few remaining leaves overhead, and a faint shimmer appeared between the trunks, like a veil parting to reveal something hidden. Bella gasped beside me, and I felt a thrill of triumph wash over me.

"Harper, you did it," Bella murmured, her voice hushed with awe.

I grabbed her gloved hand. "*We* did it. Come on."

I tugged Bella into the small clearing. The large tree in the middle hadn't been visible before, but whatever spell was masking it must've been powerful because I don't know how magic could've kept something so impressive hidden. The branches stretched skyward and seemed to...pulse. Not with light exactly, although that's probably the closest word I could give the sensation. The tree positively vibrated with life, beating like the very heart of the forest. I don't know why I felt that way, but as soon as I thought it, the feeling stuck with a *rightness* I couldn't shake.

It towered above the other trees, its enormous trunk wide enough to block the view of anything behind it, easily dwarfing the largest oaks I'd ever seen. The bark was a deep, impossibly rich brown, interwoven with intricate patterns that looked almost like ancient runes, faintly glowing with a warm, golden hue that shimmered on the snow. The sheer size of the tree made it feel like it could cradle the entire forest within its embrace, exuding a vitality that defied the winter's chill.

As I moved closer, I felt it—a deep hum that resonated through the air, through the ground, right into my bones. It was as if the entire forest was holding its breath, waiting. The temperature, too, seemed to shift. Despite the snow all around, there was a gentle warmth emanating from the tree, enough to melt the snow around its roots. Patches of vibrant green moss and grass peeked through the thinning snow, impossibly alive in the middle of February.

I knelt down, brushing aside a layer of snow, and my breath caught in my throat. Scattered around the base of the tree were small, heart-shaped leaves—vivid green and impossibly alive against the stark winter landscape. Almost without thinking, I tugged off my glove. For a moment, I hesitated, the chill biting at my exposed fingers. But the sight of those leaves—so vibrant, so unexpected—was too striking to ignore. I brushed my fingers against the moss. To my amazement, it felt warm against my fingertips, like it still contained residual heat from summer. Or that it was brimming with magic. I laid my bare hand on the trunk and sucked in a breath. The warmth enveloped me like the tight embrace from a friend you hadn't seen in years. It was like a corner of my heart I hadn't realized was dormant had suddenly been illuminated with love. The tree was alive in a way that I could feel deep inside me. There was no doubt in my mind—we had found the heartwood tree.

"This is it, isn't it?" Bella asked softly.

"Yeah," the single word was all I could manage as I rocked back on my heels and looked up at the tree. I could almost imagine what it would look like in spring, heart-shaped leaves dancing in the breeze and the warm glow from the trunk melding with the sprinkle of sunshine tickling the grass underfoot.

"It's beautiful," Bella sighed.

I nodded, feeling that anything I said wouldn't do the tree justice. Silently I stood, keeping my fingers in contact with the tree as I walked around it, mesmerized by its beauty, by its vitality.

"I wonder what it looks like in the summer. Oh! The autumn! Can you imagine the leaves? We should definitely do something out here next fall," Bella said from behind me.

"Yeah..." I trailed off as something caught my eye when I rounded the trunk. "Umm, Bella?"

She looked up from the leaf she was examining, her brow furrowed. "What is it?"

I didn't answer right away. My eyes were fixed on the other side of the tree, where the once majestic trunk was blackened and charred, a deep scar running from the roots all the way up into the branches. The tree, so vibrant and alive on one side, was scorched and broken on the other. Among the charred wood, faint embers still glowed, pulsing softly in the darkness of the burnt bark, as if the tree's life force on this side was holding on by a thread. My stomach churned as I took in the damage.

Bella came up beside me, her eyes widening. "Harper? What is it? Oh, my goodness! What happened here?"

"I don't know," I whispered. "But it's not good."

Bella swallowed hard, her hand reaching for mine. "We need to tell someone."

The sight of the damaged tree, so stark against the snow, was like a punch to the gut.

I nodded slowly, unable to tear my eyes away from the charred wound in the trunk of the heartwood tree. "Yeah...we do."

But as we stood there in the stillness, I couldn't help but wonder if we were already too late.

Get Cursed

Hastily, I took several steps backwards to get a better view of the damage and then spun around in a slow circle, trying to take in everything at once from the crushed snow and fallen leaves, up the charred trunk, and then to the forest beyond.

"What are you doing?" Bella asked.

"Looking for clues," I murmured, continuing my slow spin.

"Clues? What for? This is obviously a lightning strike." Bella leaned in closer, noticing the faint sparks of embers glowing against the blackened wood. "And it looks like it's still hot enough to burn. We need to call the fire department." She pulled off her gloves with her teeth, digging in her jacket for her phone.

"Lightning? There hasn't been a storm in weeks," I said.

Bella gestured at the tree. "How else would you explain this?"

"I don't know…" I trailed off, stepping back to examine the damage.

Bella's hand shot out toward the scorched trunk, her words spilling over themselves. "It has to be lightning! What else could do this? Should we call someone? What if this starts a forest fire? Can that even happen in winter? I mean, I don't know! Do you?"

Her voice had pitched high enough to rival a fire alarm, and I held up a hand, trying to ground us both. "Maybe. But let's not jump to conclusions just yet." I crouched, brushing snow aside as I pointed at the ground. "Look at these footprints. There's at least two—no, make that three different sets."

"So?" Bella asked, lifting her phone up towards the sky and turning around, obviously searching for a signal.

"Well, it means that the heartwood's location isn't as forgotten as we first thought."

"Or maybe someone just wandered by and thought it was pretty."

"What about the concealment spell?" I countered.

"Okay, I'll grant you that, but what does that have to do with a lightning strike?" Bella asked, her eyes fixed on the screen in her hand.

My mind flashed back to what had happened last Halloween with Isadora Silverthorne, Gabriel's little sister and my friend. She was an elemental mage who had inadvertently set a handful of fires around town when she'd lost control of her emotions. Not that I thought Isadora was responsible for this. She was away at a fancy magical academy. But if something like that could happen to her, who's to say it couldn't happen to someone else?

"Maybe it's nothing," I admitted.

Bella looked up. "I know that tone of voice. What are you thinking, Harper Sullivan?"

I hesitated and then explained my theory that this could be the result of a loss of magical control. If that was the case, we could be facing more fires or lightning strikes or whatever caused this damage in the very near future.

Bella's face was grim by the time I finished. She nodded seriously. "I see your point, but one problem at a time. We need to make sure that the embers in this tree are put out completely and there's no chance of a fire spreading. That would be catastrophic for the tree, the forest, and possibly all of Havenwood."

"You're right. You call the fire department, and I'll keep an eye on the tree to make sure a spark doesn't spread," I said. I'd also keep looking for clues before the fire department washed anything away.

"Fine, but I'm not getting any bars here. I'm going to have to hike back the way we came until I get a signal. Will you be okay?"

"Don't worry. I'll be fine."

Bella shot me a stern glare. "No heroics, okay? I'm still not over what happened at Christmas."

"There're no armed jewel thieves around here. It'll be okay," I promised as I scooped up my glove and tugged it back on. "See? I'm not even risking frostbite."

"Fine. Keep making safe choices until I get back," Bella said before turning and hurrying back the way we came.

I drifted around the tree, looking for anything that might give me a hint about what had happened here. There were several tracks around the tree. Most were various sizes of animals, but I could pick out three human prints. One was a large boot with a distinctive crosshatch tread. On instinct, I grabbed my phone and snapped a picture of the print. From the size, I guessed it belonged to a man. The second was a sort of shuffling trail through the snow, like a child was scuffing her feet and dragging a sled behind her. I followed both prints to where they disappeared deeper into the forest.

At the edge of the clearing, I gasped when I saw something unexpected. There, next to the shuffling trail, was the distinct imprint of something heavy that had rested in the snow. I bent forward to get a better look. I couldn't be one hundred percent positive, but that looked like a basket weave pressed into the snow. My mind flashed to the old woman I'd seen in the woods. Could she have been here? Did she see anything?

The final set of prints was both the most intriguing and the most unsettling. I snapped some more photos before crouching down to examine them. They crisscrossed the snow around the tree, but when I examined the tracks more closely, I saw they led to the trunk and then vanished—no trail leading away. It was as if whoever had left them had climbed straight up the tree and disappeared into the branches above. These prints were small, about the size of mine. But what made my stomach twist was that whoever made them had been barefoot.

Who in their right mind would walk around without shoes in the middle of winter?

With no answers presenting themselves, I turned my focus back to the damage. If the damage to the heartwood was an act of nature, lightning was the obvious answer, just like Bella assumed. But what if it wasn't? This was Havenwood after all. I stretched my mind as far as I could. A magic user like Isadora was an obvious suspect. But there were plenty of tracks around. What about some sort of shapeshifter? I knew Sheriff Jackson was a werewolf, and Finn had even mentioned that advanced druids could shapeshift. However, animals didn't carry fire-starting equipment. No, they'd need some mundane help to cause damage like this.

Other than the footprints, there was nothing. No discarded matches, no scorched can of accelerant, not even a cigarette butt. My eyes swept the area again, looking for any overlooked clues. A lightning strike, like Bella suggested? Maybe. But how could a storm have targeted the heartwood tree so precisely while sparing the rest of Havenwood? The odds didn't seem right.

I knelt, inspecting the damage more closely. The marks weren't jagged like I imagined lightning might leave, but what did I know? I'd never seen the aftermath of a lightning strike up close. My mind raced, flipping between possibilities—magic, nature, or some strange coincidence I wasn't equipped to understand. Or maybe I was just letting my imagination run wild, looking for conspiracies where there were none.

A sharp voice cut through my spiraling thoughts like a slap. "What have you done?"

I whirled to see an unexpected figure dash out of the forest and fling herself at the tree. "Wait! It's hot! It was struck by lightning, and there're still embers in there," I warned, my voice ringing through the clearing as my gut twisted. Anyone throwing themselves at the still smoldering tree would be badly burnt, but it would be monumentally worse for this woman. Person. Creature?

The...being...whirled to face me, giving me my first good look at her. Her bark-like skin was a muted blend of browns ranging from walnut to maple. Her hair, a cascade of frost-touched, dark green tendrils, hung limply down her back, intertwined with bare twigs and the last remnants of autumn leaves, now brittle and faded. It was her eyes that caught my full attention though. They were the same shade of vibrant green as the moss beneath the heartwood tree and blazed with fury.

"This was no lightning strike. No natural lightning touches the heartwood. This was sabotage," she spat out.

"You're a nymph." It slipped out before I could help myself. Thistle was the nymph who lived in the tree behind Spellbooks, but she didn't look quite so...treelike.

"I'm a dryad, and you're a murderer!"

That snapped me out of my stunned examination. "What? No! I didn't kill anyone!"

She threw her hands forward angrily. "And yet the heartwood tree is dying."

"This wasn't me!" I protested.

"Exactly what a perpetrator of such a heinous crime would say." The dryad glared at me. She reached out a hand towards the charred side of the tree.

Despite the accusation, I couldn't let her get hurt. "Wait! It's burning still! You'll get hurt."

The dryad ignored me and placed her hand directly on the glowing embers, closing her eyes. "It's not burning," she murmured. "It's magic. A magical leak from the damage. The tree is...dying." Her head snapped up. "The heart!" she gasped. In an instant, she scampered around the tree and disappeared. I tried to follow her but wasn't as quick in my heavy winter gear. I glanced down noticing the footprints. Well, at least that explained the bare feet in the middle of winter. They belonged to the dryad. But given the footprints, she must've spent a considerable amount of time here. Why?

Before I could ponder the situation further, she reappeared behind me suddenly. "The heart! The heart is gone. Do you know what you've done?!"

"Me? I didn't do anything! I found it like this," I protested.

The dryad cut a hand through the air. "No! Don't lie to me. I know what I see. You're responsible! Give me the heart, and I might have enough time to save the heartwood tree." She thrust out her hand.

"One, I'm not responsible. I just walked up. And two, I'm—"

"Lies!" screamed the dryad, her eyes wild with fury. Her hair, once calm and still, now whipped around her like angry vines in a hurricane. "How dare you deny it! If not you, one of your root-withered townsfolk stole the heart. Bring it back to me! If you don't, the balance will crumble, and your termite-infested town will pay the price."

"No, please! I didn't do anything! I'm just trying to help—"

"Help?" The word spat from her lips like a curse. "After what your kind has done?" She flung a hand toward the charred half of the tree, her bark-like fingers trembling with rage. The surrounding air crackled with energy, and the ground beneath my feet seemed to tremble.

I took a step back, my hands raised in a placating gesture. "Please, just listen. No need to release any sort of magic. I don't even know what the heart is. If you tell me, I can help you find it. Let's just talk about this and—"

"The time for talking is over!" The dryad's voice cut through the air like the snap of a breaking branch, sharp and final. Her eyes bore into mine, filled with a seething anger that left no room for doubt. "The heart is gone, and you—your kind—are to blame!"

"I'm not to blame! I didn't even know the heart was missing until now! Or that trees even *have* hearts!" My voice wavered as I desperately tried to reason with her, fear clawing at my insides. "But I want to help. Please, just tell me what to do—"

"Find the heart, or the tree will die!" Her voice rose to a fevered pitch, each word reverberating through the clearing as the air thickened with her fury. The forest seemed to tremble in response, branches creaking and leaves shivering as though alive with her wrath. "And if that happens, everyone in your root-cursed town will be loveless forever! So swears the guardian of the heartwood!"

Her voice dropped to a low, menacing growl, her gaze locking on me with the weight of ancient power. "And you," she hissed, her words dripping with venom. "Your heart will wither like leaves in the autumn wind. Love will surround you, but you'll never hold it—slipping through your fingers like grains of sand. Longing will be your only companion until the heart is returned, or you fade into nothing."

The forest seemed to close in, her words crawling under my skin. "You will know longing and loneliness like never before, until the heart is returned—or until you yourself are nothing but a shadow of what you once were."

"Wait! You can't do this!" I cried, taking a step forward, but it was too late.

The dryad's form wavered, her outline flickering like a flame in the wind. The wild magic around her intensified, swirling leaves and snow into a chaotic dance as she stepped around the trunk of the heartwood. Her last words echoed through the clearing, chilling me to the bone.

"Remember my warning, human. The forest is watching, and it will show no mercy."

I dashed around the tree. "Wait!"

But she was gone, leaving me alone in the silent, snow-covered grove, the weight of her curse hanging heavy in the air.

The Missing Heart

I STOOD THERE, DUMBFOUNDED, staring at the charred damage to the heartwood in front of me, trying to comprehend what had just happened. The once-serene forest around me seemed to shift, the air growing colder, the shadows deepening with each passing breath. Trees, which moments ago had stood as silent sentinels, now loomed closer, their bare branches clawing at the sky like skeletal fingers. The soft, muffled blanket of snow underfoot felt suddenly treacherous, like a trap waiting to be sprung.

The wind picked up, whistling through the trees with a mournful wail that sent shivers down my spine. It felt as if the forest itself was watching me, judging me, the dryad's curse echoing in the rustle of the dead leaves clinging to the branches. I could feel it—an ancient, primal anger stirring in the woods, as if the very ground beneath me was recoiling from my presence.

A wave of panic washed over me, tightening my chest. What else was lurking out there, hidden among the shadows and the twisted roots, besides an enraged dryad? The thought that the entire forest could turn against me, that all of Havenwood could suffer because of a curse I didn't even understand, sent a jolt of fear through me.

My hands trembled as I tried to steady my breath, but the chill in the air seeped into my bones, making it impossible to think clearly. The forest, so recently a place of quiet solace, now felt alive in the worst way—watching me, judging me, its anger as raw and primal as the dryad's fury.

The realization hit me like a blow, snapping me out of my shock. I had to move, to act, before the forest's wrath escalated—before this curse, whatever it was, took root and spread. The dryad's warning echoed in my mind, and I knew I couldn't stand here, paralyzed by fear. I needed to find the real culprit and the dryad's missing heart.

Desperately, I circled the tree again, scanning every inch of the ground, every root, every scrap of bark for something I might have missed. A clue, a sign, anything. But other than the footprints, there was nothing. No trace of magic, no glimmer of hope.

I stopped, closed my eyes, and tried to breathe through the panic rising in my chest. It was like an ocean inside me, waves crashing against my thoughts and pulling me under. Every instinct screamed at me to run, to get as far from the forest as I could, but I forced the feeling back, one shaky breath at a time. Slowly, the tide receded, leaving me with just enough space to think.

I was out of my depth here—completely unprepared for anything involving forests, dryads, or a heartwood tree. I needed help, but who could I turn to?

Gabriel and the Silverthornes came to mind first. They had knowledge, resources, and probably records that could shed some light on the dryad's accusations. But going to Gabriel meant involving his mother, Vivienne, and the thought of facing her made my stomach twist. She'd already called me out more than once since I moved to Havenwood, accusing me of putting the town's secrets at risk—always with that cold, piercing stare that made me feel like a schoolkid caught sneaking out of class. And while I hadn't done anything wrong, not really, how long would it take before coincidence stopped being a good enough excuse?

No. The Silverthornes were my last resort.

My thoughts spiraled again, grasping for anyone else who might help. Martha Morningstar? No, we'd already tried that. The panic flared, choking me, but I forced it down with a sharp inhale. What about Aunty Agatha? She'd been in Havenwood forever and knew its history better than anyone. Maybe she'd heard something—some old legend or forgotten story that could lead me to the dryad's heart.

But what if she hadn't? What if no one could help?

Then, like a lifeline cutting through the haze, a thought pierced the fog of fear—*Finn.*

Of course. Finn.

He was a druid, connected to nature in ways I couldn't even begin to understand. If anyone had an insight into the heartwood, it had to be him. A flicker of hope sparked in my chest, momentarily dimmed by the thought of our recent distance, but there was no time to dwell on that now.

As I considered Finn, another name came to mind—Thistle. I nearly facepalmed myself. How could I have overlooked Thistle, the nymph living in the tree behind Spellbooks? If anyone had a direct line to the world of trees and plants, it would be her. The panic ebbed further, replaced by a growing sense of purpose.

And then, almost as if the pieces were falling into place, another thought occurred. Two members of my book club were involved with plants. Stella owned a flower shop, and Jeremy was a botanist. Their love of nature had been what had drawn them to one another in the first place. And Jeremy's uncle—how could I forget? Jeremiah, the treant. He was a unique being that reminded me of the dryad in someways, but much less angry.

As the ideas spun through my mind, I realized something. Going to all of these people for help to find the missing heart would take time—time the heartwood tree might not have. What if, instead of trying to bring everyone to the tree, I could bring the tree to them? The thought felt crazy, but also somehow right. I didn't know if it was even possible, but I had to try.

I gathered my strength and jumped. It took me a couple of tries to reach the lowest hanging branch with my heavy winter gear, but I did it, clutching at the slender, flexible wood. I wanted a sample, something I could bring back to those who might be able to help. Gently, I tried to snap it off. Maybe it was my fingers going numb with the cold, but the branch refused to break, bending easily under my fingers. I gritted my teeth, pulling a little harder, but it was as if the tree itself was refusing to let go.

Frustration bubbled up, and I muttered, "Come *on*! I don't know enough. I need something to show the others, so they can figure out how to save you." My voice was barely a whisper, more a plea than anything.

Suddenly, I felt the branch give way, almost as if the tree had finally relented, understanding my intent. The moment I broke it free, I felt a subtle pulse of magic—a connection between the tree and the piece I now held. Maybe, just maybe with the help of my friends, this small sample would be the thing we needed to help save the heartwood.

I barely had finished securing it inside my jacket when Bella returned, her cheeks flushed with the effort of running through the snow.

"Hey!" she called. "I couldn't get a signal but didn't want to go too far away from you in case that fire spread."

"What fire?" I asked dumbly.

Bella gave me a strange look, holding up her phone. "You know, the embers? The fire department? Calling for help?"

I swallowed hard, shaking my head. "The fire department can't help with this," I muttered. The tree wasn't burning—it was leaking magic. And that meant there was only one person in Havenwood equipped to handle it.

Panic clawed at me again, my thoughts spiraling as I wrestled with what I needed to do. I didn't want to call Vivienne Silverthorne. I'd firmly put her in the 'last resort' category of my mental list. But as much as I hated to admit it, nerves couldn't stand in the way right now. This wasn't just some supernatural mishap I could stumble through on my own.

If the heartwood's magic was leaking, we needed someone with both authority and knowledge—someone who could handle a situation like this. And no matter how much she intimidated me, that person was Vivienne Silverthorne.

I grabbed Bella's hand and started pulling her toward the Oasis. "Come on. We need a signal."

"What are you doing?" Bella exclaimed, stumbling as she tried to keep up.

"I'll explain everything, but right now, we need to call Vivienne Silverthorne."

"What?! I thought you were terrified of her."

"I'm not terrified," I said quickly. Bella raised an eyebrow, giving me *that* look, and I sighed. "Okay, fine. Maybe I am. A little. But I'm not wrong. We can't deal with this on our own, and if that means facing Vivienne, then I'll just have to deal with it."

Bella studied me for a moment, her expression somewhere between amusement and concern, before letting out a low whistle. "I don't know whether to be impressed or worried. Either way, let's go before you change your mind."

wild magic

In a shorter time than I would've thought possible, Bella and I hurried along the boundary fence, retracing our steps toward the Oasis. My gaze flicked to the multiple jagged breaks in the fence, ones I hadn't noticed earlier in our rush to reach the heartwood. Had they been there before, or was the damage spreading? The thought made my stomach churn, but I couldn't afford to dwell on it now.

I had a phone call to make.

As soon as my phone showed a flicker of signal, I called Gabriel. The words tumbled out in a rush as I explained everything that had happened. He listened quietly, his steady voice a balm when he finally replied. "You did the right thing," he said firmly. "We'll be there as soon as possible. My mother and I will meet you at the Oasis."

It said something for our state of mind that Bella and I sat in silence after I put the tree branch in a vase of water. Neither of us touched the treats Honey tried to entice us with, so lost in our thoughts of angry dryads and curses. We'd agreed not to say anything to Honey or Antonio until we knew more, but it was hard to make small talk with something so big looming over us. Silence was easier.

Honey must've sensed our tension because after a few minutes of coaxing, she squeezed my shoulder and left us to our thoughts. Luckily, we didn't have much time to wait as the crunch of tires on snow outside announced the arrival of a car.

Bella and I glanced at each other and then raced for the front door, opening it as Gabriel and Vivienne strode up the porch steps, matching grim expressions on their faces.

I took a breath, stepping forward. "Thank you so much for coming. Like I told Gabriel, we discovered—"

Vivienne sliced a hand through the air. "Not here. If the situation is as you described, we must hurry. We can talk on the way."

In short order, Vivienne, Gabriel, Bella, and I rushed back through the woods towards the damaged tree. The dryad's curse still echoed in my mind, her furious voice and the eerie rustling of the forest's magic clinging to me like a second skin. Every step felt heavier, the surreal events in the forest crashing against the more familiar, grounded rhythm of Havenwood life.

Vivienne had insisted no one else accompany us, her tone sharp and final. That, more than anything else—the dryad's rage, the strange and wild magic we'd witnessed—drove home just how dire this situation really was. Vivienne tended to close ranks when trouble arose, keeping only those she deemed necessary in her circle of trust. On the one hand, my ego preened a little at being included, even though I knew it was because of our discovery rather than my abilities. On the other, Vivienne still intimidated me. To be this close to her only added to my nerves.

On the way, she demanded that we recount everything that had happened in detail. I glanced at Bella, but she gestured for me to speak. After all, this had been my idea from the start. As quickly as I could, I explained why we'd been in the woods and what we had discovered along with our initial assumption that the tree had been struck by lightning. I flicked my eyes towards Vivienne when I said that to get her reaction. A small puff of air formed in front of her as her lips tightened and thinned, but other than that, she gave nothing away.

I continued, my heart rate climbing as I reached the part in the story where the angry dryad appeared. I kept my voice steady, careful not to linger on the more personal aspects of the curse. Instead, I focused on the dryad's fury, the threat to Havenwood, and the danger to the heartwood tree itself. Even so, my breathing quickened, and a knot of unease tightened in my chest, pressing harder with each word I forced out.

Gabriel reached out, his gloved hand gently squeezing mine. The quiet gesture steadied me, as though he could sense there were things I wasn't ready to say aloud. His touch wasn't demanding—just a silent reminder that he was there, ready to listen if and when I chose to share.

I squeezed back, the simple connection easing the tension knotting in my chest.

I didn't want to appear weak in front of Vivienne—not now, not when we needed her help—but Gabriel's quiet support reminded me that I didn't have to carry this alone.

As I finished the story, the air seemed to grow colder, the icy breeze whistling through the bare, almost skeletal tree branches. Vivienne's expression remained inscrutable, her eyes narrowing slightly as she considered my words. Gabriel opened his mouth, but his mother raised a hand, cutting him off before he made a sound and continued to stride through the snow. As I led the way towards the clearing, I noticed I could see the heartwood from a greater distance this time. It looked as if the concealment enchantment only worked on first-time visitors. Vivienne strode past me, not hesitating as she entered the clearing, giving me the distinct impression that was not her first time under the boughs of the ginormous tree.

I felt my stomach twist into knots, a gnawing sense of unease creeping up on me. I didn't know what Vivienne was thinking as she circled the tree, examining the damaged section at length. She started on a second circuit, her mouth turning downwards. A realization hit me like a punch to the gut. Vivienne didn't know what had caused this either. Her uncertainty made me even more anxious. Her reputation as a formidable force in Havenwood was well-earned. The set of her jaw reminded me of by-the-book teachers on the army bases where I grew up. Suddenly, I felt like a student again, one who was awaiting judgement.

Finally, Vivienne broke the silence, her voice calm but edged with a sternness that made my pulse quicken. "I see nothing to contradict your story. Unless I miss my guess, someone with great power has deliberately sabotaged the heartwood. You girls obviously had nothing to do with this except being in the wrong place at the wrong time."

Bella grabbed onto my sleeve, and a silent breath of relief whooshed out of me.

Vivienne held up a finger, drawing my attention back to her. "However, angry dryads are not to be trifled with. They are ancient beings, magically tied to the very essence of the forest. If this dryad has cursed you and the town, it means she believes the situation to be dire."

I swallowed hard, my mouth suddenly dry. "I understand. We didn't mean to—"

"I know you didn't," she interrupted, her tone softening slightly, though her eyes remained sharp and calculating. "But intention doesn't matter to a dryad, especially one who believes her charge is in danger. I will do what I can to find her, reach out and try to reason with her. But we must find this heart, and quickly."

She paused, her gaze steady and unyielding as she continued. "The heartwood's magic is ancient and powerful, but it is also fragile. If the heart isn't recovered soon, the damage could become irreversible. The wild magic leaking from the heartwood will only grow stronger, and if it continues to mingle with the dryad's curse..." She hesitated, her lips pressing into a thin line.

"What happens then?" I asked, my voice barely above a whisper.

Vivienne's eyes flicked to mine, her expression unreadable. "Let's just say the results could be... unpredictable. The dryad's curse may have been aimed at you and the town, but wild magic is chaos—it has no boundaries. Together, they could twist and warp the very fabric of the town, in ways none of us could foresee. If left to fester, Havenwood could become something unrecognizable."

Her words hit me like a punch to the gut. I had already felt the weight of responsibility but hearing it from Vivienne made it more real. The idea of wild magic running rampant through Havenwood was terrifying, and the thought that it was all connected to the heartwood made my stomach churn. And the curse... I couldn't even bring myself to contemplate the personal ramifications of that—not now. The air seemed heavier, and I forced myself to steady my breathing.

"Then we have to find the heart," I said, my voice coming out more confident than I actually felt.

Vivienne nodded once. "Precisely. And quickly."

I nodded, my throat tightening with the effort to hold back the surge of emotion threatening to overwhelm me. Bella stepped up, squeezing my hand and giving me a bit of courage. Thank goodness for her.

"What can we do?" she asked, her voice steady.

Vivienne nodded her approval. "The first thing is to keep this quiet. We don't want to start an emotional response that spirals through town."

I couldn't stop myself. "But what happens if we can't find the heart? Shouldn't people get out of town before the dryad's curse takes effect?"

Vivienne's gaze was strong, but there was a hint of pity in the depths of her eyes. "It has already taken effect. Anyone who was within the town when the curse was uttered now has it hanging over their heads like a sword of Damocles. Unless we find the heart or convince the dryad to withdraw her curse, there is nothing those people can do and nowhere they can go to escape it. We're not yet sure of how far her curse or the wild magic extends, but dryads are powerful. Leaving town is likely fruitless. No, letting them know now would be the height of folly and incite a panic."

I froze, my thoughts spinning as the dire curse replayed in my mind. Was I really destined to be loveless forever unless we found the heart? How much power did a dryad really have? Enough to cast a curse to last a lifetime? My breath started to come fast and hard, and my gaze flitted around the clearing, landing on Gabriel. His calm, steady presence was like a lifeline pulling me back from the edge. Did I love him? I didn't know. It was too new, too fragile. But I wanted the chance to find out—wanted time to figure out what we could become.

When our eyes met, the clarity in his expression made me close mine for a moment. I thought of my dad—his unwavering belief in my strength and the lessons he taught me about facing challenges, no matter how overwhelming.

I drew in a deep breath and straightened my shoulders. No. This wasn't the end of the story—not for me, not for Havenwood. I wasn't going to let a leafy dryad throwing a temper tantrum full of chaotic magic tear apart my life.

"Let's not waste any more time," I said, my voice steady. "We need to find the heart."

Vivienne nodded, meeting my eyes. "Agreed."

Gabriel pushed to his feet. "Harper and I can search for it. Maybe we get lucky, and the dryad misplaced it or the thief dropped it somewhere in the forest. We'll start there."

Bella glanced at the sky, her brow furrowing. "We don't have enough time for a prolonged forest search. It'll get dark soon, and we only have our phones for light. Their batteries will drain fast, and besides, it'll be freezing out here after sundown. Tramping through the forest at night is a great way to get lost or worse."

Vivienne nodded. "You're right. Besides, anyone brazen and powerful enough to attack the heartwood, wouldn't drop their prize as they escaped. No, Gabriel, what I need you to do is return to town and call Lucas. The two of you will be the first line of defense to combat any wild magic. Magic like this can be unpredictable. Even volatile. We must keep the tourists ignorant as to the nature of our town and the residents as calm as possible. I'm depending on the two of you."

Gabriel nodded. "What about you, Mother?"

Vivienne's eyes narrowed. "I'm going after the heart. There are only a handful of people in town who are powerful enough to do this," she waved at the charred half of the tree. "I will discover who is responsible and...*convince* them to return the heart immediately."

Bella stepped forward, her expression thoughtful. "If it's an outsider—someone new in town—I might hear something at the Oasis. People talk. I can ask discreetly if anyone unusual has been spotted or mentioned recently."

Vivienne regarded Bella for a long moment before nodding. "Good. Follow that lead. But be cautious. If someone has the power to steal from the heartwood, they'll have no qualms about protecting themselves—or their prize."

I shivered, both at the look in her eyes and her tone. Vivienne wasn't just one of the most powerful mages I'd ever met—she was one of the most powerful mages in the country. I didn't even want to think about what she might do to convince the thief to hand over the heart. For an instant, I almost pitied them. Almost.

"What about me?" I asked, glancing between Vivienne and Gabriel. "I can't just sit around doing nothing."

Vivienne's lips pressed into a thin line, and for a moment, I thought she might dismiss the idea of me helping outright. But Gabriel spoke before she could. "Harper could coordinate with Bella and look for anything unusual around town. She has a knack for spotting things others overlook—like she did at the ball with the jewel thieves. If there's a lead to find, she'll see it. I have confidence in her abilities."

I blinked, caught off guard by the trust in his voice. A quiet warmth spread through me, momentarily pushing back my earlier doubts.

Vivienne arched an eyebrow. "Whoever is behind this is dangerous. This isn't a task to take lightly."

Gabriel's gaze stayed on me, steady and reassuring. "I trust her instincts. And if anything seems off, she has my number. Lucas and I will be nearby if backup is needed."

I nodded, my chest tightening with equal parts determination and gratitude. "Okay. I can do that."

Vivienne's sharp gaze turned toward me, pinning Bella and me in place. "Stay discreet. We can't risk the thief catching wind of this—or worse, spooking them into doing something reckless. If you find anything, bring it to Gabriel or me. Do not act alone."

"I won't," I promised quickly, though a flicker of doubt crept in. Staying subtle wasn't exactly my strong suit. Ever since I moved to Havenwood, trouble seemed to find me. And when it came to magic, I was painfully aware that my small gifts didn't compare to the Silverthornes' raw power. I was in over my head, and we all knew it.

Bella shot me a warning look. "Just don't go overboard. Whoever did this went after the heartwood—that's not someone you want to mess with. We've got enough going on without you adding 'reckless heroics' to the list."

I offered her a faint smile. "Don't worry. I'll stick to asking questions. And if anything feels even remotely dangerous, I'll get out of there right away."

Gabriel stepped closer, his gaze steady and warm in a way that made my stomach flip. "Good. And remember, you're not alone in this. If anything happens, call me. I'll be there."

His calm confidence in my abilities given the gravity of the situation did strange things to my nerves—both steadying and unsettling me all at once. I nodded, managing a quiet "Thanks," even as my chest tightened with the important task looming before us.

Vivienne's sharp gaze swept over us, her tone cool and authoritative. "Remember, our goal here is to protect Havenwood. With wild magic on the loose, the stakes are higher than you can imagine. Mistakes are a luxury we cannot afford."

Her words struck like a cold wind, leaving no room for doubt. I swallowed hard, the enormity of her statement settling in. There was no room for mistakes. No room for hesitation. Ready or not, I had to rise to the challenge—for Havenwood, and for myself.

Secrets Underfoot

BELLA AND I LINGERED on the porch as Vivienne and Gabriel's car disappeared down the driveway, its tail lights fading into the dusk. The sun was sinking fast, casting long, weak shadows across the snow. Bella tilted her head toward her car, silently asking if I wanted a ride back to town. I shook my head, adjusting my coat as the branch tucked inside pressed lightly against my chest, its faint hum of magic a steady reminder of everything that was at stake.

"I'll walk," I said, offering a faint smile when her brow furrowed. "I just...need to clear my head. Besides, who knows? Maybe I'll spot something useful on the way back. The sooner we can sort this out, the better, right?"

She studied me for a moment, then sighed and handed me the spare gloves and scarf she'd brought along earlier. "Be careful, okay? And remember what the Silverthornes said—no playing hero."

"I won't," I promised, tucking the scarf securely into my coat.

After a quick wave, I turned and headed toward Arcadia Avenue, my boots crunching softly against the snow. The cold stung my cheeks, sharp and biting, but I welcomed it. It was a bracing contrast to the swirl of unease in my mind. Each step carried me deeper into Havenwood's quiet streets, my eyes scanning the growing shadows for anything out of place.

Gabriel believed I had a knack for noticing details, and I clung to that confidence, hoping it might lead me to something—anything—that could help us.

The streets were eerily still as I wandered, warmth spilling from shop windows and the faint scent of dinners wafting through the air. It should have felt comforting, but it didn't. The normalcy of it all clashed against the chaos I knew was brewing beneath the surface, leaving me with a hollow unease.

As the last rays of daylight faded completely, I let my gaze linger on alleyways and shop doors, searching for anything unusual among the familiar sights. Was the thief out here somewhere, blending into Havenwood's everyday rhythm? Or was I just trying to distract myself from the growing fear that wild magic might already be spreading beyond the heartwood?

Eventually, the cold seeped into my bones, urging me to seek shelter. I quickened my pace toward Arcadia Avenue, Spellbooks' inviting glow drawing me in like a beacon. Gideon, the small gargoyle above the door, called out a welcome. I think I muttered a response. However, my thoughts were so consumed by dryads and curses that I couldn't be sure.

The moment I stepped inside, the shop's warmth enveloped me, easing the tension in my shoulders. I pulled the branch from my coat, holding it for a moment as its gentle pulse of magic seemed to transfer to my hand. It was a small connection to the heartwood, a reminder of how much work lay ahead. Carefully, I set it on the counter, my fingers brushing its bark one last time before letting go. Mr. Wigglesworth descended from of his normal lounging place in the front window and greeted me with a pitiful meow. He wound through my legs, making a valiant impersonation of a purring trip wire. I crouched to scratch him behind the ears and then scooped some food into his bowl.

"Sorry, boy," I murmured. "I bet you've been lonely. I'm sorry I was gone so long. It's been a strange day."

With the cat satisfied and Luna nowhere to be seen, I went in search of a vase. Eventually, I found one tucked high on a shelf in the broom closet. I fished it down, filled it with water, and plopped the branch of the heartwood into its temporary home. Cupping my chin in my hands, I considered the fragment of the heartwood as my mind wandered.

Where could the missing heart be? Who would steal it? I doubted it was random thievery, but what was the point? Why target the heartwood? Did the culprit bear a grudge against the dryad? If she was always as prickly as she'd been today, I could see why someone might want revenge. Maybe the thief hadn't wanted to risk getting cursed by her. I couldn't blame them for that.

But their actions had left the heartwood—and Havenwood—vulnerable. Wild magic from the heartwood leaking throughout town and causing who knew what kind of chaos. Combine that with the dryad's curse looming overhead, the town's ability to love would wither, leaving everyone disconnected and cold. And then there was my curse: cruel, personal, and devastating in its specificity. A life surrounded by love but never able to hold it? The thought sent a shiver down my spine, but I pushed it away. That was a nightmare I couldn't afford to dwell on.

A quiet knock at the door pulled me from my spiraling thoughts. My head jerked up, and I was surprised to see Finn peering in. He lifted a hand and gave a little wave before gesturing between himself and the interior of the shop with a questioning look. I nodded and hurried over as he stomped the snow from his boots outside.

Seeing Finn standing there made my heart squeeze unexpectedly. Earlier, I'd been so careful to sidestep the complexities of relationships—the tangled mess of emotions, unspoken expectations, and unresolved histories. But now, the dryad's curse loomed over me like a storm cloud, threatening to make even those complications a distant, unattainable dream. The thought sent a pang through my chest, sharper than I wanted to admit. Not that it might matter if we couldn't find the missing heart. Without it, Havenwood's warmth would fade, love replaced by emptiness and apathy. And as for me, the dryad's curse promised a far crueler fate—always yearning, never holding. I couldn't let that happen. Not to the town, and not to me.

Still fumbling with my composure, I unlocked the door and pulled it open, letting Finn step inside out of the cold.

"Hey," I said, awkwardly holding out my hand for a handshake.

"Hi there," Finn said, moving in for a one-armed hug. He froze, looking at my hand and then dropped his for a handshake at the same time I stepped forward into what I expected to be a friendly squeeze. Instead, it was an awkward muddle of arms and murmured apologies as we extricated ourselves.

A blush burned my cheeks, and I tried to distract both of us from the embarrassment. "What are you doing at work so late? Did you have an appointment?" I asked, tipping my head towards his tattoo shop next door. Havenwood might be small, but Finn's reputation as a tattoo artist extended beyond the town limits. The mundane humans thought his designs were pretty, but they were more than pretty. I knew that he also infused his magic into his work. Nothing big or world changing. Just some runes to help his customers get over colds faster or to bring a little luck their way, that type of thing.

Finn lifted a shoulder. "I had some paperwork to do. I saw you through the window, and Gideon said you seemed out of sorts when you got home, so I thought I'd check on you. You know, as a...um...friend." He hesitated over the last word, and I couldn't tell if it was because he still wanted something more or because he was working hard to adjust to the boundaries we'd already set. Either way, his smile softened into a look of concern as he examined my face. "Is everything okay? You look worried."

"I am," I admitted. "Everything is definitely not okay. Not even close."

"Want to talk about it?" he offered.

I hesitated, Vivienne's words about avoiding a panic ringing in the back of my mind. But this was *Finn.* He'd always been so supportive, ever since I moved to Havenwood. Besides, as a druid, he might know something about what could damage the heartwood tree or, at the very least, how to placate an angry dryad.

Ten minutes later, I'd finished my story with very few interruptions from Finn. He was a good listener and seemed to understand half of my story was me trying to process everything that had happened. The silence stretched after I finished, and he examined the small heartwood branch in the dusty vase sitting in the middle of my counter.

"So, what are you thinking?" I asked.

Finn scratched the back of his head. "Well, I've never heard of a dryad cursing an entire town before, so she's either incredibly powerful or this is a massive bluff."

My heart leapt into my throat, hope flaring. A bluff? That could change everything. "Really? You think she was lying? That would make so much sense! I mean, it'd explain why she was so dramatic about it, and maybe—"

"Harper." Finn's voice was calm but firm, cutting through my rambling. I froze mid-step, realizing I'd started pacing the shop. With a sheepish glance, I sat back down.

"What is it?" I asked, trying to rein in my over-eagerness.

"You said wild magic, right?"

I nodded and Finn's brows drew together in that frown of his that always meant trouble. "Well…on second thought, maybe not," he murmured.

My stomach dropped. "Why not?"

He sighed, not meeting my gaze and running a hand through his long hair. "I forgot about the ley lines."

"The ley lines? What are those?" I leaned forward, my heart sinking with the sense that this was about to get worse before it got better.

"It's a system of branching and intersecting lines of natural magic," Finn explained. "Havenwood happens to be situated on a nexus where several ley lines converge. Personally, I think it's what drew the town's founders here in the first place."

"What does that mean, exactly?" I asked.

"Magical creatures are drawn to them instinctively. Humans, on the other hand, tend to avoid places like this. They feel…off, like their gut instinct is warning them away. Most people don't even know ley lines exist."

"How is Havenwood such a tourist town then?" I asked.

Finn shrugged again. "Personally, I chalk it up to a number of factors. The town's charm does a lot of the heavy lifting. Back in the old days, people would get uneasy and leave before they even made it past the welcome sign. But now? The internet hypes it up, travel bloggers rave about Havenwood's 'unique energy,' and most folks just assume the weird feeling is part of the experience. Maybe some blame it on bad seafood, others on small-town quirks. But the wards the Silverthornes place around the town? I think they keep the worst of it from driving people away."

"You're telling me Havenwood's sitting on top of a magical hotspot, and somehow I'm only just now realizing how much that actually affects the entire town? Maybe even the whole region?" I said, exasperated with myself.

Finn sighed. "Not many people can actually tap into ley lines, Harper. The magic in them is raw, primal—dangerous, even. You'd need serious training, abilities, and protections to handle that level of magic safely. So, no, it's not exactly common knowledge."

I paused, the weight of his words settling uneasily in my mind. "If they're so dangerous, why would anyone build a town on top of them? Isn't that asking for trouble?"

"Ley lines aren't dangerous if they're left alone," Finn said quickly. "They naturally balance themselves, creating a steady flow of energy that's harmless unless someone actively tampers with them. But when they're disrupted, they release wild magic and that balance collapses. That's when things get dicey."

I frowned, recalling how Benny O'Rourke once claimed the Hideaway's runes had stayed strong because it was built on an unexplainable magical hotspot. Now, Finn's explanation cast that claim in a new light—more logical, but also far more unsettling.

"Well, I've definitely never heard of ley lines before," I admitted.

"And that makes sense," Finn replied with a faint smile. "For most folks, it's just background noise. If I'm right, this sounds like it could be linked to ley lines. Maybe the heartwood acts as some kind of filter for the magic? I don't know. But for someone like the dryad or anyone tampering with the heartwood...well, they'd know exactly what they're dealing with—and how much power is at stake. It's dangerous to mess with ley lines unless you have the proper training and magical abilities."

"Could someone like Vivienne Silverthorne manage it? Is that the power level we're talking about?" I asked.

Finn shook his head seriously. "Not even her."

I blinked in surprise. "But isn't Vivienne the most powerful mage around? She left the council of mages or whatever, didn't she?"

Finn nodded. "Yeah, but she's a mage. The magic in ley lines is wild magic. A druid would have a better chance at safely tapping into a ley line than a mage because of our affinity to the natural world. Even then, it would have to be one of the top tier druids who's devoted most of their life to studying and perfecting their craft, and it would still be incredibly dangerous to tap even the smallest ley line."

"So, you're saying someone with an ability in natural magic would be able to use one of these lines?" I asked.

Finn tipped his head and waggled a hand back and forth. "Hypothetically, yes. I've never seen or even heard of it being done before."

"Do you think that's why someone did this? To gain access to the ley lines' power?"

Finn shook his head emphatically. "It's just too much power for one person to handle without some sort of magical filter. Any magic user who attempted it without the proper preparation would be setting themselves up for failure at best."

"What if it's not a person? What about a dryad?" I asked.

Finn nodded grimly. "That's where my mind went. Because dryads are normally so shy, no one ever thinks of them doing big magic, but from what I know, yeah. It's possible. An elder dryad would be one of the few creatures who could tap into a ley line and use its magic safely."

"Great. So, she's either bluffing or has the magical equivalent of a super power-up behind her curse. How do we know which it is?"

Finn blew out a breath and shook his head. "Wait and see if wild magic starts causing havoc around town, I guess."

"And here I was wishing for more excitement just this morning. Now, I'd be happy with boring again," I said, throwing my arms out as if speaking to the whole of Havenwood.

Finn patted my shoulder awkwardly. "Look, I could be wrong. She might not be able to access ley lines at all. Why don't I make some calls? I still have a couple of friends in the druid community who'll talk to me. Maybe they'll have some more information."

I closed my eyes and nodded. "That would be helpful. Anything that helps in breaking her curse as soon as possible is great in my mind."

Finn nodded, but before he could say anything else, I straightened and added quickly, "But Vivienne was very clear—we need to keep this quiet. The fewer people who know, the better. If word gets out, it could make things worse."

His smile faded slightly as he considered my words, then he nodded again, more seriously this time. "Fair enough. I'll be careful. I'll reach out to the people I trust, but I'll make sure to keep it discreet."

"Thanks," I said, exhaling a breath I didn't realize I'd been holding.

"Who knows? It still might be a bluff," Finn said after a moment, offering me a small, reassuring smile.

I tried to smile back, but it felt forced and unnatural. "Yeah. It might be," I agreed. I don't think either of us believed it.

Silence stretched uncomfortably between us. Finn shifted his weight from foot to foot. "Well, I'd better go make those phone calls."

"Yeah. Thanks," I murmured.

He turned, one hand on the door. "Harper?"

"Yeah?"

"Probably best to stay inside and out of the forest. Just until I get a clearer picture of what's going on," he said.

I nodded silently as he headed out into the cold February night, ducking his head against the icy wind. I locked the door behind him and rested my forehead on the smooth wooden panel. It wasn't the most comforting way to end the conversation, but I couldn't really be upset with Finn. He was just looking out for me after all, but I didn't like the idea of hiding away in my shop until he got word back from his contacts.

A rumble under my fingertips pulled me out of the beginnings of a spiral. "I hear you, Spellbooks," I murmured.

A strong vibration shook the floorboards under my feet, making me stumble a few paces backwards.

"Woah! What's going on?" I asked, surprised. Normally, the spirit in the shop wasn't this forceful.

Another rolling vibration shuddered through the floorboards, pushing me back another step. Behind me, the back door leading to the garden behind the shop banged open, letting in a blast of freezing air.

"Spellbooks! What are you..." I trailed off, as the back door banged against the frame again and again. "There's something you want me to see?" I guessed.

The banging stopped immediately.

"Okay, I get it. But what's in the backyard that—" I broke off as the pieces clicked together. "Thistle! You're telling me to go see Thistle!" I exclaimed. The vibrations under my feet shifted into what felt like a satisfied purr, confirming my guess.

I hesitated, glancing at the back door. Vivienne's strict orders about keeping this secret loomed large in my mind. I'd already brought Finn into the fold, and now, obviously, Spellbooks too. But this wasn't just anyone—it was *Thistle*. If anyone could shed light on an angry dryad, it would be her.

Still, the thought of defying Vivienne again made my stomach twist. "Spellbooks," I muttered, lowering my voice, "I was not supposed to talk about this with anyone, and now I'm pulling you and two others into my circle of trust. You're not going to rat me out to Vivienne, are you?" The shop gave no response, but somehow the steady hum beneath my feet felt like quiet encouragement.

I sighed. Spellbooks was right. If anyone knew more about a furious dryad than the druid next door, it was the tree nymph who lived in the oak behind the shop.

I just hoped she was home—and that including her wouldn't come back to haunt me.

The Race Is On

I KNOCKED LOUDLY ON the rough bark of the oak tree, shivering as another gust of wind pierced my sweater. I really should've grabbed a coat before heading outside, but excitement and anxiety had defeated my common sense. Loose snow kicked up as the breeze turned into a blast, whistling around the corner of the shop. Was this biting February wind in Connecticut normal, or was it somehow influenced by the turmoil surrounding the heartwood? It was hard to tell past the chattering of my teeth. The dryad hadn't cursed the weather, but with wild magic seeping from the ley lines, even the wind seemed to carry a sharp, unnatural edge.

I was just about to turn back to get my coat or possibly even a parka when part of the trunk slid back, revealing a pair of leafy green eyes.

"Harper?" Thistle asked in disbelief. "What are you doing out here? And without a coat? You'll catch your death!"

"H-h-hey," I managed as a shiver shook me from head to toe. "Mind if we have a quick chat? Something's happened."

I don't know what she saw in my face, but whatever it was must've been convincing because suddenly Thistle reached out a hand, grabbing mine with surprising strength and pulling me forward. For a moment, I thought I was going to crash face first into frozen bark. I closed my eyes and flinched away, but instead of scraping up my nose, all I felt was a breath of blessed warmth that carried the scent of rich earth, moss, and a hint of something floral. I opened my eyes in surprise and realized I was standing inside Thistle's home for the very first time.

I would've assumed that living in a tree would be a squished affair, especially when inviting guests over. Nothing could be further from the truth. I don't know how, but the interior of Thistle's home far exceeded the exterior. The walls, though formed from the living oak, were smooth and flowed seamlessly into the floor, which was carpeted in a soft, verdant moss that was thicker than the plushest of carpets. The wood had a subtle glow, as though lit from within, casting a gentle amber light that bathed everything in a warm, welcoming hue.

Furniture seemed to grow naturally from the tree itself—graceful chairs and a long, curved bench made from smooth wood with cushions woven from leaves and vines that looked surprisingly comfortable. A low table, its surface polished to a mirror-like sheen, sat in the center of the room, adorned with a delicate arrangement of fresh flowers, each one seemingly plucked from the forest just moments before despite the snow outside. It was hard to believe I was inside a tree. The space felt more open than I would've imagined possible, like I'd just pushed through a dense thicket to discover a secret grove hidden deep within the woods, untouched by the cold world outside.

Thistle herself blended perfectly with her surroundings from the walnut of her hair to the leafy green tint in her skin. Despite the weather outside, she wore a dress woven from layers of leaves, each one overlapping the other, giving her the appearance of a living, breathing part of the oak tree itself.

"Thistle, this is beautiful." The words escaped me on an awed breath.

"Thank you. But tell me what's happened. You look like you've seen a ghost—and not one of Mason's drinking buddies." Thistle's tone was light, but there was a hint of worry in her deep green eyes.

I swallowed hard. "I need your help." The words felt heavier than I wanted them to. "I found something in the forest, and I think something may be terribly wrong." I saw the flicker of concern in her expression morph into full-blown trepidation.

She grabbed my hand. "Tell me everything. What's happened?"

I took a deep breath, trying to steady myself as I rushed through the story. "The heartwood tree is withering. Its heart has been stolen," I finished.

Thistle's eyes widened, and she sucked in a breath. "Stolen? That should be impossible. The heartwood's heart is deeply connected to the tree's guardian," she gasped.

I froze. I'd read a little about a guardian, but didn't know much. "What are you talking about?" I asked, my mind flying back to the books I read in the restricted section of the library.

Thistle's hand flew to her mouth. "Oh no," I heard her mumble past her fingers. "I really shouldn't have said that."

"Said what? What's going on?" I asked.

Thistle's wide eyes met mine, and she clapped her other hand over her mouth, shaking her head back and forth.

"Thistle, I need to know," I pressed.

She shook her head more violently, peeling her fingers away from her lips long enough to say, "I gave my oath to the nymphs to not talk about it with the uninitiated. Even now, I fear I've said too much."

Sensing she had the answers I needed, I took a desperate stab in the dark. "Is this about the ley lines under Havenwood?"

Her mouth dropped open, and her hands fell to her sides. "How do you know about them?" she whispered.

I waved a hand through the air, not wanting to admit I'd only dis-covered their possible existence mere moments before. Instead, I drew on my extensive knowledge of reading fantasy books and the oaths typically included therein. "It doesn't matter *how* I know, only *that* I know. See, I'm not uninitiated, so you can talk about it with me, right?" It was another wild conjecture on my part, but at this point in time, wild conjecture was the only thing I had going for me.

Thistle's brows drew together. "I suppose that's true. The oath was meant to keep me from discussing the matter with those in Havenwood who didn't know, but since you already do..." she trailed off.

Before she could talk herself out of it, I snapped my fingers and pointed at her. "Exactly. You didn't tell me the secret. But now that I know it, could you please connect some dots for me? What does the heartwood have to do with ley lines? Who is the heartwood's guardian? Why should it be impossible to steal the heart?"

Thistle hesitated, glancing around as if the walls themselves might be listening. I reached out and gently touched her shoulder, lowering my voice.

"Please, Thistle. I need to know."

When she met my eyes, I could see the inner battle she was fighting. However, she must've seen something similar within me because she sighed and spoke in a soft voice. "The heartwood tree isn't just a symbol or a powerful magical object. It's the anchor point for the ley lines beneath Havenwood, a focal point where all the magic converges. The ley lines are the lifeblood of the magic in this town, and the heartwood is the very core that keeps that energy flowing smoothly. The combination of the heartwood and the ley lines are the reason Havenwood can function as it does, with magic occasionally slipping into the open without the normal humans really noticing or remembering."

"I thought that was because of the Silverthornes' spells," I said.

Thistle tipped her head from side to side. "Yes and no. The spells focus the energy of the ley lines. Without the lines, the Silverthornes would need a veritable army of mages to keep the charms running at the level they do."

"I'm confused. What's the point of the guardian then? Who is this guardian?" I asked, my mind flashing back to the dryad who had laid the curse.

Thistle shivered. "Her name is Rowena. From all accounts, she used to be quite sweet. Now? Well...I wouldn't want to get on her bad side."

Before I could ask another question, Thistle wove her fingers together. "Think of it like a symbiotic relationship. The Silverthornes protect the forest from development, infrastructure, and other destructions masked as progress. In return, the heartwood, protected by its guardian, filters the magic of the ley lines into useable...umm...fragments? Pieces of magic small enough that mages like the Silverthornes can use them without fear of magically overloading."

"And what happens if someone magically overloads?" I asked, not sure I wanted to know the answer, but knowing I needed to.

"It's not pretty. The best case is they go mad. Usually, they just release the magic before it gets to that point."

"And then what?"

"Magic runs amok until balance can be restored," Thistle said with a shrug.

"But what does that mean?" I pressed.

Thistle toyed with the ends of her long hair. "It's magic. Wild magic at that. It could mean anything. It would depend on the situation."

I nodded, trying to process the gravity of what she was saying. "So, without the heart, this symbiotic relationship is disrupted and the magic in the ley lines can what? Do whatever it likes?"

"Basically," Thistle confirmed, her voice grave. "If the connection between the ley lines and the heartwood has become unstable, it would cause magic to spiral out of control. You say the tree is withering? That means its connection to the ley lines is already tenuous or it would be able to repair itself. Without the heartwood acting as a filter, a protection against the wild magic inherent in the ley lines, chaos will spread, affecting not just the tree but the entire town and everyone in it."

"But the guardian," I pressed, needing to understand. "I'm guessing that was the dryad? Why did she allow this to happen?"

"The guardian is...*was*," Thistle corrected herself, "Rowena. She was bound to the heartwood tree, tasked with protecting it. As long as she remained true to her oath, the heart could not be taken. But something must have happened, something that weakened her bond."

Thistle remained silent for a moment, her gaze drifting to the flowers on the table. "The guardian's anger is understandable," she said quietly. "The heartwood tree is her charge, and without its heart, the tree—and the magic it holds—cannot survive."

"What happens then?" I asked, not wanting to hear the answer.

Thistle's expression softened with a touch of sadness. "Then the curse will take root, and Havenwood's future will wither along with the tree. The heart must be found and returned to its rightful place, or the town—and everyone in it—will be lost to a life without love."

"So, whoever stole the heart was trying to gain control of the heartwood? To what end? To allow wild magic to spread through Havenwood?"

"Perhaps," Thistle allowed. "Or perhaps there's something else going on."

"Which is?"

"The heart is more than just a source of power; it's like a living entity, attuned to the magic and needs of the town. If it sensed that Rowena could no longer protect it, or that the tree was in danger, it may have sought a new guardian, someone it deems worthy to protect it and, by extension, the town."

I took a deep breath, trying to put the pieces together in my mind. "So, the heart could be stolen, or it could be hiding and waiting for someone to prove themselves? Is this like an Arthur and Excalibur thing? We'll know who the new guardian is if they can pull a sword out of a stone in the middle of the forest?"

Thistle nodded, her expression somber. "Something like that, but if it is hiding, finding it won't be easy. The heart won't reveal itself to just anyone. It will require someone who demonstrates not just power, but a true understanding of the responsibility that comes with being its guardian."

"How do I know where to start looking? Or even if it's hiding? Couldn't it be that someone has taken it?"

Thistle stepped closer, placing a hand on my shoulder. Her touch was light but grounding, like the gentle strength of a growing vine. "You won't know until you start. I'll do what I can to help by finding out what is happening with Rowena, but you need to find the heart."

"How?" The word slipped out, sounding more plaintive than I would've liked.

Thistle's eyes softened. "Start by listening to the tree, Harper. It's alive, connected to the ley lines, and it speaks through the rustle of its leaves, the creak of its branches. The heartwood tree may guide you if you're open to hearing its call."

I already knew the heart was missing, but the magnitude of it truly hit me now. I had known we needed to find it fast, but urgency ignited within me like a spark catching dry tinder.

"We need to find the heart as soon as possible!" I exclaimed.

Thistle nodded in agreement. "Exactly. The town's magic, its very essence, is tied to the heartwood. Without the heart to anchor the magic, the ley lines will continue to destabilize, and Rowena's curse will tighten its grip."

"We need to spread the word, get as many people searching as possible," I said. "With all the magically gifted people in town, I bet we can find someone with a knack for finding lost items, but—"

Thistle's expression turned stern. "No. You cannot speak of the ley lines unless it's with someone who already knows about them. The knowledge is dangerous, Harper. It's a secret that must be protected at all costs. Swear to me that you won't breathe a word of this."

I sucked in a breath, biting back my instinct to argue. Vivienne's earlier warning echoed in my mind, cold and unshakable. First her, now Thistle, both repeating the same warning.

I let the breath out slowly, forcing control into my voice. "But who can I ask for help if I can't talk about it?"

"You can speak to those who already know, but no one else. Not a soul," she said, her voice low but filled with an earnest urgency. She glanced around the oak as if worried someone had snuck into her home without either of us realizing. She dropped her voice. "If word of this spreads, the repercussions could be catastrophic. For both of us. Swear it to me, Harper."

I swallowed hard, the urgency in her eyes pinning me in place. "I swear," I said, my voice steadier than I felt. "I won't say a word to anyone about the ley lines."

Thistle nodded in relief and took a step back.

I rubbed at my upper arm, not sure of what the next step was. "So, I guess I'm on my own?"

"Not entirely," Thistle reassured me, her voice gentle. "You have allies—those who understand the importance of the heartwood and what's at stake. You're not in this alone."

I tilted my head, curiosity mingling with a glimmer of hope. "Like who?"

Thistle's gaze shifted, thoughtful. "Nymphs, dryads, druids—those connected to the forest and its magic. The heartwood is a lifeline, even to those who don't live in Havenwood. They would understand what's at risk. But finding the heart won't be easy."

My stomach sank. "Other than you and Finn, I don't know any of those people." An idea occurred to me, and I leaned forward. "If I can't ask for help, can you?"

Thistle hesitated, her fingers brushing over the bark of her oak as though drawing strength from it. "I'll do what I can. I need to consult with some of my contacts, those who might have insight into what's happening with Rowena. But if I bring you with me, I fear they might run away. Humans haven't always been kind to those of the forest. And to be fair, those of the forest aren't always kind, even to their own." Her voice dipped, and her hand stilled on the bark, tension radiating through her frame.

Her words struck me like an arrow, guilt blooming in my chest. How could I have been so thoughtless? Thistle had fled the forest to escape the pain of isolation, the bullying she'd endured from her own kin. Havenwood and Spellbooks had become her sanctuary, a place where she could live without fear of rejection or judgment. And now, here I was, pulling her back into the very world she'd tried so hard to leave behind.

"I understand," I said softly, my throat tightening. "I don't want to make this harder for you."

Thistle's expression softened, and she gave me a small, reassuring smile. "We all do what we can, Harper. You're trying to help. That matters. I will see what I can do."

She paused, brushing her hands down the front of her dress as though trying to shake off the heaviness of the moment before squaring her shoulders and nodding at me.

I returned the gesture but couldn't quite shake the pang of guilt lancing through me at what I was asking of her. However, I didn't see a better way and if we didn't find a solution, then all of Havenwood would suffer, including Thistle. "You reach out to your contacts, and I'll do some research on the heartwood. First thing tomorrow, I'll go back to the tree and see what I can find."

As we stepped out of Thistle's oak tree, Spellbooks' backyard stretched out before us, bathed in silvery moonlight. The wind that usually whispered through the trees had stilled, leaving the leaves frozen mid-sway. Shadows clung tightly to the garden's edges, and not a single noise broke the silence. The air pressed down, heavy, like a held breath waiting to exhale.

Then I noticed it—an unsettling flicker in the streetlamps, their lights dimming and flaring as though struggling to stay lit. The snow that had fallen earlier was no longer a pristine white; it seemed to shimmer with a strange, iridescent green glow. A low, almost inaudible hum vibrated through the air, making the hairs on the back of my neck stand on end.

Thistle froze beside me, her eyes widening as she scanned the surroundings. "The wild magic...it's already leaking into the town," she whispered, her voice filled with alarm. "The ley lines are destabilizing faster than I feared. We don't have a moment to lose. We need to find and replace that heart. Now!"

The town I knew so well had suddenly taken on an ominous edge, the wild magic warping everything it touched. A sudden crackling sound made me jump, and I turned to see a large branch splinter and fall from the oak tree, crashing to the ground. I barely dodged out of the way in time. Before I could react, the branch leapt up as if it were a child that had just played a prank on me. It skittered away towards the woods, running faster than I would've imagined on its leafless branches.

"Thistle?" I turned to her instinctively, my heart pounding. Her wide, unblinking eyes followed the rogue branch as it disappeared into the forest. The serene calm she usually carried was gone, replaced by a stark, almost fragile stillness.

I reached out and gently touched her arm. "Are you okay?"

Her voice trembled, barely above a whisper. "Oh no. This is bad. So very, *very* bad."

I swallowed hard, forcing the panic clawing at my throat to subside as her words sank in. This wasn't just about saving the heartwood tree anymore—it was about stopping the wild magic from unraveling Havenwood entirely. Standing beside Thistle, both of us rooted in place as the runaway branch vanished into the dark woods, one thing became crystal clear: the wild magic wasn't some distant threat. It was here—alive, relentless, and spreading. The race against time had begun, and we were already losing.

Shreds of Hope

I HURRIED BACK TO the shop before the cold could set in too much, shutting the door behind me with a breath of relief at the warmth and sense of normalcy the shop exuded.

A pair of white ears poked around a shelf, followed by Luna's sharp eyes. "Fluff and furballs, what's got your tail poufed? You look like you've seen a ghost."

"Not this time," I quipped, my mind flashing back to Benny. However, I wasn't about to get distracted by a ghost when a curse was on the horizon and quickly filled the rabbit in on everything that had happened today.

"Everyone with an ounce of sense knows that hosting an event outside in February is a bad idea," Luna sniffed.

"*That's* what you're focused on? Not the curse?" I asked. I hadn't said anything explicit about the ley lines. I'd forgotten to ask Thistle about the repercussions of talking about them, but based on my vast fantasy book knowledge, it probably wasn't cuddles with a teddy bear in front of a crackling fire while drinking hot chocolate. Breaking an oath like that usually came with a heaping helping of mortal peril, a side of possible death, and a sprinkling of intestinal distress. I'd kind of been hoping Luna would give me some indication she already knew about the ley lines so I could ask her some of my mounting questions.

Luna's ears twitched. "You live long enough, and curses, though rather unfortunate, do happen. Especially in this town. Why, even Agatha went through a rough patch where she was casting hexes about every other day. Not that they ever worked exactly how she intended, but they were there, just hanging about and waiting to ambush unsuspecting people."

"Hexes can ambush people?" I asked.

"Of course. How else do you think they get cast? You don't suppose people volunteer to be on the receiving end of a hex, do you?"

"Well, no, but—"

Luna waved a paw, cutting me off. "Enough about Agatha and her ill-spent seventies. What are you going to do about this missing heart and the wild magic?" Luna demanded.

"Try to find it and do whatever I can about the wild magic and its...um...source." I put an extra emphasis on the last word, raising an eyebrow at Luna.

"What's wrong with your face?" Luna asked. "Did that fish last night not agree with you? I told you it looked suspicious. You should never eat anything that can watch you."

"You eat potatoes. They have eyes," I pointed out.

"Not the same thing and you know it," Luna sniffed.

I held up my hands in surrender. "Fine. I concede. But about the source of the wild magic. It's a secret that I can't discuss openly. Do you happen to know what it might be?" I left the question hanging in midair, hoping she'd offer some sort of illuminating insight, and I wouldn't have to break my promise to Thistle.

Luna narrowed her eyes at me. "The first rule of magical secrets is you don't talk about magical secrets."

"But how do you know who knows what you know if you can't talk about it? Can you write it down? Act it out like charades?" I really should've gotten more details from Thistle.

Luna twitched her nose. "I'll admit, it *is* a bit of a conundrum. Generally, the person you swore the oath to would let you know who was safe to talk to and who wasn't."

I groaned and dropped my head into my hands. Thistle hadn't given me any clues except it was an oath that bound tree nymphs. I assumed Finn was safe to talk to because he already knew about the ley lines, but I couldn't be one hundred percent sure of anyone else.

Luna patted my arm in an uncharacteristically sympathetic gesture. "Whatever's going on, I'm sure you'll figure it out. If you run into a wall, I find a cup of tea and a good night's sleep work wonders."

"Thanks," I murmured as she hopped down the hall towards her special rabbit door, disappearing outside. Where the familiar went in this weather was always a mystery to me, but I knew better than to pry. A low, eerie hum filled the air, like the wind was singing, but it wasn't a melody I recognized. The streetlights flickered for a split second, plunging the town into darkness before snapping back on. My breath hitched, and I rubbed the back of my neck, trying to ignore the tingle of dread creeping up my spine.

Something Luna said niggled at me. "If you run into a wall..." I mused aloud, dragging my fingertips along the smooth wood of the wall behind me. I felt Spellbooks give a little shiver to let me know it was listening.

Listening. Spellbooks was listening. *Had been listening.*

Spellbooks had been here when Finn was talking about ley lines. Which meant I wouldn't be breaking my oath to Thistle if I talked about the ley lines with my magical bookshop. Score one for loopholes.

"Spellbooks? Do you remember what Finn said about ley lines?" I said to the empty shop. Another rippling vibration tickled my fingers in what I recognized as Spellbooks version of an affirmative. "Do we have any books here that could give me a better idea of what they are, how they work, and how to manage a potential, um, magical leak?"

A rumble shook the shop, followed by the thump of several books hitting the floor. Spellbooks used its abilities to shimmy the books over to the counter, even being considerate enough to flip them open to the relevant pages. Sometimes, I still couldn't get over how cool it was to have a sentient shop. For a bibliophile like me, it was better than having a magic wand. A place where the bookshop itself wanted to help you solve the mysteries of the world? That was pure bliss.

"Right," I said, scooping up the armful of books and plopping down in one of the comfy armchairs I kept for customers. "It looks like I've got some reading to do."

As I flipped through the pages of the first few books Spellbooks had thoughtfully selected, I quickly realized just how elusive solid facts on the ley lines truly were. The information was all over the place, with much of it contradicting itself or veering into the realm of pure speculation. From what I could gather, ley lines were like the earth's natural arteries of magic, invisible channels of energy crisscrossing the globe. They were said to operate on a constant, low-level leak, kind of like how a river saturates the surrounding land without washing everything away. This gentle flow of magic was what sustained the environment, quietly supporting life and various forms of magic without drawing too much attention.

As I read, Spellbooks gently nudged another book toward me, its pages fluttering open to a section on magical catastrophes. I glanced up, half smiling at the shop's insistence, before diving into the text. The warnings in this book were clear—and unsettling. While ley lines usually did their thing harmlessly beneath the surface, providing a stable foundation of magic, messing with them was a whole different story. Breaching a ley line without the proper safeguards could be catastrophic, like taking a wrecking ball to the middle of a dam. The energy that normally seeped out in a controlled, manageable way could be unleashed in a destructive wave, causing anything from localized magical chaos to outright disaster.

Just as I was beginning to grasp the gravity of the situation, another book slid across the floor, opening itself to a page filled with lore about ley lines. I skimmed through the passage, which spoke of gates and access points—closely guarded secrets known only to a few. These gates, where ley lines could be accessed directly, were protected by powerful wards, ancient spells, and, in some cases, physical guardians. The texts made it clear: you didn't mess with ley lines unless you were either extremely powerful, had the intricate know-how, or were at least partially desperate—and maybe a little crazy. Possibly all the above. The thought of someone having the audacity or recklessness to breach a ley line sent a shiver down my spine.

Was that what had happened? Someone deliberately stole the heart from the heartwood in order to breach the ley lines under the town? Or, as Thistle had implied, had the guardian somehow been deemed unfit, and the heart was seeking a new companion?

I closed the last book, placing it on the stack next to me as I contemplated the situation. Spellbooks, ever the diligent assistant, began reshelving the volumes I'd already read, as if eager to clear space for the next round of insights. It was hard to know what to believe, but one thing was certain: I needed to tread carefully. With every page turn, Spellbooks seemed to reinforce that point, its subtle guidance reminding me just how high the stakes were. The more I learned, the more it became painfully obvious that tampering with ley lines was a dangerous game—but one I was going to have to play whether I liked it or not.

I yawned and stretched the kinks from my back as my eyes started to burn with exhaustion. It had been a long, eventful day. As much as I'd like to find the answers I was searching for, I wasn't going to be much use unless I got some sleep. Goosebumps rose along my arms as the temperature seemed to drop sharply, despite the fact I was ensconced in the warmth of the bookshop. There was an unsettling stillness around me, the kind that made the hairs on the back of my neck stand up. Even the familiar creaks of the building seemed to have changed, sounding more like whispered warnings carried on the wind.

I looked over at the branch of the heartwood sitting in its dusty vase on my counter. "If only you could communicate like Spellbooks, then maybe you could just tell me where the heart is," I said aloud.

Unsurprisingly, the branch didn't speak. Although, I'm not sure I would've been all that shocked if it had. It certainly would've made my task of finding the heart easier if the branch had jumped up and ran off like the branch from Thistle's oak tree. Unfortunately, I wasn't that lucky.

"Well, if you don't know where the heart is, maybe you can tell me what's going on with the heartwood. What's causing it to wither? Is it just the missing heart, or is it something more?"

The branch stayed woodenly silent.

I blew out a sigh, making a mental note to go see Jeremy Rowan tomorrow morning. The friendly botanist might be able to shed some light on what was happening with the heartwood. Part of me hoped he'd tell me it was a typical thing, like the common cold but for trees, and could be cured with some rest and lots of fluids.

I knew it wouldn't be that easy, but with little else to go on, I clung to my shred of false hope like it was a life raft as I headed upstairs to bed.

A Storm Is Coming

AFTER A FITFUL NIGHT filled with dreams of angry trees stalking through the streets of Havenwood, I was almost glad when I saw the gray light of dawn chasing away the stars. I groaned as I grabbed my phone, squinting at the time. How could it still be this early? It felt like the night had stretched for a week, and not in a good way. All sane people were still asleep at this hour. Just as I was about to put it down and try to get some more shut-eye, a message from Bella popped up—a funny meme that made me smile despite myself. At least I wasn't alone in this early morning misery.

You can't sleep either? I typed back.

Her response appeared within seconds. *Come over for breakfast?*

I sent her a thumbs up before dragging myself out of bed. Today was definitely a caffeine-before-anything-else type of day. While I waited for the coffee to brew, I sent a message to Finn asking what he'd found. He didn't respond right away, not that I blamed him. If he was sleeping, more power to him. I wished I was. Sleeping that is. Not with Finn. I sighed and ran a hand through my hair. Even though I'd ended any sort of romantic situation, he was still one of the first friends I'd made here in Havenwood. I wondered what these new boundaries would do to our friendship.

A cheerful little beep let me know my coffee was ready. I scooped up the mug and inhaled the rich aroma gratefully. Whoever discovered how to make coffee was right up there with Einstein and Newton when it came to great discoveries as far as I was concerned.

I hurried to get ready, the promise of breakfast at the Oasis giving me almost as much energy as the coffee. As I finished putting food out for the animals and tugged on my boots, Luna hopped onto the counter, eyeing me with her usual sassy expression.

"Skipping out on work already? The day's barely begun," Luna said archly.

I rolled my eyes, grabbing my coat. "I'm not skipping out, just delaying a little. I barely slept. Thoughts of wild magic running rampant through Havenwood kept me up most of the night. If I'm going to function at all today, I need a good breakfast in me."

Luna tilted her head, her whiskers twitching. "If you're going to thrive in this town, you're going to have to learn to juggle your responsibilities. I've got some ninja stars in the back if you need a head start."

I blinked at her. "What do you use—no, I don't want to know." I exhaled, shaking my head. "Until I become a master like you, Luna, I'm going to focus on one thing at a time." I laid a hand on the wall. "Spellbooks? I'm opening late today."

Luna hopped down from the counter with a graceful leap. "You do realize that it's your shop, right? If it doesn't open on time, you're the only one losing out."

At that moment, Spellbooks rumbled softly.

Luna flicked an ear. "See? Spellbooks agrees with me. So what's your plan? Run around town fixing the magic while also staying here and operating your business? Or were you expecting me to solve all your problems for you?"

I let out a tired chuckle. "It would be nice if you could, but somehow I think this might be beyond even your impressive capabilities."

She gave me a look. "Flattery won't distract me. You should consider getting some help around here—at least part-time. Unless, of course, you've figured out how to be in two places at once."

I scrubbed a hand through my hair. "Fine. I hear you. I'll think about it. I just need to deal with this current crisis first."

Luna's eyes sparkled. "Now you're talking sense. But whoever it is, you'd better tell them that carrots and cabbage are fine offerings to stay on my good side, but *always* radishes over rhubarb."

"I'll keep that in mind," I said with a grin, heading toward the door. "But for now, breakfast calls. Try not to get into too much trouble while I'm gone."

"I'll assume that was directed at the hairball you call a cat," Luna called after me, with a haughty sniff.

As I stepped outside, the cold air bit at my cheeks, sharp enough to sting, but the promise of a warm breakfast at the Oasis kept my feet moving. The streets were unnervingly quiet at this early hour—no voices, no distant hum of cars, not even the usual sound of wind rustling through the trees. Instead, the world was saturated with an unnatural stillness, amplifying every crunch of snow under my boots.

The absence of human sounds made the subtle noises of nature seem overwhelming—the creak of ice settling on branches, the faint crackle of frost spreading across frozen leaves. A strange hum seemed to vibrate just at the edges of my perception, setting my nerves on edge. I scanned my surroundings, my breath fogging in the frosty air, trying to decide if it was the wild magic in Havenwood—or just my overactive imagination—making things feel so off.

I shook my head, brushing off the thought and forcing myself to focus. After last night, it made sense that every shadow felt spookier, every sound sharper. If anything strange did happen, I reminded myself, I could call Gabriel. Should call Gabriel. But I didn't want to bother him if it was all in my head. After all, he had enough on his plate at the moment.

Still, I couldn't shake the feeling that something was watching, hidden in the shadows just beyond the edges of my vision. A shiver ran up my spine and I glanced over my shoulder at the empty street behind me. However, that didn't stop me from increasing my speed as if trying to outrun the creeping paranoia.

By the time I reached the Oasis, my cheeks were flushed, and my neck ached from glancing over my shoulder so often. Seeing Bella at the door, her usual bright smile lighting up the early morning, brought a welcome wave of relief. For the first time all morning, something felt normal again.

"There you are!" she said, grabbing my arm and pulling me inside. "Come on, help me with these trays. The faster we get things set up, the faster we get to eat."

I gladly left the sensation of restless energy outside the Oasis, surrendering gratefully instead to the hustle and bustle of the B&B this early in the morning. It must've all been my imagination doing its overactive thing again, right?

Honey was bustling around the breakfast nook, arranging trays of treats that looked like they'd been pulled straight from a fairy tale. The air was thick with the scent of freshly baked pastries and the sweet tang of citrus.

"Morning, Harper!" Honey called cheerfully as I shrugged out of my coat and joined her and Bella in setting up. "Hope you're hungry!"

"When you're cooking? Always," I said as my stomach gave a rumble of confirmation.

With all of us working together, it didn't take long to arrange everything. The kitchen table brimmed with an array of delectable breakfast items, each one clearly crafted by Honey's magical touch. Golden-brown cinnamon swirl buns glistened with sticky icing, begging to be tasted. Flaky white chocolate and cranberry scones crumbled perfectly with each bite. At the center stood a tower of delicate macarons in enchanting flavors—rose, lavender, and honeyed lemon—practically glowing with allure.

Rich, buttery croissants, still warm from the oven, filled the table beside a platter of honey-drizzled fruit tarts that sparkled faintly with a dusting of edible gold. Honey stood near a bubbling pot of hot chocolate, the scent of melted dark chocolate mingling with hints of cinnamon and vanilla wafting through the room. A basket of fresh bread rolls, their crusts perfectly crisp, nestled in a napkin-lined basket next to a beautifully baked spinach and cheese quiche topped with crumbled bacon.

"Are those your famous honey-glazed pecan rolls?" I asked, my mouth watering as I eyed the pastries.

Honey beamed with pride. "Fresh out of the oven. Help yourself. There's plenty."

I glanced around at the impressive spread. "I thought this was Havenwood's slow season," I said, raising an eyebrow. "But you're cooking enough to feed a small army."

Bella laughed, leaning against the counter. "It *is* the slow season. Normally, the Oasis is about half full this time of year. But today? Closer to seventy percent."

I widened my eyes. "So, I should be grateful you saved some for me?"

"Exactly." Bella nudged me towards the table with a grin. "It pays to have connections."

She passed me a plate, which I shamelessly piled high with a little of everything before following her toward the kitchen where we could talk in private.

"Hot chocolate or coffee?" Honey called from near the stove.

"Would you judge me if I said both?" I asked.

"I'd judge you if you didn't," Bella said with a wink.

Honey chuckled. "Coming right up."

Antonio pushed through the backdoor to the kitchen, stomping snow from his boots and peeling off his jacket. "All the walks are plowed and salted," he announced.

"Perfect timing. Breakfast is served," Honey said, setting down a plate filled with quiche and a huge cinnamon swirl bun for her husband.

Antonio caught her around the waist, planting a kiss on her cheek. "How did I ever get so lucky? Thank you, *amore*. Girls! Did I ever tell you that I'm the luckiest man alive?" he called.

"At least twice a day," Bella said with a good-natured smile.

"Well, I'm slipping then," Antonio said, giving Honey a little twirl. She giggled and headed towards the coffee machine to get him a cup. "The day I met your mother was the best day of my life and every day since only reinforces that. Why she chose me, I'll never know, but I'm eternally grateful every day."

"Likewise, sweetheart," Honey said, sliding a mug of coffee in front of her husband as she settled down at the table across from me. "So, how are you feeling after your adventure in the woods yesterday?" she asked.

I bit the inside of my cheek, unsure of what I could say. After all, Finn hadn't sworn me to secrecy, but Thistle had. After a moment, I decided to avoid mentioning the ley lines. Discretion was the better part of valor after all.

"Well, it wasn't what I was anticipating, that's for sure," I said.

Antonio blew on his steaming coffee. "I don't think anyone could've anticipated that. Never in all the time we've lived in Havenwood has anything like this ever happened."

I shot Bella a look over my mug. She shrugged, unapologetic. "I had to tell them. They're my parents."

Antonio arched a brow. "And you think we'd just sit quietly and *not* ask questions?"

I let out a breath, setting my mug down. "Fair point. So... you mean everything with the heartwood?"

"The heartwood, the dryad, all of it," Antonio said, waving an all-encompassing hand.

Honey nodded, cupping her hands around her mug of hot chocolate. "The heartwood was always this rumored place for young lovers to go. You know, like the make out points you see in the movies. By the time we moved here, we were too busy running the Oasis to go hunting for some fabled tree so we could carve our initials in it."

"Not that we'd do that anyway with all the nymphs and dryads in the forest," Antonio added. "We wouldn't want to go upsetting our neighbors in the woods."

Bella snorted softly. "Good call. We learned that the hard way."

Honey reached across and gave her daughter's hand a squeeze. "You didn't do anything wrong," she said firmly. "That dryad just over-reacted."

"It doesn't change the situation though. All of Havenwood will be loveless unless we find this missing heart," Bella said, worry evident in her voice.

Honey shook her head, a confident smile on her face. "I don't believe that for a second. I think the dryad is just trying to scare you. Nature is a dryad's realm, not love."

At that moment, the back door creaked open, and Alex stepped into the room, looking slightly awkward as he took in the cozy scene of everyone gathered around the table.

"Sorry, I didn't know there was a breakfast party going on," he said.

Antonio jumped to his feet. "Not a worry. It wasn't a party until you got here. Now the festivities can really begin."

Everyone chuckled at his effusive welcome as Antonio clapped Alex on the back and helped him out of his coat. Alex fished a cream envelope from his pocket as Antonio whisked his coat away.

He cleared his throat and looked around before handing Bella the envelope. "I know you were a little worried that I was going to Vegas, even though you tried to hide it. I also know you like old-fashioned gestures," he said, his cheeks a little pink, "and since I'm going to be gone for little while, I wanted you to know that I'll not only be calling and texting, but I'll also surprise you with letters. Even though I'll be on the other side of the country, I never want you to doubt how much you mean to me."

I ducked my head to hide my smile. Alex and Bella were so perfect together. He didn't even seem to care that he was making such a declaration in front of me or her parents. He only had eyes for Bella.

Her face flushed with warmth as she took the letter from him. "You wrote me a letter?" she asked, clearly touched. "I actually wrote you one too," she said, grabbing a similar envelope from the sideboard. "I wanted to get all my feelings down, and sometimes my tongue just gets tied up in knots."

Alex's eyes lit up with surprise and delight. "You did?"

Before Bella could respond, Antonio, who had been watching the exchange with a grin, clapped Alex on the back. "Great minds think alike, my friend. I often write love letters to Honey, too. She thinks it's a waste of a stamp, so I just put it in with the mail when I bring it in these days."

Honey rolled her eyes affectionately. "He's right. It is a waste of a stamp. We live in the same house for goodness' sake."

"Gestures of love know no logic," Antonio said grandly.

"Isn't that the truth?" Honey murmured, but the twinkle in her eye as she looked at her husband belied her words.

"Speaking of," Antonio added, pulling a similar white envelope from his pocket and handing it to Honey, "here's one for you."

Honey took the letter with a fond smile. "You never cease to amaze me."

Alex, still holding Bella's hand, looked down at her with a soft smile. "I'll be thinking of you the whole time I'm gone."

"And I'll be counting the days until you're back," Bella replied, squeezing his hand gently.

Antonio chuckled, shaking his head. "You two are almost as bad as we were at your age."

As Alex settled into his seat, we shuffled things around to make room for the plates of breakfast treats. A sudden gust of wind blew open the back door and through the room, rattling the windows. The chill of the outside air carried with it the same crackling sensation of wild magic I'd felt outside Spellbooks.

"Whoa!" Antonio exclaimed as the gust of wind sent the letters scattering across the floor.

"I must not have shut that all the way," Alex said, hurrying for the door. "Sorry about that."

"Not to worry," Honey said, as we all scrambled to catch the fluttering papers.

Antonio passed one envelope to Bella and the other to his wife with a flourish. Bella opened hers with a small, excited smile. But as she read the first few lines, her smile shifted into something more tender, her eyes widening slightly.

"Um...this isn't from Alex," Bella murmured. She glanced up at her parents, her cheeks flushing slightly.

Antonio, noticing her expression, grinned. "Ah, that's for your mother. I hope you weren't too shocked by your papa's sweet talk."

Bella laughed softly and shook her head. "Not at all. If anything, you two are the very definition of relationship goals." She handed the letter back to her dad, her eyes shining with admiration.

Honey smiled, reaching out to take Antonio's hand. "He does have a way with words."

Alex, having retrieved his own letter, watched the exchange with a sheepish grin. "I'll try to make sure my letters don't go flying off next time."

Bella gave him a reassuring smile. "No harm done. But I have to say, reading that made me appreciate you both even more," she said, looking at her parents with a soft expression.

Antonio winked at her, clearly pleased. "Well, I'm glad to know that my words still have some impact. I know you and Alex will make your own kind of magic."

Bella's smile faltered for the briefest moment as her gaze flicked to mine. The unspoken worry in her eyes was a clear reflection of the nerves she'd confided in me about Alex's potential trip to Vegas. I held her gaze, offering a small, reassuring nod, trying to remind her that she wasn't alone. The moment passed as quickly as it came, and Bella's smile returned, brighter and more confident. She turned back to the conversation at hand, just as Antonio leaned back in his chair, a mischievous twinkle in his eye.

"For the record, I don't mind someone reading my love letter," he said, grinning at Honey. "I'd shout it from the rooftops—or better yet, hire a singing telegram to do it for me."

Honey snorted, shaking her head with a fond smile. "Been there, done that, and I still have the video evidence."

Antonio's laughter filled the room, and even Bella cracked a genuine smile at her parents' banter, the tension easing just a little more.

The mood around the table lightened as we all settled back into our seats. No one else seemed to notice the crackle of wild magic that I had sensed, but an uneasy feeling lingered in the pit of my stomach, making it hard for me to concentrate on the rest of my breakfast.

I offered to help Honey with the dishes, but she waved me away, saying she and Antonio would handle it. It only took a glance at Bella and Alex to realize that they'd like some time alone to talk, so I made my excuses and slipped away.

Standing on the porch of the Oasis, I pulled my coat collar up and shivered as a gust of wind whipped a flurry of snow around me. At the rate the snow was falling, Antonio would need to plow the walkways again before noon. I should've headed straight to Spellbooks—there was a stretch of sidewalk outside the shop that would need shoveling soon, and the shop itself wouldn't open on its own—but instead, I lingered, drawn in by the quiet tension in the air.

Something felt...off. The town was unusually still, like the world was holding its breath. Even the wind, cold as it was, seemed hesitant, pausing between bursts as if waiting for something to happen. I scanned the street and the edges of the forest in the distance, my nerves on edge. After Vivienne's warning to keep an eye out for anything strange, every shadow, every sound seemed magnified, setting me on high alert.

I looked around, having the unnerving sense of being watched. There was something in the air, something I couldn't quite name. It felt like the moment before a thunderstorm, when everything is too still, too quiet—like the world is holding its breath, waiting for something to happen. I didn't know what, but I could feel it.

A flicker of movement out of the corner of my eye caught my attention. There, at the edge of the trees, was an old woman, hunched over and stuffing something in the bag slung across her body. As if she sensed me watching her, the woman's head snapped up, sending wild gray curls flying as she scanned the area.

My pulse quickened as I watched her, the memory of yesterday flashing through my mind. I sucked in a breath as I recognized her. It was the same old woman I'd seen in the woods. The same day the heart had gone missing. It didn't take a genius to piece it together. An old woman skulking around the forest in the middle of winter, the very same day we discovered the heartwood was withering and its heart had been stolen? The odds of that being a coincidence were slim.

Suddenly, her sharp eyes locked onto mine, and for a moment, the world seemed to tilt.

"Hey!" I called, my voice cutting through the stillness. Without hesitation, I stepped off the porch and strode toward the trees, my boots crunching through the fresh snow.

The old woman scuttled backwards, her shuffling gait increasing in speed as she disappeared into the woods.

"Wait! I just want to talk to you!" I called running after her.

She didn't pause, continuing her headlong dash away from me. I grunted as I forced my way through the forest after her. Given the differences in our ages, it shouldn't have been hard for me to catch up, but it seemed like the very forest conspired against me. Branches tugged at my hair as I ran, and snow filled my boots when I mis-stepped and nearly fell into a drift. I dusted myself off, but when I looked around, the old woman was nowhere to be seen. To make matters worse, I was lost.

Nervously, I looked around, searching for anything that looked remotely familiar, but in the winter, all the trees looked the same. The leafless maples and oaks stretched skeletal branches towards the sky, where thick pines stoically watched me under a light dusting of snow. Even though I'd stopped moving, my heart rate increased, my breath puffing out clouds of steam in the frigid air as I looked around. The snow fall had grown heavier, making it hard to distinguish the shapes in front of me. I looked behind me, just now noticing that my tracks were already filling up with snow. My stomach fell like I was on a rollercoaster. Had she led me out here on purpose? Was this all some sort of ploy to get me alone so she could...do what, exactly? I didn't even know who the old woman was. Maybe I'd jumped to the wrong conclusion entirely and scared her as much as she had me.

In my heart of hearts, I didn't believe that. My gut told me she was involved in this somehow. I just had to figure out how she was linked to the heartwood, the dryad, or the missing heart. Perhaps all three. I squinted, looking around in case she was trying to double back and spring an ambush on me. However, I didn't see her anywhere. Instead, something else caught my eye through the trees. My breath quickened as I slogged through the deepening snow, the wind whipping around me as the weather continued to worsen.

As I neared the broken boundary fence, I let out a silent breath of relief, reaching out to touch the cold, rusted chain link with a gloved hand. At least I had something solid to hold on to. All I had to do was follow the fence back towards the Oasis. Bella and I had just walked out here yesterday—surely I'd recognize something soon.

But the snow was falling more thickly now, the flakes swirling around me in a dizzying dance. My nerves prickled as I kept glancing over my shoulder, half expecting the old woman to reappear, her voice echoing through the trees. The rapid change in weather only heightened my anxiety, the once peaceful woods now feeling oppressive and strange. Every snap of a twig, every rustle of the wind had me on edge, my heart pounding in my chest.

I pushed forward, my steps growing more uncertain as the snow seemed to erase all traces of familiarity. The farther I walked, the more the surrounding landscape shifted, becoming increasingly unfamiliar and foreboding. I tried to shake it off, but the sense of unease wouldn't leave me. Other than chasing after the mysterious old woman, nothing had happened—nothing obvious, anyway. But the air felt thick, every sound seemed sharper, every silence more loaded. Something was off. I could feel it in my bones. Panic began to bubble up inside me. What if I was going the wrong way? What if I couldn't find my way back? How long did it take someone to die from exposure? Or worse, what if the old woman really was a witch, and she was upset I'd been chasing her? What kind of chance did I stand against an angry witch and a dryad's curse all in one week?

Suddenly, through the thick curtain of snow, I spotted the heartwood tree again. Its massive trunk stood out starkly against the whiteness, but something was different. The withering had spread, its dark, sickly veins now crawling further up the bark, draining the life from the once-majestic tree.

I hesitated, glancing around to ensure I was alone before leaving the security of the fence and approaching the tree. The air around it felt heavy, almost oppressive, and a deep sense of unease settled over me. The snow underfoot crunched louder as I stepped closer, the sound unnerving in the otherwise silent woods.

Cold air bit at my cheeks as I continued to examine the heartwood tree, searching for any clue that might lead me to the missing heart or the source of this spreading blight. But the snow had wiped everything clean, leaving only my own footprints to disturb the otherwise pristine blanket of white. My frustration grew as I circled the tree, my mind racing for answers. The stillness around me felt oppressive, like the forest itself was holding its breath, waiting for something—anything—to happen.

Someone—or something—had caused this destruction, and it was undeniably spreading. My heart pounded in my chest as I thought about what Thistle had said. If the heartwood was a gate to a conglomeration of ley lines, then this wasn't just a local issue. The ley lines were powerful, ancient, and unpredictable. If one was destabilizing because of this destruction, the consequences could be unimaginable.

I clenched my fists, determination hardening within me. I needed to find the missing heart, and fast. Failing that, I needed to find a solution. A way to stop the damage to the heartwood before it spread too much further. This wasn't just about saving the tree; it was about protecting all of Havenwood from a disaster that could tear the very fabric of our town—and maybe the whole region—apart.

Moving almost instinctively, I reached up, breaking off a small, brittle piece of withered bark. It crumbled slightly in my hand, the once vibrant wood now fragile and gray. Maybe with this and the healthy branch back at the shop, Jeremy could figure out what was going on. The sooner the better.

I carefully tucked the crumbly specimen inside my coat. The piece of withered bark in my pocket felt heavier than it should, a stark reminder of the gravity of the situation. I couldn't afford to waste any more time. I needed to get back to the Oasis, get this sample to Jeremy, and start figuring out a plan. The clock was ticking.

With one last, lingering look at the heartwood tree, I turned and began retracing my steps back towards the broken fence. The snow fell more heavily now, erasing my footprints almost as quickly as I made them. The wind picked up, howling through the trees and sending shivers down my spine. I pulled my coat tighter around me and quickened my pace.

I followed the fence towards the Oasis, surer of my path with the heartwood behind me. As soon as I broke through the tree line into the yard behind the Oasis, the heavy snowfall seemed to stop abruptly. I looked around in confusion. Behind me, in the forest, the dense snow still fell, and I could hear the wind whistling through the trees. However, from where I stood, it seemed like I was watching a giant snow globe. In the back yard of the Oasis, all was clear and still, but a veritable blizzard raged mere feet from where I stood.

I took another step back, my heart hammering in my chest, but I couldn't tear my eyes away from the chaotic storm raging just beyond the tree line. The forest felt alive, almost as if it were aware of me. Inside the trees, the storm was waiting, biding its time before it broke free and descended upon the town. The air around me crackled with energy, the kind that made my skin prickle and my instincts scream at me to run. The same kind I'd sensed outside Spellbooks.

Wild magic.

My mind raced. The dryad's curse was spreading. A ley line was leaking. The danger wasn't looming—it was already here. Magic was unraveling faster than any of us had anticipated, and if we didn't act, Havenwood wouldn't survive.

Unable to stand it one second more, I turned on my heel and bolted; the wind howling in my ears as I raced back to the safety of the Oasis. Every instinct told me to escape the forest, to get back to the B&B where it was safe, but the gnawing fear in the pit of my stomach told me that safety was an illusion. The storm was coming, and I had no idea how to stop it.

To Find a Botanist

I STOPPED IN THE Oasis only briefly to tell Bella and her parents about the blizzard in the woods. Alex closed his eyes, reaching out with his own magic. He could sense weather patterns. Not control them, just sense them.

He opened his eyes almost immediately, shaking his head in amazement. "That blew in out of nowhere."

"What's going on?" Bella asked, peering nervously out the window at the blizzard in the forest.

Alex shrugged. "We were supposed to have flurries on and off throughout the day, but this is almost as bad as the storm at Christmas. However, it looks like it will blow itself out in about fifteen minutes. It shouldn't even hit the Oasis, which is weird given how close it is."

Antonio tugged on his boots. "Nevertheless, I'd like to take a look outside, and make sure we're ready in case the winds change."

"I'll go with you," Alex offered.

Antonio dipped his head. "Much appreciated."

Bella tugged on my hand as they headed out into the snow. "What are we going to do?" she asked.

I patted my pocket to make sure the withered piece of bark was still there. "I hate to desert you, but if Alex is right, the Oasis will be just fine, and we need answers. I'm going to find Jeremy Rowan and ask him if he knows what might've caused the damage to the heartwood."

Bella nodded eagerly. "Good idea. What should I do?"

I glanced outside, the snow swirling in steady drifts. "We need to find the missing heart as soon as possible. However, if there were any clues out there, they're either blown away or completely buried now."

Bella sighed, folding her arms. "Great. So, we're back to square one."

I hesitated, lowering my voice as I leaned closer to her. "Actually...I did see something—someone. Yesterday, in the woods and again just now. An old woman, hunched over, with wild gray curls. She was acting...strange. Have you seen anyone like that?"

Bella frowned, her expression turning thoughtful. "An old woman? No, I can't say I have. Not around here. Who do you think she is?"

"I don't know yet," I admitted, my mind racing. "But she was out there yesterday when we discovered the heart was missing. I don't think it's a coincidence."

Bella's lips pressed into a thin line. "What's the plan, then? Wait until someone tries to sell the heart on the black market and track them down?"

I snorted softly, caught off guard by the suggestion. "And you're going to do this with all your black-market contacts?"

Bella rolled her eyes but couldn't hide her faint smile. "It's called brainstorming, Harper. Some of us aren't afraid to think outside the box."

I nudged her gently. "You should definitely reach out to those illicit contacts of yours if you have any. But seriously, I think the best thing for you to do until we hear from Jeremy is to make sure the Oasis is blizzard ready. After that, maybe make a list of suspects. You know this town better than anyone." I paused, considering. "Maybe someone held a grudge against the dryad? Or had something to gain from destroying the tree? I don't know, but any link you can think of might point us in the right direction."

"You still want me to ask around?" Bella's expression turned serious, and she lowered her voice. "What about Vivienne and her decree to not talk about what's going on?"

I hesitated, glancing toward the window where snow was still swirling outside. "She said not to involve anyone else. But if the heart is gone, we don't have time to sit back and wait for answers to fall into our laps. Besides, I'm not suggesting a town-wide announcement. Just...discreet inquiries."

Bella nodded, though the furrow in her brow lingered. "Okay. Discreet. Got it. I can do that."

I offered her a small smile and gave her a quick hug. "Thanks, Bella. With the, um, wild magic from the dryad's curse getting stronger, it's probably best if I hurry to find Jeremy." I carefully avoided any mention of ley lines.

"Good idea," Bella nodded, pulling out her phone. "I'll start making a list and text them to you as soon as possible."

"If anyone can Sherlock Holmes the thief's identity, it's you," I said.

Bella snorted. "Between the two of us, you're definitely Holmes. I'm one hundred percent Watson in this relationship."

I pretended to frown at her. "Wait a second. Watson was the more normal of the two. Holmes was neurotic at best. What are you saying exactly?"

Bella didn't lift her eyes from her screen, but a small smile played around her mouth. "If the deerstalker hat fits..."

I laughed. "How about we leave the crazy detective stereotypes to Sir Arthur Conan Doyle and just be Bella and Harper?"

"Deal," Bella said, holding out her fist.

I grinned and bumped my knuckles to hers. "I'll touch base if Jeremy has any useful information."

"And I'll text as soon as I have a viable suspect list," Bella assured me.

"We got this," I said with a confident smile as I stepped out of the Oasis. My smile froze in place and then slowly died as I caught sight of the blizzard still inexplicably trapped within the forest. Despite Alex's assertion that the storm wouldn't hit the Oasis, it was hard to believe him when I could see it raging just behind the house. Seeing the whirling snow reinforced the urgency of finding Jeremy and some answers.

I tucked my scarf a little more tightly around my throat as I turned my back on the storm and hurried into town, texting Jeremy as I walked despite the cold numbing my fingertips. I was on a mission and a little winter weather wasn't going to stop me now.

The snow might not stop me but the half-giant peering into my shop's front window definitely could.

"Grimgor?" I called as I approached, instantly recognizing the man's distinctive height.

He turned and relief washed over his face. "Harper! Have you seen Thistle? We were supposed to have breakfast this morning, but I can't get ahold of her."

I frowned and shook my head. "She, um, said she was going to check some things out last night, but I thought she'd be back by now."

"What kind of things?" Grimgor asked, his bushy brows drawing together in concern.

I winced. "I really can't say, I'm sorry. But I'm sure she's fine. If I see her, I'll tell her you're looking for her."

Grimgor gave me a hard look as if he was weighing whether or not to press me for an answer, but eventually he blew out a breath. "Well, do you mind if I go around back and knock on her tree? Maybe she slept in or something."

"Come straight through the shop," I offered, hurriedly opening the door for him. I followed Grimgor as he made a beeline for the garden and knocked loudly on the trunk of the oak tree. There was no answer. He shot me a worried look.

"Where did you say she went?" he asked.

I shifted from foot to foot, not meeting his eyes. "Just to check on some things with the other nymphs. I really can't say more than that, so please don't ask."

Grimgor glanced between me and the tree. "Whatever you two have got going on, I sure hope it's not tied to the strange happenings around town."

"Strange happenings?" Was it my imagination, or had my voice suddenly jumped an octave. I swallowed and continued. "What are you talking about?" This time, my voice was too low. Lying really wasn't my thing.

Grimgor's brow furrowed, and he crossed his arms, his concern clear in his stance. "You haven't noticed? The weather's been all over the place—sunny one minute, snowing the next. And don't even get me started on the animals—pets are skittish, and the birds are flying like they've lost their minds."

My stomach twisted. Other people were noticing. It wasn't just me, Thistle, Bella, or the Silverthornes keeping an eye on things anymore. If Grimgor had picked up on it, how long before the rest of Havenwood did? How long before the wards started buckling under the strain placed on them by the wild magic?

"That...doesn't sound good," I managed to say, trying to keep my voice steady.

"That's an understatement," Grimgor grunted. "If you or Thistle know anything about this—"

I shook my head quickly, cutting him off. "I believe you. You're right—it's serious. You know what?" My mind raced as I searched for a distraction tactic, grabbing the first one that popped into my head. "I'd better call Gabriel and let him know what's going on."

"Gabriel? As in Gabriel Silverthorne?" Grimgor raised an eyebrow.

I swallowed hard, trying not to facepalm myself. Not everyone knew that Gabriel and I were...well, not even *I* knew what Gabriel and I were. "Yeah. Him. We met at the Pumpkin Parade and—"

My phone vibrated in my pocket, cutting me off. I pulled it out, shocked to see Gabriel's face on the screen. I waved it at Grimgor. "Would you look at that? I bet he's calling with a solution right now."

Grimgor grunted. a noncommittal noise that seemed to convey both skepticism and reluctant trust. "I hope so. This town's got enough problems without adding magic running wild to the mix."

With that, Grimgor turned and lumbered away, leaving me standing there with a sinking feeling in my gut. The strange happenings he mentioned were just the beginning—I could feel it in my bones. Whatever was going on, it was up to me to stop it before things spiraled even further out of control.

My phone buzzed again, pulling me from my thoughts. I flicked the green icon to answer. "Hi, Gabriel."

"Harper." His voice was soft but carried an edge of urgency. "I don't know how much you've heard this morning, but things in town are getting...chaotic. I'm sure you've noticed. I just wanted to check on you. You didn't call me, and I wanted to make sure you were okay."

A smile tugged at my lips, a wave of warmth spreading through me. It was sweet of Gabriel to call. For a moment, I let the comfort of his voice settle around me like a warm blanket.

Not that he was ever inconsiderate. In fact, he was one of the most thoughtful people I knew. But he usually kept his worries tucked beneath that cool, unshakable confidence of his. Hearing the concern so plainly in his voice now was different. If Gabriel was checking in like this, then things were worse than I had thought.

Guilt crept in, needling at the edges of my thoughts. We had already pulled in the DeLucas, Finn, and Thistle. Now I was planning to reach out to Jeremy. Vivienne's warnings about involving others echoed in my mind, sharp and clear.

I pushed the feeling aside. The town needed answers, not hesitation. If Gabriel was worried enough to reach out, then I couldn't afford to second-guess myself. The magic wasn't just unraveling. It was spiraling out of control.

"I'm fine," I said, trying to portray a calmness I didn't feel. "But I appreciate you checking in. It's been...a morning. Grimgor was just here, talking about some strange things happening in town. Have you heard anything?"

Gabriel exhaled, the sound soft but unmistakably relieved. "Good. I mean, good that you're okay—not about the strange things. It's just...I know you can handle yourself, but with the dryad's curse and the wild magic acting up, I didn't want to take any chances."

My stomach tightened. "It's that bad?"

"Yeah," he said, his voice turning grim. "I wouldn't bother you if it wasn't, but things are getting out of hand. Just today, we had two incidents that were...well, let's just say they're not normal, even by Havenwood standards."

A chill ran down my spine. "What happened?" I asked, my voice sharper than I intended. My mind raced through worst-case scenarios, trying to anticipate what we were up against.

"There was a blackout in a residential neighborhood," Gabriel said, his tone heavy. "At first, we thought it was just a power outage. But when we got there, we realized it wasn't just the lights—every single flame, every source of light, had gone out. Lanterns, candles, even the streetlamps with magic redundancies were snuffed out. It was pitch dark, and nothing we did could get them to relight until the sun started coming up. People are scared, Harper. It's like the darkness was alive."

I tightened my grip on the phone, my pulse quickening. A wave of unease swept over me, and I found myself pacing the length of the shop as Gabriel continued, his voice lowering as if he didn't want anyone else to overhear.

"And then, there's the issue with the forest. Some of the trees have started moving—actually uprooting themselves and shifting positions."

I stopped pacing, the weight of his words settling like a stone in my chest. "Trees moving? Thistle and I saw a broken branch get up and run off into the forest last night. That's—" My voice faltered as I searched for the right words.

"Bizarre? Tell me about it. We've cordoned off the area, but it's only a matter of time before someone sees the moving trees, gets hurt, or worse. Lucas and I are doing what we can. Even my mother is helping, but it's overwhelming."

I could hear the frustration in his voice, the weariness from trying to hold everything together. "Gabriel, you're doing everything you can," I said softly, hoping to reassure him.

"I know," he sighed. "But it's hard to feel like I'm making a difference when the magic is this wild. Until we can figure out how to stop it, I'm afraid things are just going to keep getting worse."

I swallowed hard. "We'll find a solution," I promised. "But you need to be careful too, Gabriel."

He let out a small, humorless laugh. "Right back at you, Harper. Just...stay safe, okay? We'll talk soon."

As the call ended, I stood there for a moment, the silence of the room pressing in on me. The situation was deteriorating faster than I'd thought, and Gabriel's concern only confirmed it. The longer the heart remained missing, the more volatile the town became. The wild magic was escalating. If we didn't stop it soon, I wasn't sure we would be able to contain the chaos.

We were running out of time, and I needed answers.

I hurried back inside, not even pausing to say hello to Spellbooks or Luna. Instead, I grabbed the healthy tree branch from the counter and immediately left again.

I had a botanist to question and no time to waste.

Circle of Trust

Jeremy's message said he was at Stella's flower boutique, so when I reached the end of Arcadia Avenue, I turned right, rushing past familiar shops in my haste to get answers. As I opened the door to Blossom and Bloom, I froze at the unexpected sight.

In the middle of the shop, Professor Edmund Hawke bent over a display of roses, his disheveled hair shaking as he murmured, "Remarkable. Simply remarkable."

"Yes, isn't it just," Stella replied, her voice strained. Her anxious glance darted between me and two men near the door. One of them inspected a Valentine's bouquet with exaggerated interest, while the other pretended to study the heart-shaped trinkets. Their casual demeanor didn't fool me—one of them kept glancing over at the professor, clearly intrigued by his enthusiasm.

I didn't recognize them, which immediately set me on edge. Tourists, maybe? Havenwood didn't seem to attract many out-of-towners during the slow season, but given the occupancy of the Enchanted Oasis, Valentine's Day could be an exception. Still, the way Stella kept shooting anxious glances in their direction, like she was afraid they might overhear something they shouldn't, told me she was more concerned about keeping Havenwood's secrets than about selling roses.

I stepped forward with an easy smile, hoping to diffuse the situation. "What's going on here?"

Professor Hawke straightened, gesturing wildly at the roses as though I'd asked him to defend his life's work. "You must see this! These roses! What extraordinary specimens! Look at how they respond."

He leaned closer and breathed on the flowers. Instantly, the petals shifted from pale yellow to deep crimson. The man holding the bouquet nudged his companion, and they edged closer to the excited professor. Stella, meanwhile, looked ready to faint.

"That's incredible," I said smoothly, shooting Stella a reassuring glance before adding, "But maybe we should keep it low-key? Wouldn't want to spoil the surprise for other customers." I tried to catch the professor's eye and tip my head towards the tourists, but he either didn't see the signal or ignored me completely.

Jeremy appeared from the back, a clipboard in hand, and froze at the scene unfolding in front of him. His eyes darted to Stella, who gave him a look that could only mean *Help!* Setting down his clipboard, he stepped forward with a tight smile.

"Ah, I s-s-see you're interested in our new arrival. Those roses," he began, his voice slightly strained. "They're part of an experimental p-p-project. A mix of natural and holographic t-t-technology." Jeremy always had a slight stutter, but his anxiety seemed to be making it worse.

Professor Hawke's brow furrowed. "Holograms? But they reacted to me!"

"Yes, that's, uh, part of the illusion," I said quickly, waving my hand over the roses as though pointing out something hidden.

"Exactly," Jeremy chimed in. "The, um, light refraction mimics interaction. It's quite cutting-edge."

The tourist with the bouquet leaned closer to the roses, his brow furrowing. "Holograms, huh? Looks pretty real to me."

His companion sighed. "You're really grilling them over flowers?"

"Judy would love them," the first man said with a shrug.

"Judy would love *you* remembering Valentine's Day. Period. Don't overthink it. Holographic roses? Please. She'd be happier with a nice dinner or a new necklace."

"Still, you've gotta admit it. That's really something," the first guy said, pulling out his phone.

Stella laughed nervously, her hands fidgeting with her apron. "It's just a prototype. Please, no pictures—it's not ready for public release yet."

The tourist shrugged, slipping his phone back into his pocket. His buddy tugged on his arm and both of them wandered back to the Valentine's Day trinkets at the front of the shop. Stella visibly relaxed, but her gaze lingered on them, wary of any sudden moves.

The professor, however, wasn't so easily deterred. "I could've sworn they were reacting to me, not some sort of...algorithm. I've dedicated my life to researching rare and unique plant species, you see. It's what drew me to this area in the first place. Havenwood's microclimate is unique—perfect for nurturing rare cultivars that can't be found anywhere else. I thought perhaps I'd stumbled upon something truly extraordinary here."

Jeremy latched onto his shift in tone. "You're right about Havenwood, though. Its microclimate is p-p-perfect for unique plants. That's why we're t-t-testing the technology here."

The professor sighed, his shoulders slumping slightly. "I see...well, I suppose it's still remarkable in its own way. Just not the botanical breakthrough I was hoping for."

Stella offered a polite smile. "But that doesn't mean there aren't other incredible plants here in Havenwood. I'm sure with your expertise, you'll find something just as fascinating."

The professor nodded, though he still looked somewhat deflated. "Yes, perhaps you're right. I've already found some remarkable samples. I was just hoping for something...more. The natural world is extraordinary enough without the addition of artificial embellishments."

Stella seized the opportunity to usher him toward the door. "That's true, but I'm sure Havenwood has more surprises in store for you, Professor. You'll find something amazing—I'm sure of it."

The professor nodded reluctantly, muttered a goodbye, and left, his curiosity tempered for now. The two men lingered a few moments longer before heading to the counter to make their purchases of chocolates and cards. As the door finally closed behind them, the tension drained from the room.

Stella let out a long breath. "Thank you. I froze—I didn't know what to do."

Jeremy gave her a sheepish smile. "I-i-it's nothing. Just glad it worked."

"That was some quick thinking," I said, but as the unease lingered in the back of my mind, I couldn't help but reflect: *This was just one, relatively small incident. How long before the wild magic became something we couldn't explain away?*

Jeremy blushed. The lanky man wasn't used to being the center of attention. "I-I-I, well, you see, I just did what...well, what I mean is, that it s-s-seemed like the most logical thing."

Stella smiled at him. "It was. You did great." She gave him a peck on the cheek. As soon as she turned and saw the color-changing flowers, her smile faltered. "What are we going to do about those?"

"Call the Silverthornes?" Jeremy ventured.

I toyed with my scarf, thinking of everything Gabriel was dealing with. "Maybe, I don't mean to intrude, but perhaps you could stick them in the back? For now, at least?"

"Good idea," Stella said, scooping up an armful. "Then we can call the Silverthornes. Hopefully, they'll have an answer as to why my roses are lighting up like a disco."

Jeremy moved to help her, but I cleared my throat and tipped my head to the side, indicating I'd like a private word. His eyebrows crept up nearly to his hairline, but the lanky botanist followed me without question.

"What's going on, Harper? Your message was more than a little c-c-cryptic."

I tipped my head back towards the color changing roses and cut to the chase. With incidents like the roses, there was no time to waste. "I know what happened here. It's wild magic. It's sweeping through town at the moment, and the Silverthornes are doing everything they can, but I fear it's not enough. I need your help."

"M-m-my help? What can I do that the Silverthornes can't?" Jeremy asked.

"Don't sell yourself short, Jeremy. You are a good friend, an insightful reader, and a brilliant botanist." I carefully withdrew the two specimens I'd collected from the heartwood tree from my jacket. "The last is why I called you."

"What're those?" Jeremy asked.

"These are the reason magic is running wild," I said, holding out the two pieces as I carefully selected my words to dance around any mention of ley lines. "There's a very angry dryad in the forest who laid a curse on the town because someone or something damaged her tree, and we think the damage released this surge of wild magic Havenwood is experiencing. I need your help to figure out what's wrong and how to stop it."

Jeremy's eyes lit up as he took the two pieces, one supple and strong, the other brittle and crumbling. "Tell me everything," he breathed.

I told Jeremy as much as I dared, not wanting to break my oath to Thistle or draw Vivienne's ire by spreading panic. Jeremy listened intently, but his eyes never left the two pieces of heartwood he held in his hands. Stella, as if sensing my need for a private word with Jeremy, busied herself with tidying the shop.

As I concluded my abbreviated version, I ended with a question. "So? What do you think? Can you figure out what happened?"

Jeremy shrugged and then bobbed his head in a gesture that might have meant yes or no. "It would be easier if I could see the tree itself. Is that possible?" I noticed whenever his attention was focused on plants, his stutter seemed to vanish.

I thought back to the blizzard in the woods and shuddered. No way I wanted to get caught in that. "Um...maybe. But I think I might need to call in some back up before we could go there safely."

Jeremy nodded as if he'd expected such an answer. "Speaking of back up, I'd like your permission to show these samples to my uncle. He's a treant you know."

"Yes, I had the pleasure of meeting him a few months ago," I said, my voice softening as a pang of bittersweet nostalgia surfaced. I thought back to the day Finn took me to the botanical gardens that Jeremy's uncle, Jeremiah, managed—how thoughtful Finn had been, how easy it was to laugh with him. For a brief moment, regret tangled with gratitude, poignant and fleeting, before I pushed it aside.

"I might be a decent botanist, but I'll never be able to match his magic when it comes to plants," Jeremy admitted. "He might have some insights that could help me figure out the root cause of the decay faster than I could on my own."

"The faster, the better," I replied earnestly. "But maybe keep the circle of trust small. Vivienne really doesn't want people panicking."

"Panic about what? A little wild magic running loose? Trust me, the good p-p-people of Havenwood can handle a bit of errant magic," Jeremy declared confidently.

I almost blurted out the full extent of the dryad's curse but caught myself just in time. If Jeremy and Stella only had a few days of their loving relationship left, I wasn't going to spoil that for either of them. And if we could figure out how to stop the decay eating at the heartwood or find the missing heart, it wouldn't matter anyway.

Jeremy smiled, unaware of the storm brewing just beneath the surface of what I hoped was my calm façade. "Don't worry, Harper. We'll get this fixed."

I forced a smile in return, my mind racing. "Yeah...we'd better."

But deep down, I knew—this was only the beginning. And if we didn't find a solution soon, wild magic would be the least of our worries.

Special Delivery Disaster

With part one of my plan in place, I headed back towards Spellbooks. Stopping the decay might not be possible, but with zero leads on where the missing heart might be, it was the best I could do. The longer it took me to find the heart, the more I felt like I was suffocating. Havenwood wasn't just my home—it was my responsibility, and the wild magic was threatening that security. The people I cared about were counting on me to find the missing heart, whether they knew it or not. But every lead I chased down crumbled to dust before I could grab hold of it. The urgency thrummed through my veins like a drumbeat, pounding louder with each passing second. I wondered if Bella had made any progress on a suspect list and pulled out my phone as I neared the shop.

"Hey Harper," the mailman, Marty, called.

I looked up from my screen and smiled warmly. Marty was a good soul and always happy to stop for a chat. He was on the downhill slide from fifty and claimed he only did the mail delivery because it was a job where he got paid to walk and talk to people. In my opinion, it was the perfect position for the friendly man.

"Hi Marty, anything good today?"

"Just the usual. Some junk mail and a couple of official-looking letters," he said, reaching into his bag to retrieve my mail. He was old-school, preferring to load up an old satchel and stroll down the street rather than inch the official post office vehicle along his route.

But as soon as he lifted the flap of his satchel, a veritable explosion of letters and cards burst forth, launching into the air in all shapes, sizes, and colors. The envelopes seemed to have minds of their own, fluttering and spinning in the wind as if they were playing some sort of game.

"Stamp my socks! Those aren't meant to be air mail!" Marty exclaimed as he tried to grab at the escaping envelopes, but they slid through his fingers, flying off as a gust of wind took them out of reach. Marty refused to give up and gave chase. "Those letters are postmarked for chaos, I swear!"

I hurried to help him, but the letters were surprisingly elusive, darting down the street as if taunting us. We chased after them, the wind aiding their escape, making it feel like we were trying to catch a flock of particularly mischievous birds. A few of the letters even danced just out of reach, teasing us before slipping away again.

Eventually, we managed to corral most of them, stuffing them back into Marty's bag, though a few stubborn ones continued to flutter just out of reach. It took us a few extra minutes, but we finally got them all.

Marty shook his head, puffing slightly from the unexpected exercise. "Well, slap a stamp on my forehead! I think this might be the day I should've brought the truck. These letters have a mind of their own! Thanks for the help, Harper."

"No problem," I replied, still holding onto a couple of the more obstinate letters. "At least they kept things interesting." I carefully handed them over so they couldn't make another break for freedom.

Marty chuckled as he accepted them, giving a mock salute. "Much appreciated. You take care now. Hopefully, the rest of the route won't be as lively."

I waved goodbye, careful to keep a tight grip on my stack of mail as Marty headed back down Arcadia towards his vehicle.

"Radish ruckus! What was that all about?" Luna demanded the moment I unlocked the shop door.

I held up my handful of mail. "Marty. He was just dropping off the mail when all the letters decided to go flying out of his bag. This wild magic is really causing havoc."

"Are you sure it was magic and not just Marty, being, well…Marty?" Luna asked with a sniff. "That boy is rather careless."

I hid a smile behind a colorful flyer. No one in their right mind would've called Marty a boy, except for the cantankerous familiar. To be fair, I had no idea exactly how old Luna was. She'd been Granny Bea's familiar for as long as I could remember. Which was long enough for me to have learned that asking the rabbit her age wasn't a sensible idea unless I had an hour to listen to a rant about the uncouth behavior of today's youth.

"Well, I'm not sure it was Marty's fault," I said mildly. I set the mail down and started to unbutton my coat.

Luna pointed a paw. "You dropped one."

"No, I didn't," I said instinctively, but when I turned, I saw a large pink envelope sitting in the middle of my welcome mat.

"Really, Harper. You need to eat more carrots," Luna said as she turned and hopped away.

"Why? So I can meet the quota to finally be initiated into the rabbit ninja club?"

She froze and slowly swiveled her head to look at me. "The first rule of rabbit ninja club is to *never* speak of rabbit ninja club. And don't be ridiculous. Carrots aren't how you'd join anyway."

"Then how—"

Luna cut me off. "Carrots are good for your eyesight, and you obviously need the help if you missed that giant envelope," she said before disappearing into the stacks with a sniff.

I glanced at the envelope. "That's not what I was going to ask. I was going to say…" but when I looked up again, the familiar had vanished. Like a ninja.

Maybe I did need to up my carrot intake.

With a sigh, I grabbed the letter from the floor, curiously turning it over to see who it was from. There was no return address, just a single name, and it wasn't mine.

Hortense Puddleton.

My stomach dropped. The Puddletons, who owned the other bookshop in town, hadn't exactly rolled out the welcome mat when I moved to Havenwood. If anything, their cold attitude had only deepened over the past six months. With Spellbooks being direct competition with their shop, the Dusty Tome, probably didn't help matters—especially considering we were both on Arcadia Avenue, fighting for the same customers. Whenever either Oswald or Hortense walked by, I could feel their sour glances practically burning through the windows. I had to admit, the winter weather had been a small blessing. Instead of sharing their usual glares, they'd taken to driving into work, the snow keeping them away from their ritualized walks past my shop. Entire days had gone by without a single sneer in my direction.

Thinking of that, I stuck my head outside, searching for Marty so he could return the letter, but the mailman was nowhere to be found. I sighed. A little part of me wanted to toss the large pink envelope back into the wind and shut my door on the whole affair rather than deliver it to the Puddletons by hand. After all, they'd publicly accused me of jewel theft just a couple of months ago with absolutely no proof. What would they come up with next if I knocked on their door with some of their mail? Stealing their letters? Wasn't that a felony? Sure, it wasn't my fault that there'd been a mix up, but little pesky things like the facts never seemed to be of much importance to Oswald or Hortense.

I glanced down at the large envelope in my hand. Without a magical breeze bent on mischief, there was no way this thing was blowing anywhere. I blew out a sigh, already knowing that I couldn't just toss it away and forget about it. My parents had been very particular on correct behavior and helping out a neighbor. If my dad, Master Sergeant Edward Sullivan, witnessed me tossing a neighbor's misdelivered mail into the wild, I'd be running obstacle courses for a month—likely while carrying Marty's mail satchel.

I re-buttoned my coat with a resigned sigh. Hopefully, the Dusty Tome had a mailbox, and I could drop off the letter without the Puddletons catching a glimpse of me.

As I ducked my head against the stiff breeze, something caught my eye—a flash of red hair, unmistakable against the sparkling white of fresh snow. I frowned, recognizing her instantly. The woman from the library. The same one who had been talking to Martha, trying—unsuccessfully, from what I'd overheard—to gain access to the restricted section.

I narrowed my eyes, watching her for a moment. She sprinted down the street, her expression frantic as she waved her arms in the air. "Help! Please, help!" she called out, chasing after something. A bright blue envelope skittered ahead of her, dancing through the snow like it had a mind of its own.

Without thinking, I darted forward and managed to step on the edge of the envelope, trapping it beneath my boot as the woman came to a breathless halt.

"Thank you," she gasped, bending over to catch her breath. "That thing's been determined to get away for over a block."

I gave her a tight smile and leaned down to pick up the envelope, but as soon as I did, it started wriggling in my hands, pulling as if it were trying to free itself. "What the—?"

Before I could stop it, the envelope ripped itself open, the contents spilling into the snow. I quickly grabbed the paper, inadvertently catching a glimpse of the words written in bold, angry script:

"Vivienne Silverthorne is nothing more than a power-hungry fraud!"

I blinked in shock, my mind scrambling to process what I'd just read.

"That's strange. I could've sworn I sealed it." The woman pushed a strand of red hair back into place and smiled in gratitude as I silently handed the letter back. "Thank you for catching it. I've been trying to craft the perfect letter for an hour or so and didn't relish the idea of starting over. I need to make a good impression, and I fear I'm failing miserably in this town. I'm Cassandra Bellamy, by the way," she said, sticking out a hand.

Instinctively I took it. "Harper Sullivan." I paused, and then added. "I know it's not any of my business, but if you want to make a good impression, I don't think that's the way to do it." I tipped my head toward the letter in her hand.

"What do you—" Her eyes went wide as she scanned the page, her already pale face turning ashen. "This isn't what I wrote! Oh no, can you imagine if this was delivered?"

I grimaced, thinking of my run-ins with Vivienne Silverthorne. The mere thought of her displeasure had been enough to keep me awake at night more than once. To actively and intentionally insult her wasn't something I was brave enough to contemplate, let alone do.

"I don't think it would go over well," I said tactfully.

"If she thought I wrote this, I'd be done in this town. Probably not just this town but the entire state. Maybe even beyond. This is *Vivienne Silverthorne* we're talking about here," Cassandra said, tearing the letter in half and stuffing it in her purse before emphatically zipping it closed.

"Oh? Do you know her?" I asked, trying to keep my tone casual.

Cassandra shook her head. "Not personally. I know *of* her. She was…a friend of my, um, former teacher. I thought she might be able to…um…give me some advice."

I tried to keep my face blank. Cassandra wasn't a very good liar. Given it was Vivienne, I guessed that at least part of the reason Cassandra wanted to see her was magical in nature. However, she didn't know that I knew that the Silverthornes were mages, and I didn't feel like outing myself as a witch to a complete stranger in the middle of the street. After writing insulting letters, publicly admitting to magic was how you drew the wrath of Vivienne Silverthorne down upon yourself.

"Well, I don't think the pen is mightier today," I said, nodding at her purse and the offensive letter. "Perhaps try an email? Or a cookie? There's a great bakery called Pixie Pastries in town."

Cassandra chuckled. "Even a burned cookie would probably do less damage than that letter." She frowned and shook her head. "I can't figure out how it got changed. What a strange thing."

I bit my lip, wondering how much I could safely say. But she seemed like she genuinely wanted to make a good impression, and Vivienne wasn't the kind to offer second chances after an insult.

"Maybe try that cookie or talk to her in person. You know, to avoid any misunderstandings?" I suggested.

Cassandra shot me a grateful smile. "I think I'll take your advice on that one. Thanks for the help."

"Anytime," I murmured as she lifted a gloved hand and hurried past me down Arcadia. I glanced at the large pink envelope. Could I give it the same treatment Cassandra had hers? The thought was tempting.

I shook my head, annoyed I'd even thought it. I wasn't a coward, and the Puddletons weren't that scary. Annoying, rude, and usually obnoxious, but not scary. I could handle returning their misdelivered mail.

Although, I still had every intention of anonymously dropping it in their mailbox and beating a hasty retreat. Good intentions only went so far—and mine definitely didn't extend to a face-off with the Puddletons if I could avoid it.

Tinder at the Tome

As it turned out, the Dusty Tome didn't have a mailbox out front, and the door wasn't equipped with a mail slot either. I paused, considering my options. I could just leave it on the mat and call the deed done, but that seemed a bit rude considering I was already here, and the shop was open. Deciding there was nothing for it, I steeled my nerves and pushed through the door.

When I stepped inside, the difference between this shop and Spellbooks hit me like a brick wall. Where Spellbooks was calm and cozy, inviting you to linger and get lost among its shelves, the Dusty Tome felt like sensory overload. The space was cramped, with towering stacks of books looming over narrow aisles, threatening to topple at any moment. Garish displays cluttered every available surface, shouting for attention with bright sale signs that clashed with each other in a chaotic mess.

There was no cozy nook to curl up in with a good book, no comfy chairs begging you to settle in for a chapter or two. Instead, harsh fluorescent lighting buzzed overhead, casting everything in an unforgiving glare. The shelves were stuffed to the brim with books, but they seemed to be arranged with no rhyme or reason, making it impossible to find anything without a struggle.

An upbeat tune blared from a speaker behind the counter, loud enough to make casual browsing feel like a race against time. And despite the shop's name, there wasn't a speck of dust in sight—every surface gleamed, almost to the point of being too clean, as if the place was trying just a little too hard to scream, Look at me!

It was the polar opposite of what a bookstore should be, in my opinion. Spellbooks and I worked hard to create an experience for readers akin to a warm hug. Entering the Dusty Tome felt like trying to read a novel in the middle of a carnival with a marching band parading down the street.

Luckily, neither Hortense nor Oswald Puddleton was at the front counter. I laid the envelope on the counter, turning to go when I spotted a familiar figure. I caught my breath. What was Finn doing here?

"Oswald? Did you find that book?" Hortense's shrill voice was unmistakable, even though the overly upbeat music.

Oswald's nasal voice answered her from behind a nearby shelf, causing me to jump. "Coming my darling. Where are you?"

"Near the cookbooks," Hortense called.

"Where'd we put those again?" Oswald yelled back.

Hortense's voice was tinged with scorn. "Next to the mystery books, naturally."

I couldn't think of a less compatible pairing, but it wasn't my business how they ran their bookshop. Silently, I headed toward the door.

"Harper? What are you doing here?"

Finn's question stopped me in my tracks, and I turned, a faint blush sweeping over my face.

"Oh, hi. I, um didn't see you there," I said, keeping my voice soft so as not to draw the attention of the Puddletons.

I glanced down at the books Finn had just set on the shelf. The titles jumped out at me immediately—Mending Fractured Relationships and Finding Your Inner Peace. A pang of awkwardness flickered through me. Finn caught the direction of my gaze and gave a nervous chuckle.

"Uh, yeah," he mumbled, scratching the back of his neck. "Not exactly light reading, right?"

I raised an eyebrow but decided to play along. "Well, self-help is all the rage these days." I gestured to the towering shelves around us. "Apparently, the Dusty Tome has you covered."

He nodded, clearly uncomfortable, then cleared his throat and glanced around, changing the subject. "Actually, I needed to talk to you. I heard back from my contacts in the druid community about the heartwood tree."

My pulse quickened at the mention. "Oh? What did they say?"

"They're pretty sure the heartwood is deeply connected to the ley lines that run beneath Havenwood," Finn explained, his tone more serious now and all traces of awkwardness gone.

I tried to keep my expression neutral, but my mind raced back to my promise to Thistle. *Don't speak of the ley lines unless it's with someone who already knows.* "Is that...common knowledge?" I asked, my voice careful.

Finn paused, considering. "Well, in the druid community, yes. Ley lines are something every druid knows about because that's where we get much of our power."

"Do you think everyone does? Is it a secret?" I asked.

Finn lifted a shoulder. "Not among the people I know, but you're right. It's probably prudent to be cautious, especially with everything going on." His voice dropped slightly as he glanced around the shop, even though there was no one else in sight.

I nodded, but my worry only deepened. "That confirms what you told me. Do they know how many ley lines there are?"

"If my sources can be believed, three," Finn said, his voice grim.

Three.

My stomach tightened. "That's not good. Three ley lines? What happens if I can't find the heart?" I asked, forcing my voice to stay steady.

"If the tree heals, it should be fine," Finn said, his brow furrowing. "The heartwood acts like a gateway to the ley lines. As long as the gateway stays intact, it maintains a balance between the magic of the town and the ley lines' power."

"But what if I don't find the heart?" I pressed.

Finn hesitated, his gaze hardening as if considering the worst-case scenario. "If you don't find the heart, the magical gateway could collapse," he said quietly. "It'll either shut off the dryad's and the town's connection to the ley lines completely or—"

"Or?" I prompted, dreading the answer.

"Or it could overload," Finn finished, his voice grim. "Flood the town with uncontrolled wild magic straight from the ley lines."

A cold shiver ran down my spine. This was already happening. For a moment, the cramped, chaotic shop seemed even more oppressive, the clutter closing in around us as the reality of the situation settled over me like a heavy fog. If I didn't find the heart, Havenwood might face a magical disaster unlike anything we'd seen before.

"Well," I said, forcing a smile that didn't quite reach my eyes. "No pressure, right?"

Finn managed a jerky nod, but I could tell he wasn't any more reassured than I was. "What are you going to do?"

"Everything I can to find the heart, but other than an old lady I saw in the woods, I don't know where to start looking," I admitted.

"I can ask around with my contacts. See if anyone has a grudge against the dryads?" Finn suggested.

I nodded, even though I could tell he didn't sound confident in his own idea. "I'll take all the help I can get. I've already been to see Jeremy, and he promised to look at the samples of the heartwood I brought back. Maybe he and his uncle can figure out a way to heal the tree or at least buy us some more time so we can find the heart."

"Good idea. Calling in a treant for a plant problem is a smart move. In fact, he might know something about the dryad situation. I should swing by and have a chat with him," Finn said.

"Give me a call the second you hear anything," I said as we headed towards the door.

"Harper?" an unfamiliar voice called out from behind me. I froze for a moment before realizing it didn't have the distinctive shrill or nasal timbre of the Puddletons' voices. I glanced over my shoulder to see Sandy, the volunteer from the library heading our way.

Finn's eyes flicked over my head. "I'll catch up with you later," he murmured before pulling open the door and heading down Arcadia Avenue towards his shop.

I nodded and then turned to greet Sandy. "Hi there. You must really love books. Looking for anything in particular?" My smile felt forced. I wanted to be out there, searching for a solution to the heartwood problem, not stuck in the Dusty Tome making small talk.

"No, just browsing. But that's a good thing, I think. If I was actually searching for something, it would be nearly impossible to find it in this clutter." Sandy's eyes went wide. "Oh, I'm sorry. This isn't your bookshop, is it? I didn't mean to offend. It's...lovely...and so full of things to read."

"No," I chuckled. "I run Sullivan's Spellbooks. It can be confusing though, especially since our bookstores are so close together."

Sandy's face relaxed. "Oh, that's right. Now I remember. Well, I'll have to swing by and browse through your collection as well." She dropped her voice and cupped a hand around her mouth. "But I do hope your establishment is better organized."

Before I could respond, a nasal voice cut through the shop. "I thought I recognized your voice, Harper Sullivan. Just how long have you been sneaking into my shop and trying to poach my clients?!"

I groaned inwardly. Of course. Oswald Puddleton, in all his odious glory, came stomping up with a familiar scowl plastered across his face. He was a small, round man with a perpetual air of self-importance that seemed to grow more unbearable every time I encountered him. Today, he was wearing a mustard-colored vest that did nothing to soften his harsh glare.

"I'm doing no such thing," I said, meeting his accusation head-on. "We were just having a friendly conversation."

"Friendly conversation?" Oswald scoffed. "In my shop? You're just here to undermine my business, steal my customers, and ruin my livelihood! Admit it!" His nasal voice grew more strident with every word, grating on my nerves almost as much as the false accusations.

"I'm not here to steal anything," I replied, doing my best to remain calm. "I came to drop off some misdelivered mail, and that's it."

"A likely story," Oswald sneered.

Sandy, visibly flustered, looked between the two of us and held up the book in her hands. The cover had a distinctive green and purple color palette, but I couldn't quite see the title. "I think I'll just take this and be on my way, if you don't mind."

She hurriedly handed the book to Oswald, who seemed all too pleased to ring her up, eyeing me with a smug smile. Sandy gave me a small, apologetic wave before beating a hasty retreat out the door, no doubt eager to distance herself from any continuing drama.

I turned to follow her, ready to escape the heavy atmosphere of the Dusty Tome, when my elbow caught a precariously balanced stack of books on a nearby table. The whole pile wobbled dangerously before tumbling to the floor with a resounding thud.

Oswald's sigh was so loud it could have rattled the overstuffed shelves. He paired that with a withering glare, as though I'd ruined his entire day. Heat rushed to my cheeks as I knelt to pick up the fallen books. "I'm so sorry," I said quickly, my voice instinctively softening as I started stacking them again. It wasn't as if I could just leave them there—no matter how much I wanted to make a quick exit.

As I carefully stacked the books back on the table, Hortense returned to the counter, escorting another customer toward it. My breath caught when I glanced up to see none other than the disheveled Professor Edmund Hawke, cradling an armful of books on rare flora. He deposited the stack on the counter with a satisfied thump, looking as if he'd just struck gold.

"Ah, Professor Hawke," she said in a sickly sweet voice, though her eyes shot daggers at me. "I'll be happy to assist you—unless our little distraction here gets in the way." She looked me up and down, clearly unimpressed, and added with a sneer, "Some people just don't know when they're not welcome."

I bit back a retort, opting instead to smile tightly. "For the record, I wasn't here to cause any trouble. I was just returning a misdelivered letter."

Oswald's eyes narrowed further, if that was even possible. "A convenient excuse! I bet that's just what you *want* us to think. That so-called 'letter' probably doesn't even have anything written on it. You're here snooping, trying to steal our business secrets!"

I exhaled slowly, trying to keep my frustration in check. "No, I'm not here to steal anything. This—" I pointed the envelope slightly for emphasis, "—was delivered to me, and I'm just dropping it off. It's a letter you wrote to Hortense."

His face twisted into a sneer. "I wrote no such thing!"

"Well, it's addressed to her and looks like a Valentine. My apologies for jumping to conclusions," I said sharply.

Whoops. My frustration was getting the better of my self-control. I needed to make my escape before I said something I'd regret.

Before I could excuse myself, Hortense's sharp voice cut through the tension. "Let me see that!" She snatched up the envelope, ripping it open with the same efficiency as a cat shredding a toy mouse. Professor Hawke shifted to the side to allow her some space as he paged through a book titled *The Guardians of the Grove* without looking up.

Hortense yanked the card out of the envelope. As her eyes skimmed the contents, her expression shifted from curious to livid in a heartbeat. "What's this supposed to be, Oswald?" she demanded, thrusting the card in his direction.

Curious, I craned my neck to get a glimpse of the inside as Oswald came around the counter to take it from her. As I suspected, it was a Valentine's

Day card. Inside, there was a handwritten personal message penned in a cramped, bold style. Only, instead of sweet nothings or affection, the note was a mess of rude, snarky remarks I could easily read from over Oswald's shoulder.

> *To my dear Hortense, your shrill voice makes my ears bleed, but*
> *hey, no one's perfect. Hope you have a decent Valentine's Day.*
> *If anyone can tolerate you, that is.*

My jaw dropped. The Puddletons weren't my favorite people in town, but at least I was civil to them both. If this is how they spoke to each other, no wonder they were both bitter, odious people.

Oswald's face turned beet red as he gaped at the card. "I—I didn't write that! It's not—" He rounded on me, eyes blazing with accusation. "This is your doing, isn't it? You forged this to make me look bad!"

I reeled back, my voice incredulous. "Me? I didn't write that! I found it mixed in with my mail and just brought it here like I said. Why would I go out of my way to do something like this?"

Hortense's face had turned an alarming shade of purple as she glared at Oswald. "This is how you feel about me, Oswald? After all the years we've been married?"

"I didn't write it!" he protested.

She snatched the card from him and waved it under his nose. "Don't lie to me. I recognize your handwriting!"

Oswald sputtered, backing away slightly. "I swear, it wasn't me! This has to be some kind of trick!" he jabbed a finger in my direction. "I bet *she's* behind this. First, you come into my shop, then you try to make me look like a fool. This is sabotage!"

Hortense crossed her arms, glaring at me as well. Her ire seemed to shift in my direction in an instant. "It wouldn't be the first time someone tried to undermine us. Remember the Pumpkin Parade and what happened with our candy? We were the laughingstock of the town! I distinctly remember *her* being there as well."

"Undermine you?" I echoed, exasperated. "I didn't write that letter, and I certainly wasn't responsible for what happened to your candy last October!" That was mostly true. I hadn't turned their float into a habitat for candy frogs, spiders, and snakes, but I hadn't been completely blameless in the debacle either. I snapped my mouth closed before I said something I'd regret.

Behind her, Professor Hawke shifted the first book to the side and opened the second. I caught a glimpse of the gold-foiled lettering on the cover. *Secret Beneath the Roots.* He must really love plants. He was muttering to himself as he reached into his jacket pocket.

"You! You're behind everything, aren't you?" Hortense snarled at me, her shrill voice reaching an ear-piercing pitch.

"Yes, that must be it. You're trying to turn us against each other," Oswald said, joining his wife in her accusations.

"Me? Why would I do anything of the sort?" I protested.

"Who knows? Maybe you can't bear to see your competition thrive," Hortense said, waving a hand proudly at the cluttered bookshop.

"That's right," Oswald chimed in. "Or you bear a grudge because we helped your cousin. It's a shame *he* didn't inherit Spellbooks. Thaddeus would've been a *nice* neighbor."

My breath caught in my throat as I glared at him. Thaddeus, my obnoxious, long-lost cousin, had proposed some ridiculous collaboration with the Puddletons if he had inherited the shop. The very thought made my blood boil.

I opened my mouth to retort when something behind the Puddletons caught my attention. My jaw dropped as I completely forgot what I was going to say and watched dumbfounded as Professor Edmund Hawke pulled out a small candle and a lighter. With an absent-minded air, he lit the candle and started running it under the pages of a book—just like my dad used to do when he'd written me secret messages in "invisible ink," which was really lemon juice.

"Is he...?" I mumbled, blinking in disbelief and pointing at the professor. The Puddletons' anger melted into confusion, and they turned as one.

Hortense's piercing voice cut through the shop, shrill and indignant. "Professor Hawke! Put out that candle this instant!"

The disheveled professor looked up, mildly surprised by the interruption. "What? Ah, yes, but you see, it's the only way to know if a book is of...a certain nature," he replied, waving the candle slightly as if the matter were perfectly self-evident.

Oswald's eyes bulged in his pudgy face. "What on earth are you talking about? No fire in the bookshop!"

"But I really must check the authenticity of this tome. For research purposes, you understand," the professor said, turning the page and starting to run the candle along the underside of the next one.

"Stop!" Hortense screeched. "I already told you that the book is authentic. We got it delivered directly from the publisher. I've pulled all the books you requested on the history of Havenwood, and rare plants. I swear they're all authentic!"

Professor Hawke, seeming unperturbed by the shouting, waved the candle under another page, utterly unbothered. "Yes, yes, I appreciate that. But you see, some books have a way of hiding things in plain sight. A little heat can reveal...well, let's just say, hidden knowledge."

I watched in growing horror as he waved the candle around, the small flame dancing dangerously close to the edges of the book's pages.

"You're going to set something on fire!" I hissed, trying to keep my voice down but failing miserably. I'd had my own close calls with fire in Spellbooks in the past few months and had no wish to relive that trauma. Or be blamed for anything that happened in the Dusty Tome. Knowing the Puddletons, they'd probably claim I was solely responsible for trying to burn the shop to the ground around their ears.

The professor gave me a thoughtful look, as though the idea of a fire had only just occurred to him. "Ah. That would be...unfortunate." Before I could say another word or urge him to blow out the candle, the inevitable happened. One careless flick of the candle too close to the book, and the corner of the page caught fire.

"Oh, no—" I started, lunging forward, but it was too late.

The fire spread quickly, licking up the edges of the brittle paper, the flames dancing in the too-bright light of the Dusty Tome. Hortense let out a piercing shriek, while Oswald stood frozen in shock.

"Fire! Fire!" Hortense screeched, flapping her arms like a panicked bird. "Someone do something!"

I didn't have time for their dramatics. I had to act, and fast.

The professor, still holding the burning book, seemed oddly fascinated by the flames. "Well, this is...unexpected. But on the bright side, I can now say with authority, this is an authentic copy."

I ignored him and, channeling my focus, I reached out with a small pulse of magic, feeling for the metal objects nearby. I sensed a familiar cylindrical tube behind the counter. Perfect.

Without asking permission, I dashed behind the counter while Hortense flapped and screeched like an irate bird at the bemused professor, and Oswald just stared in shock as the pages slowly curled and blackened. I grabbed the handheld fire extinguisher and, with a concentrated effort, manipulated the mechanisms to shoot a small, very directed spray of white foam at the flames licking up the spine of the book on the counter. The fire died almost immediately under the deluge as the professor stood there, staring down at the mess with a fascinated expression.

"Well, that's one way to solve the problem," he said cheerfully, blinking at the foam-covered pages.

I let out a breath I didn't realize I'd been holding. I just hoped no one realized I'd used magic to prevent *the Dusty Tome* from burning down.

Hortense glared at the mess; her face flushed from all the screaming. "What...what did you do?"

"I saved your merchandise, your customer, and likely your shop from a fire," I said, not trying very hard to hold back a smile of relief. If I'd been a lesser person, I might've made a comment about how that should prove to them I wasn't interested in any form of sabotage, but I felt it was an unnecessary point to make. My actions spoke louder than any words.

Oswald and Hortense, however, were too busy flapping about, fussing over the foam and frantically trying to reassure and reprimand Professor Hawke in turn. Oswald waved a rag at the professor, his voice rising in pitch as he stammered something about "health and safety protocols," while Hortense tried to salvage the soapy pages of the singed book.

"Really, Professor! What were you thinking?" she shrilled, snatching the rag from Oswald and trying to dab at the foam. "You could've ruined this valuable book!"

"One that you will only find at the preeminent bookshop in Havenwood," Oswald added, shooting me a nasty look.

As Hortense wiped the foam from the pages, I managed to steal a glance at the book. Sure enough, on one of the exposed pages, a message shimmered into view—the familiar brown of invisible ink, now revealed by the heat. It wasn't anything overtly magical, but the words made my heart skip a beat: *Order No. 47—initiated by the Council. Further inquiries require authorization.*

I furrowed my brow, trying to make sense of it. Order numbers? An unnamed Council? Authorization? It sounded official, though I had no idea what it referred to. A vague memory of gossip about Vivienne serving on the mage council sprang to mind. Could this be a reference to that magical body? Is that why it was hidden and still so obscure?

Before I could process the meaning of the note, Hortense barged in, practically pushing me aside. "I'll handle this. You're in the way," she snapped, her hands flailing as she attempted to clean the mess with little success. No thank you, no acknowledgment—just more chaos.

I decided I'd had enough. I'd accomplished my goal and returned the letter. Staying any longer would likely only result in more erroneous accusations. Who knows? The Puddletons might even twist the story in such a way that they convinced themselves *I* set fire to the shop. There'd already been more drama this week than I'd bargained for. No need to incite anything additional. With a quiet sigh, I turned to leave.

As I made my way to the door, a book on a cluttered table near the entrance caught my eye. The title was simple but striking: A History of the Silverthorne Family. Intrigued, I picked it up and flipped it over, scanning the back cover.

The Silverthorne family, one of the oldest and most powerful lineages, traces its roots back beyond the founding of Haven-wood itself. Their influence extends far and wide, bringing both powerful allies and formidable enemies. Most notable among their rivals is the Wraithmoor family, whose grudge has spanned decades, sparking conflicts that echo through time.

A shiver ran down my spine as I read the words. The Silverthornes weren't just any family. They held sway in Havenwood and possibly beyond. That made me glad I'd worked so hard to not get on Vivienne Silverthorne's bad side. If this book was anything to go by, I was grateful I'd been able to help avoid the formation of a grudge between Vivienne and Cassandra Bellamy earlier today as well. No one needed more animosity, not in the current climate. I glanced over my shoulder. Maybe I'd even done some good and started mending fences with the Puddletons—though I wasn't holding my breath. Admittedly, being on their bad side didn't seem nearly as terrifying as being in Vivienne's crosshairs.

Then again, here I was, considering a relationship with her son, Gabriel. If that wasn't putting myself squarely in Vivienne's sights, I didn't know what was.

Another loud crash came from behind me, followed by more frantic shouts from Oswald and Hortense. I winced and quickly placed the book back on the table. No sense in sticking around for more drama.

With a final glance around, I slipped out the door, eager to leave the chaos behind. The crisp winter air stung my cheeks as I crunched along the short lane toward the sidewalk. That's when I saw it—a boot print, the tread leaving a distinct crosshatch pattern in the snow.

My heart thudded as I crouched, brushing my gloved fingers against the edge of the impression. The pattern tugged at my memory. Yanking off my glove with my teeth, I pulled out my phone, scrolling frantically through my gallery. There it was—the photo I'd taken at the heartwood tree. I held the phone up to the print in the snow, my breath catching. A perfect match.

I straightened slowly, scanning the snowy street. The arguing voices from inside were muffled now, just background noise. My mind leapt to the nearest suspects. Had Oswald or Hortense been out here? Unlikely. As odious as the Puddletons were, I couldn't imagine them traipsing through the woods much less risk exposing Havenwood's secrets. Their selfishness had limits, and jeopardizing the town wasn't in their playbook.

But someone had been here and at the heartwood. A name surfaced in my mind, sending a chill down my spine: Edmund Hawke. His recent antics both in the Tome and at the library came flooding back. He had magical powers, there was no doubt in my mind. But what were they? More to the point, could he have been at the heartwood? Could he be responsible for the damage? The possibility gnawed at me.

Behind me, the door creaked open, and Hortense stepped out onto the stoop, her sharp glare slicing through the winter air. I didn't wait for her to speak. My boots crunched faster against the snow as I headed down Arcadia Avenue, my thoughts a swirling storm of questions and unease.

As I moved away from the Dusty Tome, one thing became clear—Edmund Hawke had just secured the top spot on my suspect list.

Wandering Into Trouble

As I walked back to Spellbooks, I was pleasantly surprised to see more pedestrians out window shopping along Arcadia Avenue. Perhaps I should get back to my own shop and try giving the Puddletons a real run for their money. My competitive spirit normally lay dormant unless I was watching the Olympics, but imagining the Puddletons' smug smiles invigorated me to figure a way out of my current business slump. Admittedly, running around town with Spellbooks shut wasn't helping matters any.

I slowed to a stop, catching my breath as reality crept back in. Running around town was the only way I was going to stop the dryad from cursing Havenwood indefinitely. The wild magic felt stronger now, like static electricity crawling across my skin. People would start to notice soon—first with whispers and wary glances. If we didn't find the heart soon, it wouldn't be whispers for long. They'd be screaming for answers I didn't have.

Still, so far, my search hadn't turned up anything of note—except for the footprint. My gut twisted at the thought. Could it really be a coincidence? My instincts told me no, but logic tried to nudge its way in. Maybe I was just reading too much into it. After all, plenty of people walked through Havenwood every day.

I pulled out my phone, my finger hovering over Gabriel's number. Should I tell him about my suspicion that Hawke might somehow be involved? But I hesitated. Gabriel had enough on his plate, and the last thing I wanted was to pull him into a wild goose chase based on a hunch.

I stuffed the phone back into my pocket, shaking my head. No. Not yet. There was still the possibility it was just a coincidence, even if my gut insisted otherwise. Besides, if I called him every time my imagination ran away with me, he'd start screening my calls. I straightened, forcing myself to take a steadying breath. If I was going to solve this—and keep the town from falling apart—I needed to follow the facts, not just my instincts.

Starting with Spellbooks. Maybe tending to the shop for a bit would help me clear my head and refocus. Saving Havenwood at the cost of running Spellbooks into the ground wouldn't do me any good either. Maybe I should start looking for some part-time help. But that was going to have to wait until after I dealt with my current crisis. Crises.

I glanced up at the sky, where soft flakes were just starting to drift down. Going out into the woods now wasn't the best idea. What if something happened to me? A tree branch could fall and knock me out, or worse, the dryad could ambush me and curse me again. No, going alone wasn't smart. Better to bring someone with me.

Bella? She'd come if I asked, but she was working at the Oasis until the evening. Finn? He'd probably say yes too, but after seeing him at the Dusty Tome earlier, I got the feeling he could use some space. Aunty Agatha? That was a possibility, though she might be off on one of her frequent trips. Even if she was home, was it fair to drag an older woman into the woods in winter to face an angry dryad? Probably not.

I squared my shoulders and made a swift decision. I'd leave Gabriel to his magical duties. In the meantime, I'd give Agatha a quick call—maybe she'd have some insight. But for the rest of today, I had other responsibilities to focus on. With the Valentine's Day blind date with a book event coming up, the shop needed some love, even if customers had been scarce these past few weeks. If things stayed as quiet as they'd been, I'd have plenty of time to get everything ready. Maybe Luna and Spellbooks would lend a hand. After that, I'd settle in with my computer and dive into researching ley lines, dryads, curses, and anything else that might save the heartwood tree.

Decision made, I started walking again, feeling slightly foolish for having stopped in the middle of the sidewalk. I glanced around, hoping no one had noticed my odd pause. But as I scanned the street, my eyes snagged on a familiar figure at the end of the road. An older woman, wearing a long dark dress, wild silver hair falling across her face, and a gray shawl wrapped snugly around her shoulders.

It was the same woman from the woods.

My body moved before my brain caught up. I found myself half jogging toward her, my voice rising as I called out. "Hey! Hello! Can I talk to you for a minute?" I waved, my overly wide smile making my cheeks ache.

The old woman's head snapped up, her expression sharp, and she scuttled backward, the basket on her arm swaying as she quickly retreated. I picked up the pace, trying to catch her before she slipped away.

"Hey! Wait! I just want to talk!" I called again, my voice echoing in the crisp winter air. A few window shoppers glanced at me like I'd lost my mind, but I didn't care. My gaze was fixed on the woman.

She looked both ways, and in a movement so speedy that it surprised me, darted across the road. For someone her age, she moved with surprising agility, disappearing between two buildings across Arcadia Avenue faster than I thought possible. By the time I reached the spot, puffing from the effort of running in snow boots, she was gone.

Panting, I glanced around, my breath coming in visible clouds in the chilly air. The alleyway she had vanished into was empty—no sign of her anywhere. But as I retraced her path, something caught my eye in the snow.

I crouched down, brushing aside the fresh powder she'd kicked up in her hasty departure to reveal a small pile of twigs and herbs, neatly bundled together with twine. Among them, a few pieces of bark that looked oddly familiar—smooth, thin...and blackened. My stomach dropped as I realized what I was looking at: dead bark from the damaged heartwood tree.

I inhaled sharply and brushed the twigs aside to uncover something else beneath them. A small silver pin glinted in the snow. It was shaped like a crescent moon, simple and unadorned but eerily familiar. I squinted at the pin, holding it up to the light as I tried to remember where I'd seen it. All of a sudden, the memory clicked into place. It had been in one of the old books I'd discovered in Granny Bea's office. One of the ones related to magic.

But which one? And what did it mean?

My heart raced as I glanced back down the empty alleyway where the woman had disappeared. The snow-covered ground held no fresh tracks, as if she'd simply evaporated. How was she so quick—and why had she left no footprints? I gripped the pin tightly, my mind spinning with questions. Was she somehow connected to the missing heart? To the damage at the heartwood? But if she wasn't, why had she run? Who was this woman? Why did she keep turning up? More importantly, what was she hiding? And how was I going to get any answers if she kept disappearing?

I shook off the swirling thoughts and slowly started heading back towards Spellbooks when I spotted someone familiar hurrying down the street.

Cassandra Bellamy.

She was moving quickly, her face flushed with what looked like a mix of anger and tears.

"Cassandra?" I called out, stepping toward her.

She halted, as if she hadn't seen me until that moment, and wiped hastily at her eyes. "Oh, it's you. Hi again."

"Is everything okay?" I asked.

She shook her head, red hair flying with the gesture. "No, not really. I just got a message..." her voice cracked and spiraled upwards. She swallowed hard and wrapped her arms around herself. "It's completely irrational and over the top!"

"Oh," I said softly.

"It's just ridiculous!" she burst out. "She accused me of doing something I didn't even do, and her tone—ugh! It's like she's not even the same person everyone always raves about."

My stomach dropped. Cassandra had been trying to speak with Vivienne Silverthorne recently, hadn't she? Maybe something had gone wrong. Vivienne wasn't exactly known for being warm and fuzzy.

"That sounds...unfair," I ventured cautiously.

"Tell me about it! Everyone always said I'd get so much out of studying with her. That someone of her caliber is the only teacher I should be working with if I want to get better at my m—" she cut off, her eyes going wide. "My mastery of my subject," she finished hurriedly.

I didn't need her to spell it out. She'd been about to say magic. If Cassandra was hoping Vivienne would coach her, then she'd really picked the wrong week to ask. Vivienne still intimidated me on a good day. I didn't want to imagine what it would be like to face her ire full force. I spoke softly, feeling sympathetic for the woman. "Maybe it's worth talking to her directly. Sometimes things can sound worse in writing than they do face-to-face."

Cassandra hesitated, her jaw tightening before she let out a short sigh. "Why bother? She won't see me."

That stopped me in my tracks. Vivienne could be cold, sure, but outright refusing someone? What had Cassandra done to make Vivienne shut her out completely?

Cassandra's smile was tight and fleeting, a poor attempt to mask her frustration. "Thanks, anyway. And sorry for snapping earlier. I shouldn't have unloaded on you."

"Don't worry about it," I murmured.

Her strides were quick and purposeful as she headed towards a nearby car, but something about her posture suggested she wasn't nearly as confident as she appeared. Moments later, the engine rumbled to life, and she drove off without looking back. As the car disappeared down the road, I noticed a small piece of paper fluttering on the ground where she'd been standing.

I bent down to pick it up, brushing snow off its edge. Probably just a receipt or some scrap she'd meant to toss. Still, I figured I'd take it back to Spellbooks and throw it away—no sense in leaving litter behind.

However, as I glanced at the scrap of paper in my gloved hands, I realized it wasn't a receipt at all; it was a handwritten note. The handwriting was sharp and deliberate. The message wasn't just irrational—it was threatening. My stomach twisted as I read.

> *I know what you're trying to do, and it won't work. I'll see to that myself. Stop now, or you'll regret it.*

My breath caught as I reached the bottom of the note. It was signed with a simple L.

L? Not *V?* I stared at the letter, my mind racing. I'd assumed it was from Vivienne. After all, who else would Cassandra be dealing with if she wanted magical guidance? But the note seemed more aggressive than Vivienne's usual cold perfection. It was too brash. But...L. Who did I know that had that initial?

Not Vivienne, but perhaps *Lucas* Silverthorne?

The thought sent a ripple of unease through me. He was Vivienne's son and a mage himself, but...could he really have written something like this? His demeanor had always seemed cool, aloof, even condescending at times, but this level of threat didn't match what I knew of Lucas. And yet, I couldn't completely rule him out.

Of course, there were countless other possibilities. *L* was a common enough initial. But what was Cassandra trying to do that had sparked such a threatening response?

I folded the note carefully, sliding it into my pocket. I couldn't shake the uneasy feeling curling in my gut. Something wasn't right here. Not with Cassandra, not with this note, and not with whoever had penned it.

What exactly was Cassandra involved in, and who had she crossed to trigger such an ominous warning?

The Glitter Chronicles

As I MADE MY way back to Spellbooks, my thoughts swirled with fragments of everything that had happened. Cassandra's angry outburst, the note she dropped with its ominous message signed L, and the strange old woman I kept running into. Whoever she was, she had an annoyingly good knack for disappearing right when I got close.

When I pushed open the door to Spellbooks, the bell jingled softly overhead, a small comfort against the storm brewing in my mind. My eyes landed on the welcome mat, where an unexpected envelope lay. I froze, hesitant after my last few encounters with letters. The wild magic leaking into town was definitely causing more than a little havoc. However, the handwriting on the outside was instantly recognizable.

Gabriel.

I smiled despite myself. I shrugged out of my winter coat and slipped into the shoes I kept near the door for working in the shop before picking up the note. As I unfolded it, a familiar voice rang out behind me.

"Well, look who's finally back. Did you get lost in the forest or something?"

I glanced up to find Luna sitting on the counter, paws crossed as she stared at me with her usual unimpressed look. She twitched her ear. "I was starting to think you'd abandoned me. You've certainly been MIA around the shop recently. Interesting way to run a business."

"I wasn't gone that long, Luna. You can hardly call it an abandonment," I said, unfolding the note from Gabriel.

"'Not that long' in human time, maybe. In rabbit time, that's—well, I don't know. Rabbits don't usually tell time, unless they have a Mad Hatter for a friend and a madder Queen for a boss. I always thought the obsession with time is what makes most people neurotic. Regardless, for a familiar as magnificent as I am, it was an unacceptable amount of time."

I snorted softly. "Magnificent, huh? What happened to humble?" I teased.

Luna hopped down from the counter, running a paw along her whiskers. "Oh, sweetie. Humble doesn't suit me. But you know what does? My ninja headband. Maybe I should get it and teach you some manners."

I threw my hands up in the air immediately. "I concede! I apologize. It's all my fault. Rabbits make the best familiars. I'll bring you treats from Honey. Just don't get the headband!"

"Fine. Apology accepted. As long as it comes with chocolate chip cookies." Luna glanced at the note in my hands. "What's that? A love letter from Prince Charming?"

I rolled my eyes. "No, Gabriel."

"Like I said..."

I ignored her, opening up the letter and reading Gabriel's short but heartfelt message.

Harper,
I've been thinking about how to say this for a while now, but I realize there's no perfect time. You are everything I admire—brave, smart, independent. You don't need anyone to lean on, but I want you to know that I'm here. I want to be the one you call, the one who stands by your side. I want to be the person you don't have to be strong for. Not because you need me, but because you deserve someone who will stand by you, no matter what.
You face the world head-on, and I can't help but admire that. But I also see how much you carry, and I want you to know—you don't have to do it alone. I'm here, whenever you need me. I believe in you, completely.

Just know that you have all of me.
Yours,
Gabriel

I couldn't help but smile, but as I reread Gabriel's words, my pulse quickened. This was...a lot. A *lot*. My heart did a flip, then stuttered in confusion. We hadn't known each other that long—sure, there was chemistry, but this? This was deep. Vulnerable. Unexpectedly strong, especially for Gabriel. He was sweet, but usually more reserved than this.

I swallowed, glancing down at the letter again, my hands trembling slightly. Was this really how he felt? Or was he swept away by the romance of the season with the approach of Valentine's Day?

Or was there another answer to the unexpected letter?

My thoughts stuttered as the faces of the Puddletons and Cassandra Bellamy flashed through my mind—people who had enchanted letters appear suddenly, potentially causing havoc. Maybe Gabriel hadn't written this at all. Maybe this was another trick of the wild magic.

The possibility sent a cold shiver down my spine. My fingers tightened on the edges of the letter, and I drew a shaky breath. Could I trust what I was reading? Or was the magic in town warping the note in my hands? What if these letters weren't just words but unfiltered thoughts, the raw truth stripped of society's polished veneer and polite falsehoods?

I stared at the letter a moment longer, my mind racing, and then folded it neatly, shoving it into my pocket before I could second-guess every word. There wasn't time for this right now.

"I see someone's in a good mood," Luna remarked, her tone teasing but with a hint of her usual sharpness. "Don't tell me the world's about to end, and you've decided now's a good time to try your hand at writing love letters."

I chuckled halfheartedly, though my thoughts were still tangled up with Gabriel's letter. "It's not exactly the end of the world, Luna," I said, dodging the issue of the letter completely. It wasn't something I wanted to share until I knew where Gabriel's thoughts and feelings truly lay.

"Just a curse and wild magic running, well, wild," she said dryly. Her eyes sparkled, but there was something like concern in her voice. "You know what? You might want to focus on one crisis at a time."

I sighed, rubbing my temples. "Yeah, I know." I hesitated for a moment, feeling the weight of everything pressing down on me. I really needed to find this missing heart and fast, but with no leads, where was I even supposed to start looking? Actually, I had no idea where to start, and every lead had either dried up or circled back on itself. The heart was out there, somewhere, but how was I supposed to find it when I didn't even know where to look?

A thought occurred to me, and I spoke slowly. "Actually, focusing on one crisis at a time is excellent advice."

"I know. That's why I suggested it," Luna said with a sniff.

I glanced toward the shelves, trying to push Gabriel's words from my mind. "Can I count on both you and Spellbooks for help? We're going to need all hands on deck. Between running the business and researching this heartwood mess, I'm stretched thin."

"Well, it's a good thing I've got paws then," Luna said, waggling them at me with a sly grin. "But don't expect me to dig through dusty old books. I'll leave the boring research to you and Spellbooks."

"Thanks, Luna," I said dryly, rolling my eyes.

"Don't worry, though." She leapt onto the counter with leporine grace and tapped a paw to her chest. "I'll manage the crucial work of making this place look amazing for your Valentine's event. Ribbon curling is a rare and underappreciated talent, and lucky for you, I'm a master."

"How are you...what about the thumb thing? Isn't that—" I stopped myself mid-sentence and shook my head, laughing. "Never mind. Thank you, Luna. I accept your help."

Luna gave a little bow. "You're welcome. Now, if you'll excuse me, I have adorable chaos to spread." With a flick of her tail, she hopped off the counter and hopped toward the craft supplies at the back of the shop.

As soon as she was out of earshot, I turned toward the shelves and lowered my voice. "Spellbooks, it's just us now. I need your help. I've got nothing solid to go on for the missing heart. I remember reading something about crescent moon symbols in one of Granny Bea's books upstairs. I can't remember the details, but I need to research that too. And while you're looking, I could really do with some more information on ley lines. I need to understand their connection to the heartwood tree. Is there anything in the shop that would be useful for me to read?"

A soft hum passed through the floorboards, reassuring me that Spellbooks was listening. A few books slid from their places on the shelves, shuffling and flipping open to specific pages as the shop started conducting the research I'd requested.

"Thank you," I whispered, feeling the familiar comfort of Spellbooks' quiet magic. "While you work on that, I'll handle any walk-in customers and get some social media posts ready for the blind-date-with-a-book event. Let me know when you find something."

It didn't take long before a book thumped onto the counter, its pages flipping open to a section about ley lines, curses, and the delicate balance of magical forces. I nodded, taking a seat and diving into the research. Every now and then, I glanced up to greet a customer or answer a question, but my thoughts kept returning to the missing heartwood heart—and the looming sense that time was running out.

The rest of the day passed in a blur of activity. *Spellbooks* hummed quietly in the background, its shelves shifting every so often as it continued its research, flipping through page after page of magical lore from the minimal selection of books downstairs and the wider range of magical tomes Granny, and now I, kept upstairs. Some of what I read was pure speculation, while other tidbits ranged from mildly interesting to absolutely fascinating. However, nothing was particularly helpful for my current predicament.

Spellbooks seemed to exhaust our resources at the shop, the books coming slower and the information less relevant. While Spellbooks searched, I focused on helping customers, managing the shop's social media, and trying to make some eye-catching graphics for the "Blind Date with a Book" Valentine's promotion.

Meanwhile, Luna had set up a wrapping station, her precision and flair on full display. Each book she wrapped looked like a gift you'd find under a Christmas tree—perfectly folded paper, shiny ribbons curled to perfection, and bows tied with just the right amount of a festive touch. I watched her work for a moment, marveling at her skill.

Luna caught my eye and smirked. "What? Never seen a rabbit out-wrap a human before?"

"When you told me Christmas was your favorite holiday, I didn't realize you took it this seriously. To be honest, I thought your gifts came pre-wrapped from the store," I said with a grin.

"Christmas is the only holiday that matters," she declared, using her paws to nudge a glittery ribbon into place. "Valentine's Day is...fine. Even if it is a made-up holiday. I like chocolate as much as the next girl, so I can't really complain. But nothing beats the holiday spirit of Christmas. The lights, the decor, the gifts. It's practically my raison d'être."

I chuckled as I saved my latest set of graphics. "You realize this is a Valentine's event, right? We're wrapping books, not stuffing stockings."

Luna gave me a withering look, eyes narrowing as she placed the final touch on her latest masterpiece. "Details. I'm here to bring a level of class to your humble shop, no matter the occasion. Although thumbs would make it easier, I dare say, I'm doing an excellent job." She laid a paw on the newly wrapped book, the glittery ribbons glimmering under the lights.

I had to admit, she had a point. The packages looked incredible—like they'd been done by a professional. Each one was unique and still left plenty of space for me to add a little card with the generalized tropes as customers selected a wrapped book. Luckily, Luna had left post-it notes labeling each book, or it really would be a completely blind selection.

"I'll admit it," I said, raising my hands in surrender. "Your wrapping skills are unparalleled. But don't get too smug, or I might hire you for Christmas next year."

Luna sniffed, nudging another ribbon into place. "As if you could afford me."

I smirked and then considered the crafting chaos surrounding her. "Although I still don't understand why the glittery ribbons needed to be dragged around the entire shop. I think I've got enough in my hair to be considered a disco ball in the right light," I said, running a hand through my long wavy hair. A shower of shimmering sparkles drifted lazily to coat my sweater.

Luna sniffed. "And that is why I am the *artiste,* and you are manning the phones."

Before I could protest the excessive use of glitter further, Mr. Wigglesworth jumped down from his preferred spot in the front window and wound his way through my legs. Unlike Luna, he didn't offer much in the way of help, but his calm presence was at least soothing. I crouched down and ran my hand along his soft fur, scratching in his favorite place behind his ears before returning my attention to my phone.

Just as I was finishing up my last post for the day, my phone buzzed with a new message. I swiped to open it and smiled at the name that appeared on the screen: Gabriel.

Exhausted. Could really use a cup of coffee. Any chance I can interest you in one?

I grinned, already typing my response.

Sure. I've got coffee here if you want to stop by.

Almost immediately, the familiar dots appeared to show he was typing. I waited patiently until another message popped up.

If I'm asking you out for coffee, I'm not expecting you to make it for me, Harper. I'll pick you up in ten.

I glanced at the clock and realized it was nearly closing time anyway. "Well, that works," I said aloud, flipping the sign on the door to Closed and locking it. "It looks like I've got about ten minutes to not look like a disaster before Gabriel picks me up," I said to Luna as I headed towards the stairs.

Luna barely glanced up from her wrapping. "Fluff and furballs, if the man thinks a little glitter is a disaster, then what's he going to say when we start hanging heart garlands from the ceiling?"

"Wait. I thought you were anti-Valentine's Day. And what do you mean 'we?' You've been avoiding decorating since I moved in. The lack of thumbs always seemed to be an issue, but judging on the wrapping, I think you might have been pulling my leg."

Luna ran her paws over her whiskers and shot me a smug smile. "You had to learn somehow."

I rolled my eyes. "Seriously? Well, in the future, I'm putting a limit on how much glitter you can use. Call it retribution for dodging decorating duty."

Luna shrugged. "I call it teaching by doing. Namely, forcing you to do it. But you should really get upstairs. Your hair is a mess. Did you lose your hairbrush again?"

"What? No. Why would you—"

"Oh good. Make sure you put it to good use then," Luna advised, hopping away from the wrapping station and towards her spot in the window opposite Mr. Wigglesworth.

"Wait, what about all the ribbon and wrapping? I don't suppose—"

"Radish ruckus, you can't really expect me to do it *all* for you, especially without thumbs!"

"But—"

Luna cut me off. "But don't worry—I look fabulous, and that's what really matters."

"Thanks," I muttered, eyeing my outfit covered in stray bits of sparkle from the earlier wrapping. "And for the record, this glitter situation is your fault."

She yawned, her paws gracefully tying off another ribbon. "Glitter is the spice of life. Just accept it."

"I think I'll pass," I said, moving toward the stairs to freshen up. "But seriously, Luna—thanks for wrapping everything. You've got this whole place looking like Valentine's Day exploded in here and I love it."

She flicked her tail, satisfied. "Valentine's Day is all about making an impression. And nothing ruins a good first impression like being late. Don't you have eight minutes now?"

I glanced at the time and hurried toward the stairs. "Eight minutes is all I need."

Her voice followed me, dripping with amusement. "Are you sure? Bold of you to assume miracles work on a timer. Especially when you look like you just lost a fight to a glitter bomb."

Suspects Everywhere

As it turned out, eight minutes was not plenty of time. Fifteen minutes later, I was back downstairs in a new sweater and having shaken most of the glitter out of my hair. Luckily, Gabriel had been delayed as well. I flicked open the message on my phone.

Sorry, will be there as soon as I can. I'll explain when I get there.

I shot him a thumbs-up emoji and a brief reassuring message before turning my attention to the wrapping station Luna had left in disarray. Hopefully, I'd have enough time to tidy it up and make it look like a Cupid-themed party hadn't descended into chaos, complete with runaway ribbons and glittery hearts gone rogue.

A soft knock at the back of the shop pulled my attention away from returning everything to its rightful place. I frowned, glancing at the back door. Now, who could that be and why weren't they coming to the front door?

Curious, I headed towards the back and the sunroom leading out to the snowy garden beyond. To my surprise, Thistle was standing at the back door, hand raised for another knock. She wore only her leafy green dress and didn't appear to have any sort of proper protection from the elements. I rushed to open it for her, pulling her in out of the cold.

"Thistle! You don't have to knock, especially in weather like this. Here, let me get you a coat and warm you up," I said, shutting the door firmly behind her.

Thistle lifted a slim shoulder. "Nymphs don't often feel the cold. I mean, we do. But not in the same way you humans do. It's one of the nice things about our connection to the trees." Her grim expression didn't lighten despite her words.

"Did you find anything out?" I asked, hoping for some kind of good news.

Thistle met my gaze, her normally vibrant green eyes dull with worry. "It's worse than we thought."

I felt my stomach drop. "What do you mean?"

Thistle sighed and shifted, her expression uneasy. "Rowena's not just angry, Harper. She's...devastated. Her husband's tree was damaged."

"What?" My voice cracked. "Her husband? Is he okay? What kind of damage?"

"He's weak but recovering," Thistle said, her voice gentle. "Sometimes this happens—it's unfortunate, but trees can be damaged by natural caus-es. Heavy snow, falling branches, maybe even an animal. It's rare, but it's not unheard of. However, the damage weakened him, and Rowena's livid. She's convinced it's not just an accident."

Her words sent a ripple of unease through me. A damaged tree—like the heartwood? A chill ran down my spine. Was there a connection, or was this just another terrible coincidence?

"That poor man. And Rowena! No wonder she's so upset," I mur-mured, though my thoughts churned. If someone was behind this, what did it mean?

Thistle lifted a shoulder, not meeting my eyes. "Not just that. She thinks there's a conspiracy against her. That someone's out to hurt her and everyone she loves."

"Oh my," I breathed, startled that Rowena and I had leapt to the same conclusion. But could she be right? Or was grief clouding her judgment? "But do you think that's true?" I asked.

Thistle's eyes flicked to mine. "I don't know, but given the circum-stances, can you blame her? This is more than just upset. Grief and rage can cloud a dryad's mind like a storm. She's not thinking clearly, Harper. Her emotions have taken over, and she's lashing out at everyone she thinks might be conspiring against her. The longer this goes on...well, I don't want to even consider the possible outcomes," she finished with a shiver.

I rubbed my arms, trying to absorb the gravity of it all. "This is so much worse than I thought. Is there anything we can do to help her or her husband?"

Thistle hesitated. "From what I've seen, she won't listen to reason. The best thing we can do is figure out what happened to the heartwood. As fast as possible."

I nodded, my mind already racing with possibilities. "Okay, let's do that then. What about the heart? Did you find out anything about it?"

Thistle's face darkened, and my hope dwindled. She looked down at the floor, her voice heavy. "That's what took me so long. I've been reaching out to everyone I could think of—other nymphs, dryads, forest creatures—no one's seen the heart, Harper. No one even knew it was missing."

My legs wobbled, and I sank into one of the nearby chairs. "How can it be missing, and no one's even heard of the theft? It's the heartwood's heart—isn't it supposed to be incredibly powerful?"

Thistle shifted from foot to foot. "Honestly? I don't know. But given how Rowena is reacting, I'd say that's a fair guess. The ley lines are leaking wild magic, and it's fueling her. That extra power is making her curse even stronger. We're running out of time, Harper."

I swallowed hard, the weight of her words pressing down on me. "So, the wild magic isn't just leaking—it's amplifying her. She's drawing from it?"

Thistle nodded grimly. "That's what they are whispering in the forest. The wild magic is acting like fuel to a fire, and Rowena's grief and rage are the spark. Until we find the heartwood's heart, that magic is going to keep seeping out—and she'll keep growing stronger."

The gravity of her words hit me like a punch to the gut. The town, the heartwood, the people I cared about—everything was at risk. And still we had no leads, just a lot of suspicion.

My thoughts turned to Edmund Hawke, the plant-loving professor. Did he have something to do with what was happening, or did he have a knack for being in the wrong place at the right time? I couldn't prove it yet, but something about him had been gnawing at me since I left the Dusty Tome. For now, he still sat squarely at the top of my suspect list.

I stared at the floor, frustration boiling inside me. "So, what do we do? Just...keep looking?"

Thistle placed a hand on my shoulder, her touch grounding. "We keep trying. I believe the heart will reveal itself when the time is right. But we can't stop. We can't give up. I'll do what I can, but I fear I will discover nothing more than another dead end."

I nodded, but the knot in my stomach tightened. The race against time felt more impossible than ever.

"We'll figure it out," I said quietly, though the words felt hollow.

Thistle smiled softly, but it didn't quite reach her eyes. "I know we will. I am going to try to talk to some more of the forest folk but wanted to fill you in on what I'd found out so far."

"Thanks, Thistle," I said softly, "You're a loyal friend."

She paused, her gaze flickering toward me with that same sad, sweet smile that didn't quite reach her eyes. I hesitated, debating whether to tell her about Grimgor stopping by. But something in the weary slump of her shoulders stopped me. She'd already gone above and beyond, even going back to face the others—her tormentors—for answers. I couldn't burden her with more.

"Take care of yourself, okay?" I added, my voice quieter.

Thistle gave a small nod before slipping out the door, her footsteps light and swift across the snow. She disappeared into the large oak tree at the edge of the property, leaving only a faint trail behind her. As I watched her go, my heart sank even lower. I'd been skirting around the edges of the problem, asking questions, seeking advice, but what had I really done to find the heart? Not much. And that wasn't good enough—not anymore.

I took a deep breath, clenching my fists at my sides. If I wanted answers, I needed to go after them. It was time to stop waiting for something to happen and start taking control of my own fate.

I jumped up from the chair and hurried to the desk, grabbing the notebook and pen I kept under the counter. It was time to start thinking like an investigator again. First: motive. Someone had a reason for attacking the heartwood tree, and if I could figure out why, maybe I could trace it back to who. I scribbled "Motive" at the top, my pen hovering as I thought. Revenge? Power? Desperation? The heartwood wasn't just any tree—it was deeply tied to the ley lines and Havenwood's magic. Destroying it couldn't be random. There had to be something tied to someone's specific intent. But what and who was behind it? I underlined "Motive" twice, then moved down the page, writing "Suspects."

First on the list: the person behind the damage to Rowena's husband's tree. I hadn't wanted to say this to Thistle, but Rowena could be right. Maybe it wasn't natural damage at all, but a deliberate attack. But who would have done such a thing? I wrote it down, frustration gnawing at me because I had no idea where to even begin. That lead would be hard to chase without Thistle's help, and she needed rest after everything she'd been through.

I tapped the pen against my chin, my thoughts shifting to those with the knowledge and power to harm the heartwood itself. The Silverthornes came to mind immediately. Vivienne's magical expertise and fierce control made her capable, but her outrage over the tree's damage felt genuine. Lucas, though... Could the note signed with *L* point to him? He was Vivienne's son, a powerful mage, and had the means. But the Lucas I'd seen was distant, not brash. Besides, he always seemed to have the best interest of Havenwood at heart, even if we didn't always see eye to eye. I highly doubted Lucas would've done anything to hurt the heartwood, especially if it hurt Havenwood.

But what about Cassandra Bellamy? She was new in town, a magic user with unknown motives. I'd run into her more than once, and something about our interactions had left me uneasy. She seemed on edge and had been searching for Vivienne. Not only that, but she'd also been rebuffed. Perhaps this was her way of getting the Silverthorne matriarch's attention? That note she'd dropped only deepened my unease. There was definitely something going on with her, but did it tie back to the heartwood? Maybe. I wrote her name on the list and circled it.

I cast my mental net even further. What if this wasn't a magically driven act at all and had nothing to do with the ley lines or revenge on the dryad? Could it be something to do with the tree itself? I bit my lip. I didn't know enough about plants to be sure one way or the other. Scribbling a reminder in the margins to talk to Jeremy tomorrow, I let my mind wander through the possibilities. If someone was interested in the tree from a botanical point of view, why attack it? Could it be that pieces of the heartwood were used in some spell or other?

I glanced at the bundle of twigs and the pin that belonged to the old woman from the woods. She kept turning up at the most suspicious times, and I still hadn't figured out who she was. There was something magical about her presence—something that made my instincts scream she was more involved than she let on. I wrote "Old woman in the woods" at the bottom of the list, underlining it.

But she wasn't the only person who was interested in plants. Professor Edmund Hawke kept crossing my path as well, looking into magical texts about rare plants. First, he'd been at the library where his annoyance at Bella and me for being too loud resulted in him lashing out with his magic. Then he'd been perusing texts at the Dusty Tome, researching old lore about plants and the town's history. Not to mention the footprint I'd spotted in the snow. Coincidence? Maybe. But it also seemed like he was looking for something specific—something related to the magic here. If the heartwood tree was tied to a ley line, Edmund might see it as a gateway. I jotted his name down too, putting a large star next to it.

I stared down at the names, tapping the pen against the paper as my mind churned. Motives, suspects, and tentative leads. It wasn't much, but it was a start. Whoever was behind this couldn't stay hidden forever. I needed to figure out more about each of these people and determine whether they had the means or the motivation to steal the heart. The race against time had already begun, and, if I didn't act fast, Havenwood was going to spiral further into chaos. If I didn't fix this, Havenwood's future—and it seemed even my own shot at happiness—was at stake.

My grip tightened on the pen. I wouldn't let that happen. I couldn't. A life without love? It was too terrible to contemplate.

Hocus Mochas

My phone buzzed, jarring me out of my thoughts. I flicked open the notification, smiling when Gabriel's name popped up.

I'm so sorry. This is taking longer than I thought.

I sighed regretfully, glad he couldn't see my face right now. Knowing him, Gabriel was probably off dealing with something regarding the wild magic or the town. I couldn't really fault him for being busy, but I was disappointed I might not get to see him tonight. My fingers hovered over the screen, ready to tap out a conciliatory reply, but before I could, another message popped up.

Meet me at Hocus Mochas? Anything you want, on me. I've already arranged it with the owner.

I knew we both had bigger issues to deal with, but the thought of trying out a new coffee shop with Gabriel, especially one with such a cute name, was enticing. I shot him a thumbs up and then tapped out my reply.

Sounds good to me. Where is it?

His text was almost instant.

It's two streets over from Spellbooks. Think you can walk it, or should I call you a car?

I glanced out the window. Nighttime had settled over Havenwood, wrapping the town in a starlit embrace, even though it was barely six. The streetlights were already on, and a warm light illuminated Arcadia Avenue as shops wrapping up their daily business. Havenwood was typically a safe place, even at night. Besides, the walk would probably do me good after hunching over a computer and research books all afternoon.

I sent him a quick text to confirm that I'd walk and then grabbed my coat. Some people might raise an eyebrow at drinking coffee at six in the evening, but I wasn't one of them. Coffee was good at any point of time in the day and if it was in the evening with a handsome man who was interested in me, well that's why decaf was made, wasn't it?

I was surprised to see Hocus Mochas was still bustling. Havenwood was a small community that seemed to close down around six, but maybe that had just been my impression because of working in Spellbooks. As I glanced around the lively coffee shop, I realized that I'd been so consumed with thoughts of learning the business, running the business, expanding the business, that I hadn't allowed myself much time for exploring the hidden gems of Havenwood. Based on what I saw in Hocus Mochas, that was a problem I needed to remedy immediately.

Warm light spilled from vintage glass sconces, illuminating the brick walls and worn, wooden floors. The space was inviting, with mismatched plush armchairs gathered in small clusters and shelves brimming with books, mugs, and quirky decor. The air was thick with the smell of rich coffee threaded with notes of luxurious chocolate, the kind of place where time seemed to slow down, encouraging you to sit and savor each moment.

As I waited for my turn to order, my jaw nearly dropped at the array of decadent treats in the display case. Rows of artisanal chocolates were arranged like jewels including dark chocolate pieces topped with sea salt, truffles dusted with cocoa powder, and white chocolate bark studded with dried fruit. Steam rose from oversized mugs as baristas skillfully crafted drinks, from frothy cappuccinos to rich, velvety lattes. Customers filled nearly every table, talking softly as they enjoyed their desserts.

It wasn't flashy or overwhelming, just warm and inviting—like a neighborhood secret you were lucky enough to stumble upon. The hum of conversation, the clinking of spoons against ceramic, and the scent of melting chocolate made the whole place feel like a world apart, completely untouched by the wild magic running through the streets of Havenwood. But even in this cozy café, a gnawing unease lingered at the edges of my mind, refusing to be soothed.

As I reached the front of the line and approached the counter, the barista—a young guy with bright eyes and a friendly smile—said, "I haven't seen you around here before. What's your name?"

"Harper," I replied, a little confused. Didn't they only ask for names *after* they took your order?

His grin widened. "Ah, Gabriel Silverthorne called ahead. Said anything you want is on him tonight." The barista cupped a hand around his mouth and whispered. "If I were in your shoes, I'd order at least three boxes of truffles." He winked, his charming smile putting me instantly at ease.

A flush of surprise and warmth spread through me. I wasn't sure whether to feel flattered or overwhelmed. A small line was forming behind me, and I didn't want to hold them up. "Uh, any recommendations? Apart from the truffles?" I asked quickly.

The barista's eyes gleamed. "How about a slice of our signature dark chocolate peanut butter cake with a cup of the house special mocha? It's the perfect pick me up for a cold night like this."

"Sounds great," I said. It really did. My mouth was already watering as I glanced at the luscious cake topped with a decadent dark chocolate ganache.

"Fab. I'll give you a call when it's ready," the barista said, bustling off to make my coffee.

I moved to one of the few empty tables for two near the door, unbuttoning my coat and sitting in the plush purple armchair with my back towards the door. The small café was lively, and I could feel the settled magic of the place as a comfortable hum in the background, though my mind kept drifting back to Gabriel's thoughtful gesture.

As I waited for my order, the bell above the door chimed and, to my surprise, in walked Antonio and Honey holding hands. They didn't see me, but headed straight towards the counter, talking animatedly with one of the servers behind the display case who swiftly worked to compile a box of truffles based on the treats Honey indicated.

The DeLucas turned, matching smiles on their faces, and I waved as they headed towards the door, catching their attention.

"Hi! What are you doing here?" I asked, standing and giving them both a hug.

"Baking has always been my thing," Honey confessed, glancing over at Antonio with a warm smile. "But chocolate? That's my weak spot."

Antonio leaned in, his voice playful. "That is exactly why it's *my* job to ensure my beautiful wife is always happy. Chocolate is but a small price to pay for her joy." He winked and held up the box of truffles.

Honey chuckled. "Good thing I've got a fey metabolism, or all this sugar would go straight to my hips."

I grinned, feeling a little of the tension from earlier slip away. "What did you get?"

Honey opened the box to reveal a selection of beautifully crafted truffles, each one more decadent than the last. She pointed to a few with a wink. "These are my favorites—the sea salt caramel, dark raspberry, and Antonio's personal weakness, the hazelnut praline."

Antonio chuckled, already eyeing his selection. He plucked a hazelnut truffle from the box and popped it in his mouth. "It's the perfect bite," he said, though his words were a little muffled.

"So, how long have you been buying chocolates for Honey?" I asked.

Antonio held up a finger, chewing slowly and deliberately. He swallowed with a satisfied sigh. Suddenly, his eyes widened, and he blurted, "Since the night of our first date. I accidentally forgot the flowers and was so nervous that I ate half the chocolates meant for her!"

I blinked, caught off guard by the sudden confession. Judging by the look of shock on his face, Antonio was just as surprised by his own words as I was. For a moment, the words hung in the air between us, like they had slipped out before he even realized what he was saying.

Honey burst out laughing, clearly amused by the memory. "I remember that! When I opened the door, you had a little smear of chocolate on your cheek, but you were so upset about the flowers I didn't have the heart to tell you."

Antonio's cheeks turned a little pink, but he laughed along, shaking his head. "I guess I've always had a fondness for sweets, which is why I knew we'd be perfect together from the moment I met you."

Honey squeezed his arm, brushing the moment off with a smile that made it clear their relationship was as strong as ever. "And I wouldn't have it any other way," she said.

Their easy affection was a reminder of how solid they were, no matter what happened. I smiled as I watched them, feeling a twinge of something I couldn't quite name.

Antonio brushed his wife's cheek with a kiss. "Speaking of sweet moments, we have a delectable cheese board paired with a bucket of gourmet popcorn just waiting for us to return home."

"It's my turn to choose the movie, isn't it?" Honey asked, doing an excited little wiggle. "I was thinking about that mystery rom-com. You know? The one where they go on a cruise and get caught up in a smuggling ring on the high seas?"

Antonio chuckled and rolled his eyes. "I was hoping for the latest Tom Cruise movie, but for you, *amore*? Anything."

"Well, I could always watch the boat one with Bella. She's into that kind of thing," Honey offered.

"Let's talk about it in the car, shall we?" Antonio said, ushering his wife towards the door.

"Good idea. See you later, Harper," Honey called, giving me a little wave. Her voice was warm as always, but it did little to soothe the gnawing worry building in my chest.

"Take care!" I managed to call back, my voice more strained than I intended. I couldn't stop the thoughts spiraling in my mind. If Rowena's curse really was affecting everyone in Havenwood, what would it mean for Antonio and Honey? Their love was the kind of story people dreamed about—deep, enduring, the type of bond that could weather any storm. But what if even they weren't immune to the magic? What if their love met a tragic end because of all this?

"Harper!" the barista's voice broke through my spiraling thoughts. He waved toward the tray sitting on the counter, a generous slab of chocolate cake perched alongside a steaming mocha

"Oh, right! Thanks!" I hurried over, grabbing the tray with an appreciative smile. The sweet, rich aroma of chocolate wafted up, momentarily cutting through my worry like a soothing balm.

I returned to my comfy chair, setting the tray on the table before me. The worry nagged at the edges of my thoughts, refusing to let go. I couldn't let this curse unravel the lives of everyone I cared about. Antonio and Honey found their happy ending. They deserved to live it. The entire town deserved better than this magical curse hanging over their heads. And if I didn't figure out how to stop it, who knew how much harm it could cause? How many lives and relationships it could destroy?

With my thoughts far away, I picked up my fork, cutting into the rich chocolate cake. The first bite was nothing short of divine, the layers of chocolate and peanut butter melting together in perfect harmony. I let out a soft sigh of contentment; the sweetness offering a fleeting reprieve from my swirling concerns. I sampled the mocha next—smooth, velvety, and just the right balance of coffee and chocolate.

Hocus Mochas was quickly becoming my new favorite spot. Though if I wasn't careful, these indulgences would mean either longer runs or more training sessions. Probably both. *Definitely both because I'm going to eat every single crumb of this cake*, I thought, taking another bite of cake and savoring every decadent morsel. I closed my eyes in sheer bliss as I chewed, deciding to add an extra run to my weekly training program just so I didn't feel even a little guilt at enjoying my sugary treats.

While I savored the cake, I pulled out one of the books on rare magic that Spellbooks had found. I'd skimmed it in the shop, but, beyond a few obscure mentions of the heartwood tree, there wasn't anything overtly helpful. I'd hoped by doing a deeper dive into the tome, I'd uncover some other hidden clue. If nothing else, I had something interesting to read while I waited for Gabriel.

I was halfway through the introduction when I heard a familiar voice behind me.

"Are you sure you want to get coffee this late? You'll be up all night."

I blinked in surprise. That was Finn. Before I could turn around to greet him, a soft female voice answered.

"With the business still getting settled in its new headquarters, I wouldn't mind the extra jolt. I think a little extra sugar might be in order too." A tinkling laugh accompanied her words, and I froze. I knew that laugh. It was Seraphina, Finn's ex. I sank lower into my armchair as they paused behind me.

Suddenly, I remembered my run-in with him at the Dusty Tome. He'd been looking at self-help books about mending relationships and finding his inner peace. Did that mean he'd made a decision about Seraphina? Was he getting back together with her? Although I'd seen him a few times, I suddenly realized that I hadn't seen much of the two of them together lately. Was that because they were not a thing, or they were a thing and avoiding me? After all, Finn had been in the Dusty Tome looking for books when it would've been much easier to browse Spellbooks' collection or even do an online search. Whatever was going on, I had no interest in getting tangled up in their relationship drama. Deciding it was best to avoid them when it seemed like they'd been so obviously avoiding me, I pressed backward into the armchair and used my book to hide my face, hoping they wouldn't notice me.

They passed me without comment on their way to the counter. I held my breath as they ordered and snuck a look. It seemed like the barista was making their coffees in paper cups versus the ceramic mug I had. I let out a little sigh of relief. At least they weren't staying too long.

I tried not to stare as they collected their coffees, and Seraphina selected some truffles from the gorgeous display. I held the book up to block my face again as they turned, feeling a little foolish as they walked past. Maybe I should just greet them. Would that be weird now that they were leaving? No, I should probably just let things be, right?

But of course, they stopped right behind me. I couldn't help but overhear Seraphina's voice, soft but insistent.

"You should try this one," she said, her tone light. "The hazelnut pralines are my absolute favorites."

"I don't know..."

"Trust me, you haven't lived until you've had one," Seraphina said.

Although I couldn't see what was going on behind me, I heard the faint rustle of paper and imagined Finn selecting a chocolate.

"See? Delicious, right?" Seraphina's voice was triumphant.

"Well..." Finn trailed off, his words muffled through a mouthful of chocolate.

"Well, what? Tell me the truth. What did you think?"

"I think..." There was a pause, then Finn's low voice broke through. "I don't know if us getting back together is the right thing, Seraphina."

My stomach dropped, and I froze as the awkwardness behind me thickened. Seraphina's reply was barely above a whisper, but I could hear the hurt in her words. "What are you saying, Finn?"

"I care about you, I do. But revisiting the past? I'm just not sure." He paused. "I don't know why I said that. It's not a conversation for this place, but I...I couldn't stop myself." Finn's voice was filled with confusion.

I felt my chest tighten, their discomfort practically smothering me. What was going on? My mind flashed back to Antonio and his sudden revelation about his first date faux pas. Was the wild magic affecting the chocolates in the shop? Had the praline somehow made Finn blurt out the truth? Or was I looking for magic when it was just the mundane?

A sniff interrupted my thoughts and Seraphina's quiet voice murmured. "You're right. I think this is a conversation to be had in private."

The bell tinkled above the door, announcing their departure, leaving me with a strange mix of sympathy and anxiety.

I set my book down, blowing out a breath as I glanced at the half-eaten cake on my plate. Was it just the pralines, or were all the treats in Hocus Mochas causing people to spill the truth? Was I about to confess something to Gabriel without intending to? Or was I just seeing wild magic where there wasn't any?

Feeling the need to investigate, I stood and hurried over to the display case, my eyes landing on the tray of pralines. They looked innocent enough, but after hearing Finn and Seraphina, I wasn't so sure.

From behind the counter, I caught a snippet of conversation between two of the servers.

"People are, like, super chatty tonight. Whenever someone asks a question, it's like they're incapable of lying," one whispered. "Some of the stuff I heard tonight is going to be great gossip. I can't wait to tell you all about it."

"Yeah, it's like some kind of sugar-induced honesty boost," the other responded with a giggle. "Or maybe it's a full moon. People always get weird around a full moon—makes them spill their secrets."

I frowned. Sugar and caffeine didn't make people blurt out the truth. And a full moon? That wasn't exactly scientific. But either way, this wasn't an isolated incident. It felt more like the wild magic leaking through Havenwood, pushing everyone to confess things they weren't ready to say.

Before I could dwell on it further, the bell chimed again. My heart lurched as I saw Gabriel step inside, scanning the room until his eyes landed on me. A flash of nervous energy shot through me. I didn't feel that usual burst of excitement. Instead, dread coiled in my stomach.

What if he asked how I felt about his letter? I still didn't know. The declarations were flattering, sure, but I wasn't ready to be forced into telling the truth—not when I didn't even know what that truth was yet. What I really needed was more time. Time to figure out what I wanted from the relationship, from him.

Gabriel spotted me and hurried over, a warm smile lighting up his face. I did my best to return it, though a knot twisted in my stomach. I'd have to be careful—every word from here on out mattered. If I wasn't on guard, I might find myself loveless long before the curse had its way with me.

Caught in a Spell

GABRIEL CAME TOWARDS ME, a soft, genuine smile on his face. He wrapped his arms around me before I could say anything.

"I am so glad you could come and so sorry I kept you waiting. Things have been crazy around town," he murmured, his low voice rumbling with exhaustion.

"Why don't you tell me all about it?" I offered. Partially because I really wanted to hear about his day, and partially because the more he talked the less likely it was I could blurt out something I didn't intend to. Like my true feelings, which I was still unsure about.

"Sure but let me get a cup of coffee first. And maybe some of those truffles," Gabriel said, eyeing the display case.

"No!" I exclaimed.

Gabriel shot me a strange look, and I immediately modified my tone. "What I meant was, you don't want just sugar after a long day, do you? Think about the inevitable crash. Better to get a cheese and smoked turkey croissant or maybe even one of the quiches. You know, something with a little protein to keep you going?"

Gabriel's expression softened, and he brushed my temple with a kiss. "It's sweet you're always looking out for me. Let me order, and I'll be over to join you in a second. Do you want anything else?"

I mutely shook my head, afraid of what might tumble out of my mouth if I opened it. Were the croissants even safe from the wild magic? I didn't know. Gabriel tugged at his scarf as he considered the menu posted behind the counter. I silently returned to my seat, pushing the remainder of my chocolate and peanut butter cake around with my fork.

Gabriel came over with his croissant and coffee, a small smile still lingering on his lips despite the weariness in his eyes. He set his tray down and leaned back in his chair, watching me carefully.

"So, how are things?" he asked, his voice gentle.

I shifted uncomfortably in my seat, trying to find a way to dodge the question. "Oh, you know...expect the unexpected in Havenwood." Not a lie, but not the whole truth, either. My voice sounded thin, even to my own ears. "But enough about me. What about you? You look exhausted. Has it been rough out there?"

Gabriel sighed, looking thoroughly worn out. "You could say that. It's been nonstop. First, there were the singing heart-shaped balloons. They popped up all over town, following couples and serenading them. People loved it at first, until they realized they couldn't make them stop." He shook his head, clearly exasperated. "Then, over by the park, the ice sculptures decided they weren't content with just standing still. Now they're moving around, posing for pictures like some kind of magical performance art."

He let out a breath and gestured at the falling snow outside the window. "And this? Heart-shaped snowflakes. Harmless, right? Except I can't make them stop. I've been casting illusions all day trying to make the tourists think it's normal, but I'm running out of tricks. Tourists are going to start asking questions soon if I don't figure out how to turn it off. Thank goodness it's winter and gets dark early. At least most of the tourists are indoors."

He shook his head, his voice dropping to a whisper. "I know it's the wild magic—it's seeping into everything. But this curse is amplifying it somehow. It's like the two are feeding into each other, making the magic more...unpredictable. And Havenwood is caught in the middle of the storm they're creating."

My mouth went dry. "That doesn't sound good," I managed.

"It's not," Gabriel said, running his hands through his hair.

Silence settled over the table, and I glanced outside. I hadn't even noticed the heart-shaped flakes until he pointed them out. It must've said something about my level of distraction. Guilt settling in my chest like a stone. Where was the missing heart? My list of suspects felt ridiculously small, and the clues I'd discovered seemed tenuous links at best. I needed a breakthrough, anything to point me in the right direction. But right now, I had nothing.

As Gabriel sipped his coffee, I couldn't help but think about the strange magic swirling around Hocus Mochas, affecting everyone who stepped through the door. Could I be sure it was wild magic? No. Could I be sure it wasn't? Also no. Maybe I should've said something sooner. Before I could stop myself, the words tumbled out.

"I think the wild magic might have invaded this place too."

Gabriel paused before taking a bite of his croissant, eyebrows knitting in confusion. "What are you talking about?"

I took a deep breath. "People have been acting strange, saying things they wouldn't normally say. It's like...like the magic is making everyone speak their minds. Too much truth, if that makes any sense."

Gabriel set his croissant down, concern flickering across his face. "That could be serious. Have you noticed anything specific?"

I hesitated, unsure if it was the guilt gnawing at me or something more that was pushing me to spill everything. In the end, I just sighed and shook my head. "A couple of things. Something Antonio said and then some things I overheard. But I can't be sure."

Gabriel's frown deepened. "If the magic has ramped up from moving sculptures to forcing the truth out of people, that's quite an escalation."

I ran a hand through my hair. "Yeah, I figured. It was too much to hope that the wild magic was wearing itself out already. But I can't be sure that's what's happening. Just...do me a favor? Can you not ask me any personal questions right now? Please?"

He studied me for a moment, his gaze searching, but then he gave a slow nod, completely understanding. "Of course. I won't press you. When you want to tell me something, you will. I'm happy to wait until that time."

"Thanks." I managed a small smile, relieved, but still uneasy.

"I do want to look into the magic though. A truth spell is pretty powerful. To cause several at the same time is even more significant, obviously. From what I've seen so far today, I'd imagine that there isn't enough wild magic in town yet to keep the spell going for more than an hour or two. Definitely not overnight."

A sigh of relief escaped me. At least this wasn't permanent. Forced truth telling would reveal lies. Not that I lied much—I was terrible at it anyway—but a little white lie now and then wasn't exactly a crime. Gabriel sipped his coffee, his calm gaze making me feel like he could see right through me. I kept my eyes on the crumbs of cake on my plate, trying to look busy.

The silence stretched, and before I knew it, the words tumbled out of my mouth. "I've been working on a suspect list."

I froze, my eyes widening. That statement wasn't supposed to happen.

"A suspect list?" Gabriel leaned forward, setting his mug down, curiosity lighting his face.

I stammered, scrambling for an explanation. "I...I wasn't planning to tell anyone yet. It's just rough ideas, and I'm not even sure they're right."

His expression softened, but his interest didn't waver. "So, what's holding you back?"

I glanced down at the notebook in my bag and pulled it out, my fingers fidgeting with the edges. "I don't want to accuse someone who is innocent or waste your time or your mother's. You've seen what happens when she's angry."

He nodded, a trace of understanding in his eyes. "And yet, you just told me."

He had me there. I couldn't backtrack easily now. With a small sigh, I flipped the notebook open to the correct page and twirled it around to face him. "It's not much, but it's a start."

Gabriel picked up the notebook. "Cassandra Bellamy?" His brow furrowed as he shook his head. "I don't know her. She's new?"

I shrugged. "I think so. The first time I ran into her, she was attempting to access the restricted wing of the library, but Martha Morningstar wouldn't let her in. I get the impression she's trying to get your mom's attention, but to what end, I have no idea."

"Well, attacking the heartwood would certainly do it, but I'm not sure that's the kind of attention she wanted," Gabriel said grimly.

"Yeah, *I* sure wouldn't," I said with a little shiver. Then, realizing my words, hurried to add, "want to get on your mother's bad side. Or attack the heartwood."

A faint smile tugged on Gabriel's lips. "Good to know. What about this next name? Edmund Hawke? What did he do to get on your list?"

"He keeps showing up looking for obscure plant lore. First, I bumped into him at the library. Then, in the Dusty Tome. With the attack on the heartwood, I found it hard to believe that his interest was just a co-incidence. If he's into plants, maybe he concocted a targeted poison or something to attack the heartwood."

Gabriel frowned, rubbing the back of his neck. "Edmund is...eccentric. He's been fascinated with old plant magic for as long as I've known him. But as far as being capable of this? I don't know. He's more of a scholar than an actual practitioner of magic. Besides, the damage to the tree didn't look like poison."

"I suppose so," I admitted. "But based on what I saw in the library, he has magic capabilities and he's not afraid to use them. It was like he conjured a mini hurricane because Bella and I forgot to whisper."

Gabriel's frown deepened. "That doesn't sound like Edmund at all. Still, you were there, and I wasn't, so far be it from me to contradict you." He let out a breath and leaned back. "For the record, despite my opinions on the man, I'm inclined to agree with you. There's too much overlap to dismiss it as mere coincidence. It's worth keeping an eye on him. Maybe I could enlist my mother to have a conversation with him. They've known each other a very long time. Not friends exactly but definitely cordial acquaintances."

I nodded, adding a mental note to not go accusing Edmund Hawke without more proof. If he was on good terms with Vivienne Silverthorne, that probably meant he was well respected in Havenwood and not some-one I wanted to upset. "Maybe. But perhaps one of us could keep an eye on him. Or casually try to snoop around for information." A thought occurred and my eyes flicked to the display of truffles. "Maybe we could slip him one of the pralines and then ask him if he was involved."

Gabriel chuckled. "Truth chocolate as an interrogation technique?"

"Why not? It's nicer than what they do in the movies," I pointed out.

"You have a point. But it's entirely unethical." He held up a hand as I opened my mouth to protest. "Regardless of the ethics, there's an issue of practicality. If wild magic is to blame for the truth chocolates, assuming there's no indication of sabotage to prove it isn't, then the spell will likely wear off long before we find him, let alone convince him to eat a truffle."

"Oh," I said, feeling a little deflated. It seemed that everywhere I turned, I met a dead end.

As if sensing my mood, Gabriel tapped the sheet between us, distracting me from my failure to find the merest crumb of a clue that could lead me to the missing heart. "What about this old woman in the woods?" Gabriel asked.

I explained swiftly about what I'd seen, wrapping up by sliding the charm and the bundle of sticks across to him. "I have no idea who she could be, but she's obviously involved somehow. I think this is part of the damaged heartwood," I said, tapping on the burned piece of wood.

Gabriel picked up the fragment and turned it around in his fingers. "I see your point. This does look like it's a match for the heartwood."

"So, do you know who she could be?" I asked.

Gabriel thought for a moment before shaking his head again. "There are a fair number of women in Havenwood who could fit that description, even without magic thrown into the mix. We'd need more to go on."

"What about the pin?" I asked hopefully, passing it over to him. "Do you recognize it at all? Is it something, you know...*magical*?" I whispered the last word, just in case any of the other patrons in Hocus Mochas were listening. I didn't think they were, but I wasn't going to be the one to give away Havenwood's grand secret.

Gabriel examined it and then shook his head, passing it back to me. "If it is, I don't recognize it. I also can't sense any magic on it, although my brother is better at sensing residual magic than I am."

I sighed, sliding the pin back into my bag. "I was hoping it would be some kind of clue. At least the wild magic isn't being more than a nuisance at the moment. I mean, we can handle some extra honesty and the occasional flying letter if need be."

Gabriel's expression grew serious. "Wild magic isn't something to mess with. It has a way of snowballing—gathering strength the longer it's left unchecked. This truth spell you suspect is running amok in the shop? As serious as it is and as much magic as it takes, I have a feeling that's just the beginning. With wild magic, things can get out of hand fast."

My heart sank. If what we were experiencing was just the start, then Havenwood was in even more danger than I'd thought. "I didn't realize it would escalate this quickly."

"Can you tell me more about these flying letters?" Gabriel asked, redirecting the conversation.

Swiftly, I explained, filling him in on everything, but stuttering awkwardly to a stop when I got to the part where I found his letter in my shop. The folded page of paper in my pocket seemed to dig into my leg.

Gabriel gave me a searching look, his brow furrowing slightly. "Is there something else on your mind? I don't want to press, especially with you being suspicious about the cake and truth spells." He nodded toward the half-eaten slice of chocolate cake on the table.

I hesitated. There was no easy way to approach this without feeling vulnerable. But the note sat heavy in my pocket, and if I didn't show him now, it would eat away at me. Slowly, I pulled out the folded letter and slid it across the table.

"I found this just after all the kerfuffle with the letters. Did you mean this?" I asked softly.

Gabriel's brow furrowed as he took the paper, his confusion growing. "A chef's table dinner tasting for Valentine's Day?" He smiled, glancing up at me. "Of course I meant it. I've got a friend who hooked me up. The food is supposed to be incredible, and the chef supposedly studied with some of the greats from our side of the world." He dropped his voice and whispered. "The magical side."

I swallowed, shaking my head. "That's not what's on the note you left me. I hadn't heard about any dinner invitation until this moment."

"What are you talking about?" Gabriel asked as he unfolded the final crease.

I watched in silence as Gabriel read the letter and then read it again, his expression shifting as the words sank in. His cheeks reddened slightly, and, when he finished, he set it down on the table, not meeting my eyes at first.

I braced myself, expecting him to deny it, to brush it off as a mistake or wild magic playing tricks. And that would've made sense. It would've been easy. But a small part of me—the part I hadn't quite confronted yet—felt an unexpected twinge of disappointment at the thought.

Now, what did that *mean?*

Gabriel paused, his expression softening as he rubbed the back of his neck, looking at me with a quiet intensity. "That wasn't exactly how I planned to say it," he began, voice low but steady. "And definitely not the timing I would have chosen, but none of it's untrue, Harper."

I blinked, my thoughts swirling, trying to process what he was saying. "Oh," I managed, not quite sure how to respond.

"Look, this wasn't how I wanted to bring this up. There should've been flowers and a nice dinner. At least I got the chocolate part right," he said ruefully, waving at the shop.

"I definitely want to come back to this place. Once everything calms down," I said. I bit my lip, hesitant to say more. How could I respond to Gabriel's declaration when I couldn't even put a name to my feelings for him?

Gabriel's smile grew tender as he tilted his head, studying me for a moment. "You look tired. Let me take you home. With the way this truth magic seems to be affecting people, this probably isn't the best time for this conversation, anyway."

I hesitated but nodded, grateful for the out. He was right—everything was too uncertain right now, especially with wild magic creeping into places like Hocus Mochas. What was real? What was being twisted by magic? Was he telling me this only because of the wild magic? Is that how I wanted to find out about his feelings—because a spell forced him? And what might the spell force me to tell? I couldn't be sure and that, more than anything else, was the most terrifying of all.

Even though we were close, Gabriel drove me back to Spellbooks, the steady hum of the car engine filling the silence between us. It wasn't an uncomfortable silence, though—more like a mutual understanding that when we talked, it wouldn't be in the midst of a crisis or because of a spell. When we arrived, Gabriel parked and walked me to the door, his hand lingering on mine as I fumbled with my keys.

Before I could say anything, he leaned in, brushing his lips gently against mine. The kiss was sweet, but over too soon, leaving me breathless and wanting more.

"Get some rest," he said softly, pulling away with a smile that made my heart flutter despite everything. "We'll figure this out. All of it."

Despite the chaos, I found myself looking forward to the next time I'd see him, even if it meant navigating the complexities of his world. Because some things were worth the effort.

Some *people* were worth the effort. What I really needed to do was take the time to sit down and honestly evaluate my feelings for Gabriel. After what he just shared, I felt even more of a pressure to find an answer within my own heart.

Time.

That was the problem, wasn't it? With the curse hanging over Havenwood, wild magic running rampant, and the heartwood's missing heart, time was slipping away faster than I could catch it. The night stretched on, my mind circling through possibilities, leading only to a restless sleep filled with images of the heartwood tree withering and wild magic spilling out into Havenwood. Time was running out. Could I really afford to spend some of that precious time attempting to sort out my relationship?

Could I afford not to?

Flying Flowers

I WOKE THE NEXT morning before the sun rose, tired from a restless night. The feeling from the night before crept in slowly—so slowly I almost didn't notice it at first. But there was a tension in the air, like the whole town had slipped slightly off balance. It was subtle, like a faint hum just at the edge of hearing, but it was there, threading its way through everything. I needed to find answers now, more than ever. Failing that, I'd settle for a clue. Or even a clue-lette, if that was a thing. But I wasn't going to figure out my problems or solve the mystery of the missing heart by staying in bed. I grabbed my phone and texted both Gabriel and Bella with a rough sketch of a plan before I could second guess myself. Almost immediately, I received an affirmative response from both of them. By the time I'd had a quick shower, blow-dried my hair enough that it wouldn't freeze in the cold, and poured coffee into my oversized travel mug, I was practically bouncing with nervous energy.

I grabbed my coat and clattered down the stairs, hurrying to set out food for Luna and Mr. Wigglesworth. The Maine Coon rubbed against my leg affectionately before diving face first into his bowl of dried food. Luna, on the other hand, arched an eyebrow as I slid on my boots.

"Heading out again? The shop won't run itself you know," she said with a sniff.

"The heart won't find itself either," I pointed out.

"Well, if you are going to keep running all over town trying to solve every mystery that comes up, you're going to need help around here. I prefer my help tall, dark, and handsome with an air of deviltry and a love for carrots."

I rolled my eyes. "If I hire anyone, it'll be to help run Spellbooks. Not to be your personal valet."

Luna's whiskers twitched. "Tell yourself what you like." She disappeared into her hutch with a paw full of cabbage before I could formulate a response.

Rather than engage in a fruitless debate about the purpose of hiring help, I pulled a hat over my wavy hair and headed towards the Enchanted Oasis.

Bella opened the door as I tromped up the steps of the porch. Her hair was in wild disarray, stray strands slipping from the hasty bun perched atop her head. Dark circles smudged under her eyes, which darted anxiously around the room, never settling for more than a second. Her shirt, untucked and wrinkled, looked like it had been thrown on in a hurry, and she clutched her phone in one hand as if it were a lifeline.

"Bella! What's going on?" I exclaimed.

"Nothing good. I hadn't realized how bad it was, or I wouldn't have invited you over," Bella said, going to run a hand through her hair and obviously forgetting that she'd tied it up. A chunk of hair fell out of the messy bun and the whole thing slid to the side. She sighed and quickly rearranged it as I stepped inside and closed the door behind me.

"How can I help?" I asked.

"Can you catch a flower?" Bella asked.

"The baking kind or the plant kind?"

"Plant," Bella clarified.

"Normally, I'd say try a garden, but given the temperature outside and your general air of frustration, I'm guessing that won't help. Why do you need to catch a flower?" I asked.

"Follow me," Bella said, waving me towards the kitchen.

Intrigued, I slipped out of my coat and boots and padded after her as she hurried down the hall. As soon as she opened the door, I saw the problem.

A vibrant bouquet of roses and lilies was floating through the air, weaving between chairs and counters as Honey squealed, dodging left and right.

"What the..." I trailed off in amazement.

"Antonio brought me flowers," Honey called out, laughing as she barely escaped a floating rose that nearly grazed her head. "And now they won't leave me alone!"

I blinked, taken aback. "But how...?"

Bella threw her hands up, her voice dripping with exasperation. "It's the wild magic of course! It's not just the flowers either. The curtains keep billowing like there's a hurricane inside, the fireplace lights itself every ten minutes, and don't even get me started on the dishes. They're stacking, unstacking, and restacking faster than I can blink! Yesterday, the coffee mugs were marching across the counter like they were in some kind of parade!"

I stared, wide-eyed, as a stem of lilies drifted past my head, serenely oblivious to the surrounding chaos. Wild magic at play and not in a good way.

"What can I do to help?" I asked, already moving toward the table.

Bella caught my arm gently. "Don't worry about that. I've tasted your cooking, and once was enough, thanks."

"Hey!" I protested.

Bella shot me a look that had the lilies darting out of the way to rejoin their flowery friends.

"Fine. You have a point. My skills are not in the kitchen," I admitted.

Bella nodded just once. "Alex is on his way over. Mama can't cook without petals dropping into the food, so he's volunteered for breakfast duty."

I glanced at the hovering bouquet, now performing an aerial ballet around Honey's head as she tried to take a sip of coffee. A pair of roses twirled too close, causing Honey to jump back. She narrowly avoided splashing coffee down her front. Antonio swept through the door with a butterfly net in his hands.

"I've got it, *amore*!" he called triumphantly.

Honey swatted away an overly zealous lily. "Oh, thank goodness! Maybe I can actually have a drink of coffee without fear of spilling or getting a thorn in the eye."

Antonio kept his eyes on the floating flowers. "I made sure the thorns were removed. Only the best for my wife."

"Aw, Antonio," Honey said with a smile.

Bella tugged on my arm, pulling me off to the side as Antonio carefully swung the net, attempting to capture the flowers.

"Let me help," I said. "I can set out plates or something."

Bella shook her head, more serious now. "Look, I can't help you find the heart right now, but that's the best thing you can do to help. This madness isn't stopping until you do."

I glanced at her parents as Antonio fought to keep a pair of roses in the net while the other flowers sped towards the ceiling.

"You may have a point," I admitted.

Knowing that Gabriel was on the way, there wasn't any point in returning to Spellbooks just to come back so we could look for clues near the heartwood. Instead, I spent the next few minutes trying to help corral flying roses with a broom, which was every bit as ridiculous and difficult as it sounded. We'd nearly captured all the flowers when a knock at the back door announced Alex's arrival.

Antonio captured the last of the rogue roses with a triumphant whoop, holding the bouquet aloft as if it were a prized trophy. Alex had already set to work in the kitchen, his movements fluid and efficient as he cracked eggs, chopped vegetables, and had a quiche ready in what seemed like a blink of an eye. Meanwhile, Honey, now out of immediate danger from the flower assault, had resumed her pastry-making in the corner, sipping gratefully from a steaming mug of coffee.

Crisis averted—for now.

Bella shot me a look, wiping her brow dramatically before shooing me toward the door. "You've done your part here, Harper. Now, go find that missing heart before this chaos gets any worse. I've got to keep the guests blissfully unaware of the magical insanity unfolding in the kitchen."

I nodded, pulling on my coat and gloves and preparing to face the cold. As I opened the door, ready to step out into the winter chill, I found Gabriel standing on the other side, hand raised, about to knock. His eyes met mine with a hint of surprise, his cheeks flushed from the cold.

"Perfect timing," I murmured, feeling my heart skip a beat.

"I try," he replied with a grin, offering his arm with a gentlemanly bow. "Could I interest you in a hike through the snowy forest to search for clues in order to find a missing magical heart and stop a curse?"

A laugh bubbled up in my chest despite the tension hanging in the air. "When you put it like that, how could I refuse?"

He tucked my gloved hand into the crook of his arm, squeezing it gently. The warmth of his touch seeped through the layers, grounding me. "What can I say? I know the way to your heart. Apparently, curses and clues beat chocolate."

"Hey, don't knock chocolate," I said with a smirk. "That cake yesterday was divine. When this is all over, I'm going back for another slice. Maybe even two."

Gabriel's smile widened. "Deal. I knew you'd like that place." His tone shifted. "Speaking of last night, how are you feeling? Still on the verge of telling me the truth about everything?"

I bit the inside of my lip, the weight of the letter tugging at the back of my mind. The warmth from our banter faded slightly, making me feel a little more exposed than I was ready for. I shrugged, trying to play it cool. "I guess the only way to know is to test it. Ask me a question," I suggested.

He raised a brow, his response immediate. "What color is the snow?"

"Purple," I deadpanned, lips twitching.

He pressed a hand to his forehead in mock distress. "Oh no! The wild magic has gotten worse than I thought!"

I shook my head, feeling a little lighter again. "You're in a good mood today."

"Why wouldn't I be?" He glanced down at me with a soft smile that made my chest tighten. "Despite everything that's going on, I get to spend the morning with you."

For a moment, I couldn't tell if the warmth in my cheeks was a reaction to the cold or something entirely different. I cleared my throat, refocusing. "Speaking of wild magic, you won't believe the chaos in the kitchen of the Oasis I just walked in on."

His lips tightened in concern. "What happened?"

"Antonio brought Honey a bouquet, and it literally chased her around the kitchen. Bella and I had to help corral the flying roses with a broom," I said, quickly filling him in on the rest of what Bella had told me.

Gabriel sighed, rubbing the back of his neck. "It's spreading faster than I thought possible."

I nodded. The situation was getting worse, and fast. "That's what I was afraid of."

Gabriel glanced around as we entered the forest. "The number of occurrences Bella and her family are experiencing at the Oasis might be due to their relative proximity to the heartwood, but wild magic escalates. If we don't find a way to stop it, these sorts of incidents will spread, both in range and in quantity."

My stomach knotted. "Exactly. But it's not just the wild magic. I think there's a possibility the wild magic might be fueling the dryad's curse."

Gabriel's frown deepened. "That's not good," he muttered.

I nodded. "That's what worries me the most. It's also why I'm glad you could come with me this morning. With two of us searching, maybe we can find a clue to the missing heart faster."

Gabriel cast a glance around the snow-covered forest. "I'm not sure how much we'll find out here now, but I'm willing to try anything to stop the wild magic and repair the heartwood," Gabriel said.

"Speaking of that, can you tell me anything about the heartwood? It seems important, but I can't find much information about it that goes beyond speculation."

Gabriel spoke as we continued to crunch through the snow. "I didn't know much myself before all this happened. My mother filled me in on some of its history, but she prefers to keep the circle of trust small."

I drew an "x" over my heart and pressed a gloved finger to my lips. "I won't spill any secrets."

Gabriel raised an eyebrow. Now that it was obvious the truth spell from the chocolate was no longer in effect, I felt a bit freer. At least I wasn't unintentionally blurting out half my thoughts anymore, but I'd still have to tread carefully. Especially when it came to Vivienne.

He nodded, accepting me at my word without hesitation. "As you probably guessed, the heartwood isn't just any tree. It's the core of Havenwood's protections. I don't know if you've heard of something called ley lines, but the heartwood sits at a rare convergence of three lines, meaning that the magic running through this forest is tied to the tree and therefore the ley lines. Without the heart to stabilize it..." His voice trailed off, and I finished the thought for him.

"Without the heart, everything falls apart."

He glanced at me, his jaw tight. "Exactly."

The conversation paused as we continued deeper into the woods, each lost in our own thoughts. At least he'd told me about ley lines so now I could talk about them with him without breaking my promise to Thistle. I wondered how secret they must be if both Gabriel and Finn knew of them and spoke of them so openly. To that point, I asked, "Are ley lines common in the magical world? Or the heartwood for that matter?"

"Ley lines, yes. No one really knows how they came to exist or how they seem to have endless magical energy. I think of them like the Mississippi River or the Atlantic Ocean. No one asks how those bodies of water came about. They just are. I feel the same way about the ley lines in the magical world."

I nodded, letting his words wash over me. "What about the heartwood?"

Gabriel shrugged. "As far as I know, it's the only one of its kind. It's not something people talk about much. Maybe because they don't know about it, or it's so rare to have one still thriving."

A thought occurred to me. "Do you know if Havenwood formed around the heartwood, or was the tree planted here intentionally?"

"I never thought to ask," he admitted.

I felt excitement sprout within me. "If someone planted it, then there must've been a seed. Maybe your mother knows how or even who planted the heartwood. If they're one of the long-living supernaturals, we could talk to them. Failing that, we might be able to find some old records. Just think! If we can figure out who planted the heartwood, maybe they know a way to cure it without the missing heart."

Gabriel nodded thoughtfully. "It's a good idea and a creative solution to the problem. I'm not sure it will work, but there's no harm in asking. I'm willing to try anything if it gets the wild magic to stop."

We walked in silence for a moment, my mind spinning with the implications. When we reached the clearing, I stopped in my tracks. The moment we stepped into the open space, dread pooled in my stomach. The tree looked worse than before—its bark was darkening, its branches brittle, and its leaves curled in on themselves at an alarming rate. The heartwood was dying.

A sharp pang of helplessness surged through me. Was I too late? Panic swirled beneath the surface as I took a shaky breath, trying to steady myself. If we didn't find the heart soon, everything Havenwood stood for could crumble.

The dryad appeared suddenly, her form emerging from the shadows of the withering heartwood, her eyes blazing with anger. Beneath the fury, though, was a deep weariness, as if the weight of the tree's decay was pulling her down. Her voice cut through the clearing like a sharp wind. "Are you here to scatter more rot? Haven't your actions uprooted enough already?"

I flinched, the accusation stinging. "No, absolutely not," I protested, shaking my head. "I'm trying to help. We're trying to stop this."

Her eyes narrowed, her expression unyielding. "Help? You call this helping?" She gestured to the brittle branches, the sickly bark. "The heartwood is wilting before our eyes. The magic of this land is unraveling, like a vine torn from its roots. All of this is happening because of you." Her voice cracked like a branch under pressure, exhaustion creeping in despite her anger.

"I didn't—" My throat tightened, panic threatening to rise, but I pushed it down. "I didn't cause this."

The dryad's eyes flashed, her fury snapping like a wildfire through dry grass. "Didn't cause this? All of this decay took root with you. Your meddling, your interference! The heartwood withers, and the magic in this place is fraying like leaves in a drought. And you dare stand here, denying the part you've played?"

Her words hit me hard, leaving me breathless as if the wind had been knocked out of me. My hands clenched at my sides.

"I care about this town. More than you know." My voice trembled, but I didn't stop, heart pounding loudly in my ears. "I'd never let anything happen to Havenwood, to the heartwood, if I could stop it. I love this place. It's my home, and I'll do whatever it takes to make things right."

Tears burned behind my eyes, but I held her gaze, desperate for her to see the truth. Gabriel moved beside me, his quiet presence a reassurance. His voice was steady when he spoke. "She means it. We're here to help. We'll do everything we can." His unwavering gaze met the dryad's. "We want to make this right, for you and for the town."

The dryad's anger flickered, the weariness in her eyes growing more pronounced. She looked between us, traces of her doubt still lingering like storm clouds on her face, but something in her posture softened, just a little. Exhaustion overtook her fury, her energy wilting like a flower that had been in bloom too long. "You better hope you can."

I stepped forward. "We're doing our best. We're here looking for clues, trying to figure out what's happening." I hesitated, glancing at Gabriel before continuing, "But with the blizzard caused by the wild magic, most of the signs are gone. Maybe...maybe you noticed something? Someone lurking near the heartwood?"

The dryad shook her head. "No one has been near the heartwood to the best of my knowledge other than you and your friends."

"But there were three sets of footprints here the first time we came," I pressed. "I've seen an old woman in the woods, but I'm not sure who she is..."

The dryad scoffed, her lips curling as if the name itself left a bad taste. "Blasted brambles! Mad Mads is at it again," she scoffed, waving her hand dismissively. "She's harmless. A wandering weed, talking to herself as she moves through the forest. She's not the one who poisoned these roots."

I bit my lip, unsure of how to proceed. Before I could reach a decision, the dryad's brow furrowed like a wrinkled leaf, as if dredging up an uncomfortable memory.

"Not near the heartwood, but in the woods. An odd sort of man. He moved through the trees like a beetle lost in the canopy. He didn't belong among the roots and leaves. He looked like he came from town, not the forest. I saw him snipping at the trees, as if he were a scavenger leeching something from the land. Poking around, searching for something he had no business taking."

My pulse quickened. "What did he look like?"

She frowned, her face pinched with distaste. "Thin as a sapling in poor soil, and as awkward as a rabbit caught in a bramble patch. He wore thick glasses and his hair was unkempt, as if a windstorm had swept through it—definitely in need of a good pruning. He didn't make it to the heartwood, but something about him...he was completely out of place in the forest. His clothes were worn and impractical for a hike. He looked as if he belonged among books, not the wild."

Gabriel and I exchanged a glance, an unspoken understanding passing between us. Could the man she saw be Edmund Hawke? The silent exchange lasted only a moment, but when we looked back, the dryad was gone.

Disappearing Suspect

ALTHOUGH WE SPENT THE next fifteen minutes examining every inch of the heartwood tree, we didn't discover any more new clues. I sighed, having expected as much after the storm, but there had been a kernel of hope that I'd been wrong.

Armed with new information but no additional leads, Gabriel and I made our way back to the Oasis. On the way back, the temperature dropped significantly, and the wind picked up, almost seeming to blow us on our way, urging us to leave the forest and find the missing heart. With every step I took through the snow, I felt the weight of time pressing down on me. The heartwood tree was dying—the dryad's curse spreading like wildfire through the town. And I still had no idea where the missing heart could be. If I couldn't find it, I doubted my ability to stop the curse before everyone, me included, became loveless.

I was relieved when I saw the familiar slope of the Oasis' roof against the overcast sky. Hopefully, Bella's morning calmed down. I thought about knocking on the door, but I had so little new information, it seemed like a waste of time. No, it was better to see if we could follow the information the dryad had given in the hopes of turning up an actual clue.

Gabriel caught my eye. "I'm going to search for Edmund Hawke. See if I can tie him to the heartwood. Want to come along?" He pulled out his car keys as we walked around the corner of the Oasis. "Who knows? Maybe he really is responsible for the attack on the heartwood. From what I know of the man, he doesn't seem the type, but I've been surprised before. In a worst-case scenario, maybe he saw something while he was prowling around the woods doing, well, whatever he was doing. Hopefully, he'll have some answers when we track him down."

"That's a good idea," I agreed. "But with the wild magic around town amping up, we should really divide and conquer, don't you think?"

He frowned slightly, a hint of confusion crossing his features. "Am I missing something? Who or what other than Edmund do we have to investigate?"

I took a deep breath. "This Mad Mads person. No one seems to know who she is. Do you?"

He shook his head. "No. Never heard of her before."

"I can't shake the feeling she's connected to this. While you go talk to Edmund Hawke, I want to see if there is any way I can track her down."

Gabriel beeped the fob in his hand and we both slid into the car. I was thankful when he switched on the heating right away. The temperature had continued to drop dramatically. "How are you going to find her if no one knows who she is?" Gabriel asked.

I shrugged, holding my hands out to the vents blowing warm air. "If anyone knows about a woman wandering in the woods, it'll be Aunty Agatha. I meant to call her earlier but got distracted. Let me see if she knows anything." I pulled out my phone, finding Agatha's number, but there was no answer.

"Anything?" Gabriel asked.

I shook my head. "No answer. I'll try again later or, better yet, swing by her house. She needs to know what's going on." I paused, my thoughts already whirling ahead. "If we find out Professor Hawke is responsible, I have no doubt you'll be able to handle him. But if he's not, we'll already have a head start on the only other lead we have."

Gabriel nodded, understanding the logic. "Okay. I'll drive you part of the way, so you don't have to walk through the cold."

"Thanks," I said, grateful for his company, and the heat in the car as he pulled smoothly into traffic.

As Gabriel drove me down the snowy road, our path took us right past Stella's flower shop. A small crowd had gathered outside, voices raised in confusion and concern. Even through the closed car windows, I could hear snippets of their startled exclamations.

Gabriel slowed the car, his brow furrowing. "That doesn't look good," he muttered, glancing at me. "What do you think? Wild magic?"

I leaned forward, watching as Stella herself stood at the entrance, surrounded by a flurry of floating flowers that danced in the air as if caught in an unseen breeze. "Definitely," I replied.

Gabriel pulled over to the curb and shifted into park. "I'll handle the crowd and smooth over any memories if needed. Can you get Stella and the flowers under control?"

"On it," I said, already stepping out into the biting cold. Gabriel moved toward the gathered onlookers, his calming tone quickly drawing their attention as he began weaving his illusion magic.

I hurried toward Stella, who was waving her arms frantically at a particularly bold bouquet that had taken flight. "Get back here!" she shouted, her voice laced with frustration. The flowers, however, seemed intent on performing an impromptu aerial ballet.

Dodging the bouquet, I managed to snag it mid-air and whisk it through the shop's door. Stella followed close behind, and once Gabriel rejoined us and the crowd began to disperse, he shut the door firmly, snapping the window blinds shut.

Stella's shoulders slumped, and her voice wavered. "This is a disaster! I can't afford to close down, especially not this close to Valentine's Day. It's our busiest time of year! If I can't provide flowers for people's loved ones, I'll lose customers—and probably my sanity."

Gabriel stepped forward, his expression serious. "What if I cast an illusion spell over the entire shop? It'll buy you some time while we figure this out, and it should help mask the chaos if anyone else stops by."

Stella didn't look reassured. "But what if it doesn't blow over? I've been hearing rumors about strange things happening all over town."

I exchanged a glance with Gabriel, my unease deepening. The wild magic wasn't just spreading—it was making its presence known in every corner of Havenwood.

Gabriel's tone was calm and measured as he spoke. "There's been some unusual magical energy lately, and it's causing some disruptions. My family and I are looking into it and working on a solution."

"Magical energy?" Stella asked, her eyes darting toward a vase that had started to wobble on its own. "What does that mean? Is this going to get worse?"

"Think of it like…static electricity in the air," Gabriel said smoothly. "It's unpredictable but temporary. If we keep things under control for a little while, it should dissipate on its own."

Stella's expression softened slightly, though the worry didn't completely fade. "Are you sure?"

Gabriel nodded firmly. "Absolutely. I'll cast a temporary illusion spell to help for now, and we'll stay on top of this."

Before Stella could respond, Jeremy burst out of the back room, a look of urgency on his face. "Avoid the orchids at all costs! I think they might've turned carnivorous overnight!" he warned, his eyes wide as he waved a bloody finger in the air. He stopped in his tracks, blinking in surprise at Gabriel and me. "Oh hi, I didn't see you there. Did Stella call you two to help with whatever is causing this?" he asked, waving an arm at the shop.

"Not exactly," I said, forcing a smile. "We were just passing by and thought we'd lend a hand."

Gabriel pointed at Jeremy's injury. "My illusions can make everything look normal, but I don't think they can stop carnivorous plants."

Stella grabbed a paper towel from behind the counter, wrapping it around Jeremy's hand. "Better stay out of the back room until this wild magic has blown over. We don't need a re-boot of *Little Shop of Horrors* right now."

"T-t-totally," Jeremy said, putting pressure on his wrapped hand.

Stella gave him a tight smile and then moved towards Gabriel, who was speaking in low tones as he started to weave his illusion magic around the shop.

While Gabriel worked, I turned my attention to Jeremy. "Are you sure you're okay?"

"Yeah, it's just a scrape. I was more surprised than anything else. You don't expect a flower to bite, you know?"

I nodded in sympathy. "I can't imagine a worse surprise to be honest. Hey, as long as I've got you, did you have a chance to check in with your Uncle Jeremiah about that sample I gave you?" I asked, seizing the opportunity.

He nodded, brushing a few errant petals off his shirt. "I did! He's a whiz with all things plant related. He t-t-took a look at it and was intrigued.

He thinks there's something unusual going on, and thinks he might be able to help, but he wanted to run a few tests first."

"Any idea when that might be?" I pressed, feeling a mix of hope and urgency.

"Not yet, but I'll keep you p-p-posted," he said, offering a reassuring smile.

Gabriel returned, a look of satisfaction on his face. "The illusion spell is in place," he announced. "I've woven it so you can say this dismissal word, and the illusion will vanish. Until then, it's probably best to keep the shop closed." He handed Stella a scrap of paper with a hastily scribbled word. She stuffed it into the pocket of her jeans.

Her eyes lit with gratitude. "Thank you! It was perfect timing that the two of you were passing by. I don't know what I would've done without your help. I can't believe how chaotic everything around town has gotten in the past few days."

A thought struck me. Maybe there was a clue here we were missing. "Speaking of chaos, did you notice if anyone else was around earlier? Anyone unusual?"

Jeremy shook his head. "No one has been in t-t-today."

Stella frowned slightly, glancing at the bouquet trying to escape. She scooped it up, pushing it into a glass display case and firmly shutting the door. "That's not quite true, remember? Professor Hawke popped in earlier."

Gabriel and I exchanged surprised glances. "What did he want?" I asked, my curiosity piquing.

Jeremy nodded as a look of recollection passed over his face. "That's right. He...what did he want again?"

Stella pressed her back against the door as the bouquet started throwing itself against the glass. "He wanted to talk with Jeremy about some rare plant or other."

"Do you remember which plant?" Gabriel asked.

Stella shrugged, distracted by the flowers. "It wasn't anything I recognized. But that's when I noticed things going crazy with the flowers. They were shooting little lightning bolts all over the place!"

"Really?" I leaned in, intrigued.

Stella nodded as the bouquet slammed against the glass again, causing a spray of petals to fly up. "Yeah, we were so distracted by the chaos that by the time we got the flowers under control, he had slipped out."

"Any idea where he went?" Gabriel pressed, his expression serious.

"He was researching plants, so maybe the library?" Stella suggested, glancing at the now scraggly bouquet of crushed leaves and stems, which lay wilted in the display case, completely devoid of blooms.

"He likes his plants almost as much as I do," Jeremy chipped in.

As I looked at Gabriel, a thought began to gnaw at me. Another unexplained occurrence of wild magic had coincided with Edmund's presence. Was it really just the wild magic causing all this chaos, or could he be to blame? What if he was using the wild magic as a cover for something more sinister? The sooner we tracked him down and got some answers, the better off everyone would be.

Every hour that passed without finding the heart seemed to pull Havenwood closer to the brink, the wild magic thickening in the air like a gathering storm and Edmund Hawke seemed to be at the center of it all. Time wasn't just running out—it was slipping away faster than I could chase it. If we didn't find him soon, there might not even be a town left to save.

Smoke Signals

As we settled into the car, the warmth enveloped me, but my mind buzzed with speculation. "Do you think Professor Hawke really has something to do with the wild magic?" I asked in a rush. "It seems too coincidental that the chaos started after he showed up, doesn't it?"

Gabriel nodded, his grip tightening on the steering wheel. "It definitely seems like he's connected somehow. But before we can get answers, we need to find him."

I glanced out the window, weighing the options. "I agree, someone needs to find him, but if it's not just wild magic and he's behind all of this, I'm not sure I'm the best back up for you."

Gabriel shot me a sidelong glance. "I don't know. You handled yourself pretty well against two jewel thieves if memory serves. I'm pretty sure you can handle one scholar."

I smiled despite myself, warmed by the praise. "Okay, you may have a point, but we're talking about magic here. Your brother Lucas would be better back up than I would, don't you think? If Professor Hawke is really that dangerous, I'd just be a liability."

"You're never a liability," Gabriel said instantly, easing the car to a stop at a red light. "But I see your point. I'll give Lucas a call."

"And then you can drop me at the corner up there before heading to the library," I said, pointing.

Gabriel gave me a surprised look. "You don't want to come?"

"No, it's not that." I said, hesitating. "Despite what just happened at the flower shop, dividing and conquering might still be our best option. The library is on the opposite end of town, and I'm close enough to Aunt Agatha's to walk now. You could head to the library with Lucas, and I can check in with her."

Gabriel frowned slightly, clearly not thrilled with the idea. "Are you sure? I'd rather not let you go off alone. Especially with wild magic ramping up."

"I'll be fine," I reassured him, forcing a smile. "Who knows? If you and Lucas find the professor, we might have some answers as to where the heart is anyway. If you hit a dead end, maybe I'll turn up something at Aunty Agatha's."

Gabriel hesitated, his eyes narrowing slightly. I could sense his concern, and for a moment, I debated bringing up the note—the "L" scrawled at the bottom and my fleeting suspicion about Lucas. But what if I was wrong? What if I accused him unjustly? Vivienne's wrath was bad enough without adding unnecessary accusations to the mix. I swallowed the thought, deciding to keep it to myself. For now.

Reluctantly, Gabriel sighed. "Okay, but keep your phone handy. Call me if anything feels off."

"Deal," I said, feeling a mixture of excitement and anxiety as he eased the car over, and I stepped out, waving goodbye when he pulled away from the curb.

The cold air bit at my cheeks as I started through the woods, the snow crunching sharply underfoot. The eerie silence pressed in around me. It wasn't the peaceful kind of quiet I usually associated with a picturesque forest—it was heavy, unnatural. The kind of quiet that makes the hairs on the back of your neck stand on end. But I pushed the thought away, focusing on the reason I was here. Agatha needed to know what was happening, and if she knew who the old woman was, I needed answers. I didn't have time for distractions—or to dwell on the creeping sensation that I wasn't entirely alone.

The glow of Agatha's cottage soon peeked through the trees ahead. Normally, I'd pause to appreciate the charm of her home, but now, even its welcoming blue shutters and festive wreath couldn't shake the unease in my chest. The last time I'd been here, everything had been draped in Halloween cobwebs and flickering jack-o'-lanterns, but now the snow-blanketed scene should have been idyllic. Instead, it seemed even spookier than it had in October. I hurried toward the door, my boots slipping slightly on the icy path.

The feeling of eyes on my back didn't leave me until I knocked on the door.

Aunt Agatha opened the door wide as soon as I knocked, her warm smile instantly easing some of the tension in my chest. "Harper, dear! I didn't expect you today. Come in, come in!" she exclaimed, ushering me inside. I stepped into the cozy cottage, the inviting scent of herbs and spices wrapping around me like a comforting blanket.

She led me to the table, bustling about her small kitchen before setting down a steaming cup of tea and a plate of store-bought cookies. Baking wasn't Agatha's forte any more than it was mine, but the tea more than made up for it. That was her magical gift: brewing excellent tea. Over the years, she had collected an array of enchanted objects that made her seem more powerful than she truly was, several of which she'd crafted alongside Granny Bea, but making tea was her specialty.

I wrapped my hands around the thick, warm mug and inhaled the fragrant steam gratefully. The tea had a rich, earthy aroma with floral notes and a warm hint of spices—maybe cinnamon or cardamom. There was also a refreshing undertone of herbs, perhaps mint, that mingled with the sweetness of dried fruits. As I breathed it in, I savored the promise of comfort and warmth.

Agatha settled across from me with her own mug of tea. "Now, what catastrophe has brought you to my door this early in the morning? It must be something truly terrible. You didn't try to slip rhubarb in with Luna's cabbage, did you?"

A surprised giggle escaped my lips. "No, I know better than that," I said. As quickly as I could, I explained the situation—how wild magic was causing chaos in town and how we were searching for clues related to the damaged heartwood.

Agatha nodded, her brow furrowing slightly. "I've been wondering what was going on. It felt like the magic in the air was thicker than usual."

"It is, and it's spreading throughout town. At first, the incidents were so small, not many people noticed. Heart-shaped snow or letters flying away in the breeze, that type of thing. But now, things are escalating. I'm worried that the wild magic might even be fueling the dryad's curse."

Agatha nodded briskly, squaring her shoulders. "And Havenwood needs me to jump into the fray once more. Just like the time with your Granny and the magnets and peanut butter."

I hesitated a moment before shaking my head. "As much as I want to hear that story someday, we need to stop the wild magic. And I'm looking for answers more than jumping into the fray."

Agatha glared at me. "Is this an ageist thing? Because I'll tell you now that I'm just as capable of fray-jumping as I've ever been. Don't let the white hair and the wrinkles fool you."

I held up my hands to show in immediate surrender. "No, nothing like that. You and Luna can hold a jumping contest and invite the whole town if you like."

Agatha narrowed her eyes. "Are you insinuating that the hopped-up excuse for a sassy familiar can beat me?"

I waved my hands vehemently. "No, I'm sure you could take her."

"Of course I could. Anyone who says differently has a few too many screws loose. And that counts for Luna as well."

A piece of advice my mother used to tell my father when I was younger floated to the front of my mind.

The first rule of holes—when you find yourself in one, stop digging.

My mother was a wise woman. I shifted topics, adding in a heavy dose of flattery. "Actually, the reason why I'm here is because you know everyone in town."

Agatha sniffed. "I should hope so. I've been here long enough."

"Well, I keep seeing this old woman in and around the woods. Long dark dress, wears a shawl, wild white hair? I think she might have something to do with what happened to the heartwood. The dryad mentioned someone named Mad Mads. Does that mean anything to you?" I asked, crossing my fingers under the table and hoping for a lead.

Agatha sighed, a fond smile creeping onto her face. "Oh, you mean Maddie."

"Maddie?" I asked, my heart skittering in excitement. I'd been right to come here!

"Madeline Greaves. She prefers Maddie, and she's not mad—eccentric, maybe, but not mad. She's a witch like us. You'd probably call her a hermit, which isn't too far off the truth. She likes her space, that's for sure, but she wouldn't hurt a fly. She comes up with the most interesting combinations for tea I've ever experienced. Always out in the woods collecting this or that. Roots and herbs, that type of thing. Although, this time of year it's more likely bark and a runny nose from being out in the winter weather."

I nodded, thoughtfully. "Ah, that explains a lot. Do you think she'd attack the heartwood?"

Agatha's eyes narrowed. "Don't tell me she's a suspect."

I lifted a shoulder, not wanting to offend Agatha, but also feeling the pressure of the curse. "She's been seen in the forest more than once…"

Agatha scoffed. "You don't know Maddie. She chooses to be out here, but she's a good soul. No one could force that woman to do anything, and she wouldn't do anything to hurt the forest. Or Havenwood, for that matter."

"You speak as if you know her well," I observed.

"I do. We've known each other for a long while. She's not part of my weekly mahjong group, but I wouldn't be upset if she wanted to join. She's always been good company and a better neighbor," Agatha said firmly.

"Can you introduce me? I really need to talk to her."

Agatha scowled at me, shaking a finger in my direction. "You aren't going to do something silly like accuse her of this nonsense with the heart-wood, are you?"

I held up my hands to protest my innocence even though that possibility had been in the forefront of my mind before I knocked on Agatha's door. "I trust your judgement in people, Aunty Agatha. But she is in the forest quite a lot. She might've seen or heard something that could give us a clue as to who is behind the theft of the heart and the destruction of the heartwood tree. We don't have much else to go on, and if we don't figure this out soon, the dryad's curse will take root. No one should be loveless the rest of their lives," I finished with a little shudder. To my dismay, tears flooded my vision, and I hastily blinked them away before they could fall.

Agatha's eyes filled with sympathy, and she patted my hand.

"Of course you don't want to live without love, dear. No one would. Love is the thread that weaves our stories together; without it, the fabric of life unravels."

This time, a few tears did manage to spill down my cheeks before I could brush them away. "I don't know where else to look. Everywhere I turn seems to be a dead end. I know I may be grasping at straws, but

Maddie might be my best hope at a lead to finding the heart and stopping the wild magic."

"And you understandably want to follow every possible avenue." Agatha suddenly clicked her tongue and shook her head.

"What is it?" I asked, noticing her expression shift.

"Well, Maddie doesn't have a cell phone or email. She's never been one for technology, so reaching out to her takes a bit more time."

I frowned. "So how do you get in touch when you need to?"

Agatha smiled wryly. "Mostly luck. Sometimes smoke signals."

I raised an eyebrow. "No, seriously. How do you do it?"

"I *am* being serious. It's either that or wander around the forest hoping you'll bump into her."

I glanced at my phone. No new messages from Gabriel. Probably too soon for that anyway. I hesitated, weighing the options, but not for long. If Edmund Hawke ended up being a dead end, Maddie was our only other lead.

"Okay, I'm in. Let's try the smoke signals."

Sever the Roots

To my surprise, Aunty Agatha shooed me out of her house in short order. Apparently, the smoke signals weren't only a real thing, but also magical and private. Who knew? Certainly not me.

That was how I came to be standing on the sidewalk, unsure of what to do or where to go. Meeting up with Gabriel was the obvious choice, but if he was in the middle of talking to Edmund or doing some illusion magic, I didn't want to interrupt him. Better to wait for him to call me. I could head back to the Oasis. Bella looked like she might be able to use an extra hand today, but with Alex already there, I might just get underfoot. I could swing by Blossom and Bloom to check on Stella, but how much would've really changed since I left? Of course, there was Spellbooks. A seed of guilt took root and sprouted in an instant. I was ignoring the shop, my livelihood and my legacy. What would Granny Bea say if she could see me now?

That you made a hard decision and put the needs of the many above your own.

It was like I could hear her voice echoing in my memories. I squared my shoulders, trying to summon some of Granny Bea's determination. If wild magic continued to run rampant through Havenwood, we might not have much of a town left. Shutting the shop for a day or two meant I could dedicate my entire attention to finding the heart. But the truth was, I didn't even know where to start. The heart, the leads, the clues—they all felt like they were just out of reach.

I let out a slow breath, pulling out my phone. Maybe I should call Mom. Just hearing her voice might help ground me—or remind me of what I was fighting to save. The thought sent a pang through me. What if this curse was strong enough to erode even those bonds someday? Would I forget the love I shared with my mom or my dad's gruff warmth? Tears clogged my throat and threatened to pour down my cheeks as the implications swirled around my mind.

My phone vibrated in my pocket, startling me. I dug it out and glanced at the screen, relief flooding through me when I saw Gabriel's name. Yanking my gloves off with my teeth, I answered the call.

"Gabriel? Hi. Did you find him?" I asked in a rush, pacing anxiously as I talked.

"No." The single regretful word pricked the balloon of hope that had been rising inside me.

"Oh," was all I managed. My fingers were already going cold, so I awkwardly tugged my glove back on.

"Yeah, I was hoping we'd locate him, he'd confess, and this whole thing would be over. But by the time I made it to the library, he'd already left. Lucas met me there, and we're going to drive over to Eastford. Hawke works at the university over there. Maybe he went back to the school. If not, maybe we can track down his home address."

"Okay," I murmured. I didn't know how much use I'd be hunting through a university in a town I'd never visited, but I was willing to help if it meant finding the heart faster.

"Any luck with your lead?" Gabriel asked.

I shook my head even though he couldn't see it. "Not exactly. Aunty Agatha mentioned something about a Madeline Greaves?"

"Never heard of her," Gabriel said. His voice shifted as if he'd pulled the phone away from his head for a moment. "Have you ever heard of Madeline Greaves?"

I waited in silence for a beat until Gabriel came back on the line. "Lucas says the name sounds familiar. Some lady who lives out in the woods?"

"That's the one. I think that might be the Mad Mads the dryad mentioned. Anyway, Agatha's going to try to get in touch with her. Until then, I'm at loose ends."

"I'd offer to pick you up, but we're already on our way. We can swing back if you like," he offered.

"No, I'm fine. Just let me know what you find in Eastford, okay?"

"I'll call as soon as I have something," he promised before saying good-bye and hanging up.

I shoved the phone back into my pocket, my thoughts turning over like the pages of an unsolved mystery. The library was the last place Edmund had been seen, and there was a chance he might have left a clue behind that Gabriel and Lucas had missed. If he'd left even a hint of a trail, it might be waiting there. I could almost picture him in the restricted area, poring over tomes on Havenwood's history, ancient spells, and hidden truths.

It wasn't much of a lead, but it was something. Standing still wasn't going to get me anywhere. I squared my shoulders and took a steadying breath, determination pushing aside any lingering doubt. I had to do something; waiting around wouldn't solve anything.

I set off down the path, my footsteps crunching in the fresh snow. Each step brought me closer to the library and the possibility of discovering something that could change everything. The thought of uncovering a clue kept my spirits buoyed despite the weight of uncertainty hanging in the air.

As I stepped into the library, the familiar scent of aged paper and polished wood enveloped me, offering some comfort amid the chaos brewing in Havenwood. I headed straight for Martha's desk, my mind racing with thoughts of Edmund Hawke.

"Hi Martha," I said as I crossed the empty foyer to the front desk. She looked up, a hint of surprise crossing her features.

"Harper! What brings you back so soon? And on such a cold day too," she said, drawing her soft pink cardigan a little tighter around her shoulders. "No one is out in this weather. Not that I usually mind an empty library. It allows me to get work done. Except today."

"What do you mean?" I asked.

"I know there's some sort of weird magical energy going around town. Everyone's whispering about it, but whoever's behind it seemed to target the library in particular today. I had a whole stack of fantasy books fly off the shelves and circle the reading room before forming an impressive castle. They took me nearly an hour to reshelve," Martha said, shaking her head. "And the lights keep flickering, while strange sparks of energy crackle in the air, making it feel like a storm is brewing inside the library. It's unsettling to say the least, but thankfully no one else is here or I don't know what I'd do to explain what's going on."

"Oh dear," I murmured.

"Don't worry. Gabriel and Lucas Silverthorne were just in. Hopefully, the spells they cast will help everything return to normal," Martha said. Her tone was confident, but her eyes shifted around uneasily, as if she expected more books to leap off the shelves at any moment.

"Actually, that's why I'm here. I'm working with Gabriel to try to stop all the magic causing chaos around town. He was asking about someone. Edmund Hawke?"

Martha nodded, setting aside the book she'd been scanning into the system. "Yes. He mentioned that Professor Hawke might be somehow tied to the strange magical occurrences around town."

"That's what we're trying to figure out, but we can't find him. I know this might be a long shot, but I was wondering if something in the books he was reading might give us a clue as to his whereabouts. Do you have a list of the books he was reading last time he was here?"

She shook her head, looking thoughtful. "Because you can't check out items from the restricted area, I don't have that information at my desk, but I might be able to pull something from the card catalogue. Is it important?"

"I can't say for sure, but it might be the clue we need," I replied, my fingers tapping nervously on the desk.

Martha nodded, her expression turning serious. "Come with me then. Let's see what we can find."

We made our way to the restricted area, and Martha gestured to a cart piled high with books. "It might be a long shot, but do you think these will be useful?"

As I scanned the titles, my heart raced—I recognized several of the books from Edmund's research table. "Wait, are those...?"

"The books from the day Edmund Hawke was here? Yes. I haven't had time to take care of these yet. With the shortage of volunteers, I've been swamped with the mundane side of the library. You're lucky. It's on my to-do list for today, though."

"Lucky?" I asked.

"If they'd been reshelved, it would've been much harder to track down which ones Professor Hawke borrowed. Here, let me show you," Martha said, pulling a book from the top shelf of the cart. "Every request for books is magically logged on the inside back cover," Martha explained, her voice taking on a nostalgic tone. "Think of it like the old-school libraries before everything went digital."

"That was before my time I think," I said, leaning forward curiously.

She chuckled softly. "I forget how young everyone is these days. Back then, we wrote the name and the date on a little card and tucked it in a pocket on the back cover." She opened one of the books to reveal a blank back page and squeezed the upper right corner. To my amazement, a glowing list of names appeared on the blank page.

"Wow," I breathed, taken aback by the magic at play.

Martha smiled at my reaction. "I think this may be the best I can do. If the books had already been reshelved, we'd have to go through every title in the restricted section to find what you're looking for. I'll try to manipulate the card catalogue to see if we can get a full list of his searches, but that's a finnicky piece of magic."

"Okay. I'll start here and see if I can find anything that looks like a clue," I said, slipping out of my coat and settling cross-legged on the floor.

As I began to sift through the stack, I quickly became overwhelmed. There were countless books on plants with titles like Whispers of the Verdant Realm, The Enchanted Flora of the Forgotten Woods, and Herbology of the Arcane. None of them looked familiar, and without something conveniently handy like his notebook, I couldn't track which pages Edmund had read. A thought struck me. Sandy mentioned putting Edmund's notebook in lost and found. If it was still there, it might hold the exact notes I needed to connect all these threads. Unless Edmund had come back to retrieve it. I made a mental note to ask Martha about the notebook as soon as she returned as I continued to sort through the books. Slowly, I accumulated a pile, each book glowing with Edmund's name at the bottom of the inside cover.

My initial enthusiasm for finding a clue began to wane. I grabbed a book with a striking purple and green cover, glancing at the title: Tendrils of Power: Forgotten Pathways of Ancient Magic. It looked intriguing and oddly familiar. I flipped to the back cover, tracing a finger down the glowing list of names, and my heart skipped when I saw a name I hadn't expected: Vivienne Silverthorne. That came as a surprise; I would've thought she had her own magical library. Maybe there were books here that she didn't have? The next name made me pause—Samuel Bellamy. Could this be a relation to the Cassandra I'd met or was it just a coincidence? My gut told me not to dismiss it as such. The smallest clue might prove to be the very thing I needed to unravel this mess. I made a mental note to ask Martha when she returned.

The other names on the list didn't ring a bell. Margaret Jameson, Sorrel Aetherwyn, Felix Carter, Lysandra Wraithmoor, Edmund Hawke. This book seemed to be more popular than the rest of the stack I'd examined. While I waited for Martha to return, I flipped back to the beginning, scanning the list of chapter titles. My eyes snagged on one chapter title and my breath caught.

Sever the Roots, Sever the Magic.

Why did that sound familiar? It only took me a moment to place it. Edmund Hawke scribbled something remarkably close to that in his notebook! Quickly, I flipped to the chapter, scanning it eagerly for anything that might give me a clue. There was a lot of magical and herbology references that mostly went over my head, but I paused my frantic skim reading as I reached the last page of the chapter.

Magical plants possess a remarkable resilience, often returning with renewed vigor when faced with adversity. However, this tenacity hinges on the health of their roots. If the roots are compromised, the plant's chances of recovery diminish rapidly, leaving it vulnerable to decay and death. Severing the roots can spell disaster; it disrupts the very foundation of the plant's magic, making revival nearly impossible.

A glimmer of hope flickered within me. If the heartwood's roots remained intact, perhaps it could still recover. But the darkened wood surrounding it painted a grim picture, looking more like a disease spreading through the tree. We had to stop that encroachment—fast. This might be another avenue to save the tree if we couldn't find the heart, but time was not on our side.

I took a picture of the final paragraph and sent it to Gabriel with a brief summation of my thoughts. I received a reply almost instantly.

Thanks. I've forwarded this to my mother, and she'll take care of this. Looks like we're going to be here a while. No one has seen Edmund today. Trying to track him down.

I tapped out a quick message wishing him luck. Martha returned just as I hit send.

"Did you find anything?" I asked hopefully.

Martha shook her head. "The card catalogue is a very useful enchantment, but it wasn't built for tracking requests, and I couldn't alter the spell to pull a backlog of data. I'm sorry."

My hope dimmed, but didn't extinguish. "I thought of something else. Professor Hawke had a notebook with him that he left behind. We put it in lost and found. If it's still there, maybe we could check his notes."

Martha frowned. "I'm sorry, but I just cleared out Lost and Found this morning. There wasn't a notebook—if it was there, he must've come back for it."

My spirits sank. "Well, it was worth a try. I think we might have just hit another dead end."

Martha nodded sympathetically. "Don't get too discouraged. I remembered something I think you might find interesting." She held out a slim book. "I hope you don't think me presumptuous, but I overheard the Silverthorne brothers talking about magic and plants around Havenwood. I didn't put two and two together until coming back here. This book is kept in a highly classified area that only I can access, but I thought it might be useful."

I accepted the book, my fingers sliding along the rich leather and title embossed in gold. I gasped as I read it: The Enchantment of Havenwood: A History of Magic and Its Roots.

"The card catalogue wouldn't have pulled this for anyone," she explained. "I have to personally find it and unlock it. I haven't done that in at least a decade—last time was for Vivienne Silverthorne herself."

I took a deep breath, clutching the book to my chest. Was the information in this book what Edmund had really been searching for? I moved to the reading table, already scanning through chapter titles as I went. Martha settled in the chair next to me as I flipped through the pages, searching for any clues. The words danced in my mind, but the connections felt just out of reach. After a few minutes, I finally stumbled upon a passage that discussed the effects of disrupting ley lines and their importance to Havenwood's magic.

"Ley lines are the lifeblood of magic in Havenwood," I muttered to myself, piecing together the fragments of information.

"You're interested in ley lines?" Martha asked, surprised.

I blushed. "Um, well, yeah. I guess you could say that."

"Ley lines are a particular fascination of mine," Martha admitted. "One I don't often have the opportunity to discuss."

"Do you know what happens when a gateway to a ley line is destroyed?" I asked.

Martha looked thoughtful. "It's never been formally documented because most scholars aren't foolish enough to disturb a ley line. However, it's been hypothesized that the line might self-heal and find a new gateway elsewhere. The other theory is that it erupts like a magical volcano. No one is quite certain."

I felt a chill run down my spine. "That's not good."

Martha shook her head firmly. "No, it is not. Which is why the gateways always have a guardian and are reinforced with magical redundancies like a magical focus. A gateway could never be destroyed as long as the focus was secure."

Although part of me didn't want to hear the answer to my next question, I needed to know. "What would happen if someone possessed the magical focus for a ley line? What could they do?"

Her answer sent a shiver of dread through me. "Anything they want."

Reality Calling

I QUICKLY SKIMMED THROUGH the rest of the book, hoping to unearth any additional clues before reluctantly handing it back to Martha. She accepted it with a somber nod, carefully returning it to its secure location. Seizing the moment, I stepped outside the restricted area and called Gabriel, eager to fill him in on my discovery.

"I think I may have found something," I said, barely able to keep the hope from creeping into my voice.

"Good news," he said. "Let's hear it."

"Have you ever heard of anyone named Bellamy?"

He paused briefly before responding. "No, I don't think so. Why?"

"I ran across the name at the library. Just curious if it rang any bells," I said, brushing the thought aside for now. "Anyway, I think I found—"

"Hold that thought," he interrupted. "I've got everyone on the line. Let's make sure we're all on the same page. Just give me a second." He paused and when he spoke again, his tone was steady. "Mother? Are you there?"

I swallowed hard, trying to calm my breathing as Vivienne's chilly voice echoed through the receiver. A shiver ran down my spine, and I felt my stomach tighten. I struggled to mask my emotional reaction, reminding myself that this was about the heartwood, not her.

"I'm listening, Gabriel," Vivienne said.

Lucas' voice came next. "I'm here too. Gabriel has us on speaker."

Vivienne's words were clipped and urgent. "The wild magic is escalating at a rapid rate. We must find that heart. Tell me you've caught the perpetrator."

Gabriel replied. "Not exactly."

Lucas chimed in. "From what we've discovered, we don't think Professor Edmund Hawke could've attacked the tree. He's been at a rare plant symposium in New York. He only got back the same day we found the heartwood and apparently went straight to the Havenwood library. His colleagues say he wouldn't step on an already dead branch, let alone hurt a living plant. He loves all things plant related."

"He doesn't seem like our guy," Gabriel confirmed. "The timeline and the motive just don't fit."

"I'm inclined to agree," Lucas said.

"What did you find out, Harper?" Gabriel asked, and I felt a jolt of anxiety course through me, compounded by Vivienne's presence on the call. It was incredible how she still managed to rattle me, even from a distance.

I took a deep breath, forcing myself to focus. "I came back to the library and, with Martha's permission, went through Edmund's stack of research. I found a book that warns the ley line could explode if it's not contained."

Vivienne's tone turned sharp, cutting through the air. "Yes, we already know that's a possibility. Which is why we've all been working so hard to find this missing heart."

I blinked, momentarily taken aback by her intensity. I hadn't realized that was a potential outcome until just now. The fact Vivienne and possibly even Gabriel hadn't told me was jarring.

Gabriel interrupted my thoughts, asking, "Did you find anything else?"

I refocused on the conversation. "Yes, but it might be a long shot." I hesitated for a moment. "I found someone named Samuel Bellamy in the records on one of the same magical plant books Edmund Hawke was looking at."

Lucas' voice was sharp. "Who is Bellamy?"

"I don't know," I admitted. "But there was a Cassandra Bellamy hanging around town. She tried to gain access to the restricted section of the library and also seemed very intent on finding you, Vi…erm…Mrs. Silverthorne."

Vivienne's voice turned contemplative. "Bellamy, you say?" There was a brief pause, and then she continued, "That name is familiar." Another pause followed, longer this time, as if she were sifting through memories.

"Oh, I remember now," she finally said. "Cassandra Bellamy. She's a student of an old…acquaintance of mine. She's been seeking a different approach to magic, but unfortunately, my schedule has been so packed with this current crisis that I've had to put her off."

Silence fell, and I wrestled with whether to mention Madeline Greaves. I had no new information from Agatha, so I decided against it.

Gabriel spoke next. "Any more wild magic occurrences, Mother?"

Vivienne's voice turned urgent. "Yes, unfortunately. This morning has been chaotic. We've noticed strange fluctuations in the weather patterns—unseasonable gusts of wind that sent snow swirling through town like miniature tornadoes, knocking over market stalls. Then, we had the bizarre sight of raindrops shooting up from the ground, creating puddles in mid-air before disappearing entirely. Streetlamps flickered on and off, casting odd colors that illuminated strange words in the air. And to top it all off, animals have been acting wildly—dogs howling in harmony, cats pretending to be mimes, and squirrels boldly entering grocery stores to enact audacious nut heists with an almost theatrical flair."

Lucas chimed in, "It's as if the wild magic is having a field day."

"That's all since I left?" Gabriel asked in disbelief.

"And it's getting worse," Vivienne said grimly.

"Well, there were instances at Blossom and Bloom, the Enchanted Oasis, and the library this morning as well," I added.

Vivienne's voice turned steely. "We can't let this situation fester. We've been trying to keep this under wraps, and perhaps that was the wrong approach. This is now a code red crisis. We need everyone in town helping out. I'll arrange for a town meeting first thing tomorrow morning. That'll give you boys enough time to get home and help me plan a multi-pronged approach to dealing with the wild magic until we can find the missing heart."

"We'll be home as quickly as we can, Mother," Lucas confirmed.

"See that you are," Vivienne said grimly. "I have a feeling things are going to get worse before they get better."

The call abruptly disconnected, leaving me staring at a black screen. A wave of frustration washed over me. With the news of what Gabriel and Lucas had discovered about Edmund Hawke, it felt like another lead withered away before my eyes, leaving me with more questions than answers. Now, all my hopes rested on a woman in the woods who may or may not be mad. I just hoped Agatha could get in touch with Madeline Greaves soon.

As I turned to leave the library, a shiver ran down my spine. What if I was chasing shadows and Madeline had nothing to do with what happened at the heartwood? The thought settled uncomfortably in my mind. If she turned out to have no ties to the heartwood, I'd be at a loss for where to search next.

Just then, the ground beneath me vibrated slightly. I glanced around in surprise. Earthquakes shouldn't be happening in Havenwood. We weren't on a fault line which meant...the wild magic was gaining power by the hour. I noticed dark clouds gathering ominously over Havenwood. A flash of lightning split the sky, followed by an unnatural crackle that made the hairs on my arms stand on end. Maybe it was just my imagination, but it was almost as if I could feel the wild magic stirring, ready to unleash its fury. The heartwood tree was dying, the curse was spreading, and here I was, left clutching at straws.

A gust of wind whipped through the trees, carrying with it an unsettling energy that prickled my skin. I couldn't shake the feeling that something was about to happen—something big. With each step, a sense of foreboding grew, leaving me to wonder whether I could withstand the storm that was brewing on the horizon.

Holiday Hodgepodge

I'D BEEN RIGHT ABOUT the weather, at least. By the time I turned onto Arcadia Avenue, I was hunched against the biting wind. Snowflakes whipped through the air with such force that it felt like tiny needles stinging my cheeks. I fumbled in my pocket for the shop keys, struggling to shield myself from the gusts while trying to unlock the door.

The moment I stepped inside Spellbooks, a warm hush enveloped me, cocooning me from the chaos outside. The familiar scent of paper, ink, and rich coffee wrapped around me like a comforting blanket, offering a fleeting reprieve from the storm. For a heartbeat, I allowed myself to savor the cozy atmosphere, even as the winds howled relentlessly beyond the door.

"Fluff and furballs! Careful!" Luna admonished, throwing herself over strips of colorful paper as the wind blew me into the shop.

"I'm sorry," I murmured on reflex and then took in the creative chaos in front of me. "Umm, Luna? What's going on?" I asked, trying my best to keep my tone light.

Luna looked up from a pile of mismatched ribbons, scrapbooking paper, and more tubes of glitter than should be allowed in one room without triggering an apocalyptic event. Her eyes sparkled. "Harper! Perfect timing! I've decided your Valentine's event needed a little...upgrade. Quick, come here. I need a finger to tie this bow properly."

I blinked, taking in the colorful chaos as I pressed down on the ribbon where she indicated. "Upgrade? It looks like a holiday threw up in here. Possibly more than one holiday," I said, picking up a candy cane and looking at it in surprise.

"Exactly! Why have only one holiday when you can have two? I thought combining the generosity of Christmas with your Valentine's Day event was the perfect mashup. Who wouldn't love a little festive flair mixed with romance?"

"Because nothing says, 'I love you' like a garland of twinkling lights and peppermint hearts," I said, trying not to smile as I twirled the candy cane between my fingers. "But don't you think we might overwhelm people?"

"Overwhelm? Pfft! I prefer to call it an 'immersive experience,'" Luna shot back.

I couldn't help but chuckle. "So, candy canes with hearts on them? Is that the plan?"

"By the long ears of Lord Bunbury Fluffington, yes! It's brilliant, isn't it?" Luna hopped onto the counter, knocking over a spool of ribbon. "This is exactly what the people need to lift their spirits with the weather going crazy—love and giving all wrapped in one festive bow. Oh, and your book thing, I guess," she said, waving a dismissive paw.

"Thanks," I said dryly. "I wouldn't want to impede upon your creative masterpiece."

"Very thoughtful of you," Luna said, completely missing my sarcasm. "I'm calling it 'Valentine's Wonderland.' It's got everything—romance, presents, and enough sparkle to blind a squirrel. A surprise everyone will undoubtedly adore. You're welcome."

"You're right, it is surprising," I said, nodding at the chaos of paper and glitter.

"Exactly. Now, if you'll excuse me, I have to bring this concept to life. The world needs to see my genius!" She hopped down, heading back to the table set with her craft supplies.

"Umm, Luna? What about all this?" I called, gesturing at the mess in the shop.

"Don't worry! The disco ball will really tie it all together!" Luna called back.

"Disco ball?" I asked, looking around. "Where would we hang a disco ball? Scratch that. Spellbooks has a disco ball?" As if in answer, Mr. Wigglesworth cautiously poked his head out of his cozy cat apartment and meowed pitifully.

"I know, buddy. It's a lot." I scooped up his food bowl and tucked it in his refuge. He ducked back inside in a rare show of fear at the sight of Luna's chaotic creative process. I sighed. "My sentiments exactly. If I could join you in there for a little less glitter and a little more peace and quiet, I would."

A thought tickled the back of my mind: could the wild magic have gotten to Luna too? I glanced over at her, fully immersed in her crafting chaos, ribbons and glitter flying in every direction. No. This wasn't wild magic. This was just Luna being Luna—chaotic, stubborn, and entirely herself.

"Excuse me?" Luna's voice cut through my attempt at commiseration like a laser beam. I froze, realizing too late that her sharp ears had caught my muttering. I coughed and scrambled for a quick save.

"Nothing!" I called quickly,

However, Luna's idea, while over the top, wasn't a bad one. With a winter storm blowing outside, I should probably make good use of the time by working on the Valentine's Day event. I tried to ignore the spread of glitter as Luna hopped all over the shop, muttering to herself. Instead, I got busy scribbling key phrases for the books Luna had wrapped earlier, to give patrons a clue as to what tropes they could expect on their bookish blind date.

As I worked, my thoughts kept drifting back to the mystery at hand. If Edmund wasn't behind the stolen heart, who was? Cassandra? The Bellamy name kept popping up in the most unexpected places. Or, despite Agatha's assurances, was Madeline Greaves somehow involved? More to the point, how could I find the responsible party, preferably before the wild magic or the winter weather wiped Havenwood from the face of the map?

In between note cards, I kept a vigilant eye on my phone, half expecting Agatha to call with news about the smoke signals. But in this weather, I doubted a message of that kind would reach Madeline. While I waited, I busied myself with other shop preparations, arranging items for the event and drafting social media designs that I could later print and plaster around town or across the internet.

Just as I shut my computer nearly two hours later, my phone buzzed. It was a text message from Gabriel.

It took three times longer to get back from Eastford than it should have, but I'm home safe.

Relief flooded through me. *I'm glad you're safe.* I wrote back. Was a heart emoji too much to add? Probably. Right?

His reply popped up before I could decide. *It was touch and go a couple times. The upside is that a storm like this will keep people indoors until it blows over.*

That was a good thing. Fewer witnesses for any potential wild magic, not that it was enough to keep Gabriel home and safe.

Glad to hear it. I responded.

Are you okay?

I smiled as I typed my reply. *Yes. Luna's just taken over the shop. We'll see if it can survive the deluge of glitter.*

A laughing face greeted my message. *Can't wait to see it.*

Another message popped up nearly immediately. *Mother says the town meeting is at 9 at the library. Pick you up at 8:30?*

I tapped on the thumb's up emoji. It would be easier to drive than to walk to the library. As long as the streets were cleared, that is.

My phone buzzed again in my hand. I glanced down, expecting another message from Gabriel, but was surprised to see Agatha was calling. I quickly answered the phone.

"Ah, good. I caught you," Aunty Agatha said in greeting.

"Hi. Are you safe?" I asked.

"What? What do you mean?" Agatha asked, surprised.

"With the storm," I clarified.

"Oh, that," Agatha said dismissively. "I've survived much worse than a little magically induced snow. What I'm calling about is Maddie. I managed to get a hold of her. She's coming to my house tomorrow around eleven, assuming this storm blows itself out by then. I suggest you come early. She isn't great with time or patience."

"Okay. Vivienne Silverthorne's just called an emergency town meeting tomorrow at nine at the library. I'll swing by afterwards," I said.

"Emergency? What's got that girl's knickers in a twist?" Agatha asked.

I had to suppress a chuckle. It always made me laugh when Agatha called Vivienne a girl, even though the Silverthorne matriarch was clearly well over middle age. "I think it's all the wild magic," I supplied.

"Oh. Well, I suppose that's a sensible rationale. I thought she was being dramatic again," Agatha muttered.

There wasn't a scenario in which I could imagine the stoic Vivienne being dramatic, but then again, I hadn't lived in Havenwood nearly as long as Agatha.

"Thanks for setting this up. I'll see you tomorrow morning," I promised, feeling a mix of excitement and apprehension. First the town meeting, then a get-together with a madwoman. Tomorrow was shaping up to be an interesting day.

I hung up, glancing around the shop. Today had already turned out to be more interesting than I'd anticipated. The disco ball, the twinkling lights, and the candy canes scattered across the counter gave the room an absurdly festive vibe that clashed with the growing tension swirling outside. At least, with the weather this bad, I doubted anyone would be out shopping for books, so I didn't have to feel guilty about keeping Spellbooks closed or the mess in the shop. But it *was* a mess.

Sighing, I set to work cleaning up the glitter and ribbons strewn about, while Luna continued to enact her genius vision with complete focus. As I tidied up, my thoughts kept drifting back to the heartwood. What possible motive could Cassandra or Madeline have for harming it? I felt a knot of uncertainty tighten in my chest. With the wild magic escalating and the heartwood's condition worsening, we were running out of time. The storm outside wasn't the only threat looming. If we couldn't figure out where the missing heart was, what would that mean for Havenwood? Would it unravel the lives of everyone here? And if love truly was at risk, how would any of us survive that—myself included?

It was a question I hoped I'd never have to confront, yet it occupied my thoughts for the remainder of the day.

This Town Ain't Big Enough

MUCH TO MY SURPRISE, the next day dawned clear, crisp, and beautiful with a fresh blanket of fluffy snow on the ground. Somehow, the storm had blown itself out in the night. Not only that, but someone had been busy because Arcadia Avenue was already plowed.

I glanced at the clock. I'd inadvertently slept in. Likely lulled into a deep sleep from the excitement of the day and the stillness after the storm. I barely had time to shower, blow-dry my hair, and grab a quick cup of coffee before I saw Gabriel's dark car cruising down the street. I waved at him through my window, although I wasn't sure he could see me, and dashed downstairs.

To my surprise, the shop looked much better than I'd left it last night and at least ten times cleaner than I'd imagined possible after Luna's creative chaos of the day before. Knowing who was likely responsible for the assistance, I laid a hand on the wall.

"Thanks," I whispered to Spellbooks. A familiar warmth and a small vibration rippled under my fingertips.

Luna stuck her head out of her hutch, yawning widely. "You're welcome. I take thank-you gifts in the form of chocolate, radishes, and diamonds. I prefer the latter."

I blinked in surprise. "I'll make a note of that." A larger vibration tickled the palm of my hand, Spellbooks' version of a chuckle. At least the shop wasn't mad at Luna for making a mess last night.

"See that you do," Luna said, her whiskers twitching. "And like any rabbit worth their whiskers, I appreciate size in both carats—whether they're the vegetable or the gem variety."

Gabriel knocked on the door, interrupting any response I might have made, not that I had one ready for such a statement. Dealing with Luna wasn't a one-cup-of-coffee type of job, even on a normal day.

"I have to go to an emergency town meeting," I said, as I opened the door for Gabriel. "Please try not to make a mess in the shop again."

"Mess?" Gabriel asked as he stomped snow from his boots. "This place looks amazing!"

"Thank you," Luna said primly. She sniffed pointedly in my direction. "At least *someone* has taste."

"I already said 'thank you'," I protested, scooping some food into the bowl for Mr. Wigglesworth. I saw a brief flare of green eyes in the darkness of the cat apartment, but the Maine Coon didn't dare exit the cozy abode. Not that I blamed him.

Luna's ears twitched. "There's perfunctory 'thank you's' and my due. Which is awe, respect, and a dash of reverence at my genius-level execution of a plan."

"For which I have all three," Gabriel said immediately.

I caught his eye. *"Suck up,"* I mouthed.

He tapped the side of his temple. *"Smart,"* he mouthed back.

"See? The Silverthorne boy gets it. I wasn't sure of him before, but he has my stamp of approval now. You could learn a thing or two from him," Luna called.

"Luna!" I hissed, my cheeks blazing as I hurriedly shoved my feet into my boots.

"What? I'm just trying to tell you I approve of you two dating. I can totally picture you both in matching outfits, sharing romantic dinners, maybe having—"

"Luna!" I interrupted, "Let's not get ahead of ourselves!"

Gabriel stifled a laugh, and I shot him a look that was half-embarrassed, half-exasperated. "I'll see you later!" I called over my shoulder, practically fleeing for the door before Luna could say anything else.

"Aren't you curious what we'll be having?" Gabriel teased as he walked me to the car.

"A panic attack if Luna has her way," I muttered. The car was warm and inviting, a stark contrast to the frigid air outside.

"Ah, it's all in good fun," Gabriel said, shutting my door and hurrying around the front of the car to the driver's side. I took a deep breath, trying to shake off the lingering embarrassment from Luna's words.

We made it to the library faster than I would've imagined, given the snowstorm yesterday. I said as much to Gabriel. "How did the streets get cleared so fast?"

"Ice golems," he replied at once. "Mother used to make them for us to play with as children. Eventually, she figured out they have a remarkable capability for clearing streets, when given explicit directions. It takes a lot of her energy, but Havenwood hasn't been snowed in since. Well, unintentionally, that is. That thing with Aunt Elara at Christmas was another thing entirely."

"That's a handy talent," I observed as we walked into the crowded foyer.

"Less fun when you're a kid and hoping for a snow day," Gabriel said dryly.

A surprised chuckle escaped me. "Yeah, I can imagine."

Gabriel stood on his tiptoes, looking around the room. "I didn't expect it to be so crowded this early. Oh, I see my mother over there," he said, pointing. "Come on."

"I, um, I think I'm going to stay here," I said.

He shot me a knowing smile. "Okay. Wait for me afterwards, and I'll give you a ride back. Maybe we can stop for coffee and a croissant at Pixie Pastries or Hocus Mochas."

"I'd like that," I said, my stomach growling.

Gabriel winked at me, making me wonder if he'd heard the rumbling. He threaded his way through the gathered residents to where his mother stood, talking in low tones to Mayor Featherfoot.

I inched backward, looking for a familiar face. Maybe the DeLucas were here, and I could stand with them rather than awkwardly all by myself. Out of the corner of my eye, I caught a glimpse of red hair. Thinking it might be Finn, I turned to get a better look. To my surprise, Cassandra Bellamy stood outside the library doors arguing with Martha Morningstar. The redhead gestured emphatically towards the library, but Martha stoically shook her head, pointing towards the sign with the library hours. It wasn't due to open to the public until ten. I could imagine what Martha was saying. This meeting was for residents only.

The problem was Cassandra might be the entire reason for the meeting in the first place. I started heading in their direction, fighting against the flow of incoming locals.

"See? I knew she didn't care about this town," a familiar nasal voice whined, slicing through the buzz of the crowd.

Several heads turned to look, including mine. Oswald Puddleton stood there, his pudgy frame puffed up with self-importance, while Hortense, thin and pinched, flanked him like a crow at a feast.

"Perhaps that prank card that Sullivan girl delivered was meant to stir up trouble in our marriage," Oswald continued, a smirk on his face. "But the joke's on her—we're stronger than ever!"

Hortense cackled, her voice shrill and grating. "Right! We've never been better, despite her meddling!"

"I can't believe the Silverthornes let someone like her move to our beautiful town," Oswald said, his voice rising in volume when he noticed me looking.

Hortense cackled, the strident sound making me wince. "I can't imagine she'll fool them for long. They'll throw her out on her ear before she's been here a year, you mark my words!"

I gritted my teeth. The Puddletons always seemed to know what buttons to push to get on my nerves, but I wasn't about to give them the satisfaction of devolving into a full-out confrontation. Not with a potential lead to ending the chaos of wild magic just outside. I turned my attention back to Martha and Cassandra, only to see that Cassandra had turned and was already halfway down the block, her long coat flapping as she strode angrily away. A knot of frustration twisted in my stomach. If she was involved in what happened with the heartwood, I needed to talk to her, but I doubted I could catch up to her before she vanished. Still, I had to try.

"Look, she's leaving already," Oswald called as I hurried toward the door.

"Good," Hortense shrilled after me. "Maybe she's finally realized she'll never belong here. Havenwood is better off without her."

The Puddletons' snide remarks cut deeper than usual, their smug satisfaction igniting a spark of anger within me. I clenched my fists, fighting the urge to confront them, knowing I had more pressing matters at hand. I wasn't about to linger near the Puddletons any longer, so I opened the door, feeling a mix of urgency and unease as I scanned the street for any sign of Cassandra.

A hand cupped my elbow, startling me. I glanced up into a wrinkled, friendly face. "You look in need of shelter from the storm," Jeremiah murmured. I recognized Jeremy Rowan's uncle in an instant. Being a treant, he was rather striking outside of a garden or forest.

"What? Oh. Well, I'm glad the snow stopped," I stammered, confused.

Jeremiah's smile widened. "Not the storm I was speaking of." He tipped his head back towards the Puddletons before drawing me further away. "Come. There's no need to subject oneself to corruption when there is good clean air over here."

"I'm not sure I'd call them corrupted," I muttered even as I followed him to a more sparsely populated area of the library's grand foyer. Although now that he said it, I wasn't sure I could deny the observation either.

"Pettiness is a poison in the heart. Poison, left unchecked, will spread until the host is corrupted, will it not? Like a creeping ivy, it will wrap around and strangle the very essence of a soul. At least, that's been my experience," Jeremiah mused, his eyes glinting with the wisdom of a hundred seasons.

I blinked in surprise, unsure of how to answer without sounding petty myself. "I, umm, I guess I'll leave each to his or her own choices and just try to make the best ones *I* can."

Jeremiah dipped his head in approval. "Wise words. But I would expect nothing less from a guardian of nature, someone who understands the whispers of the wilderness."

"Guardian of what now? I think you've got me confused with someone else."

Jeremiah's eyes crinkled. "I most certainly do not. My nephew passed along the samples of the exotic plant you stumbled across. I must say, your endeavor yielded quite the reward. I'm afraid I wasn't able to do anything with the burned bark. However, I coaxed some saplings from the branch you supplied. Given the condition it was in, I'll admit it was touch and go for a while, but the moment their roots nestled into the rich, loamy soil of my greenhouse, the saplings took to life like a spring breeze after a long winter. They're thriving, waiting for warmer days and gentle rain to unfurl their leaves and reach for the sun."

"Umm, that's…nice?" I wasn't sure I followed everything he said. "Did you happen to find out—"

"Harper! There you are!" I turned in surprise to see Aunty Agatha pushing her way through the crowd.

"Agatha? What are you doing here?" I asked in disbelief. She rarely came to town meetings, emergency or otherwise.

"Looking for you, of course," Agatha said, grabbing my hand. "Hi Jeremiah, nice to see you."

"Well met, Agatha. May your path be lined with blossoms and your heart be full of joy," he intoned, bowing his head respectfully.

Agatha rolled her eyes but was all smiles when he looked up again. "Yeah, same to you, Jeremiah. Blossoms. Joy. All that. Mind if I borrow Harper? Thanks ever so much," she said in a rush as she dragged me away.

"Aunty Agatha!" I whispered, somewhat taken aback by her abrupt arrival and even more so by the rushed departure.

Agatha snorted. "Trust me, you do not want to get drawn in to a lengthy exchange of pleasantries with that treant. He would go on for hours about one's root system or stretching one's branches up to the sky to embrace the soft rain. I don't understand half of what he says."

"Me neither, but that's no reason to be rude," I protested.

"Don't think of it as rudeness. Think of it as me…well, making things happen," Agatha said, pulling me out the front doors of the library.

"Making what happen? Agatha, where are we going?" I asked.

"Why to meet Maddie, of course. Trust me, you're going to want to hear what she has to say."

A Hermit's Confession

THE COLD NIPPED AT my cheeks as we stepped outside. A thin layer of gray clouds covered the clear blue sky, hinting at more snow in the near future. I was grateful I hadn't removed my coat. The chilly air felt sharp and invigorating, a stark contrast to the warmth of the library.

As we rounded the corner of the building, I saw Madeline Greaves. She stood in a nook out of sight from the door, shifting awkwardly from foot to foot. Her long, dark dress swept the ground, and a tangle of wild hair framed her face.

I could see why the dryad had dubbed her with the unkind epithet "Mad Mads." Her eyes darted around as if trying to gauge the safety of her surroundings. I couldn't help but notice her fidgeting hands and the way she hugged her shawl closer, as if shielding herself from the world.

"Ah, Maddie, dear," Agatha said soothingly, stepping forward. "It's just Harper. You remember? Bea's great-granddaughter. You can relax. She's a friend. Tell her what you told me." Agatha's voice was gentle and calm.

Maddie took a deep breath, her gaze flickering between us. "I—I don't usually talk to people, do I? But there's something you need to know. Yes, you need to know. And I need to tell you, don't I now? Something important. About the magic. About the heartwood."

My eyes widened, and I opened my mouth to interject a question, possibly several. However, Agatha placed a hand on my arm and squeezed. Hard. My mouth snapped closed with an audible click.

"That's good, Maddie," Agatha encouraged. Her voice carried comforting tone one might use with a spooked horse. "Keep going."

Maddie bobbed her head rapidly, her eyes flicking to mine then sliding away, focusing on a point just over my left shoulder. "I went to investigate, I did, I did. There was a lightning strike. Out of the clear blue sky. 'Maddie,' I said to myself, 'that ain't normal. No, not at all.' So I went to investigate, didn't I? That's when I saw it."

She drew the shawl tighter around herself, and I had to lean in closer to hear her whispered words.

"I went to look, to see what had happened. It was the heartwood, wasn't it? I know enough about magic to sense when it's wrong. And what had happened there was wrong. So very, very wrong. It was fire and blood and poison and death, but the tree didn't know it. Hanging on for dear life, wasn't it? Fighting to stay alive, you understand? Fighting hard."

"What happened next Maddie?" Agatha said, coaxingly.

"I found something on the ground—strange, like it didn't belong there, all alone in the snow. I wanted to take it to Sheriff Jackson, didn't I? But towns? They're too big. Too noisy. He wasn't where he should be, not with all this wild magic stirring. Then Agatha called, and I thought..." Her voice trailed off.

Agatha put a hand on Maddie's shoulder. The other woman flinched and then blinked in surprise like she'd forgotten where she was. Agatha's voice was kind. "Show Harper what you showed me."

With a slight hesitation, Maddie reached into a pocket in her dress and pulled out a handkerchief-wrapped item. "It was just lying there, in the snow. I found it, didn't I? It was lying there, looking lost, looking for home. So I picked it up and put it in my pocket. It wanted me to. It didn't want to be there in the snow, all alone."

"Of course not," Agatha said, her tone understanding.

Maddie glanced at the old witch. "You sure I should give it to her?"

Agatha nodded. "I think it's for the best. Harper wants to help, don't you, Harper?"

I knew a cue when I heard one. "Of course I do."

Maddie's eyes flicked back and forth, resting on mine for just a moment before darting away again. Without looking at me, she held out the small, cloth-wrapped bundle. I carefully accepted it in both hands.

A sigh escaped her, and her shoulders slumped as if I'd just relieved her of a great burden.

"It feels right, doesn't it?" she murmured, her voice a soft tremor. "Like it's home now."

Her words confused me, but rather than comment on them, I focused my attention on the handkerchief in my hands. I carefully unwrapped the cloth to reveal an ornately carved wooden heart, its intricate details gleaming in the morning light. My breath caught in surprise. "Is this...?" but when I looked up, Maddie was already scuttling away, muttering about the weird energy in the air.

"Wait! Where's she going?"

Agatha shrugged, a hint of affection in her voice. "She's always been a little odd. Probably thinks the job is done now and there's no point in sticking around. Do you think that's the missing heart?"

"I think it might be," I replied, feeling a spark of real hope ignite within me for the first time in days. "The only way to tell for sure is to get it back to the heartwood. I'll go get Gabriel. Going in his car will be faster than walking."

Agatha bobbed her head. "Agreed, but these old bones won't keep up with you in a hurry. Best leave the athletic endeavors to the young. Swing by my house later and tell me how it all went."

I blinked in surprise. "Don't you want to find out for yourself?"

Agatha chuckled. "Dearie, at my age, you've seen enough close-call disasters and a couple of real ones, so you stop searching for them anymore. No, what I want is some peace and quiet and a good cup of tea. I trust you to handle the rest." She winked at me and turned, walking in the opposite direction Maddie had taken.

I stared after her, taking a moment to fully comprehend she was leaving me to deal with this on my own. Were all women who lived in the forest a little odd, or was I just special enough to find the two that supplied credence to the fairy tales about witches and hermits?

I shook myself. This wasn't the time to be lost in such thoughts. I turned and dashed back into the library, edging through the throng of residents as best I could without too much jostling. I offered a polite, regretful smile when someone protested, but I didn't stop. I needed to get to Gabriel.

Vivienne's voice was already ringing out across the gathered crowd, commanding attention like only she could. "Friends, neighbors, I think it comes as no surprise that this week has been challenging, to say the least," she said, her tone steady and authoritative. Murmurs of agreement rippled through the assembly. Vivienne paused, waiting for the whispers to settle. "We stand at a crossroads, and I'm here to ask for your help. We must come together as neighbors..."

I wove my way through the crowd as she continued. It wasn't easy to squeeze through—Havenwood had turned out in force—but I kept my focus on finding Gabriel.

Finally, I spotted him off to the side, standing tall and composed, the picture of a supportive and serious community leader. Relief and a strange flutter of hope washed over me. With Gabriel by my side, we could do this.

We'd return the heart, stop the wild magic, and save the heartwood. The thought of Havenwood going back to its sleepy February doldrums had never sounded so appealing. After everything we'd been through, I couldn't think of anything I'd want more.

Gabriel noticed me as I closed the distance between us, and his brow furrowed. He leaned down as I stood on tiptoe to whisper to him.

"I think I have the heart." His eyes shot wide as I opened my hand, showing him the wooden carving before shoving it deep into my pocket for safekeeping.

"We need to get this to the heartwood as fast as possible," he whispered back urgently.

Just then, Vivienne's voice rose above the murmurs, commanding and reassuring. "I know you will stand strong through this trial. Together, we can overcome anything, as long as we stand united!"

Suddenly, a blinding flash of lightning illuminated the slightly overcast sky outside, followed by an earth-shaking thunderclap. The power went out, plunging the room into darkness. Gasps and a few screams echoed through the crowd.

I looked around, heart racing, when a flicker of movement caught my eye—a flash of red hair as someone outside dashed past the library doors. A figure was running off into the storm, a long coat flapping around her legs.

"Did you see that?" I whispered to Gabriel, dread creeping into my chest.

He nodded, tension coiling between us. "We need to find out who that was."

I swallowed hard. "I think I already know. Cassandra Bellamy."

Chasing the Lead

IGNORING THE GASPS OF the surrounding crowd, Gabriel and I dashed for the door. We had to catch Cassandra before she could cause any more chaos, and getting the heart back to the heartwood was paramount. Every second counted.

As we neared the exit, a nasal voice sliced through the air behind me. "Look! Running away from the scene of her crime. She's always stirring up trouble and chaos!" Oswald's words dripped with malice.

Hortense's shrill echo of her husband's sentiment cut through the noise of the crowd. "Havenwood would be better off without her."

My heart raced. The urgency of the moment drowned out their taunts, but I couldn't shake the feeling of dread curling in my stomach. I turned to glare at them both, but in doing so, I lost focus. I bumped straight into someone with long blonde hair, nearly knocking her over.

"Sorry!" I blurted out, grabbing the woman's shoulders and steadying us both. I glanced up to see Sandy, the volunteer from the library, looking startled. Her face was white and pinched. I didn't think I'd bumped into her hard enough to cause pain.

"It's fine," she muttered, annoyance flashing in her eyes.

Gabriel grabbed my arm, his expression serious. "Are you okay?"

"Fine. Just bumped into—"

"Do you still have the heart?" His tone was sharp, his eyes scanning mine for confirmation.

I patted my pocket, feeling the reassuring lump. "Yeah, it's safe."

"Good. We need to get the heart back before it's too late!" His voice was low, but urgent.

"I'm right behind you!" I said, as he pushed the door open. The instant we stepped outside, a chill wind tore at my coat. Dark clouds swept across the sky, racing toward the library with an almost unnatural speed.

A sudden crack of lightning lit up the horizon, blindingly bright. I flinched, instinctively raising my arm to shield my eyes, and the deafening roar of thunder followed a moment later, shaking me to my core.

As I blinked away spots, I felt Gabriel grab my hand. "Stay with me. I've got you," he called, pulling me towards his car.

With Gabriel at the wheel, we raced through the streets of Havenwood, the wind howling around us, as if the storm itself were pursuing us. Every flash of lightning lit up the encroaching darkness, and I couldn't shake the feeling that time was truly running out.

My phone buzzed in my pocket. I pulled it out and glanced at the screen. It was Bella. "Harper! I saw you tear out of the library. What's going on?"

"Bella! I have the missing heart!" I exclaimed, my voice loud in the confines of the car as I shouted to be heard over the thunder. "I think Cassandra Bellamy is behind the attack on the heartwood. She's a magic user—she must have weather magic!"

"That's not good," Bella replied, her voice tightening. "Alex said this wasn't a normal storm. We were supposed to have clear skies all week."

"This storm is *definitely* not normal. I think it's Cassandra trying to stop us from getting to the tree to return the heart."

"Okay, we're coming to help," she said.

My stomach dropped. "No!" I exclaimed, panic rising in my chest. I couldn't think of anything worse than Bella, with her minor talent for baking, going up against a vengeful weather mage. "I need you to get Vivienne. Tell her where we've gone and what we're doing. Find Lucas too. Tell him I saw Cassandra running away from the library—red hair, long coat. They need to find her ASAP. Gabriel and I will take care of the heart."

"Yes, we will," Gabriel affirmed, his grip on the wheel tightening. He put his foot down, skidding slightly on ice as he took a corner a little too fast.

"Got it," Bella said. "You be safe."

"You too," I said, hanging up the phone.

The storm loomed ominously behind us, dark and roiling towards us like a hungry beast. My heart pounded in my chest, each thud a reminder of the danger closing in. A cold sweat trickled down my back. Cassandra was still out there, and the thought twisted in my stomach like a knife. If we didn't act fast, the heartwood—and Havenwood—might be lost forever.

I shot a glance at Gabriel, his jaw set in determination, and it sparked a flicker of hope amidst the rising dread. Without thinking, my fingers brushed his sleeve—a quiet reassurance, not just for him, but for me too. I had to believe we could outrun this storm, that we could save the heartwood and everything we loved. But as the wind howled around us, I felt the chill of fear creeping in, threatening to drown out that hope.

Gabriel eased the car to a stop outside the Enchanted Oasis. My heart raced, and the storm loomed closer, a dark reminder of the chaos we were about to face. To our shock, Vivienne stood there, waiting for us, her presence both reassuring and intimidating.

"How did you get here so fast?" Gabriel asked, disbelief etched on his face.

"Ice golems are good for more than one thing," Vivienne replied tersely, flicking her hand at the hulking figures behind her. Their bodies were a jumbled mess of snow-caked ice, as if they had been hastily assembled and used as an impromptu sleigh to navigate through the drifts of snow. Vivienne looked exhausted, dark shadows under her eyes betraying the toll of the magic she'd been wielding, but she still stood tall and proud. "The DeLuca girl said you had the heart, that you know who's behind this. Tell me that's true."

I stepped forward, pulling the heart out of my pocket to show her. "We think so," I said, my voice steady despite the knot tightening in my chest.

She studied first me and then the carving closely. I felt small under her scrutiny. Finally, she nodded slowly. "We need to get this to the heartwood and hope it works. On the way, tell me who did this to Havenwood?"

I took a deep breath, steadying my nerves. "We think it might be Cassandra Bellamy."

"What possible reason could she have for doing all this?" Vivienne demanded, her intensity making me feel exposed even though I wasn't responsible.

I tried not to waver. "She's new in town, trying to see you. I thought she was just a nice, if forceful, young mage looking for a mentor. Now, I think this might be an act of vengeance or some twisted way of trying to prove herself to you."

Vivienne shook her head, a frown deepening the wrinkles around her mouth. "It just doesn't make sense."

"There isn't time for that now," Gabriel interjected, urgency lacing his tone. "We need to get the heart to the tree and stop the wild magic. Once the heartwood starts to heal, we can search for this Cassandra."

"Lucas is already looking," Vivienne said, striding towards the forest, the ice golems falling into line behind her. "She'd better hope he finds her before I do."

As we neared the tree line behind the Oasis, Gabriel glanced at the ice golems. "Speed is of the essence. Maybe we could use the golems to get through the forest faster." I clutched the heart in my pocket instinctively, half expecting her to turn and demand it. But Vivienne's focus stayed on the task ahead.

"Precisely my intention," Vivienne said. She snapped her fingers, and the ice golems lumbered forward. However, as soon as they entered the forest, the golems fell apart, crumbling into shards where they stood.

"What happened?" Gabriel asked.

Vivienne's frown deepened as she glanced around. "I don't know."

"Could it be the wild magic?" I ventured. "Or maybe the dryad set up some sort of magical defenses in the forest."

"Unlikely," Vivienne murmured, her eyes narrowed as she scanned the area. She snapped her fingers again, but this time it was at us. "Come now. We don't have time to waste. We'll have to go on foot and hope we beat the storm."

I glanced over my shoulder. The dark clouds were nearly upon us. Was it my imagination or were they following us like some sort of aerial hunting dogs, nipping at our heels?

"Harper! Come on!" Gabriel said. I turned to see he and Vivienne were already several yards ahead of me.

The tension in the air thickened as we took off, racing against the storm toward the heartwood tree. The drifted snow in the forest made it slower going than any of us would've liked. The storm soon caught up with us, tossing snowflakes around like ninja stars and rattling the bare branches of the trees. At least the trunks gave us a little protection, or the fury of the wind might've knocked us over. My heart pounded with every step, fear gripping me tighter as the wind howled around us. If the wild magic had escalated to this point, time was running out. Failure was not an option. We had to get the heart to the heartwood.

Now.

Havoc at the Heartwood

AFTER FIGHTING OUR WAY through the storm and the winter bound forest for what seemed like hours, I was sweaty, cold, on edge, and exhausted as the slog burned away the adrenaline coursing through my bloodstream, leaving behind only a gnawing anxiety that seemed to grow with every step.

Would we get there in time? Would the heart reverse the damage to the heartwood? Would the dryad drop the curse?

I didn't know. That uncertainty troubled at me more than I cared to admit. The questions played over and over again in my mind, increasing in tempo as we drew closer to the heartwood.

Suddenly, Vivienne raised a fist, halting us just as we crossed into the clearing. My dad's training kicked in, and I stopped in my tracks, the movement automatic. The abrupt shift in the atmosphere hit me like a wall, and I realized instantly what had made her pause.

Moments ago, the snowstorm had been raging, snow whipping through the air in a chaotic frenzy. But here, inside the clearing, the storm stopped dead. No wind. No snow. It wasn't just calmer—it was eerily still.

Snowflakes that should've been carried in by the wind hovered unnaturally at the edge of the clearing, suspended like they'd hit an invisible barrier. It wasn't quiet—it was silent. Even in a winter forest, there should've been the crunch of snow underfoot, the creak of ice-laden branches, the distant howl of the storm. Here, there was nothing but silence.

"Do you feel that?" I murmured, my voice barely louder than a whisper. Even that small sound seemed wrong, hanging in the still air like an intrusion.

"Yes," Vivienne said, her voice tight as her gaze swept the clearing. "Something's off." She moved cautiously, her posture sharp and deliberate, the way a soldier might approach enemy territory.

Ahead of us, the Heartwood loomed, massive and ancient, but wrong. The darkened veins snaking through its trunk pulsed faintly in the eerie stillness. Around it, the snow lay untouched and pristine, as though the clearing had been frozen in time.

"Do we turn back?" Gabriel asked, his voice low, barely cutting through the oppressive quiet.

Vivienne slowly shook her head, continuing her surveillance of the area. "No. We have to return the heart." She glanced toward me, her expression unreadable but her tone sharp. "I should've left you in town, Miss Sullivan. This is no place for—" She stopped herself, her sharp eyes scanning the edges of the clearing. Her tension was palpable, every muscle poised for a fight.

"What is it? What's going on?" Gabriel demanded.

Vivienne's words were clipped and tense. "I'm not sure. I can't help feeling like we're being watched. And whatever's out there isn't friendly."

The air crackled with anticipation, thickening with unspoken dread. I glanced back at the swirling storm behind us, the chaos contrasting sharply with the eerie calm of the heartwood in the clearing ahead. It felt like we were standing on the edge of a precipice, teetering between two worlds. I paused, just outside the clearing. Gabriel came up behind me, silently taking my gloved hand and squeezing it, offering his support.

"Harper," Vivienne said, her voice steady but urgent. "Take the heart to the tree. Gabriel, be on guard."

I nodded, reaching into my pocket to pull out the ornately carved wooden heart. My fingers curled around its smooth edges, grounding me for a moment. But as I stepped forward, a slim figure detached itself from the shadows of the trees, stepping into the clearing just as we did. Whoever it was approached with a gliding step that barely whispered through the snow.

Vivienne crouched in front of us, her hand outstretched to keep both Gabriel and me behind her. Long, platinum blonde hair caught the light, turning into a silvery waterfall. Recognition crashed over me.

It was Sandy, the volunteer I'd met at the library. What was *she* doing here?

"Lysandra Wraithmoor!" Vivienne hissed.

"Indeed," Lysandra purred, an unpleasant smile twisting her thin lips upward.

My mind flashed back to the times I'd run into her, at the library and around town. I'd jumped to conclusions that she was a resident of Havenwood, but neither Martha nor anyone else seemed to have known her. I should've been paying more attention.

"How did you get through the storm?" The words escaped me before I could think better of it.

Sandy—or rather, *Lysandra*—sneered at me, her eyes gleaming with dark amusement. "The weather is mine to command," she said. The air around us seemed to thrum with energy, and the storm outside intensified, as if answering her call. A crack of thunder echoed in the distance, and I could feel the pressure shift in the clearing, a hint of burned ozone in the air. The entire forest seemed to thrum, charged with her power.

She flicked a glance at Vivienne. Her sneer widened into a cruel smile. "As for how I got here, well, let's just say Vivienne isn't the only one who can summon—or destroy—ice golems." Her eyes gleamed with triumph as she caught Vivienne's gaze, her words dripping with venom. "Remember when I taught you that spell? Back when we were *friends*?" She almost spat the last word.

Vivienne's face remained impassive, but I could see a flicker of something—regret, perhaps, or old wounds reopening—as Lysandra's words hung in the air between them.

"The attack on the heartwood? It was you all this time?" Vivienne said, moving to the side, pulling Lysandra's attention as she moved. Gabriel grabbed my hand, squeezing hard. It was a silent warning to be ready. I wrapped my fingers tighter around the heart, edging onto the balls of my feet so I could respond at a moment's notice.

"Naturally. Whom did you suspect? Or have you made that many enemies that you can no longer keep track?" Lysandra sneered.

"I only pay attention to the ones that matter," Vivienne said coldly. Lysandra's eyes blazed in fury as she turned to follow Vivienne's progress. Gabriel subtly stepped in front of me, shielding me with his body as he inched backwards away from his mother. That small gesture spoke volumes. Both of his feelings for me and his belief in his mother's abilities.

Lysandra's sneer deepened, her eyes glinting with satisfaction as she stepped closer. "What better way to enact my vengeance than by striking at the very heart of everything you hold dear?" Her voice was low, laced with malice, and the storm outside roared in agreement. "It took years, Vivienne—years—but I found the answer. Who would have thought it'd be so simple? Killing the heartwood, severing its roots? That will destroy everything you love. And it's already begun. The magic protecting this quaint little experiment you call Havenwood will soon fade to nothing. And then what will you do, Vivienne? When everything is gone? When everyone is gone? You'll be left with nothing. No power. No legacy."

Vivienne remained poised, her chin raised, eyes sharp as steel. "You are mistaken if you think you can destroy me so easily, Lysandra. I am a Silverthorne and have always been one. Havenwood is more than its magic—its power is in its people, its spirit. You never understood that." Her voice was calm, but there was a note of warning beneath the measured tone. "You were never my enemy. There was no need for this...vengeful spiral. The old ways have always provided a path to resolve grievances, had you chosen to honor them. Instead, you seek destruction where we could have found balance."

Lysandra's snarl echoed through the clearing. Her fists clenched so tightly her knuckles were white. "Balance?" she spat, her fury breaking through. "You stole from me! Eldric was mine, and you took him. You took the guardianship that should have been mine. And now, now you're trying to steal my apprentice, Cassandra!"

Vivienne's tone softened, just a fraction, but her control remained unwavering. "I stole nothing, Lysandra. You forget—I was a Silverthorne before I ever met Eldric. I did not need to take anything from him or from you to carve my place in this world."

Vivienne's tone softened, just a fraction, but her control remained unwavering.

Gabriel nudged me backwards away from the confrontation. Vivienne paused, her gaze locked on the weather mage across the clearing.

"You have clung so desperately to the past that you could not see the future slipping through your grasp. Eldric made his choice, and it sounds like your apprentice, this Cassandra, has done the same."

"You lie!" Lysandra shrieked, thrusting her hands out, releasing her fists and splaying her fingers. To my amazement, white hot bolts of lightning shot out of her hands, straight at Vivienne.

The Silverthorne matriarch threw herself to the side, dodging the attack in a surprisingly quick response for a woman of her age. Gabriel flinched forward, but Vivienne threw out a hand, knocking Lysandra back with a burst of magic and deflecting the next round of bolts harmlessly into the sky.

"Ah, yes. It all makes sense now. You always were one to imagine a slight and then hold on to a grudge for dear life," Vivienne said, her tone flat. I noticed her eyes never left Lysandra, and she held her hands at the ready.

"It's not imagined if it's true," Lysandra said, as she regained her footing and smoothed her silvery-blonde hair back into place.

Vivienne's voice was firm and commanding. "Stop this now, and I will let you leave Havenwood in peace."

Lysandra's eyes blazed with rage, her lips curling into a bitter smile. "*Let* me? You always were so self-righteous, Vivienne. So convinced of your own wisdom. But where has that led you now? The heartwood is dying. And with it, your precious town. Your legacy crumbles beneath your feet, and there is nothing you can do to stop it."

Vivienne's gaze did not waver, her voice still calm but laced with a quiet power. "You may wound the heartwood, Lysandra, but Havenwood is not so easily broken. You never understood what truly holds this town together."

"And what is that?" Lysandra snarled.

"Love," Vivienne said simply. "Such a simple yet complex thing. Something you seem completely unable to understand. You didn't used to be this way. I feel sorry for you, Lysandra."

Lysandra's confidence flickered for just a moment, but her fury reigned supreme. "Sorry for me? *Sorry.* For ME?! You always were an insufferable know-it-all. Let me tell you, you know *nothing* about what my life's been like. You won't stop me this time."

"Perhaps," Vivienne replied, her voice smooth as silk, "but let me disabuse you of your petty grievances. Your apprentice? I assure you, I haven't the slightest inclination to take on the task of reeducating someone who has been under your tutelage. And as for Eldric, you never stood a chance with him."

"Lies!" Lysandra hissed again; her face contorted with rage.

"No. The only lies here are the ones you're telling yourself. Such as the absurd notion that I had anything to do with you being passed over as the guardian of the heartwood tree. The tree, in its infinite wisdom, chooses its own guardian. Based on the evidence before me," she said, waving a hand at the cracked and blackened tree, "I assume you decided to take out your ire on the tree. A magically charged lightning strike, was it? I should've made the connection sooner. Luckily, the heartwood saw you for what you were. It chose wisely in not selecting you as its guardian all those years ago."

Lysandra sucked in a breath like Vivienne had sucker punched her, but the Silverthorne matriarch wasn't done.

"And as for Eldric? He was never interested in you, not even before our paths crossed. The mere thought that you could ever have held his attention is as laughable as it is pitiful. Clinging to such delusions is just...pathetic."

If Vivienne had slapped Lysandra across the face in public, the impact might have been less devastating. As it was, it was as if Vivienne had lit the match and tossed it into the simmering cauldron of Lysandra's resentment. The other woman screamed, flinging her hands forward and two crackling bolts of lightning sped right towards Vivienne's heart.

I barely had time to open my mouth to scream before the lightning struck. Instinctively, I threw up a hand to cover my eyes from the painful burst of light, but it was gone as quickly as it appeared. Blinking spots from my eyes, I forced myself to refocus, half expecting to see only a scorch mark where Vivienne had once stood. However, nothing could be further from the truth.

The Silverthorne matriarch stood calmly in the middle of a nearly invisible bubble of protection as Lysandra threw bolt after bolt of lightning at her, screaming in rage. The scent of burnt ozone filled the air, and the snow melted in a ring around Vivienne's protective circle.

I watched in stunned awe as Vivienne lifted her chin and said haughtily. "Is that all you can muster? Really, age has not done you any favors, Lysandra. In the magic department or any other." She didn't need more words; the faint, disdainful flick of her eyes to Lysandra's frown lines delivered the rest of the message with devastating precision.

The blonde mage screamed in anger, throwing herself forward, the ferocity of her attack increasing as she beat against Vivienne's impenetrable barrier. I think I might have stood there for the duration of the fight, frozen in fascination, had Gabriel not tugged on my arm. He pulled me behind the broken trunk of the heartwood, pressing me back against the rough, charred bark as he peered around the edge at Lysandra.

Gabriel let out a little breath of relief, turning his attention back to me. "You need to put the heart back and then get out of here," he whispered urgently.

"What? No! I'm not leaving you!" I said, grabbing his hand.

He brought my gloved fingers to his mouth, pressing a fierce kiss against them that I felt even through the thick fabric. "I have to help my mother, and I can't do that knowing you're in danger. Please, Harper. Go."

I opened my mouth to protest again when an unexpected voice interrupted us. "Go, mage-ling. I will look after the witch." My jaw dropped open as I recognized the delicate features of Rowena the dryad, her skin shimmering like frost-kissed bark as she appeared as if by magic behind Gabriel. To his credit, he didn't lash out on instinct, but he did whirl to face her, gathering his magic.

She held out her empty hands, palms first. "Peace, mage-ling. I mean her no harm. I made that mistake once, and believe me, I have no intention of repeating it now that I know who the true culprit is behind the destruction here." The anger that had lit her leaf green eyes on our first meeting had been replaced with sincerity.

I put my hand on Gabriel's arm, gently pushing down his hand wreathed in swirling magic. "It's okay."

Gabriel looked between the dryad and me in surprise. "Are you sure?" he asked, clearly shocked.

I considered the dryad for a moment. She met my gaze unflinchingly. Sadness lingered in her eyes, and the lines etched into her bark-like skin spoke of a deep remorse. Even without her speaking an apology, something in my gut told me that the dryad deeply regretted her words and actions during our first meeting. Another snapping crack of lightning from the other side of the tree underscored the urgency of the situation.

I hurriedly nodded. "We understand each other. She won't hurt me."

Rowena bobbed her head earnestly. "I swear on my magic. I bear no ill will towards the witch."

Gabriel hesitated, obviously torn. I grabbed his arm, tipping my head towards the continuing battle. "Your mother needs you. Havenwood needs you. Lysandra must be stopped before she causes any more damage."

A war of indecision danced over Gabriel's features, his hand finding mine and gripping it tightly.

"Go," I whispered.

Gabriel groaned, suddenly cupping the back of my head with his gloved hand and pressing a fierce kiss against my lips. It was rough, conveyed all the emotions he didn't have time to speak, and was over much too quickly for my liking. He spun to look at the dryad.

"Keep her safe, or I'll come for you when I'm finished with the lightning mage," he growled.

"Deal with that horrible excuse for a woman, and I'll gladly protect this one with all that I am," Rowena replied, sincerity in every syllable.

Gabriel nodded tightly and then stalked around the tree, disappearing from sight as he did so with an illusion spell. The only way I could track his movement was the crunch of snow and the faint outline of his footprints. I turned back to face the dryad.

"Return what is lost," she whispered, her voice cracking, carrying both a command and a warning.

"Believe me, I'm trying," I said, pulling out the cloth-wrapped heart. I flinched as the sounds of magical spells behind me intensified. As quickly as my gloved fingers could manage it, I unwrapped the carved wooden heart. "Please tell me this is the missing heart," I said as I held it up.

Rowena's eyes lit up, but instead of taking it like I expected, she leaned forward, delivering a swift, hard shove to my torso.

"Hey! What gives?!" I flailed my arms backwards, expecting to hit the rough bark of the tree behind me. However, instead of resistance, I stumbled backwards into a world I never imagined existed.

Finish Line Found

I blinked in surprise as the cold of the snow-covered forest abruptly gave way to an earthy warmth. The sounds of the battle between the Silverthornes and Lysandra became muted, almost indiscernible, and the sharp scent of burning ozone was replaced by the comforting aroma of a forest tinged with a hint of sawdust. I looked around wildly, my heart pounding. A small, circular room with an earthen floor and smooth, wooden walls surrounded me. Before I could fully process what was happening, the dryad stepped through one of the walls as effortlessly as if it were a curtain of beads instead of a solid barrier.

"Where are we? What did you do?" I demanded, my voice rising as I pressed my back against the unyielding wooden wall, clutching the heart so tightly that my knuckles ached. Panic churned in my chest, drowning out any coherent thoughts. My magic flared instinctively as I cast out, searching for any trace of metal I could use to defend myself. Nothing. Just the tiny bits in my clothes. My pulse quickened further.

What was Rowena playing at? The room felt oddly familiar, but fear clouded my mind too much to make the connection. I could only focus on the dryad, whose every step made my stomach tighten.

"We're returning the heart to the heartwood," the dryad said, her eyes filled with sadness as she placed a hand on the wall. I saw now there was a long, jagged scorch mark marring one side of the circular space and a ragged crack creeping downwards.

"We're inside the tree?" I said, my voice softer now that the panic was ebbing. As my breathing steadied, I glanced around and started to notice the subtle details—the earthy warmth, the smooth wooden walls. The similarities to Thistle's oak tree finally clicked into place. Of course. This wasn't the first time I'd been inside a tree. Havenwood and its secrets never failed to surprise me, but I was still adjusting to the whole "anything can happen" aspect of the magical town.

"Yes. I swore to keep you safe. This is the safest place I know. The wellspring of magic, love, and protection for all in Havenwood," Rowena murmured, her fingers gently tracing the burned and blackened wood. Her voice caught slightly on the word love," and my mind immediately flashed back to Thistle's words about Rowena's husband.

I hesitated, then asked softly, "Was it love that bound you to him? Your husband, I mean. Thistle mentioned what happened. I am so sorry he was hurt."

Rowena's expression shifted, the sorrow in her eyes deepening as she turned to face me. But it wasn't the hollow grief of loss. It was something heavier. Regret tangled with guilt and fear. That profound, heart-wrenching sadness convinced me she deeply regretted her actions.

Taking a steadying breath, I thrust the carved wooden heart toward her. "Here," I said firmly. "I promised to return the tree's heart to you. Here it is. Now, lift the curse, and put everything back the way it was."

The dryad accepted the wooden token, pressing it to her chest with both hands as tears spilled down her cheeks. She met my eyes and slowly shook her head. "I can lift my curse, but I fear things cannot go back to the way things were."

"What do you mean?"

"The heartwood," the dryad said, laying a trembling hand on the wall. "It needs a guardian before it can heal. Without one, the damage will worsen. The wild magic isn't just leaking—it's surging, spreading faster with every moment. If it isn't stopped, Havenwood will soon be overwhelmed."

"Guardian?" I asked, the word tugging at a memory. Lysandra's bitter words suddenly clicked into place. The position she believed had been stolen from her was at the core of her resentment. I didn't know how the guardianship was assigned. Did Vivienne have a hand in it? Whether

Lysandra blamed Vivienne for influencing the decision or simply felt wronged, her anger made perfect sense now.

The dryad nodded, her tears tracing dark streaks down her bark-like skin. "Just as the heartwood lends its strength to protect Havenwood, so too must the guardian protect the heartwood. I have been serving as the guardian for years until...until I lost my way and, in anger, cursed you and the very town I promised to protect." A hiccupping sob escaped her.

I froze, unsure of what to say. "Um, well, we all make mistakes. But I'm sure Vivienne and Gabriel will help put things right," I said with as much confidence as I could muster.

Rowena shook her head, swiping at her eyes. "You don't understand. They might have caught the one responsible for the damage, but *I* broke my bond with the heartwood by using my powers in vengeance instead of loving protection. I am no longer fit to serve," she said, her voice dropping to a whisper.

I hesitated and then reached out, patting her shoulder awkwardly. "It'll be okay," I murmured, even though I had no basis for that claim.

The dryad looked up at me. "You. Don't. Understand. The heartwood and the guardian strengthen each other in a symbiotic relationship, channeling the magic of the ley lines to protect Havenwood. But they must both be working towards the same goal or the bond shatters. I fear, in my rash curse, I broke that bond. I am connected to the heartwood by only the slimmest threads, and they are fraying with each passing hour."

Her words hit like a punch to the gut. I felt the cold twist of fear knotting in my stomach, spreading through my chest, until my fingertips felt numb inside my gloves. My hands clenched into fists at my sides, as if that futile gesture could stop the rising tide of panic. Barely connected? The weight of her words—shattering the bond, fraying threads—swirled in my head, making it hard to think clearly.

What could we do? It all seemed so hopeless.

Guilt clawed at me, sharp and unrelenting. This was my fault. I should've been more focused, found the heart faster. I had to fix this. But as terrified as I felt, somewhere deep inside, a spark of determination flared. I wasn't going to let Havenwood fall apart.

Not today.

Not ever.

"That sounds...bad. Really bad," I managed, my voice shaking slightly but steadier than I expected. I swallowed hard and forced myself to keep eye contact with her. "What can we do to fix it?"

Rowena shook her head hopelessly. "We? Nothing. I'm no longer fit to be guardian. I allowed my heart to be poisoned with the rot of anger. I cannot be allowed to taint the heartwood any more than I already have. But..." she trailed off, staring at the trunk of the tree surrounding us as if she was hearing a voice that I could not.

"But what?" I asked, looking around in case anyone else had somehow wandered into the tree, which was a sentence I never thought I'd have to think.

"Are you sure?" Rowena asked.

"Sure about what?" I replied, utterly confused.

The dryad waved at me impatiently. "Hush. Not you."

My mouth snapped closed in confusion. She couldn't be talking to the *tree*...could she?

Silence filled the small enclosed room as Rowena stared at the curved wooden walls. "Yes. Yes, that could...no, you're right," the dryad murmured. "It's our only hope."

"Umm, what's our only hope?" I asked, unable to keep my curiosity at bay.

Rowena blinked and refocused on me. "The heartwood. It needs a new guardian, and it's chosen you."

Before her words fully registered, she closed the distance between us and jerked my coat aside, pressing the carved heart against the exposed skin just under my throat. I opened my mouth in protest, but before I could speak, darkness overwhelmed me.

Growing Despite the Shadows

THE WORLD AROUND ME faded, replaced by a comforting warmth spreading through my body, making me feel at peace despite being unable to see. I blinked, looking around as I realized I wasn't just standing in the darkness—I was becoming part of it, sinking into something vast and ancient. It was like stepping into a memory, but not one that belonged to me.

I felt the sensation of being something small, almost insignificant, nestled deep within the earth. It took me a moment to realize that I was a seed—tiny, vulnerable, yet brimming with potential. The world around me was dark, but I wasn't afraid. Instead, I felt a quiet, patient anticipation, as if the earth itself were cradling me, waiting for me to awaken.

Then, with a subtle crack, I split open. Roots pushed downward, finding their way through the soil, while shoots reached upward, yearning for the light. I could feel the weight of the earth above me, the way it resisted and yet encouraged my growth. When the first shoot broke through the surface, a burst of exhilaration filled me—pure, unfiltered joy. I was alive, reaching for the sky, and nothing could stop me.

As I grew, I could feel my branches elongating outward, stretching for the sun. Leaves unfurled, trembling with life, catching the sunlight for the first time. The scent of fresh earth and the crisp, green smell of new growth filled my senses, and I reveled in the sensation of being connected to the world in such an intimate, profound way.

The years began to rush by, each one a blink in the passage of time. I grew taller, stronger, my roots digging deeper into the earth. I felt the warmth of the sun on my bark, the cool caress of a soft summer rain, and the gentle rustling of my leaves in the breeze. I watched as squirrels leapt from branch to branch, their tiny feet barely touching down before they sprang again. Every season brought something new—a new scent, a new sound, a new experience. The rest and renewal of hibernation in winter, the bursting forth of life in spring, the fullness of summer, and the quiet descent into autumn.

Then, time seemed to slow as a new presence approached. A man. I felt a flicker of curiosity. It was rare for men to venture this deep into the forest. Dryads, nymphs, even the occasional elf or bridge troll, yes. But a man? What could he want?

He came closer. I could feel his warmth, his heartbeat—a gentle thrum against the backdrop of the forest. He placed a hand on my bark, and his energy merged with mine. He spoke to me, his voice soft, as if addressing an old friend. It surprised me. I didn't know men knew how to slow down enough to speak with trees. I listened quietly as he spoke of peace, of protection, of creating a haven for beings like himself—like me. I hadn't realized I was different, magical even. But his words made sense. None of the other trees had ever spoken to me, but I'd always thought that was just how it was.

The man continued, explaining his desire to weave protections through me, to anchor his spells through my roots to the magic running through the earth beneath me, to tie my essence to the protection of the town he wanted to build. I would become the heart of the magic, the focal point for a sanctuary, a safe place for others like us, those seeking refuge. In return, he promised to act as my guardian, to protect not just me, but the entire forest. The idea filled me with warmth, a deep sense of purpose. I liked the sound of that.

I blinked, and the man was gone. Scenes began to flash before me, rapid and disjointed, making my head spin. Faces appeared, then blurred away as if I was witnessing all the guardians who had come before me, each one leaving their mark, their energy intertwined with mine. I could feel their presence, their protection, their care, and it reassured me that I was never alone.

The heartwood could never stand alone.

I would never stand alone.

Suddenly, the dryad's face appeared in my—no, the heartwood's—memories on the day she became guardian. Her entire being reflected the gentle strength of the tree. Not just in her appearance, though the rich, warm tones of her skin and the green of her eyes matched the heartwood's leaves. There was a deep compassion, an open heart in this younger, gentler Rowena that radiated through the connection. She was an excellent guardian until...

A great bolt of lightning struck the trunk of the heartwood, cracking it in half. The shock of it jolted through me, sharp and sudden. The token of Rowena's guardianship tumbled onto the snow below, the pain of the strike reverberating through every inch of the tree. Rowena's cry tore through the memory, filled with anguish that mirrored the heartwood's agony. It was as though her heart had shattered along the same jagged lines as the bark of the tree.

Bitterness and anger seeped into the space where compassion and joy once thrived. And still, the heartwood struggled to survive, its memories tangling with mine. Maddie appeared, her hand darting to scoop up the token and tuck it into her basket, her gaze flicking furtively through the forest.

Then, two figures approached the tree. I—no, the heartwood—recognized them. And to my shock, so did I. My own face stared back at me as Rowena stepped from behind the trunk, her voice cold as she uttered a curse that sliced through the memory with the force of a blade.

In a rush, the connection severed, snapping me back into my own body. My breath hitched, the flood of sensations and emotions still fresh. The warmth of the sun on bark, the cool touch of rain, the weight of a man's promise—they lingered, entwined with me now. I wasn't just Harper anymore. A part of me belonged to the heartwood, its memories a part of mine, its essence guiding and protecting me as I moved forward.

I gasped and fell to my knees.

Rowena cupped my cheek, her eyes shimmering with something soft. "Before I pass on my duties, I must undo the harm I caused." She raised her hand, her bark-like fingers glowing faintly as a ripple of magic spread outward, gentle and soothing. The air seemed to shimmer for a moment, the stillness carrying a quiet sense of release. "The curse is lifted."

A sudden weight pressed against my chest, startling me. My hand flew up to find a delicate chain resting there, a small heart-shaped pendant hanging just below my clavicle.

"What...what did you do?" I rasped, looking up at her.

Her expression softened, and she brushed a hand lightly against my cheek before stepping back. "I found a guardian worthy of the heartwood. Welcome, little sister."

"But I..." Words faltered as doubt flooded in. How could I convince her—or the heartwood—that I wasn't the right choice for this?

Rowena smiled down at me. "I sense in you a good heart and a caring spirit. The heartwood has picked many a guardian over time and has never yet chosen wrong. I know you will do great and wonderful things, little sister," she said, as she stepped back, disappearing through the wall of the trunk and leaving me alone, gaping after her in shock.

Never in my wildest dreams had I imagined something like this.

In the silence that settled over the empty room within the heartwood, I once more heard the muted sounds of crackling lightning through the trunk. A sickening impact and a grunt of pain interrupted the snapping crackle followed by a scream of terror and rage.

Gabriel. Vivienne. Lysandra.

I had to get out of here.

The Price of Magic

I TOOK A DEEP breath and ran at the trunk of the tree where Rowena had disappeared, hoping I wasn't about to knock myself senseless. To my amazement, I didn't hit a wall. It was more like running down an unlit hallway. It was dark and warm, filled with a faint but lingering odor of wood smoke. A moment later, I burst out into the snowy forest, the frosty air nipping at my nose. Rowena's footprints disappeared into the forest, leading away from the heartwood. But I didn't have time to worry about her.

Another sizzle of magic and the scent of burning ozone filled my senses. Lysandra. I peeked around the cracked trunk of the tree, and my heart stuttered to a stop. Lying on the snowy ground was Gabriel, his eyes closed and his body limp. Vivienne crouched over him, one hand upraised and the other pressed against Gabriel's forehead.

Lysandra stalked forward, blood from a cut above her eyebrow traced a line of scarlet against her alabaster skin. She hammered blow after blow down on Vivienne's magical shield relentlessly; her face a mask of all-consuming hatred and vicious joy to see her nemesis down on her knees.

"Lysandra! Stop!" Vivienne yelled.

Lysandra pulled to a halt, lightning crackling at her fingertips.

"Stop," Vivienne repeated, more quietly this time. "Please." Her voice cracked, and she whispered. "He is my son."

"And you ruined my life," Lysandra snarled, her lightning snapping to punctuate her words.

"You ruined your own life with your jealousy. If you must, take out your anger on me, but spare my son. He has done nothing to you," Vivienne said, glancing down at Gabriel. My heart stuttered as I saw his jacket was singed and smoking. If he'd caught one of Lysandra's lightning bolts, what were the chances he was still alive?

Lysandra laughed tightly, and it wasn't a pleasant sound. "He should've been *my* son, not yours! But *you* stole Eldric from me. Actions have consequences, Vivienne. Something you are about to learn."

Lysandra threw both hands forward, lightning arcing out of her palms and crashing against Vivienne's protective dome. I threw up my hands, instinctively, shielding my eyes from the intense brightness.

It faded, and I forced myself to look again, seeing something I never dreamed possible. Vivienne's protective dome had shrunk by half and the powerful mage was breathing heavily as sweat ran down her face. Her outstretched hand shook with the effort to maintain the barrier between her and Lysandra while her other hand stayed firmly pressed on Gabriel's head. A ragged gasp of relief escaped me as I saw a breath from his lips form steam in the frosty air.

He was alive. Gabriel was *alive*.

But it looked as if Vivienne was using all of her strength to maintain the protective shield and whatever spell she was weaving over him.

"Just give up, Vivienne," Lysandra mocked. "Admit you're beaten and leave this town forever. I will take my rightful place as guardian and lead Havenwood into a new age of prosperity."

"By force?" Vivienne wheezed. There was a weakness in her voice I would have never attributed to the strong and stoic Silverthorne matriarch. She needed help, and unfortunately, I was the only one close enough to provide that aid. But what could one witch with a low-powered affinity for metal do against a formidable mage like Lysandra Wraithmoor?

Lysandra shrugged, sending her lightning dancing across the backs of her knuckles as a skilled stage magician might do to a coin. "If need be. But I've always found the people of Havenwood to be reasonable. Present company excluded of course."

Think, Harper! I shouted at myself, looking around in desperation. The broken heartwood still partially shielded me from view, but all I could see surrounding us was the forest and the worn chain link fence that marked the border of Havenwood's town limits, but it was too far away to be of much use even if I could figure out how to fight a mage with a fence.

"You're insane," Vivienne spat out. "The people of Havenwood will never follow you."

"They will once you make me guardian," Lysandra said confidently.

Vivienne chuckled, the mocking sound coming out hoarse and rasping. "Then you'll be waiting a long time."

Lysandra's eyes narrowed. "What do you mean?"

"I'm not the guardian, nor do I have any power to confer it upon you or anyone else. That right has and forever will belong solely to the heartwood tree." Vivienne jerked her head towards the lightning scarred trunk. "And, based on what you've done to it, I doubt it'll ever select you as its guardian."

Lysandra looked back and forth between Vivienne and the heartwood in disbelief. "You lie! You're the guardian, I know it!" she hissed, spittle flying from her mouth.

Vivienne merely met her eyes stoically, and I could almost see her pouring all of her magic into the spells in both hands, protection against Lysandra's impending attack and what I assumed was a healing spell for Gabriel.

"Wake up, wake up, *wake up!*" I muttered. A groan escaped Gabriel, but his eyes didn't open. Vivienne looked down at him, hope and surprise on her face.

In that moment of distraction, Lysandra struck.

Lightning filled the small clearing, and I flinched back in surprise, closing my eyes. When the bright white faded, I forced myself to peer out at the clearing, my heart in my throat.

Lysandra stood over Vivienne and the prone Gabriel, lightning crackling in her fists. Vivienne had half-fallen over her son, shielding him with her body, her protective shield completely shattered.

"Say goodbye, Vivienne," Lysandra snarled, drawing back her arm.

In the instant Lysandra's arm drew back, ready to unleash the fatal strike, I reached out with my magic, grasping desperately for the only metal nearby—the broken boundary fence. I already knew from experience that my gift with metal was too small, too weak to do anything significant with it, especially from this distance, but I had to try.

I reached for my magic, pulling harder than ever before. To my shock, it *erupted* within me, surging like a river in full flood, wild and untamed. The earth beneath my feet seemed to lend its strength, amplifying the power until it was overwhelming—far beyond anything I'd ever experienced, even with the power-enhancing necklace I'd used last Christmas. The force was staggering, a relentless tide that knocked me off my feet. Was this all me? It couldn't be. My magic had never been this...vast. Breathless and disoriented, I scrambled to regain control, panic creeping in with every second.

I reached for the fencepost, envisioning it pulling free from the frozen ground. If I could angle it just right, maybe—just maybe... My magic surged, wild and urgent, as I focused everything I had on that single piece of metal.

The surge of power left me reeling, and I hit the ground hard, gasping as the brilliant white flash of lightning seared the air above me. For a moment, I couldn't move, couldn't see anything besides the afterimage of the strike burned onto the inside of my eyelids. But I had to know.

I blinked rapidly, struggling to clear my vision, and when I finally managed to focus on the clearing, I couldn't believe what I saw.

There, quivering in the ground between Lysandra and Vivienne, was the metal fencepost, yanked from its place in the barrier by my magic and now acting as a makeshift lightning rod. It had intercepted Lysandra's attack, the energy of her strike crackling along its length before grounding itself harmlessly into the frozen earth. The lightning that should have ended Vivienne and Gabriel's lives was now coursing harmlessly away as Lysandra's eyes widened, first in shock and then in fury. Her scream of rage ripped through the air. Vivienne, still half shielding Gabriel, looked up, her own expression a mixture of disbelief and awe.

The power thrummed through me, an unbroken connection to the heartwood, the earth, and the metal. The realization struck with the same force as the lightning—I wasn't just Harper anymore. I was the guardian of the heartwood, bound to the ley lines beneath it, to the magic coursing through the protective spirit, and to the ancient energy that pulsed beneath my feet.

And I would protect those I loved.

Lysandra recovered quickly, her snarl aimed squarely at Vivienne. "You think you're safe because of her?" She gestured sharply at me, her voice dripping with venom. "This ends now. Say goodbye to your son."

Her words chilled me, but I refused to let them take root. A surge of power flared through my veins, drowning out my fear. I straightened, meeting her furious gaze with my own. "Not today," I said, the words quiet but firm.

Lysandra's sharp gaze landed on me. Her fury burned as bright as the lightning coalescing in her palm, but I stood my ground. The heartwood had chosen me as its guardian, and I was ready to face whatever she threw my way.

With a furious snarl, Lysandra ripped the metal fencepost from the frozen ground as if it were nothing more than a twig. She tossed it aside with a flick of her wrist. The pole fell into the snow. The air crackled with tension, charged with the building pulse of her magic. She was preparing for another strike. A final, devastating strike aimed right at Vivienne and Gabriel.

But I was already moving, instinct and the heartwood's power guiding my actions. My focus shifted to the scattered remains of the ruined fence. The metal hummed in my mind, vibrating with potential. I could feel the energy surging through me, not just my own, but the strength of the ancient tree now flowing around my power. Strengthening it, growing with my will, deepening the resolve of my intent.

Lysandra raised her arm, lightning flickering on her fingertips, but she was too focused on her intended target to notice the danger closing in. One by one, the remaining metal poles of the fence shot through the air, thudding into the ground in a rapid, dull staccato rhythm. Each one landed with precision, forming a tight circle around her.

She looked around in confusion, but before she could react, the chain link fence followed, wrapping itself around the poles, weaving a metal cocoon. The final link locked into place just as she unleashed her lightning with a shriek of rage.

The magic she had meant for Vivienne and Gabriel struck the cage instead. The lightning ricocheted through the metal, the energy bouncing from pole to pole, unable to escape the trap I made. Lysandra's eyes widened in shock as the realization hit her—she had electrified her own prison.

Sparks erupted as the lightning crackled violently through the cage. The air sizzled with the sharp scent of burnt metal. Lysandra's scream pierced the chaos, a raw mix of frustration and pain, her fury now backfiring against her as the energy she had intended to unleash upon us surged through the very barriers that contained her.

I stood frozen for a moment, heart racing, watching as the cage glowed with an intensity that matched the wild magic thrumming within. The pulse from the heartwood still resonated in my veins, steadying my resolve and reminding me that I was not alone in this fight. The tree and I were entwined, its ability to tap into the ley lines amplifying my own powers. In that moment, a promise crystallized within me: I would use every ounce of this newfound strength to protect Havenwood. I couldn't let the town fall into chaos—not while the Silverthorne family had fought so hard to preserve it. Under Vivienne's guidance, it would continue to thrive, and that meant I had to protect her, which was also protecting the son she refused to forsake.

The thought of losing Gabriel sent a fresh wave of determination coursing through me. I couldn't let anything happen to him. Not now. Not ever.

Lysandra's eyes locked onto mine, her expression a fierce storm of rage. I refused to flinch, focusing instead on the surge of power still resonating through me from the heartwood. It felt like the forest itself was standing with me, steadying my resolve.

With a primal scream, Lysandra lashed out, but the lightning crackled harmlessly along the cage's surface, unable to escape its confines. The more she fought, the more her power worked against her, ensnaring her like a wild beast.

Then she paused. A dangerous glint flickered in her eyes, and her hand shot forward, fingertips straining through a narrow gap in the cage. Electricity sparked along her fingers, and a low hiss of pain escaped her lips. A tiny, searing bolt slipped through the gap—a single, brilliant streak of light.

Everything happened in an instant that was both terrifyingly fast and seemingly in slow motion all at once. Vivienne, still half-slumped beside Gabriel, stirred. Her eyes went wide, and she surged forward, throwing herself in front of Gabriel without hesitation. A small shield weakly manifested in front of them, but the bolt of lightning tore through it, striking her squarely in the chest. The impact sent her reeling backward over Gabriel's limp form as her body crumpled.

Panic gripped me, but there was no time to lose. I didn't know if she was alive or dead, but I couldn't let Lysandra do any more harm if Vivienne had survived.

Summoning my magic, I seized the chain-link fence's wires and twisted them around Lysandra's hands, forming makeshift metal mittens. Just as she prepared to unleash another bolt, the magic ricocheted violently within the metal confines, throwing her back into the electrified cage. Even as a lightning mage, she couldn't withstand the sustained shock, her body jerking with the force of it.

"No!" Lysandra's scream tore through the clearing.

I allowed myself a brief, determined smile. She was trapped. For now.

Turning to the Silverthornes, I knelt beside Vivienne and Gabriel. Power still thrummed through me, the heartwood's magic steady and insistent. Then, something unexpected opened within me—a connection I hadn't anticipated. I felt the fierce, unyielding bond of love between Vivienne and Gabriel. The profound bond of mother and child. It wrapped around him like a shield, radiant and pure, its intensity almost blinding. Fierce and protective. Gentle and eternal. It was everything worth fighting for.

The heartwood seemed to answer in my mind, *"Love. It is the strongest magic of all. It always has been and always will be."*

It seemed to me that the spirit of the ancient tree guided my actions. I fought the unexpected intrusion for a moment, but the heartwood's magic wasn't domineering. Instead, it offered whispered suggestions in the back of my mind and allowed me to make the choice.

Not that there was much of a choice to make with Gabriel and his mother lying unconscious in the snow. I had to help them.

I yanked off my gloves and laid a hand on each of their cheeks. With the heartwood's guidance, I gathered the last remnants of our combined magic and directed it toward Gabriel and Vivienne. A warm outpouring of magic surrounded us, melting back the snow. Their bodies, previously limp and unresponsive, began to stir as the magic wove through them, mending their wounds. I poured more magic into them at the heartwood's insistence, but it felt like trying to channel a raging river through a straw. My body wasn't ready for the strain of being a conduit to such raw, infinite power.

Green grass sprouted and grew underfoot as the snow melted into the dirt. To my surprise, a daffodil sprouted and grew, blossoming right before my eyes.

I was so distracted by the unexpected flower that I didn't notice the Silverthornes stir. Gabriel was the first to awaken with a groan.

Gabriel.

Awake.

Vivienne wasn't far behind him, but she sprang from unconsciousness to awareness in the blink of an eye, her hands curled into claws and magic dancing around her fingers.

"Lysandra—" Vivienne groaned, looking around the clearing, trying to make sense of the strange scene before her eyes.

"It's okay. She's been...um...neutralized," I murmured, slumping as the magic from the heartwood receded. My body, however, wasn't so quick to recover from the ordeal of channeling it.

Gabriel glanced between Lysandra and me in surprise. "You did this?" he asked, his gaze piercing and filled with concern. When he smiled, relief flooded through me. It was all going to be okay.

The heartwood's magic might have been infinite, but I wasn't. My body, unfamiliar with channeling so much power, felt like it had been hollowed out and left trembling in the aftermath. I opened my mouth to explain, but the fatigue that hit me was overwhelming, like a riptide dragging me under.

I collapsed to my knees as the world spun around me.

Gabriel scooped me into his arms in an instant. "Harper!" His voice was laced with panic as he knelt on the ground, holding me. "Hey, stay with me. You're okay. Just breathe," he urged, his tone tender and worried.

His presence was warm, and despite the swirling darkness closing in, I found solace in his voice. "I—I'm fine," I stammered, trying to push myself upright, but my body refused to cooperate.

"No, you're not," Gabriel insisted, his brow furrowing and his arms tightening around me. He raised his voice. "Mother! I need you here!"

I saw Vivienne's head appear over his shoulder a moment later. "What's going on?" she demanded.

"I don't know. She just collapsed," Gabriel's voice was tight.

I leaned into him, grateful for his support, though a part of me felt guilty for causing him worry. "I just need a moment..." I whispered.

"Overload?" Gabriel asked his mother. "Too much magic, too fast?"

I blinked, forcing myself to focus through the haze pushing in at the edges of my vision.

Slowly Vivienne shook her head. "I don't think so. This looks…" She trailed off and then suddenly came around Gabriel, grabbing my hands.

I struggled to look at her. "What…?"

Vivienne's intense gaze captured me, and I couldn't look away. "Harper! I need you to think, to feel. Reach out with your magic. Can you feel it?"

Even as her words raced around me, I felt like I was wading through molasses, trying to keep up with her. "Feel what?"

"The heartwood," Vivienne said, gesturing at the tree and the clearing. "It doesn't take a genius to see what's happened here. You're the new guardian of the heartwood." I felt Gabriel gasp and his arms tightened around me protectively. Vivienne refused to be deterred. "Reach out with your magic and tell me what you feel. Do it now," she insisted.

I did as she asked, stretching out with my magic and reaching for the new connection between the heartwood and me. Except…

In that moment of clarity, a sinking realization dawned: in my desperate attempt to save Gabriel and his mother, I had drained the last of the heartwood tree's magic. Even though the Silverthornes were there, I alone bore witness to the ancient tree's final moments, its life force ebbing away like a tide receding from the shore. The heartwood, which had stood as a protector of Havenwood for centuries, was now faltering, having knowingly sacrificed itself to save those who called this town home.

"It will be okay, guardian. Where love endures, life endures."

The heartwood's words echoed in my mind as the last traces of its magic faded from my awareness. Grief crashed over me like a tsunami, a torrent of sorrow I couldn't withstand. I screamed as the heartwood tree died, its essence slipping through my fingers like grains of sand. Gabriel bent his head over mine wrapping his arms around me in a protective cocoon as he rocked me back and forth like I was a child.

I clutched his jacket, tears streaming down my cheeks as I gasped out the words, "The heartwood…it's gone."

The loss reverberated in the air around us, a silence that felt all-consuming, heavy with despair.

Lysandra's laughter cut through the clearing, sharp and victorious. "Oh, Vivienne, how delightful it is to see your precious heartwood wither! Just as you took everything from me, I've returned the favor in splendid fashion. Without the heartwood, the Silverthornes will be powerless to protect Havenwood. The sanctuary you built will crumble, and the people who sought refuge here will scatter like ashes in the wind. Your beloved town will die, just like your tree."

As her words lingered, a chilling truth settled in—this was not just a defeat; we had lost the very heart of Havenwood. The ground beneath me blurred as the grief became too much to bear, and the world faded to black.

A Home without a Heart

I BLINKED, LOOKING AROUND me groggily. Lace curtains, a cozy room, and a downy soft bed filled my senses. The cold and snow of the forest had been replaced by the warmth and comfort of the Enchanted Oasis. I snorted softly to myself, finding the B&B's name especially à propos today. The scent of chocolate, bacon, and freshly baked bread wove through the house, coaxing me more fully into consciousness. However, with awareness came the devastating re-realization of what had happened out in the woods. The heartwood's final words echoed in my mind, a haunting reminder of what we had lost.

Tears welled up in my eyes, blurring the room into a hazy swirl of light and color. I blinked furiously, trying to clear my vision. As the tears subsided, I heard the quiet conversations unfolding across the room and just beyond the doorway.

Through the door, Bella was wrapped tightly in Alex's arms, her face buried in his chest as his fingers gently stroked her hair. He whispered something softly, and she nodded, a faint smile pulling at her lips even as tears streaked down her cheeks, glinting in the soft light from the hall.

Somehow, despite everything, they'd made it here—together—finding their way through the storm that had threatened to pull them apart. A faint smile touched my lips at the sight of them.

Honey and Antonio stood near the doorway, their hands brushing in quiet companionship. They shared a tender glance, their smiles soft but full of a love that had weathered countless storms. There was no drama between them, no tension or doubt—just a steady, enduring partnership built over the years, as firm and comforting as the roots of the heartwood itself.

Across the room, Vivienne and Gabriel stood close, their heads bent together in intense conversation. Their words were too soft for me to catch, but the urgency between them was undeniable. Gabriel's brow furrowed in concentration as his mother whispered rapidly to him. Their relationship wasn't like mine with my own mother—playful, teasing, and open. No, theirs was a bond forged in mutual respect and strength, in a shared sense of responsibility that anchored them both.

Each embodied different facets of love—renewed love, enduring love, and familial love. Whether they knew it or not, the power of the heartwood had been woven into their lives in the same way it had been tied to mine, connecting everyone who lived in Havenwood. The warmth of those connections settled over me, a steady pulse that chased away the cold grip of doubt. Rowena had lifted the curse. Of that, I was certain. The love I saw before me—the love I could feel—was proof enough.

Yet the wild magic still hummed at the edges of my awareness, untamed and unpredictable. What did it mean now that the heartwood was dead? Would the ley lines settle, restoring Havenwood's protections? Or would the wild magic keep surging, tearing through everything in its path?

The thought clawed at me, sharp and relentless. I didn't know enough about the heartwood, about the magic it had wielded to keep this town safe. And now, with it gone, I had no way to find out. I was its guardian, but what did that even mean without the tree itself to guard?

A lump rose in my throat, grief and doubt entwining into a suffocating knot. The ache was raw, tearing at me with every thought. What if I wasn't enough? What if the wild magic overwhelmed everything, and I was powerless to stop it?

I blinked back tears, but the fear didn't ease. The heartwood was gone, and with it, any map or guide to lead me forward. I was adrift, trying to hold back an ocean with nothing but my bare hands.

"Harper?" Bella's voice broke through the haze, tentative and trembling. My eyes fluttered open, catching her wide-eyed expression as relief lit her face. "You're awake!"

She rushed over, and her voice rose, drawing the others. In an instant, everyone crowded around, their expressions a mix of concern and hope. The commotion swelled around me, but I struggled to make myself heard. Finally, I managed a hoarse whisper. "The heart—"

"Harper! We're so glad you're awake!" Vivienne interrupted. She caught my eye, her piercing gaze silencing the tumultuous thoughts swirling in my mind. My mouth snapped shut, the unspoken words dying before they could escape.

Gabriel hovered nearby, his eyes searching my face, as if he were reading the story of my recovery in the lines etched there. Bella knelt beside me, her hand gripping mine tightly, her presence a grounding force amidst the chaos.

Bella's questions tumbled out in a rush. "Are you okay? What happened out there? Gabriel said some rogue mage attacked you?"

Over her shoulder, I saw Vivienne shake her head, ever so minutely. For some reason, the Silverthorne matriarch didn't want me telling my best friend everything.

"Umm, yeah," I murmured. "You know, it's all kind of a blur."

Antonio nodded knowingly. "That will happen when you get a knock to the head. If you hadn't woken up in the next few minutes, we were going to give Dr. Stone a call."

I tried to sit up. "There's really no need to—"

Bella firmly pressed me back down. "Now don't you go doing anything overzealous and potentially stupid. Your limit on such activities is one per day, and I'd say trying to single-handedly take down a rogue mage more than fills your quota."

My eyes slid to Vivienne. Just what had she told the DeLucas? Obviously not the whole truth. What was I supposed to tell them?

"I, um..." I started to say.

Vivienne spoke over me. "It's been such a trying day, and I really do think it's important that Harper see a medical professional to ensure she hasn't sustained a concussion, don't you?"

Antonio nodded emphatically. "That's what I've been saying. I'll call Dr. Stone and—"

"No need for that," Vivienne said, waving her hand. "Gabriel would be happy to take her, won't you?"

All eyes turned to Gabriel. He hesitated, clearly caught off guard, but a subtle, expectant glance from Vivienne had him straightening. "Of course," he said, his tone firm.

"Fabulous." Vivienne clapped her hands and started towards the door. "Gabriel will see to Harper while I talk to the DeLucas about the little incident and the mage. You see, we really need to wait for Sheriff Jackson to get here. Until he arrives, we must keep your guests safe."

"I don't think anyone will be going into the woods after that unexpected storm," Honey protested.

Vivienne carried the same air of authority my father did when he was on duty. "Well, it's our responsibility to ensure they don't. Now, why don't we set up some activities in the dining room? Honey, do you think you and Alex could whip up something delectable? I know it's short notice, but..." Her voice faded as she headed down the hall, Alex, Honey, and Antonio instinctively falling in behind her.

Bella looked between the disappearing group and me, concerned. Gabriel put a hand on her shoulder. "If I were in your shoes, I'd go after them. My mother tends to turn a simple evening into a whole event."

"But—" Bella protested, glancing back at me.

"I'm okay, Bella," I assured her.

"I've got her," Gabriel said, his voice warm and confident. "No harm will come to her on my watch, I promise."

Bella narrowed her eyes at him. "I'm holding you to that. And you're not allowed to use her penchant for trouble as an excuse."

"Hey!" I protested.

"You have my word," Gabriel said sincerely, not even breaking into a smile.

Bella considered him for a long minute and then nodded once. "Fine. Harper, I'll be over first thing in the morning with fresh pastries. No more taking on dangerous mages before I get there, you hear me?"

"Got it," I said, shooting her a thumbs up.

As soon as she left and eased the door shut behind her, Gabriel let out a sigh of relief. "Thanks for going along with all that," he whispered.

"Want to fill me in on why I just lied to my best friend?" I asked, also keeping my voice low.

"It wasn't a lie. Not exactly," Gabriel pointed out.

I folded my arms and shot him a look. "Lies by omission count."

He grimaced, rubbing the back of his neck. "Okay, fair point. But before you start sharpening your pitchfork, let me explain. What my mother told the DeLucas was mostly true. She just...left out the parts about the heartwood."

"But Bella already knows about the heartwood," I pointed out.

"Not what just happened," Gabriel returned. "An unguarded ley line can be a very dangerous thing. But with multiple ley lines now exposed? We've got a day, maybe two at best to come up with a solution before things spiral out of control."

"And then what?" I asked, my mouth going dry.

Gabriel lifted a shoulder, a look of unease flitting across his face. "Not even my mother is sure. She said she needs to make some phone calls but wanted to make sure you were safe first."

"How long have I been out?" I asked.

"Since we got back to the Oasis? Maybe about fifteen minutes."

Another thought pressed in, and I sat bolt upright. "What about Lysandra Wraithmoor?"

Gabriel patted my hand. "Sheriff Jackson already has her in custody. Do you really think he'd be this delayed when Mother called him personally as soon as we got a signal?"

"Oh. Right." I didn't know what else to say.

Gabriel squeezed my hand in understanding. "I wish I had more answers for you right now, but all I can say is thank you for doing...whatever you did to protect my mother and me. I'm eternally grateful you stepped in, and someday, when you're feeling up to it, I can't wait to hear the full story."

I sighed, my shoulders slumping. Telling him everything meant reliving what happened to the heartwood, and that was still too fresh a wound.

"Maybe later?" I asked.

Gabriel nodded his understanding. "Of course. When you're ready. But in the meantime, should we make the most of the escape window my mother concocted for us? I fear if we don't leave soon, Bella may reconsider her faith in me and insist you stay here."

As much as I would like nothing more than to wallow in the comfort of the Oasis and enjoy the warmth the DeLucas would likely shower down upon me, I really needed some peace and quiet to process what had just happened.

"Okay, but I'm not going to the hospital," I said.

"I'll take you anywhere you desire. Your wish is my command," Gabriel said.

"Ireland?" I teased, a small smile unexpectedly curling my lips.

"If that's where you'd like to go, I'll book the flights," Gabriel said without missing a beat.

My smile softened, but I shook my head, exhaustion tugging at my limbs. "Maybe another time. For now, I just want to go home. Will you take me to Spellbooks, please?"

We managed to slip out of the Oasis without too much of a kerfuffle. Bella gave me a quick but gentle squeeze, reaffirming her promise to be over first thing in the morning. Vivienne had Antonio, Honey, and Alex so busy that they barely had time for a hurried goodbye. I didn't mind though. Less talking meant there was less of a chance I could say something Vivienne might frown upon.

The drive back to Spellbooks was a short and quiet, but neither of us seemed inclined to fill the silence. Gabriel shot me a concerned glance but, other than intertwining his fingers in mine, didn't say a word.

As I stared out the car window, watching the houses and the shops blur by, I wondered what the future of Havenwood might be now without the heartwood. Would it still be a haven for the magical mundanes of the world? Or would the ley lines become so unstable that the town had to be evacuated? The fact that even Vivienne Silverthorne didn't have the answers left me feeling unsettled and on edge, despite the fatigue dragging at every fiber of my being.

Gabriel helped me out of the car, and when I couldn't manage to fit the key in the lock, he took the keys from my hands and unlocked Spellbooks, ushering me in out of the cold.

Luna's sharp voice echoed through the darkened shop. "Harper! Is that you? You won't believe what that mangy excuse for a cat…Radish ruckus! What in all the green fields of lettuce happened to you?" she asked as she hopped around a corner of a bookshelf.

"Long story," I muttered, sinking into a comfy armchair.

"Fluff and furballs, I can't believe that you left me alone here all day with that cat and no lunch whatsoever while you've been off gallivanting with your young man," Luna huffed.

I sighed, letting my head fall back onto the chair. "Trust me, no one's been gallivanting. Honestly, even saying 'gallivanting' is stretching the limits of my energy."

Luna's back foot thumped an annoyed staccato on the floor. "Four syllable words really shouldn't be the undoing of a bookstore owner. If you'd just purchased that vocabulary calendar like I'd suggested, you'd already—"

"Luna?" Gabriel interrupted.

I glanced up, suddenly interested. Who would come out on top between the charming mage and the grumpy rabbit?

"What is it? I was just getting started," Luna said haughtily.

Gabriel waved his phone at her. "And I was just getting food. What would you like from the Hobbit Hole? On me, of course."

"Oh. Well." Luna looked a little deflated that he'd derailed her tirade, but the offer of food seemed to mollify her. "When you put it like that, I'll have a Fairy Garden Salad with the dressing on the side. Extra radishes, please."

"You've got it," Gabriel said. "Now, if you would be so kind, I'd like to make Harper a cup of tea. Could you please show me where the kettle is?"

"Of course, right this way," Luna said solicitously, hopping off behind the counter.

Score one for the charming mage, I thought to myself as I struggled out of my coat. I managed to escape the second sleeve just in time to accept a steaming cup of sweet and spiced chai from Gabriel. He settled into the chair next to me with his own cup of tea.

"You really don't have to stay," I murmured. "I'll be fine."

"But who would feed Luna?" Gabriel said easily.

"I could manage."

"I know you could. However, there's this cup of tea that needs drinking," he said lifting his mug.

"And then what?" I asked.

He met my eyes steadily. "Whatever you need," he said simply.

My heart gave a little flutter, and my hand rose to my throat instinctively. It brushed against unexpected metal, warmed by my skin. I startled, running my fingers along the chain until I reached the heart-shaped charm. I'd forgotten about the necklace that had appeared when I became guardian of the heartwood. Emotions that I'd been keeping at bay crashed over me. I grabbed Gabriel's hand as tears spilled down my cheeks.

"This," I said, hiccupping slightly and squeezing his hand. "This is what I need right now."

"You've got it," Gabriel said, giving my hand a squeeze back.

We sat there in silence, sipping our tea and holding hands as I tried to sort through my emotions. Eventually, I opened my mouth, and the entire story came pouring out. Gabriel sat there and listened, never interrupting me, just letting me tell the tale at my own pace. I didn't know where Luna was, but Mr. Wigglesworth stuck his head out about halfway through and padded over, surprising me by jumping into my lap.

Somehow, between talking to Gabriel and stroking the cat's soft fur, I found my way to a calmer place. I still didn't have any answers, but I didn't feel like I was on the edge of an emotional precipice, one strong gust of wind from crashing down to the depths.

A soft knock sounded at the door, and I looked up, surprised to see a delivery man peering into the shop. I'd forgotten Gabriel ordered food. My stomach rumbled letting me know that I'd neglected it almost as much as I had Luna and Mr. Wigglesworth today.

Gabriel chuckled low in his chest. "I heard that. Can you grab some dishes? I'll get the food."

"Deal," I said, heading toward my apartment. I wasn't about to admit how drained I was by the time I made it upstairs, but I wasn't the slightest bit upset when I saw a neat stack of plates and silverware already waiting for me on the counter. I smiled and lay a hand on the wall.

"Thanks, Spellbooks," I murmured.

A familiar scrape on the chalkboard drew my attention, and I patiently waited for Spellbooks to finish writing its note.

HARPER OKAY?

I patted the wall, knowing the spirit in the shop had likely overheard everything I'd just told Gabriel.

"To be honest, no. Not really," I said, tears burning in my eyes.

EAT. BETTER TOMORROW.

The words formed slowly and then the plates jiggled across the counter towards me.

"You're right," I said with more confidence than I felt. I didn't see how a meal, even one from the Hobbit Hole, was going to fix this, but it couldn't make it worse. I scooped up the plates and headed downstairs.

To my surprise, I heard two male voices drifting up towards me. With how long it took Spellbooks to write a message, I'd assumed Gabriel would've tipped the delivery guy, and he'd be long gone by now. Except the second voice sounded somewhat familiar.

Finn.

My mouth dropped open. What was he doing here? And talking to Gabriel?

Curiosity pulled me closer to the edge of the staircase and I strained to listen.

"I'm serious, Silverthorne. Just make sure you look after her," Finn said, his tone filled with an earnestness that made my heart twist.

"I will. You know I will," Gabriel replied, his voice assured and calm, leaving no room for doubt.

There was a brief pause, and I could almost visualize Finn running a hand through his hair, a gesture I'd come to recognize when he was feeling vulnerable. "She's been through so much, and it's important that she has someone she can count on," he added, his concern evident.

Gabriel's response was steady, reassuring. "She does. Believe me, Harper is my priority," he stated firmly, his tone unwavering.

A rush of emotions hit me as I absorbed their exchange. Finn's desire to protect me mixed with Gabriel's unwavering commitment, created a tension that was almost palpable. The faint sound of Finn's boots pacing across the floor reached my ears, each step heavy with unspoken thoughts. I leaned in further, heart racing, desperate to catch more of the conversation.

Finn's footsteps slowed, then stopped entirely. A heavy silence hung in the air before he spoke again, his voice quieter, almost resigned. "Just...make sure you treat her well, will you?" Finn said, his tone carrying an edge of something unspoken, raw and unguarded.

"Trust me, I intend to," Gabriel replied.

"Eavesdropping isn't nice." The whisper sounded like a thunderclap, and I jumped, nearly dropping the plates.

"Luna!" I hissed as my heart pounded. "Sneaking up on people isn't nice either."

"*Tsk*," Luna clicked her tongue. "You know I have ninja training. How else do you expect me to move? You could tie bells around my paws, and I'd still be able to sneak up on you."

"That doesn't mean you should," I pointed out.

"And you shouldn't be eavesdropping," Luna retorted.

"I wasn't eavesdropping; I was getting plates," I whispered, holding them up as proof.

"Then why are you whispering now?" Luna asked.

I rolled my eyes. "Well, what are *you* doing if not eavesdropping?"

Luna twitched her long ears. "Rabbits were built for listening in on other's conversations. It's all in the ears."

"Yeah, well—"

"Maybe I should tell that young man what I just saw," Luna said, cutting me off. "Maybe I should tell both of them."

My cheeks blazed at the thought of being outed by my rabbit. "You wouldn't."

Luna sniffed. "Then you don't know me very well. Manners are of the utmost importance to rabbits. Next to good whisker grooming and ninja skills of course." She started to hop down the stairs.

I looked around wildly. "You tell either of them and...and...I'll slip rhubarb into your hutch!" I hissed, grasping at the only thing I could think of.

Luna froze and then slowly spun to face me. "You wouldn't."

I nodded seriously. "Every day. For a month. Maybe two."

Luna's eyes narrowed. "Truce?" she asked.

"You won't breathe a word?"

"As long as I don't have to see, smell, or taste rhubarb in this shop, you have my silence," Luna said, sticking out a paw.

Solemnly, I shook it.

Have a pet, they said. It'll be fun, they said. Until the pet turns out to be a sassy witch's familiar and tries to blackmail you.

With one crisis averted, we headed downstairs. Gabriel was already setting out the takeaway boxes.

He quirked an eyebrow at me. "What do you think? Eat straight out of these? It's not as aesthetically pleasing, but it'll save washing up afterwards."

"Works for me," I said with a shrug, though my mind was still drifting back to the heartwood, the enormity of its loss gnawing at the edges of my thoughts.

Gabriel crossed the room with a few quick strides, taking the dishes from my hands and gently brushing a strand of hair behind my ear. His fingers lingered there for a moment, his eyes softening with a tender smile. For a second, I thought he might kiss me, but instead, he simply took my hand and led me to the counter.

The surface was covered in takeaway boxes—more than I could count.

I chuckled, the sound light but edged with the weight of the day. "What did you do? Order the entire menu?"

"Something like that." His shrug was unrepentant, a small smile tugging at his lips.

As we sat down to eat, the comfort food soothed the ache in my chest minutely. But no matter how good the food was, the empty space the heartwood had left still pulsed inside me. I tried to focus on Gabriel, on the simple pleasure of sharing this moment, but it was hard to ignore the sense that everything had changed.

When we finished, Gabriel insisted on cleaning up. "You go on, get ready for bed. I'll take care of this," he said, shooing me upstairs with a smile. I didn't protest too much; the exhaustion of the day had settled deep in my bones.

I'd just finished brushing my teeth and had pulled on my favorite cozy pink pajamas when there was a soft knock at the door. Opening it, I found Gabriel standing there, holding up a pair of books and offering me a warm smile.

"I don't suppose I could interest you in a reading date?" he asked, his voice low and calming. "I'd usually suggest a cozy blanket to go with it, but today was...well, a bit out of the ordinary and I find I'm unprepared."

I grinned despite the heaviness still lingering in my heart. "Lucky for you, I happen to have a cozy blanket and the perfect reading nook."

We settled next to each other on the cushioned bench in my large window, sharing the blanket between us. I tried to lose myself in the words on the page, but the events of the day clung to me. The heartwood's final moments played over and over in my mind, the echo of its last breath still reverberating through me.

I leaned against Gabriel's chest, feeling the warmth of his arm wrap around me, grounding me in the present. He pressed a soft kiss to the top of my head, the gesture simple but full of reassurance, and, just in that moment, the grief inside me quieted. As I drifted off to sleep, I held onto that small sliver of peace like it was a life raft in the eye of a storm.

After the Storm

I WOKE IN AN unexpected place for the second time in as many days. I stretched, trying to remember how I ended up in my bed last night. The last thing I remember was sitting in the window, reading and cuddling with...

I sat bolt upright, looking around. Gabriel. Where was he? My apartment was empty, but there was a bright post-it note on my bedside table. I grabbed it.

> *Harper,*
> *Don't worry. I didn't leave, but you were so tired that I thought you could use a good night's sleep. I'm downstairs with coffee when you're ready. No rush.*
> *-Gabriel*

A smile crept onto my face, warmth blooming in my chest. Relief washed over me that he hadn't disappeared during the night, and the thought of him being downstairs made my heart flutter. I had a moment to freshen up before facing the day, and I took it, glancing out the window as I brushed my teeth.

As I moved through my morning routine, an unsettling thought lingered at the back of my mind: what would the death of the heartwood tree mean for Havenwood? The town felt unnaturally calm, especially after the wild magic incidents.and the magically induced storm. Outside, everything looked picture perfect, as if it was frozen in place, waiting for something to shift.

When I finally made my way downstairs, I found Gabriel reading in an armchair. He smiled when he saw me, coming to give me a quick kiss before getting me a cup of coffee.

"Good morning, beautiful," he murmured.

"Well, well, if it isn't my favorite pair of lovebirds," Luna teased, her voice dripping with playful sarcasm. "I see the cozy blankets didn't turn into a nest for two, but I'm not one to judge."

"Luna!" I exclaimed, heat rising in my cheeks as I shot her an exasperated glance.

Gabriel chuckled, completely unfazed by the sassy rabbit. "These armchairs are surprisingly comfortable to nap in. I might need to get one or two for my home."

Luna's ears twitched. "Is your home open to *rhubarb*?"

"Rhubarb? Now why would you think that? Really, I thought we were friends, Luna." Gabriel's tone was a little hurt.

Luna nodded once, decisively. "I like you. You can stay. Harper, he's welcome in Spellbooks anytime he wants."

A bemused chuckle escaped me. "I'm not sure that's your decision to make."

Luna's whiskers twitched. "Fluff and furballs, of course it is. You've shown questionable judgement at best from the time you let that mangy excuse for a cat into the shop."

"That was Granny, not me," I pointed out.

"Well, you let him stay. And when are you going to hire that extra help? Shutting the store for days on end is bad for business, you know," Luna huffed.

I opened my mouth and then shut it again, unsure of what I could tell her. It was one thing to speak freely in front of Spellbooks. Who was the shop going to gossip with? But Luna was another matter.

Luna's back foot thumped. "Well?"

I held up my hands. "You're right. I'll look into hiring someone as quickly as I can."

"Quite right," Luna harrumphed, hopping off to her hutch.

Luna, for all her grumpiness, was a distraction from revisiting my dark thoughts from yesterday. Before my mind could wander too far down that path, Bella and Alex arrived, carrying a spread of fresh breakfast pastries. The aroma was comforting, and I appreciated their efforts to lift my spirits. As we settled around the front counter, laughter flowed, and, for a fleeting moment, I felt a semblance of normalcy. Yet, beneath the surface, a dark shadow loomed—a metaphorical sword hanging over my head, a constant reminder of my failure as the heartwood's guardian.

Gabriel eventually excused himself, promising to return soon, after a quick shower and change. He leaned down to kiss me softly, his warmth lingering even after he left. I tried to hold on to that feeling, but it quickly faded, leaving me in a room filled with friends but still cloaked in sadness.

Bella and Alex sensed that I didn't want to carry the conversational burden just now. I was thankful when they shouldered that load, chatting animatedly about Alex's upcoming residency in Vegas and Bella's plans to visit him as often as she could. I tried to be happy for them, I really did, but their enthusiasm felt distant to me, like I was watching from behind a glass wall. If good friends and good food couldn't pierce through the haze of despair that enveloped my heart, I wasn't sure what could.

We finished our pastries, and Bella invited me over to the Oasis to hang out. I shook my head, unable to verbalize all the emotions roiling inside me but knowing I needed some space to sort out my own head right now. Bella seemed to understand and gave me a quick hug, promising to call later. Alex also gave me a hug, offering to come over and cook for us all sometime before he left.

I moved aimlessly around the shop, picking up tasks only to abandon them moments later. The silence wasn't soothing; it was suffocating, amplifying the thoughts I was desperate to avoid. The idea of going to Thistle crossed my mind, but I couldn't bring myself to face her. Not yet. Not after everything that had happened. The guilt was too raw, the grief too sharp. What could I even say? That I'd failed? That I'd broken something irreplaceable? Finally, I couldn't take it anymore. I needed air, space—anything to quiet the storm in my head.

I stepped outside into the icy morning. The cold bit at my skin, sharp and unrelenting, but I welcomed the sting. It was something I could feel, something tangible amid the hollow ache that had settled inside me. I trudged through the snow without a destination, just moving for the sake of moving.

Each step felt heavier than the last, but not from exhaustion—just the sheer magnitude of what I didn't know. What was I supposed to do next? What could I do? I hadn't even been a guardian for a day, and already I had shattered the town's sanctuary in my effort to protect it. With every step, I hear the echo of Lysandra's words resonating through my mind. Before Havenwood crumbled as she predicted, I wanted to cherish one last good memory of it—a moment untainted by the encroaching darkness.

As I wandered through town, the chill of the air clung to my skin, sharp and unrelenting. Havenwood seemed oddly serene, a fragile calm settled over the streets. But at the edges of my awareness, I still felt it—the hum of wild magic, restless and waiting. It was quieter now, depleted from the surge in the forest, but its presence was unmistakable. Lurking. Watching. Gathering itself for the next storm.

Everyone I passed on the street seemed happy and blissfully unaware of what was going to happen to Havenwood soon. I wasn't about to shatter their peace. Let them enjoy their happy ignorance a little while longer, I told myself. Even if I couldn't shake the truth—without the heartwood's influence on the ley lines, I had no way to contain the wild magic. And when it surged again, Havenwood wouldn't be ready.

I paused outside Stella's shop and smiled; the flowers, once chaotic and wild, had returned to their vibrant, orderly display. At least my friends and neighbors wouldn't have to worry about attacking flowers anymore.

Stella pushed open the door and called to me, "Harper! Look! Can you believe it? Everything is back to normal. I guess the Silverthornes took care of whatever was going on around town."

My gloved fingers flew to my throat, pressing against the small heart charm. "Yeah, they must have," I murmured.

"Hey, glad I caught you," Stella said as I passed by. "Jeremy mentioned he has something important to show you. Did he call?"

I frowned, slipping my phone out of my pocket and glancing at it. I shook my head. "No, not since I was here last—and he was battling those orchids."

Stella sighed, her expression hovering between exasperation and amusement. "Figures. He probably got distracted. Flowers tend to win over his memory every time." She gestured toward my phone. "Why don't you text him? He'd be thrilled to hear from you."

I hesitated. "I don't want to bother him if he's busy."

Stella shot me a knowing look. "Trust me, you won't be bothering him."

With a reluctant nod, I tapped out a quick message. Barely a second later, my phone buzzed in my hand, and Jeremy's name lit up the screen.

"Wow, that was fast," I muttered before answering. "Hey, Jeremy."

"Harper!" Jeremy's voice was breathless with excitement. "I'm so glad you texted. I have something incredible to show you. Can you meet me at the botanical gardens' greenhouse? You won't believe this!"

I hesitated, the shadows of my worries creeping back in. But Jeremy's voice bubbled with joy and anticipation. I felt a flicker of curiosity ignite within me. I couldn't stay cooped up in the shop moping—perhaps this would be a welcome distraction.

"Okay," I said.

"Great!" he exclaimed, a beacon of positive energy that contrasted sharply with my own despondency. "Do you know the way, or should I send you directions?"

"The botanical gardens, right? I know how to get there," I said.

"Fabulous. Call me immediately when you get here," Jeremy said, before hanging up, his enthusiasm lingering in the air like a spark.

I stared at the phone, bemused. "Looks like I'm heading to the gardens," I said to Stella.

"Good. Whatever it is, he's clearly thrilled about it. Then again, Jeremy gets pretty worked up over plants. It's one of the reasons we get along so well," Stella said.

"Thanks," I said. "Well, I'd better head over there and see what's going on."

I left without really hearing whatever polite farewell Stella offered, my mind already swirling with the despair that had rapidly become my constant companion. My feet carried me toward the botanical gardens on autopilot, the crisp air biting at my cheeks.

I was startled out of my daze by the sound of my name. Blinking, I realized I had reached the entrance to the gardens, closed for the season. Jeremy stood there, practically vibrating with energy.

"There you are! I'm so glad Stella caught you," Jeremy said, his excitement spilling over as he gestured for me to follow him. "This is remarkable—no, incredible. You won't believe your eyes!" He led me through the snowy paths of the garden, his enthusiasm lighting the way.

As we approached the greenhouse, I spotted Jeremiah standing outside with Edmund Hawke. I was shocked when they shook hands, and Edmund slung a small satchel over his shoulder, a wide smile on his face.

"Safe travels, Edmund," Jeremiah said, his deep voice carrying easily through the crisp air.

"It was a pleasure meeting you," the professor replied warmly. "I'm so glad we finally connected."

Jeremiah inclined his head. "Timing is rarely convenient, but it tends to work out in the end."

Professor Hawke patted the satchel at his side. "And I'm grateful it did. This research will be instrumental for my next book."

"It was my pleasure to be of assistance," Jeremiah said, placing a hand on his chest and bowing his head.

Edmund adjusted his satchel. "I'll leave you to your work, then. Best of luck with everything." He nodded a polite greeting at Jeremy and me, before turning and heading down the path, humming to himself as he went.

I stopped short, surprised to see him here. "You know Professor Hawke?" I asked Jeremiah in surprise.

The treant shrugged. "A recent acquaintance. He's a professor at the university in Eastford and has been eager to talk with me in person. He has a touch of green magic, but his curiosity outpaces his abilities for now. Still, it's good to see young people taking an interest in nature's magic."

I glanced over my shoulder at the figure of the professor hurrying away. Pieces clicked into place as my thoughts churned. Edmund's presence in town, his time at the library, and the chaos that had followed—either that had been the wild magic starting to spiral out of control, or perhaps even Lysandra Wraithmoor, with her weather magic, had been manipulating events from the shadows.

"It is good to see you again, Harper," Jeremiah said, his voice rich and deep pulling me from my thoughts as he extended his hand.

I smiled at the treant as I shook his proffered hand, instantly comforted by his calm presence. "Nice to see you too Jeremiah."

"Come. My nephew and I have been working hard, and it's only fair that you be the first to see the fruits of our labor," Jeremiah said, gesturing for me to follow him into the greenhouse.

The door swung open, and the warm, humid air washed over me, carrying the earthy scent of soil and thriving greenery. The vibrant hues of new life filled the space, and I inhaled deeply. The clean, rich scents of growing things filled my lungs, momentarily washing away the heaviness that had been sitting on my chest. Jeremiah glided down the narrow row between abundant plants towards the back of the greenhouse. I followed him and Jeremy brought up the rear, nearly bouncing with excitement.

Jeremiah paused when we reached the back, waving a branchlike arm at a dozen or so matching pots set in neat rows on the floor. Each one contained a sapling, their slender trunks already sturdy and strong, branches nearly touching the ceiling of the greenhouse, their leaves...

I caught my breath. The leaves of each of the saplings were the same distinctive heart shape as the heartwood's. My eyes went wide as I took in the sight of them. Cautiously, I laid a hand on the trunk of the largest one, pulling on my powers. To my amazement, it pulsed with the same magic I had once felt coursing through the ancient heartwood tree.

I sucked in a breath, looking at my hand in amazement. "How...how is this possible?"

Jeremy beamed, his excitement infectious. "I told you I had something important to show you! Remember that sample you gave me to check for disease? Well, we couldn't find any infection and therefore no cure, so Uncle Jeremiah suggested trying to use it to grow more."

Jeremiah nodded, his deep eye lit with ancient wisdom. "When one tree falls, it is best if it has spread its seeds far and wide so the forest can thrive. This is the way of things. I just try to help where I can."

"Don't we all," I murmured, thinking of my own part in the drama of the past few days.

Jeremy jumped in. "I still don't know what type of tree this is, but with some help from my uncle's rather unique abilities, we managed to coax the saplings to take root. Once they did that, they've grown faster than we ever thought possible."

Jeremiah cleared his throat, rasping, "Jeremy, could you get me some water please? I'm parched."

Jeremy nodded, dashing off. As soon as he was out of earshot, Jeremiah turned back to me, his voice completely normal once more.

"I sense that you already know what my nephew does not. That these are heartwood saplings," Jeremiah said in a low voice.

I nodded, too overwhelmed to speak.

Jeremiah's eyes lit with understanding. "I thought I sensed the forest's blessing on you, although it would be wise to keep your new role secret for now."

"What do you mean?"

"Not everyone will look favorably on a witch being the guardian. The mantle usually belongs to one of the forest folk, and there are those who might harbor ill intent toward you if they learned you became the heartwood's guardian mere moments before the ancient tree died."

"How did you know about that?" I asked, surprised.

Jeremiah shrugged. "Those of us tied to nature felt the ripples in the fabric of the natural world when the old heartwood died, although not everyone knows how to interpret the sensation." He stepped forward, his hand resting gently on the nearest sapling. "You were wise to liberate an uncontaminated piece of the heartwood before the damage spread. Without it, we wouldn't have been able to save even a piece of that ancient magic. These younglings hold incredible power. If we plant them around Havenwood, they'll not only restore the town's magical protections, but strengthen them in ways even the old heartwood couldn't. The new roots will weave a network around Havenwood, protecting and nurturing it like never before."

"A new root network?" I asked, my breath hitching on the hope swelling in my chest. "Does that include the ley lines? Will they still be connected and directed?"

Jeremiah nodded, his expression thoughtful. "Yes, the ley lines will remain linked, but this network will enhance their reach and stability. Instead of relying on a single source, the magic will flow through many, dispersing its power while still reinforcing the town's protections. It's an evolution—a chance for Havenwood to grow stronger than ever."

Jeremiah fell silent as Jeremy returned, passing his uncle a glass of water. The treant shot me a meaningful look, and I decided to take his advice and keep my guardianship to myself. Especially now that I had not one, but several heartwoods to protect.

I reached out, my fingertips brushing the leaves of one of the saplings, feeling the familiar pulse of magic within. A connection bloomed instantly between us, a glimmer of hope sparking within me. Maybe...just maybe, not all was lost.

Jeremy's voice broke through my thoughts. "It's too bad the ground's frozen solid this time of year. At the rate they've grown we could replant some of the stronger ones now if it wasn't February."

I glanced at him, a smile tugging at the corner of my lips for the first time in ages. "Actually...I might have an idea for that."

Love Takes Root

As I made my way back to the clearing where the heartwood tree once stood strong, a mix of anticipation and uncertainty welled in the pit of my stomach. Gabriel walked by my side, his expression flickering between hope and determination, while Vivienne led the group with quiet authority. Her ice golems moved in perfect synchronization, pulling the sled that carried the largest of the heartwood saplings. Behind us, Jeremiah brought up the rear, his steady presence quiet yet comforting

"I want to emphasize," Vivienne said, her voice steady but low, "that this information remains confidential. The heartwood has always been somewhat of a secret in Havenwood. This must not become public knowledge, or we risk another attack like the one Lysandra Wraithmoor attempted."

I nodded, understanding the gravity of her words. The stakes were high, and keeping our plans under wraps felt crucial. Another thought occurred. "Speaking of Lysandra, what happened to her?"

Vivienne shot me a dark look. "She's been dealt with." There was a finality in her voice that cut off any further questions. I shivered and this time, it wasn't from the cold.

When we reached the clearing, a tense energy hung in the air, mixing with the remnants of magic that lingered like an echo of the heartwood's once-vibrant presence. The old heartwood still stood, but it was charred and leafless, a haunting reminder of how deeply its life force had been intertwined with the magic of the ley lines it protected.

In stark contrast, the sapling we carried was full of life, its leaves bright and resilient against the bleakness surrounding it. Jeremiah placed his hands on the thawed patch of ground. A gentle smile creased his face, and he nodded up at me.

"This is the perfect place for the first of our young heartwood saplings. You've done well, Harper," he said.

I opened my mouth to protest that it wasn't me, but Vivienne caught my eye and gave the slightest shake of her head. Her hand rested lightly on my arm, cutting off my response before it could leave my lips.

The stern look on her face softened just a touch. "He's right. None of this would be possible without the actions you took."

"But I didn't know what I was doing at the time," I protested.

"And yet, without you, none of this restoration would've happened," she pointed out, her voice losing a bit of its usual edge. There was a warmth in her typically cold demeanor that startled me. "Sometimes, all we can do is take the next right step and trust that those small, positive actions will shield our community from those who seek to harm it. You've done that, Harper. I believe the heartwood chose wisely in selecting you."

I felt my heart skip a beat, caught completely off guard by her words. The clearing's stillness felt almost unnatural, as if even the wild magic had stilled, holding its breath to watch the unfolding drama. Her unexpected approval brought a surprising sense of calm, even as the air hummed with quiet anticipation.

Gabriel surreptitiously squeezed my hand. I glanced up to see amusement crinkling his eyes, and I struggled to come to terms with the side of Vivienne that didn't leave me shaking in my boots.

"Um, thank you," I murmured.

A strange sound emanated from Jeremiah as he knelt on the ground, his fingers splayed and digging into the dirt. It took me a moment to realize he was chanting. Suddenly, the ground fell away beneath his hands, creating a hole the perfect size for the heartwood sapling.

Working together, Jeremiah and Gabriel cradled the young tree with care as they placed it in the thawed earth. Jeremiah knelt again, murmuring with his hands outstretched as Gabriel held the sapling in place. Dirt filled in around the young heartwood and the leaves seemed to glow with magic.

I felt a surge of energy flow from the sapling, intertwining with the last remnants of the old heartwood's magic still present in the clearing.

Jeremiah sat back on his heels, looking up at the glowing leaves. "I knew it. This one's special," he murmured, his voice laced with reverence.

As they finished planting, a gentle breeze rustled through the trees, almost as if the forest itself were acknowledging our efforts. For the first time in days, a flicker of hope ignited within me.

I laid a hand on the trunk of the sapling, feeling the magic flow under my fingers. Everyone else stepped back in reverence, giving me a moment with the new heartwood.

"Together, we'll protect Havenwood. I don't fully understand what it means to be a guardian or how to get it right, but I'll give it everything I have," I whispered, half to myself and half to the sapling. A glimmer of hope rooted itself within me, growing alongside the vision of a future this young heartwood could help create.

No more wild magic outbursts, a strong network of heartwoods planted in the spring that could withstand even the worst that vengeful mages like Lysandra could throw at them.

To my surprise, I heard the ancient heartwood's voice echoing softly in my mind.

"I tried to tell you that where love endures, so will life. Your love for this town is strong. Without you, Havenwood would've crumbled, just as the weather mage predicted. However, I have no doubt you will be the greatest guardian yet."

"But I let you die," I whispered.

The leaves of the sapling rustled above me, and I heard the heartwood's voice in my head.

"No, you saved me." The voice was unwavering, filled with a warmth that wrapped around my heart. *"Not only that, but for the first time in centuries, you figured out a way to create new heartwoods. Even I didn't know that was possible. For that, I and all of Havenwood owe you a great debt."*

I didn't know what to say, my thoughts tumbling over one another like leaves in a storm, yet the heartwood's faith in me flickered like a flame, igniting a spark of determination to match the hope taking root within me. I didn't have to do this alone. I had Spellbooks, the young heartwoods, Bella, Luna, the whole town. Together, we could do magical things.

Gabriel placed his hand on my shoulder, squeezing it gently. "You did it, Harper," he said, his voice filled with warmth. "This is just the beginning."

As the echoes of the heartwood faded, a gentle rustling drew my attention to the edge of the clearing. Emerging from the shadows of the forest was the dryad who had cursed the town. Except now, instead of the vengeful woodland guardian, Rowena's appearance had transformed dramatically. Gone were the frost-covered, bark-like features that had once made her seem like a warden of winter. Now, she exuded an ethereal warmth, her skin adorned with delicate blossoms and budding leaves, hinting at the promise of spring. Wisps of green intertwined with her hair, and her eyes sparkled with the vibrant life of a forest awakening from its slumber. Standing proudly by her side was another tree-like being who I guessed was her husband, his presence steady and his smile warm. The vibrant love between them was unmistakable, their bond clearly renewed. Behind me, a sudden stillness fell as all eyes focused on the pair.

The dryad smiled gently at me, her voice soft and warm. "You have done well, guardian of the heartwood. Your love and desire to protect runs deep, like roots seeking fertile ground. With these new heartwood saplings, that love will take hold, branching out to weave strength through Havenwood. As you nurture them, they will protect and sustain the town."

Rowena stepped forward, her voice rich with ancient wisdom as she recited what sounded like a blessing:

> *"As roots take hold and branches rise,*
> *The heartwood's gift in each love lies.*
> *For friendship strong that stands the years,*
> *For love renewed in joy and tears.*
> *For steadfast love, both sure and true,*
> *For love that blossoms, bright and new.*
> *And in your heart, where trust has grown,*
> *May love endure, a seed well sown."*

The words lingered in the air, soft and melodic, wrapping around me like the first breath of spring. A warmth bloomed in my chest, a quiet certainty that settled deeper with every beat of my heart.

I glanced up, catching Gabriel's gaze, and something unspoken passed between us. His eyes held an intensity that sent a flutter through my chest—not just from the magic of this place, but from something far more personal, far more real. A connection. A bond.

He stepped closer, his smile gentle yet steady, and it struck me how much my feelings for him had grown—slowly at first, then suddenly taking root deeper than I'd realized. Just like that altered letter from him, this wasn't how I'd envisioned my feelings unfolding, or how I'd imagined confessing them. But there they were—strong, undeniable, and grounded in the foundation we'd built together. Friendship, understanding, and something more. Our future felt like something that could grow and flourish, stretching out like the branches of a tree reaching toward the sky, rooted in love and belonging.

"You've done something incredible here," Gabriel said softly, his voice full of admiration that made my cheeks warm.

I glanced back at the sapling, its delicate leaves trembling in the breeze, and then back at him. "Together, we'll keep it that way," I murmured.

Gabriel's hand brushed my cheek, pushing a loose lock of hair behind my ear. The touch sent a warmth through me that had nothing to do with magic and everything to do with him. I smiled, feeling the shift in my heart—the way it settled, steady and anchored. Here, in Havenwood. With him.

The breeze stirred the leaves around us, the soft rustle of the heartwood's branches a quiet promise in the background. Whatever came next, I was ready. With Gabriel by my side, I had finally put down roots—deep, enduring roots in the place, and with the person, I was meant to grow alongside.

Thank you!

Dear Wonderful Reader,

Thank you for making it this far. I hope you enjoyed the story. Now, I'd like to share another, albeit much shorter one with you, along with a piece of my heart.

Once upon a time, I was a kid with mountains of notebooks, each one bursting with stories and dreams. Writing was my sanctuary, my escape from the world. But as I grew older, reality knocked on my door and whispered, "Writing won't pay the bills." So, I did the "sensible" thing and focused on the real world. For a while, at least.

Then came 2020, a year that turned many of our lives upside down. As an athlete and musician, I suddenly found myself unable to do the things I loved most. In a desperate bid to fight against depression, I turned back to writing. It was like finding a long-lost friend. The stories poured out of me, and I started to feel alive again.

Not that it has been without struggle. Trying to fit writing in around work, kids, and life is like juggling flaming torches while riding a unicycle. But I've kept at it. Since then, I've written and published over 20 books, each one a labor of love and infused with a piece of my heart. I'm not an overnight sensation or a best-selling author, nor do I have a stack of rejection letters from traditional publishers. Instead, I've taken a different path, connecting with incredible readers like you who cherish a good story and a touch of magic. These small victories, and the connections I make with readers like you, are what keep me going.

This is where you come in. Your review is more than just words on a screen—it's a lifeline, a beacon that helps me reach new readers and continue this incredible journey. If you could take just a few minutes to share your thoughts, I would be deeply grateful. I read every single review, and they touch my heart in ways you can't imagine.

So, if my stories have made you smile, laugh, or brought a little magic into your life, please let me know. Your support and feedback mean everything to me, and they help keep this writing dream alive for me.

Thank you for being a part of my story, for believing in my characters, and for sharing this journey with me.

With all my gratitude and a heart full of hope,

Want more Havenwood?

Stay up to date with all the latest Havenwood news!

There's no catch - you do sign-up for my mailing list but you can unsubscribe at any time.
I send out 2 emails a month (plus a couple of extra if I'm releasing a new book, just in case you're busy and miss the first one!)
There's also no spam.
Ever.

Sign up here to join!
https://www.subscribepage.io/havenwood

SCAN ME

Also By

Havenwood Paranormal Cozy Mysteries

The Mystery in the Margins
The Chaos in the Chronicles (exclusive novella)
The Puzzle in the Pumpkin Patch
The Secret of the Silver Serpent
The Riddle at the Revelry
The Manuscript in the Moonlight (exclusive novella)
The Heist of the Hidden Heart
The Mayhem in the Masquerade
The Legend of the Leaf
The Conspiracy on the Cruise (coming soon!)
The Curse at the Carnival (coming soon!)

Smoke and Shadows Series

Shadows and Relics
Pixie Pranks (exclusive novella)
Felons and Fangs
Bones and Blades
Tempest and Treason
Daggers and Deception
Sleuths and Scoundrels
Legacy and Lies
Crossroads and Curses

Children's Books

The Secret About Mistakes
Corner of the Sky
To Mom. Love, Me
To Dad. Love, Me
To Grandma. Love, Me
To Grandpa. Love, Me

About the Author

L.L. Gray writes captivating, fast-paced fantasy full of wit, warmth, and magic. Her books transport readers to charming, cozy worlds brimming with lovable characters and whimsical adventures. A lifelong enthusiast of fantasy and myths, L.L. Gray blends humor and heart, inviting readers to escape into her spellbinding stories that feel like home—cozy, magical, and impossible to put down.

Psst, it's me—L.L. Gray!

I love connecting with fellow story lovers and adventure seekers. If that sounds like your cup of tea (or coffee, or whatever magical potion you prefer), come say hello! Visit my website www.llgray.com to join my newsletter, where you'll find exclusive goodies, or join us in my Facebook readers group. And if email is more your style, feel free to drop me a line anytime at info@llgray.com.

I hope you stay in touch!

Acknowledgments

To you, the reader: thank you for stepping into this world with me. I hope you felt the magic, warmth, and wonder woven into these pages. If you'd like to stay up to date with new releases and special content, head over to my website. And if you're looking to connect with a welcoming, book-loving community, join us on Facebook—there's always room for another story lover.

To my fabulous ARC and Street teams: you've become like a second family to me, cheering me on through every twist, turn, and chapter. Your unwavering support, encouragement, and excitement fuel my creative fire—I truly couldn't do this without each of you. Thank you for believing in these stories as much as I do.

Lastly, to my wonderful husband: your support is the foundation of every story I write. Thank you for believing in me, for being my rock, and for making all of this possible. I'm endlessly grateful to have you by my side.

www.ingramcontent.com/pod-product-compliance
Lightning Source LLC
Chambersburg PA
CBHW021040310726
48969CB00006B/1745